CHRIS RYAN

GLOBAL STRIKE

CORONET

First published in Great Britain in 2017 by Hodder & Stoughton
An Hachette UK company

This paperback edition published in 2018

2

A CIP catalogue record for this title is available from the British Library

B format ISBN 9781444783810
A format ISBN 9781473670051
eBook ISBN 9781444783803

Typeset in Baskerville by Hewer Text UK Ltd, Edinburgh
Printed and bound in Great Britain by Clays Ltd, Elcograf S.p.A.

Hodder & Stoughton policy is to use papers that are natural, renewable
and recyclable products and made from wood grown in sustainable
forests. The logging and manufacturing processes are expected to
conform to the environmental regulations of the country of origin.

Hodder & Stoughton Ltd
Carmelite House
50 Victoria Embankment
London EC4Y 0DZ

www.hodder.co.uk

ONE

'I need your help.'

Terence Cooper sat bolt upright in his office on the third floor of the British embassy in Washington DC and gripped the phone hard. He recognised the voice on the other end of the line instantly. They'd spent more than twenty years working together at MI6, often operating on the same teams in the same dark, hostile corners of the earth.

A long time ago now, Cooper thought.

'Charles?' he almost-whispered. 'Is that you? What the——'

'There's no time,' Charles Street interrupted. 'Listen, I think I've found something. Something big.'

Cooper hesitated. A hundred questions pinballed around inside his head. He wondered what Street had been doing for the past six years. Where he lived now. If he'd ever remarried. Then he detected the note of anxiety in his friend's voice and decided the small talk could wait.

'How big, exactly?' he asked.

'On a scale of one to ten? Nuclear.'

'You're sure?'

'I wouldn't be calling you if I wasn't.' Street paused for a beat. 'I need your help, Terry.'

'Are you in trouble?'

'No,' Street replied. 'Not yet. But this thing is too big to keep to myself. I need another pair of eyes on it, and I don't know who else to turn to. You're still in the loop at Vauxhall. I need your advice.'

Cooper shifted his considerable weight in his executive leather chair. 'And I presume that whatever it is you've discovered, you don't wish to discuss it over the phone.'

'No.'

'Then we should meet. When are you next in town, old boy?'

'I'm here now,' Street said. 'My flight got in last night.'

'You should have told me.'

'I am. What are you up to now?'

'Nothing that can't be shifted. Not for an old friend.'

'I'll be there in thirty minutes,' Street said.

Twenty-eight minutes later, Charles Street stepped out of the rented Toyota Corolla into the oppressive heat of DC in July. He snatched up the brown A4 envelope lying on the passenger seat, hit the lock button on the key fob and made his way up Observatory Circle. A hundred metres away stood the main security gatehouse, situated on the eastern side of the grounds of the British embassy. The air was so hot and heavy he felt like he was wading through a swamp. DC in the summer, thought Street.

The damn weather.

A one-lane driveway led down past the gatehouse into the embassy parking lot. The driveway was reinforced with a red-and-white arm barrier and a flashing traffic light and a load of stop signs. Beyond it there was an automatic road blocker mounted on a hydraulic platform, designed to stop vehicles dead in their tracks. Street approached the sentry hut and handed over his passport to the duty officer inside. The guy gave him an inquiring look and made a big show of studying his ID, as if he'd just received special intelligence that Isis had gone on a recruitment drive with greying, fifty-something white men wearing cheap suits. He checked Street's name against something on his computer screen. A list of approved visitors, Street guessed. Then the guard handed back his passport and waved him through with a grunt.

The chancery building loomed directly in front of Street, a seven-floor rectangular slab of concrete and glass that looked like the regional office of a big accountancy firm. An architectural afterthought. Most passing tourists associated the British embassy with the Ambassador's Residence, the Georgian pad overlooking Massachusetts Avenue, but Street knew the real action went on deep inside the drab chancery situated to the north-west. Within those walls dozens of embassy staff were hard at work, keeping

2

tabs on assets, monitoring safe houses and feeding int back to the brains trust at MI6. Street knew all this, because he'd once worked in that same building.

Back when I still had a career to speak of.

Before everything turned to shit.

He'd joined Six straight from university and spent his early years in DC as an analyst before being assigned to Moscow. There Street had risen steadily through the ranks, eventually becoming head of the Russia Desk in the mid-1990s. He'd been the rising star at Vauxhall then, destined to one day become Chief of MI6. Then the roof crashed in on his world.

Two agents had been found dead in a Moscow backstreet after their cover was blown. An internal investigation was launched and they'd taken a long hard look at Street. He'd been shagging one of his local assets at the time, and although they could never prove anything there were rumours that the asset had been the source of the leak. Rumours that had been strong enough to derail Street's career. Six months later, he found himself out of a job. He'd spent the years since in the wilderness, doing irregular contract work for private security firms, pulling together reports from his dwindling pool of Russian contacts. Now hardly anyone bothered to return his calls. Charles Street, ex-MI6 high-flier, was yesterday's man.

He beat a path towards the entrance, passed a decorative red telephone box and stepped into the cryogenic cool of the reception. The décor inside the embassy was Late-Nineties Call Centre. Everything was bland and functional and corporate. The walls were battleship grey. So was the floor. The furniture was blocky and seemed to come exclusively in shades of beige.

Street gave the receptionist his name and got a lanyard with a visitor's tag in return. A skinny guy with a man-bun swiped him through the barrier and they rode the lift to the third floor. Man Bun led him down several identical-looking corridors, all with the same worn carpet and the same anaemic ceiling-panel lights.

They arrived outside a grey office door with stippled glass panelling to the left and a plain name plate fixed above the chrome handle.

TERENCE J. COOPER, CULTURAL ATTACHÉ, the plate read.

Man Bun nodded and left.

Street stopped outside and made himself presentable. Not easy, when you look like shit. He adjusted his tie, fiddled with his collar and brushed off a speck of dirt from his jacket lapel. Then he rapped his knuckles twice on the door. There was a moment's silence before a voice called out from the other side.

'Come in.'

Street took a deep breath and stepped into the office of the friend he hadn't seen in six years.

The room was just as drab as the rest of the building. A plain white desk occupied the middle of the floor space, with a metal bookshelf fitted to the wall on the right. Window to the left, offering a view of the leafy grounds of the US Naval Observatory. There was a faded Union Jack flag hanging from a pole next to the window. The office looked like it belonged to a small-town solicitor, rather than the senior agent for MI6 in the US.

There were the usual framed family pictures on the desk. Street noticed one of Cooper with his wife and two teenage boys, posing in front of the Grand Canyon. Next to the family snap, an old photo caught his eye. A faded shot of Street and Cooper on a fishing trip, twenty years earlier. They were standing beside a lake on a bright summer's day, Cooper looking on and smiling while Street held up his prize catch. Street was pleasantly surprised, and touched, that his old friend had not only hung on to the photograph, but kept it on display.

Terry Cooper stood up from his executive chair and spread his arms in a greeting. The smile on his lined face was big and warm and genuine. There was no awkward hesitation between the two of them. No preamble. They just moved towards each other, met in front of the desk and hugged fiercely. Then Cooper took a step back from his friend.

'Charles.'

'Terry.'

'Christ, old boy. How long has it been now?'

'Too long.'

Cooper nodded. 'You look well.'

Which was a lie, Street knew. He hadn't looked any kind of good in a long time. Not since he'd left the security services, more than a decade ago. His suit was so shiny it looked like it had been stitched together from a bunch of old bin liners. His brown leather brogues were badly scuffed. His thinning brown hair had been worked into the world's lamest combover. His appearance was that of a guy on the downward slope of his life, trying to maintain what little dignity he had left.

This is what happens when Vauxhall decides to get rid of you, Street thought to himself bitterly. Twenty-two years at MI6, and he had nothing to show for it except a crap pension and a rundown flat on the edge of Willesden Green.

I might as well have a sign around my neck that says 'Desperate ex-spy'.

One glance at Cooper told Street that his old colleague had gone in the other direction. Up, not down. His suit looked as if it had been tailor-made on Savile Row. His shoes had been polished to within an inch of their lives. His grey hair was stylishly ruffled and his chiselled jaw was so square you could have cut through timber with it. His eyes had a steely glint about them. Cooper looked like the playboy son of an ageing billionaire, readying himself to take over the family business.

None of which surprised Street. While he'd been busy wrecking his career by screwing around with Russian assets, Cooper had kept his nose clean. He wasn't the most talented agent at Vauxhall, but he'd been the perfect fit for the security services' new sleek, corporate image. Cooper had played it straight, kept his head down and toed the party line. Eighteen months ago, he'd been rewarded with a promotion to Head of MI6 ops in the US, working under diplomatic cover at the embassy. Now there was even talk of *him* one day taking over as the new Chief.

That's why Cooper is wearing a thousand-dollar suit, and you're dressed like an office junior, thought Street. *Because he played by the rules, while you pissed all over them.*

Cooper chucked a stick of nicotine gum into his mouth and gestured to the utilitarian chair facing his desk.

'Please, Charles. Have a seat. Water? Green tea? I'd offer you something stronger, but I'm off the drink these days. One needs to keep a sharp mind in this job,' he said with an ironic grin.

Street smiled at the last comment. A private joke. Something their old boss at Vauxhall used to say, inevitably prompting an eye-roll from Cooper or one of the other young officers.

'I'm fine,' said Street. 'How's the family?'

'Good, good,' Cooper replied busily. 'Stephen's starting university next month, would you believe. Durham.'

'They grow up quick.'

'They do. Anna says hello, by the way. You'll have to come around some time for dinner.'

'I'd like that, very much.'

Street sat down opposite his old friend. He noticed several framed pictures arranged on the wall behind the desk. Most of them were newspaper clippings that showed Cooper pressing the flesh with various dignitaries: a former US president, the wife of the British prime minister, an ageing Indian tycoon. They told the same story. A guy in the prime of his life, achieving all of his goals. Looking forwards, not back.

Street made himself comfortable and laid the envelope square across his lap. Cooper glanced at it before looking up at the former agent. There was a look of concern in his eyes, Street noticed. As if he was worried about something.

Or maybe I just look worse than I thought.

'You should have told me you were coming to town,' Cooper said. 'If I'd known, I would've cleared my desk. We could have even found time for a spot of fishing, you know.'

Street smiled weakly. 'You're still sore about that monster catfish I caught, I see.'

Cooper shook his head. 'Eighty-nine pounds. How you ever managed to reel that thing in, I'll never know.'

'I got lucky. That's all.'

'No such thing. You were better at fishing than me, Charles. Always were.'

I'm not so lucky now, thought Street.

'I should be done here at around six-ish,' Cooper went on, checking his smartwatch. 'We can catch up properly then, old boy. There's a new rooftop bar near Dupont Circle that serves up a bloody good Old-Fashioned.'

'Sounds great,' Street said, anxious at the thought of getting in a few rounds of overpriced cocktails.

'But you didn't come here just to swap old fishing stories, did you?' Cooper said, pointing with his eyeballs at the envelope resting on Street's lap.

Street nodded. 'I'll get right to it. I've been freelancing for a small firm here in DC, pulling together briefings on our Russian friends. Varangian Risk Assessment.'

'I've heard of them. A private security firm over in Alexandria. Small, but respectable.'

'That's the one.'

Cooper frowned. 'When did this happen?'

'A couple of months ago.'

'You mean to say, you've been in town all this time?'

Street shook his head. 'Just for a couple of briefing sessions. A day or two, here and there. I would've called, but it was back-to-back meetings.'

And I was too ashamed to meet up. To let one of my closest chums see how far I'd fallen.

'I understand.' Cooper smiled kindly. 'Well, I'm just glad to hear you've found work. After everything that happened.'

Street merely shrugged. 'It pays the bills.'

Barely, he thought.

'What sort of work have they got you doing?'

'Monthly reports on the state of the Russian security services. The FSB, the GRU, the foreign intelligence services. All the usual suspects.'

'Am I allowed to ask who Varangian's client is?'

'It's Big Oil. They're interested in any goings-on that might affect their interests in Russia. Corruption, foreign nationals under investigation, changes in strategy, that sort of thing.'

'You still have contacts over in Moscow?'

The note of surprise in Cooper's voice was obvious.

'A few. Here and there.'

'What does any of this have to do with what you mentioned on the phone?'

'One of my old sources reached out to me a few weeks ago. Told me he had information on FSB activities that I should be aware of. I thought it relevant to the work I was doing, so we agreed to meet.'

7

'In Russia?'

'London.'

'Who is he?'

'I can't say. I swore to protect his identity. He's worried about blowback.'

Cooper nodded slowly. 'Alright. Go on.'

'We spoke for a couple of hours. He told me some things that were pertinent to my paymasters at Varangian.' Street paused. 'And some things that were not.'

'I'm not sure I follow, Charles.'

Street glanced uncertainly at the envelope, as if weighing up whether to share the contents. He knew he was taking a big risk. *But if I can't trust my old mate, I can't trust anyone.* Then he took the plunge and slid the package across the desk.

Cooper stared at the envelope but didn't reach for it. As if maybe it contained anthrax spores. 'What's this?'

'A hard copy of my latest report.'

'I see,' Cooper said. He still didn't pick it up.

'The report contains everything my source told me. Most of the stuff is relevant to Varangian. But there's something else in there. Something I thought I should bring to your attention first.'

'What do you mean?'

'Take a look for yourself.'

Cooper leaned forward, took the envelope and lifted the unsealed flap. He plucked out a thin sheaf of papers, thirty or so pages held together by a couple of staples in the top left corner.

The paper was cheap toilet-paper stuff and the top page had CONFIDENTIAL / SENSITIVE SOURCES printed across the header in bold lettering, with the title INTELLIGENCE SUMMARY PREPARED FOR VARANGIAN RISK ASSESSMENT, INC. underneath.

Below that were several double-spaced bullet points. Cooper scanned them with the practised eye of someone who'd read thousands of such reports in his career.

The first two points related to a meeting between the heads of several mafia gangs and the director of the FSB. There was some speculation from the unnamed source that Russia was recruiting criminal gangs in order to carry out assassinations on its enemies abroad. Bullet points three and four repeated a rumour Cooper had heard elsewhere about an internal power struggle going on inside the Kremlin. Several hardliners were apparently unhappy with the president for failing to prevent a terrorist attack on the metro in St Petersburg a month earlier, and there was the usual talk of another purge.

The fifth bullet point was highlighted in bright green marker.

Cooper read the lines. He stopped and felt his heart skip a beat. He read through it again, more slowly. Finished. Then he looked up at Street and swallowed hard.

'Christ,' he said. 'Jesus fucking Christ.'

TWO

Cooper flicked through the rest of the dossier in stunned silence. There was a more detailed description of the findings outlined in the summary a few pages further on. Street had highlighted the passages with the same green marker pen. Cooper read through the text carefully, his brow furrowed in deep concentration. Street just sat there, watching the reaction play out on the agent's face as he took in the information. After a short while Cooper leaned back in his chair and stared levelly at Street.

'I have several questions,' he said.

'I thought you might,' said Street.

'First question. Who told you about this?'

'As I said, Terry, I'm really not at liberty to reveal my sources.'

'Which I fully understand. But you're asking me for an opinion about a document that makes some very serious accusations. It would be helpful to know whether this source of yours is reliable. Or not, as the case may be.'

Street considered, then nodded. 'He's a high-level criminal who recently fell out with the president. Before that he spent a decade working with some of the most senior figures in the Russian intelligence agencies. He's credible.'

'He also sounds like a man with an axe to grind.'

'You think he's making it up?'

'It's a possibility. Perhaps he's saying all this stuff to embarrass the president. A man with a grudge against him might say anything to get his revenge.'

'Some of his other claims are a little outlandish,' Street admitted.

'I can see that,' Cooper said as he flipped through a couple of pages. He set the dossier down on the desk and spread his hands. 'So what makes you believe this business about a tape?'

'I did some digging. As much as I could, anyway.'

'And?'

'The story he told me checked out. The dates correspond. The president was in Moscow at the time he claims. He stayed at the hotel my source mentioned. Met the same people. Moved in the same circles.'

'And the rest? The, ah, outlandish stuff?'

'He's a Russian gangster. They're colourful with the truth. I'd dismiss the rest of what he told me.'

Cooper gestured to the dossier. 'I presume none of the names in this report are real?'

'Naturally, I had to change them,' Street replied. 'To help protect my sources.'

'And the locations?'

'The same.'

'But you know the real names? If someone pressed you for them, I mean.'

'Of course.'

Cooper popped another stick of nicotine gum into his mouth and nodded. 'Fine. Let's assume this information is accurate. Do your paymasters over at Varangian know about it?'

Street shook his head. 'It's not strictly relevant to my brief.'

'They might reasonably argue otherwise. You uncovered this stuff on their dime, after all.'

'I was hired to report on the Russian security services. This isn't that. Besides, I have my concerns about taking this to Varangian.'

'Such as?'

'Let's just say that some of the senior directors are a little too cosy with the administration. If I take a report to them that alleges their new president is a sexual pervert, they might try to bury it.'

'Fair point. Which leads me to my next question. What do you want to do with it?'

'I thought you might know somebody we could take this to. Somebody local, who might take an interest in it. Another security firm, perhaps.'

'Why involve me? You could do that yourself.'

'We both know that isn't true.'

Cooper stared at his old friend. Street stared right back. They both knew what he meant. In the years since Street had left MI6, his list of contacts had shrunk faster than a coke addict's bollocks. Nowadays he could count the number of people he still knew in Moscow on one hand. Which made it difficult to pull together a full report for his employers. Street wasn't proud of it, but lately he'd started making stuff up in order to get paid. Rumours about his intelligence briefings being less than watertight had quickly spread throughout the industry. Few took him seriously now, Street knew. Not on something as explosive as this.

'I thought if you vouched for its credibility, it might help get someone's attention,' he added.

Cooper steepled his long, bony fingers on the desk. His pale blue eyes narrowed thoughtfully at the dossier. The billionaire's son, weighing up a big investment opportunity.

'How many copies of the report do you have?' he asked.

'This is the only hard copy.'

'Backups?'

'Physical storage only. No cloud. Offline and encrypted to within an inch of its life.'

'Has your source spilled his guts to anyone else?'

'He's a high-ranking criminal in hiding. The only people he's in regular contact with are his heavies and his lawyer. They're not in danger of talking to anyone.'

'So, no one else has gotten their hands on this material yet?'

'As far as I know. I've taken steps to keep it secure.'

Cooper nodded. 'You want my advice?'

'That's why I'm here.'

'You have two options. The first is to go public. Which I'm against.'

'Why?'

'The dossier might not get the oxygen it needs to make the headlines. We're talking about a president with more scandals to his name than a bishop's palace. This could easily get buried under all the other stuff.'

'This is bigger than anything else.'

'True. But it's still a risk.'

'What's the second option?'

'Selling it on, to our American friends.'

'You really think this could be worth something?' Street asked, privately relieved that Cooper had at last raised the question of money.

'Absolutely. To the right people, this stuff could be worth a fortune.'

Street tried to hide the look of greed in his eyes. 'But I don't know any of them, Terry. Not any more.'

That's what happens when you're out of the game for so long, he thought.

Everyone stops calling.

Cooper said, 'I might be able to help you out there.'

Street said, 'How do you mean?'

Cooper placed a hand down on top of the dossier. Like he was claiming ownership. 'Look, I have an idea. Why don't you leave this here with me and I'll make a few enquiries. See if we can drum up some interest.'

Street shook his head firmly. 'You're asking me to leave behind my only hard copy. I can't do that.'

'It'd be safe here. I wouldn't let it out of my sight.'

There was an eager glint in his eye as he spoke. Street's old spy instincts kicked in. He wondered why his old mate was so keen to keep hold of the dossier.

'I'd rather not,' he said.

'I thought you said you trusted me, Charles.'

'I do.' Street smiled. 'But I'm not leaving here without this document. Sorry. You know how it is.'

Cooper accepted this with a knowing nod. 'In that case ... perhaps I can arrange a face-to-face meeting with a friend of mine. Someone who might be interested in what you've got.'

'Who is he?'

'An old acquaintance from the Bureau. Chap by the name of Bill Prosser.'

Street shot a questioning look at the embassy man. 'The FBI would be willing to pay for int compromising their own president?'

'Why not?' Cooper shrugged. 'It's no great secret that there's some serious friction between the new administration and our friends over at the Bureau. They want rid of the president, quite frankly. And what you've got here, if it's true, could be enough to topple him.'

'How much are we talking, roughly?' Street asked.

'I can't make any promises, because it's not in my gift. But I'd imagine something as big as this could be worth north of say, a quarter of a million dollars.'

Street's heart did a somersault inside his chest. Two hundred and fifty grand! A life-changing sum of money. More than he could ever hope to earn cobbling together half-baked intelligence reports. With that sort of cash he could retire, sell off his pad in Willesden Green and move to somewhere warm. One of the islands in the Aegean, perhaps. He could see out his days drinking fine wine and fishing for mackerel. Maybe even find himself a young Greek woman to settle down with.

Living the dream.

He quickly masked his excitement and said, 'This friend of yours. Prosser. What's his story?'

'He used to head up the FBI's Eurasian organised crime unit until they moved him upstairs,' Cooper explained. 'That's how we met. He's high up in the Bureau's intelligence branch these days.'

'How high?'

'Very. We're talking inner circle, top-level security clearance. He'll probably make director within the next decade.'

'Can we trust him?'

'I've known Bill for years. Believe me, he's on the level.'

'And he has the authority to make a deal with us?'

'He doesn't control the FBI's purse strings. But he has the ear of the people who do. If he makes you an offer, the deal's as good as done.'

Cooper smiled.

'Here's what I suggest,' he continued. 'There's a private members' club in Georgetown. The College Club. You've probably heard of it.'

Street nodded. He was familiar with the place from his previous stint at the British embassy. The College Club was based in one of the oldest townhouses in the DC area and attracted the sort of preppy, well-connected crowd who attended Ivy League fraternities and took their holidays in Martha's Vineyard. The kind of people who could trace their heritage all the way back to the *Mayflower*.

14

'Bill's a member there,' Cooper said. 'I'll put in a call to his office this afternoon. Arrange a meeting with him at the club. You can bring along your report and tell him what you've found.'

Street weighed it up. A quarter of a million dollars in exchange for the dossier, he thought. Or I can walk away now, go public and spend the rest of my life struggling to make ends meet. If anyone would even believe what I've uncovered.

What have you got to lose?

'At least hear the man out,' Cooper went on. 'See what he has to say.'

'Fine,' said Street. 'I'll meet with him.'

'Splendid. I'll call Bill and make the necessary arrangements.'

'You're sure he'll want to meet with us?'

'Oh yes. Something as big as this, Bill will want a piece of it. Trust me.'

There was a keenness to his voice, Street noted. He thought, Cooper's excited about the meeting. That was a good sign. Cooper wasn't the type to get carried away. If he was excited, it was because he thought the dossier had real value.

He stood up from behind his desk, signifying the end of the meeting. Street just sat there, lost for words.

'Terry, I don't know what to say. If there's any way I can repay you—'

Cooper dismissed his offer with a wave of his hand. 'Not at all. What are old friends for, eh? I'm just glad to help out.'

'Thank you.'

'Thank me after Bill's made you an offer. We'll celebrate then.' Cooper broke out his winning smile. 'Now, I'm afraid I really must be getting on. I'll call you as soon as the meeting has been set up.'

Four minutes later, Charles Street strolled out of the embassy gatehouse with a spring in his step. For the first time in a long time, he felt good about life. All the shit he'd put up with since he'd left Vauxhall, all the petty humiliations he'd endured, would soon be a distant memory. The rest of the intelligence community had turned its collective back on Street, but now he was going to have the last laugh.

He was going to get rich.

And it was all thanks to the last friend he had left.

THREE

His piece-of-shit phone rang the following morning.

He was in his room in a two-star hotel on New Hampshire Avenue, on the north-eastern outskirts of the city. The room was all Street could afford on his piss-poor budget. There was a stained mattress on the bed, a rudimentary desk in one corner with a metal bottle opener fixed to the side and a Bible on top of the rickety bedside table. Stale, lukewarm air dribbled out of an old AC unit mounted above the bathroom door. It was better than a crack den, but not much.

Doesn't matter, thought Street. Soon enough, I'll be rolling in cash.

No more naff hotels.

No more pitying looks from my ex-colleagues.

Back to living the good life.

He tapped Answer on his phone's cracked screen and the voice on the other end said, 'You owe me a drink after this, old boy. Preferably something hideously expensive. A bottle of Macallan single malt ought to do the trick.'

Street killed the sound on the TV and said, 'You spoke to Prosser?'

'Just got off the phone with him now. Everything's set. We're meeting him tomorrow.'

Jesus, thought Street. That was fast. Which could only mean one thing. *Bill Prosser must be very interested in what I'm selling.*

'What time?' he asked.

'Eight o'clock. He'll be waiting for us at the College Club.'

Street felt his pulse quicken. *It's happening*, he thought. *It's really happening*. He could almost smell the money.

'We should meet beforehand,' Cooper went on. 'To discuss tactics.'

'Agreed,' said Street, pushing thoughts of the cash to the back of his head. 'Where do you have in mind?'

'Do you remember the waterfront around Georgetown?'

'Vaguely. Isn't it a bit rough around there?'

'Not any more. There's a park now, lots of redevelopment. Not quite the same as strolling along the Thames at sunset, but what is? We can meet there at seven-thirty and walk up together to the club.'

'How will I know where to find you?'

'There's a shopping district directly east of the waterfront. I'll be waiting for you outside the Starbucks on the north-western corner.' There was a pause. 'You'll need to take a few anti-surveillance measures, of course. Make sure no one has eyes on you.'

Street sat up with a jolt. 'You think I might be followed?'

'It's possible.'

'But how? I haven't told anyone else about the dossier.'

'This is DC, Charles. Half the people here are paid to keep their ears close to the ground.'

Street nodded to himself. Glanced over at the document lying on the desk. His ticket to a whole new life. He couldn't afford to take any risks, he knew. Not now.

Not when I'm so close to landing the big prize.

Cooper said, 'Do you have a car?'

Street said, 'A rental.'

'Then listen carefully. There's a car park due east of the shopping district, off the Rock Creek Parkway. It's across the bridge from Pete's Boat Hire shop. You can't miss it.'

'I know the place.'

'Drop your car off there and proceed on foot to the Starbucks. If anyone's tailing you, abort the meeting. If you don't show up, I'll assume the meeting has been blown and notify Prosser.'

'Understood.'

'Good man. I'll see you at the meeting point tomorrow night, then. And Charles?'

'Yes?'

'Don't be late. Prosser doesn't like to be kept waiting.'

★　　★　　★

17

The temperature was borderline crematorium when Street emerged from the hotel the following evening. He had showered and shaved, and he was wearing a brand-new suit for the meeting with Prosser. An off-the-rack item he'd bought at the Macy's off New York Avenue. Not as expensive as the suits he used to wear on the job, but it was an upgrade on the tired old threads he'd arrived in DC wearing. The suit had nearly maxed out his credit card, but Street felt it was worth it. He didn't want to look shabby next to the super-elite crowd at the College Club. The shoes were the same scuffed brogues he'd worn to the British embassy. Couldn't do much about those. His budget didn't extend to forking out for some new footwear. He just hoped no one would notice them.

Street subtly checked the area as he exited the lobby and paced towards his Corolla, thirty metres due east. The hotel was situated in the middle of a wide and sparsely-populated car park. Like a brick island surrounded by an ocean of blacktop. There was an IHOP to the south and a cluster of single-storey buildings to the north: a thrift store, a car wash and an attorney's office, plus a Cambodian supermarket. He made a note of all these things without being aware of it. Twenty years of taking in every detail had ingrained the habit in his daily life.

But Street noticed nothing unusual. Just a handful of pickup trucks and people carriers parked up in front of the IHOP, a couple of U-Haul vans occupying the spots further to the north. He unlocked the Corolla, slid behind the wheel.

Gave himself a final check in the sun-visor mirror.

He still didn't look good. But he looked a lot less shit than he had done yesterday.

I'm ready.

Forty metres to the west, Omar Ketsbaia sat behind the wheel of the Chevrolet Impala, watching the target head towards his car.

Two vehicles were needed for the mission. Ketsbaia was in the secondary motor. Both had been paid for using fake credit cards and documents at separate rental desks, one from Washington Dulles airport and the other from Ronald Reagan National. Both were fitted with stolen plates they had lifted from similar-looking cars across the city. Even the athletic gear Ketsbaia was wearing had been paid for in cash at an outlet where he was careful to wear a baseball cap to avoid showing his face on camera. Nothing could be traced back to the guys on the team. Or more importantly, their employers.

The people Ketsbaia worked for were not the kind you wanted to piss off.

The target gunned the engine, steered out of the parking lot and merged with the traffic shuttling south on New Hampshire Avenue.

Ketsbaia finished the dregs of his weak black coffee and tapped open the app on his phone. A loading graphic briefly filled the screen before it was replaced by a detailed map of the general area. In the middle of the screen a flashing blue dot suddenly appeared. Ketsbaia stared at the dot as it inched along New Hampshire.

He smiled to himself.

The target would be wary about being followed. But he wouldn't expect his car to be transmitting a GPS signal.

Fitting the transmitter had been easy enough. There were dozens of security stores where you could buy a tracking device the size of a box of matches, no questions asked. Ketsbaia had planted the lump under the Corolla's wheel arch in the dead hours before sunrise, when he could be sure no one was watching him. The lump emitted a constant signal that Ketsbaia could access by entering the SIM card details into the app, allowing Ketsbaia to track it from his phone. He could follow the target at a safe distance, and the guy wouldn't suspect a damn thing.

Not until it was too late.

He fixed the phone to the bracket mounted on the dash. Watched the blinking dot for a beat as it continued south. Then Ketsbaia pulled out of the car park onto the main road.

Ninety metres to the east, Denis Krashov sat up in the Dodge Grand Caravan and nodded at the woman sitting next to him.

'That's the signal,' he said, pointing towards the Impala as it turned left onto New Hampshire. 'Omar's on the move.'

There were four of them inside the Caravan. Krashov, the woman and the Vasin twins. Five if you counted the dog, Krashov reminded himself.

They were parked in front of the IHOP, along with half a dozen other sedans, people carriers and pickup trucks. They had been stationed there for the past several hours, observing the hotel entrance from a distance while they waited for their target to appear. There had been a lot of sitting around. A lot of drinking cheap coffee and listening to the Vasin twins talk shit. But now Krashov could feel a hot thrill of anticipation sweeping through his veins. The waiting was over.

They had not had much time to prepare for the op. Their employers had only learned of the target's existence a little over forty-eight hours ago and there had been no time to bring in one of their own assets. So they decided to contract it out to one of their trusted sources instead. Which is where Krashov came in.

He'd spent fifteen years of his life inside the worst prison in the world. There were no guards inside that festering pit. No rules. No order. Just a brutal daily struggle for survival, locked up with several hundred dangerous criminals and psychopaths. Either you stood up for yourself, or you took shit and ended up a bloodied corpse. Krashov was determined not to be one of the victims. In the first week of his incarceration, one of the older prisoners had dissed him behind his back. The next day at the workshop, Krashov pinned the guy to the floor, shoved a metal spike into his mouth and hammered him to the floor.

After that, no one had dared to mess with him.

Once he had been released, Krashov found himself unexpectedly on the right side of history. The world had been turned upside down while he'd been locked away. The old order had crumbled, and his particular skills were suddenly in demand. He acted as an enforcer, making sure parties honoured their side of a deal. Anyone who refused to pay their debts was dealt with, severely.

Soon his activities caught the attention of figures high up in the security services. He had expected trouble from them. Threats. Instead they'd made him an offer. There were certain jobs that the agency could not risk carrying out, the official had said. Mostly overseas work, much of it dangerous. Work they couldn't risk leaving fingerprints on.

Krashov would take on the occasional contract, as and when the official saw fit. They would supply him with documents, training and weapons for each mission. In return, the official would ensure the authorities turned a blind eye to his business dealings.

Krashov had readily agreed. He was a patriot, after all, and he was happy to serve his country's interests. As a sign of his loyalty, he hadn't even demanded a payment.

Which is why he now found himself in a parking lot in DC.

On the right side of history once again.

This op was going to be fast and smooth. A real in-and-out job. Once the target had been acquired they would take him out of the district to a rented property in Bethesda. A private jet belonging to a friend of the intelligence services would land at a nearby airfield the following morning, ready to ferry them out of the country and back to the motherland.

Twenty-four hours from now, Krashov could be back home, drinking champagne in an exclusive bar and celebrating another successful operation.

He turned to the woman. 'Get us moving. Don't lose Omar, okay?'

'Got it,' the woman said.

They pulled out of the car park. Following the Impala.

Closing in on their prey.

FOUR

The drive to the meeting point took Street thirty-two minutes.

He took a circuitous route to the park, doubling back on himself several times and taking a couple of deliberate wrong turns to throw anyone who might be tailing him. After five miles he turned onto K Street and passed through downtown DC, with its wide sidewalks lined with bland office buildings and high-rise apartment blocks. Street continued west past Washington Circle, heading towards the cobblestoned streets and elegant brick rowhouses of Georgetown. Every so often he glanced up at the rear-view mirror. But he couldn't see anyone following him.

After a quarter of a mile he turned left off K Street and motored south towards the river. Two minutes later he was pulling into the Rock Creek car park.

The car park was a rectangle of blacktop, with four bays arranged either side of a strip of grass running down the middle. Across the creek, a hundred metres away from the car park, stood the Swedish embassy and the waterfront lined with a cluster of high-end restaurants and bars. Further to the west was the water-front park. In Street's day the waterfront had been an industrial dumping ground along the edge of the Potomac River. Then the money had poured in. Now it was an oasis of green space and art installations, moments from the bustle of the city.

Progress, right there.

The Starbucks was just north of the waterfront, Street knew.

Not long now, he reminded himself. Not long at all.

He eased off the gas pedal and slow-crawled towards a cluster of empty spaces at the far end of the car park. At gone seven o'clock on a Wednesday night, the place was more empty than full. Street counted maybe a dozen cars in total. A few SUVs, plus a bunch of dated compacts and saloons decorated with political slogans and the names of college football teams.

Nothing that immediately struck him as suspicious.

He steered into a space at the end of the leftmost bay and killed the engine. Then he checked his crappy old plastic watch. 7.20pm. Street had mapped out the walk earlier and he knew it would take him six minutes to get from the parking lot to the waterfront shopping district. Which gave him a four-minute window to sit behind the wheel and wait to see if anyone had tailed him. Anyone further than a few minutes back would be too far behind to keep up their surveillance.

Standard operating procedure for agents in the field, Street knew. Always assume you're being watched.

That was why Cooper had insisted on him making the final part of his journey to the RV on foot. If someone was following him further behind, they would have to abandon their wheels in order to continue their pursuit. Which meant anyone entering the car park faced an immediate problem. *Do we stay in the car and draw attention to ourselves? Or do we get out and risk getting spotted?* All Street had to do was stay put and look out for anyone pulling into the lot and acting shifty. Or anyone who didn't get out of their car at all. Either way, they'd flag themselves up as a surveillance detail.

He watched and waited.

He saw a dark blue Chevrolet Impala steer into a space in the bay due east of Street, twelve metres behind him. A guy in full jogging gear got out and started going through a complicated routine of stretches before his evening run.

He saw a small crowd of tourists enter the park on foot, seventy metres away, taking snaps on their selfie-sticks, while their bored-looking guide lectured them on the area's history.

As Street looked around, he understood why Cooper had chosen the park as their meeting point. There were people coming and going in every direction, a transient population, lots of entrances and exits. In the unlikely event that someone did follow them into the park, Street and Cooper could easily lose them. No surveillance team could realistically cover all the entry points in and out of the park.

Two minutes passed.

The temperature on the Corolla dash read 100 degrees Fahrenheit.

He saw professional dog walkers. Young couples heading out for a romantic stroll along the waterfront. Old-timers decked out in sun visors and shades and carrying aluminium walking poles.

He saw no sign of a threat.

Just the usual comings and goings in a city park.

While Street kept his gaze fixed on the entrance, he thought about all the ways he'd spend his money. He decided he'd start by fixing himself up with a decent watch. Something respectable. A Breitling Navitimer, perhaps. He'd treat himself to a few Canali suits as well. Street figured he'd trudged around in cheap threads for long enough.

I spent ten years paying the price for shagging that Russian asset. Ten years feeding off scraps, while the rest of the world left me behind. A simple mistake had cost him his future at MI6.

But all that was about to change.

Soon he would be famous as the man whose dossier brought down the most powerful man in the world. His reputation would be restored. More than that, he'd become a celebrity in the intelligence field. Everybody would want a piece of him. The opportunities to make money would be limitless, he reasoned. He could start up his own firm. Rake in some serious cash.

He'd prove all those bastards at Vauxhall wrong yet.

After three minutes a grey wagon arrowed off Virginia Avenue and rumbled into the lot. A big old Dodge Grand Caravan with Virginia plates and tinted windows. Street observed the Caravan as it rolled past the nearest available spaces before it turned into the empty one immediately to the left of the Corolla. Which might have been due to a lazy or unconfident driver who didn't want the hassle of trying to manoeuvre a vehicle the size of a tank into a tight space, Street thought.

Or because someone was planning to make a move on him.

He stayed perfectly still, kept his hand on the wheel and focused his attention on the Caravan at his nine o'clock. Street went through the getaway plan in his head once more.

Fire up the engine. Slam the Corolla into Reverse. Pull out of the gap, bolt out of the parking lot and rejoin the traffic on the main road. Then call Cooper and tell him he'd been compromised.

He'd studied the angles on Google Maps the previous day.

Figured he could be out of the parking lot and lost in traffic in under eight seconds, if he needed to be.

But then the driver's side door popped open and he stopped panicking.

The woman who climbed out was forty or thereabouts, and she wore her age the way some people wore suits. Proud and well. She was dressed in dark tracksuit bottoms and a plain blue t-shirt underneath a zip-up hoodie with the words PENN STATE stencilled across the front in big white lettering. There was probably a photograph of her on Urban Dictionary, right next to the entry for Soccer Mom.

As Street looked on a boxer dog leapt up from the front passenger seat and jumped down onto the blacktop after her. Soccer Mom glanced over in Street's direction, saw him staring at her and gave him an All-American smile. Street relaxed his features and waved back. Then she hooked the leash onto the boxer's collar and set off in the direction of the bridge seventy metres to the south. The boxer leading the way, straining at the leash as its owner followed behind at a decent pace.

Soccer Mom disappeared out of sight behind the Caravan.

Street breathed a sigh of relief.

'Calm down,' he said to himself.

No one's following you. You're just being paranoid.

He made one last check of the parking lot. Looked towards the entrance. Clear. Checked his wing mirrors. Also clear. In the rearview he noticed that Jogger Guy had stopped to answer his phone. At a distance of twelve metres it was hard to pick up the actual conversation but Street got the gist from Jogger Guy's body language. He looked pissed off. He was waving his arm furiously and shouting at the person on the other end of the line. Street caught the words *back* and *the office* and *right now?*

As in, *You want me back at the office right now?*

He heard Jogger Guy shout, 'This is bullshit!' as he killed the call. Then the guy tossed his kit into the boot and climbed back behind the Impala's wheel. The door slammed shut.

The engine roared into life.

Street scooped up the envelope containing the dossier from the passenger seat. He was about to debus from the Corolla when he caught sight of a rapid movement in the rear-view. He glanced up and saw the Impala's rear lights glowing as the vehicle reversed at speed out of the space behind him. The wheels screeched, burning rubber as the rear of the Impala swung out in a wide arc, backing up until it filled the Corolla's mirror.

Street could see what was going to happen a split-second before it did. Then there was a shuddering impact as the rear of the Impala reversed into the Corolla at an angle.

The Corolla jolted.

Glass tinkled. Metal screeched.

Nothing happened for a moment. Then Jogger Guy cut the engine and staggered out of his ride. He marched around to the back of the Impala, spotted the damage and screwed up his face in anger.

'Motherfucker!' he yelled. 'You have got to be fucking kidding me!'

Street hit the steering wheel and gritted his teeth in frustration. This is the last thing I need, he thought. Some fitness freak pranging me five minutes before my meeting.

Prosser doesn't like to be kept waiting, Cooper had said.

He was tempted to just walk away. But the car was a rental. The damage could cost him a lot of dollars. Dollars he didn't have. Besides, who walked away from a prang? That would surely arouse suspicion. The smart play would be to get the guy's details, then quietly move on.

'Let's get this over with,' Street muttered to himself.

He left the dossier on the passenger seat and stepped out of the Corolla. The hot evening air smothered him immediately. It was like being wrapped in a stack of warm towels. Street could feel prickly beads of sweat slicking down his back, pasting his shirt to his skin as he paced around to the rear of the hire car.

Jogger Guy didn't notice him at first. He was too busy glaring at the Corolla's shattered tail light. The rear quarter panel around the light was slightly dented, Street noticed. There were various scratch marks across the rear bumper. Cosmetic damage. The kind that always cost more to repair than you figured.

Jogger Guy looked up. He didn't look much like a serious runner. The parks in DC were always full of those guys in the summer. Blokes who were jacked with muscle, decked out in the latest fitness watches and eight-hundred-dollar trainers, acting like they owned the place. Whereas Jogger Guy was tall and ungainly, with pasty white skin that suggested a serious vitamin D deficiency. Like a prisoner emerging from a long stretch in solitary. There was a tattoo running down the length of his right arm, showing a spider crawling up a web.

'Shit, I am so sorry,' the guy said.

He had a gruff, surly accent. Street couldn't quite place where the guy was from.

Not American, he thought.

But then in DC these days, who the hell is?

'It's fine,' he said. 'Really.'

'No, it's not.' Jogger Guy shook his head, angry with himself. 'It's my fault. I'm a fucking idiot. I wasn't looking.'

'It's no big deal.'

Jogger Guy nodded and scratched his jaw. 'Look, buddy, I'm kind of in a hurry here. I'm guessing you are too. Let me grab my insurance details. We can exchange and take it from there?'

'Fine,' said Street through gritted teeth, cursing the delay to his plans. And doubly pissed off because he'd been too cheap to shell out the extra for the damage waiver when he'd signed the rental agreement.

'Wait here,' Jogger Guy said.

He gave his back to Street and raced over to the Impala. While the guy reached inside the front passenger side and opened the glove box, Street consulted his watch.

7.27pm. He was running three minutes behind his schedule.

The seconds ticked by. Slowly. Then Jogger Guy came hurrying back over, waving a plastic insurance card in his right hand.

'It's all here,' he said.

Street took the card. Glanced briefly at the details printed on the front.

Then he glimpsed the movement.

A rapid blur of motion in his peripheral vision, accompanied by the hydraulic hiss and suck of a door sliding open. Coming from the direction of the Dodge Grand Caravan parked to the left.

Street looked across his shoulder.

The door on the right side of the Caravan was open.

Three figures were crouching inside.

FIVE

The figures were all decked out in matching gear. Dark grey Tactical 5.11 trousers, loose-fitting black shirts and brown Timberlands. Like they had some kind of group discount at an out-of-state hunting store. They had the sinewy, hardened definition of MMA fighters, rather than the swollen mass of guys who spent too much time lifting weights in the gym. Two of them could have been brothers. They had the same shaven heads, the same cold blue eyes. The same ring tatoos on their fingers, with a series of small dots inked on each of their knuckles.

The third guy looked older than the other two. Late thirties or early forties, Street guessed. He sported a shark-fin Mohawk and a distinctive tattoo on the side of his neck. A skull resting atop the branch of an oak tree, a crown atop its dome and a stogie sticking out of its mouth.

Mohawk and Ring Guy Two were both packing guns. Street glimpsed the polymer grips of a couple of semi-automatic pistols jutting out from their leather belt holsters.

Ring Guy One gripped a Taser.

The dart cartridges had been removed from the weapon, turning it into a close-range stun gun capable of delivering a paralytic shock to anyone it came into contact with.

Street took this all in instantly. Their appearances, the tattoos, the weapons. He saw it all in a second, enabled by his training. Years of running surveillance in the field, noticing the smallest detail. Like a snapshot.

But it didn't do him any good.

He opened his mouth to shout for help.

Too late.

Everything happened very fast. Ring Guys One and Two jumped down from the Caravan and grabbed hold of Street. Before he could get out a word Ring One hit him in the chest with the Taser. Fifty thousand volts of electric current instantly shot through his body, shredding his nerve endings. Street felt his muscles seize up in agony. His jaws clamped shut. Every part of his body locked up. Like cement hardening. He couldn't scream for help. Couldn't move.

The pain lasted what felt like a long time but in reality was no more than a second or two. Then Street felt his feet give way beneath him as he tumbled forward. In a flash Ring Two and Mohawk jumped down and seized Street by the arms, catching him before he fell away. They lifted him up then bundled him head-first into the wagon, shoving him towards the rear seats. Street collapsed onto the leather like a sack of hot bricks.

'Say a fucking word,' Ring One said, 'and I'll fry you.'

He had the same dull, surly accent as Jogger Guy.

Street recognised it now, through the pain and shock coursing through his system. It was an accent he knew very well. One he'd heard many times before, during his time overseas.

His heart sank. He knew it then. He understood who these men were. Where they'd come from.

And what they were going to do with him.

'You,' Mohawk said, snapping his fingers at Jogger Guy. 'Take the Impala. We'll follow.'

Jogger Guy took the keys from his shorts pocket and hopped out of the Caravan. Then he swept around the Impala, folded himself behind the wheel. Fired up the engine. At the same time Ring Two dived into the front of Street's Corolla and retrieved the brown envelope lying on the passenger seat. He slid out again. Climbed into the back of the Caravan. Yanked the door shut.

Trapping Street inside with his three abductors.

Ring Two handed over the dossier to Mohawk. The guy was sitting ahead of Street, in the middle row of seats. Mohawk snatched the envelope and nodded at Street.

'Cuff this piece of shit,' he said to the others.

'No,' Street groaned. 'Please. Don't.'

30

The Ring Brothers ignored his pleas. Now that Street saw them up close there was definitely a family resemblance. Ring Two swung around and ripped off Street's jacket and tossed it onto the seat next to him. Then he dug out a pair of white plasticuffs from the side pocket on his Tactical 5.11s. He used his considerable weight to press down on Street, pinning him horizontally across the leather seats. Street tried throwing the guy off. Hopeless. It was like trying to bench-press a two-ton truck. He clawed at Ring Two's face, feeling with his fingers for the guy's eyes in a desperate attempt to gouge them. Ring One stepped forward and gave him another bump with the Taser. Pain exploded between his temples, as if someone was drilling directly into his skull. His arms fell away to his sides. He felt bile surging up in his throat.

The pain seemed to go on for ever.

'Had enough, bitch?' Ring One snarled, waving the Taser inches from his face. 'Or you want some fucking more juice, eh?'

'Hurry up and get him cuffed,' Mohawk ordered, impatience creeping into his voice.

Mohawk had an air of authority about him that reminded Street of the directors at Vauxhall. Like he expected complete obedience from the rest of the team, no questions asked.

Ring One reluctantly lowered the Taser. He glared at Street and worked his lips into a cruel smirk.

'Just you wait, bitch. When we get where we're going, you're gonna be screaming like a fucking woman.' Ring Two hauled Street upright. He slapped the plasticuffs around his wrists and clinched them so tight that Street could feel the material almost cutting off the blood supply to his hands. Then Ring Two reached around for the seat belt, strapping Street in to the middle back seat.

The Ring Brothers sat down in the back seats either side of Street. Ring Two at his left shoulder. Ring One to his right, Mohawk ahead of them in the middle row.

Street was barely conscious of his surroundings. His brain registered nothing except the three toughs in front of him and the raw fear coursing through his body.

This isn't happening, he told himself.

Thirty seconds ago I was getting ready to meet one of the big shots in the US security services. Now I'm being held prisoner in the back of a minivan by a bunch of armed toughs.

He clung to the hope that someone had noticed him being abducted and was poised to raise the alarm. But nothing happened. No one came to his rescue. The whole operation had lasted no more than four or five seconds. Too fast for any casual observer to realise what had happened.

Which told him something.

These guys aren't amateurs. They're professionals.

They planned this whole thing perfectly.

The electric shock was beginning to wear off. A kind of fuzziness clouded the edges of Street's vision. He was dimly conscious of a door opening up at the front of the Caravan. Someone slipped in behind the steering wheel. Between the rear headrests Street caught a glimpse of her long brown hair and dark hoodie. A boxer dog jumped in after the woman and planted itself down on the front passenger seat.

Soccer Mom.

She was in on it too.

He realised now why she had been part of the plan. Street had been suspicious of the Caravan pulling up next to him, right up until the moment a middle-aged Doris and her dog had stepped out onto the blacktop. Then his guard had dropped.

Stupid.

His mistake.

Now he would pay for it.

Mohawk turned to Soccer Mom. 'Get us out of here. Right the fuck now.'

'Yes, boss.'

She punched the engine start-stop button, shunted the Caravan into Reverse and backed smoothly out of the parking space. A few seconds later they were rolling out of the car park and turning onto the main road. Jogger Guy was in the Impala fifteen metres ahead of them, leading the way. Street could just about see the vehicle through the Caravan's tinted windscreen. They followed the Impala as it hung a quick left and headed north on the Rock Creek Parkway.

Away from Georgetown.

Away from Cooper, and a quarter of a million dollars.

Dread seeped into Street's guts.

'Where are you taking me?' he asked in a weak voice.

No one answered.

Soccer Mom kept the Caravan to a modest forty miles per, staying well under the speed limit, clearly to avoid attracting any unwanted attention from the cops. As they breezed along the parkway Mohawk muttered something to Ring One. The latter turned in his seat and rooted around inside Street's jacket. He fished out the crap old phone from the inside pocket, laughed at it and then handed it over to his boss.

Mohawk took the handset away from him. Like all smart-phones, it was basically a mobile GPS tracking device. Which was a problem. The battery pack could no longer be physically removed, and getting the SIM card out was a bitch. There was only one way to be a hundred per cent sure that no one could use the phone to track them.

Mohawk lowered the electric window, letting in the furious roar of passing traffic through the small opening.

Then he tossed the phone out of the wagon.

Ring One grinned. 'No one can track you now, bitch.'

Street tried to stay calm. He recalled the training he'd under-gone at Fort Monckton in Plymouth as a young intelligence officer. He knew he should focus on his captors, observe them and look for weaknesses. That was what the training manual said. But that was a long time ago, when he was backed up by the full might of a national security service. Not any more. Now he was just one man.

These people are going to kill you, the voice inside his head told him. *They're going to get what they need from you. Then they're going to butcher you.* It would not be a quick death, Street knew. He was familiar enough with their training. They would want some fun with him before applying the killer blow.

Unless I can find a way out of here, I'm a dead man.

'You're making a big mistake,' he said to Mohawk, making his appeal directly to the leader. 'You don't know who you're dealing with.'

'Shut the fuck up,' Ring One snapped.

Street tried again. 'I've got colleagues. They'll come looking for me, once they find out I'm missing. You should let me go now, before things get bad for you.'

'I said shut up, bitch!'

Ring One twisted in his seat and drove his balled left fist into Street's ribs. Street bent forward at the waist, the seat belt tightening across his chest as he gasped for air. Then Ring One shoved his Taser tight against Street's groin, shocking his balls.

The pain was excruciating. Like nothing Street had ever experienced. His testicles felt as if they might explode. He thrashed around wildly in his seat between Ring One and Ring Two, howling in agony. Ring One grinned and gave him another bump from the Taser.

'That's enough!' Mohawk snapped, whipping round to face Ring One. 'We don't want to give him a heart attack.'

Ring One turned to confront the other guy. 'You can't tell me what to do.'

'Yes, I can. Or have you forgotten who you're talking to?'

Ring One stared at Mohawk, his lips trembling with rage. 'No. I don't forget. But you're not my fucking boss.'

He shot Mohawk a defiant glare and turned back to face Street. Depressed the trigger on the Taser again. Fifty thousand volts shocked through Street's body.

Street screamed. Mohawk jumped out of his seat in the middle row ahead of Street and the Ring Brothers. He swung around to the rear seats in the Caravan, thrusting out an arm at Ring One and pulling his comrade away from Street. Ring One tried to shrug Mohawk off, but the latter had a firm grip on his shoulder. The two men struggled in the confines of the wagon, wrestling for control of the Taser as they cursed at each other.

'Get the fuck *off* me, bitch!' Ring One rasped.

Up ahead, Street noticed Soccer Mom glancing back at the argument unfolding behind her in the wagon. She had taken her eyes off the road for only a split second.

But it was enough.

They were crossing the next junction. In the corner of his eye, Street glimpsed a Ford Explorer hurtling towards them. A metallic grey blur, bombing toward the junction from the east. Thirty metres away at his three o'clock. The lights were flashing red on the north–south road but Soccer Mom hadn't seen the change in signal. She was still looking over her shoulder at Ring One and Mohawk. She didn't see the Ford Explorer.

Ring One and Mohawk were both half out of their seats, wrestling in the space between the middle and back rows.

Ring Two was sat to the left of Street on the back row, shouting at the others in his native tongue.

None of them saw the Explorer tearing across the junction.

Street braced himself. He had just enough time to realise that the Explorer was going too fast. That the driver wouldn't be able to slow down in time to avoid a collision.

Then he had no time at all.

SIX

There was a bone-rattling shudder as the Explorer T-boned into the right-side of the Caravan at speed. Two thousand-plus kilograms of metal and glass collided with the minivan at its central point, lifting up the rear wheels and sending it into a violent spin as it skidded across the blacktop.

Kinetic energy rippled through the Caravan. Street was the only one wearing a belt and he felt the strap bracing tight across his front, digging into his guts as he lurched forward in his seat. Ahead of him, Ring One and Mohawk were flung around the interior like a couple of rag dolls. To his side, Ring Two was thrown forward. He slammed into the back of the seat in front of him, arms and legs flailing. Like he'd been shot out of a cannon.

The sliding door on the right side of the Caravan buckled inward, blowing out the windows and showering the interior of the wagon with glass shards. Street closed his eyes as glass rained down on him.

Metal twisted. He heard the screeching of tyres as other drivers around the junction emergency-braked.

The world kept on spinning.

Half a second later, the Caravan jerked to a halt.

So did the Explorer.

Street coughed and opened his eyes. He took in a draw of breath and felt a sharp, stabbing pain in his ribs. His hands were nicked with cuts and bruises and there was a tinny, ringing noise in his ears, but otherwise he seemed okay. A car alarm wailed somewhere close by. From the other car, Street guessed. He cleared his lungs, then glanced around the Caravan.

The three toughs were not okay. Ring One and Mohawk had smashed up against the seats at the front end of the Caravan. They were sprawled on the floor space between the front and middle rows, their clothes sprinkled with bits of broken glass. Forward of the pair of them, Street could see Soccer Mom behind the wheel, her face resting against the inflated airbag, like she was hugging a giant pillow.

None of them were moving.

Ring Two was slumped forward in the seat to the left of Street. His forehead was resting against the leather of the seat in front. Blood trickled down his face from a glistening wound to his scalp. His left eye had clamped shut. His nose had been reduced to a gout of blood and shattered bone. He looked like he'd just gone ten rounds with the Klitschko brothers. Both of them.

Then Street heard voices from outside the Caravan.

Getting louder.

He twisted in his seat so that he was facing the sliding door on the left side of the minivan and peered through the cracked glass.

Four bystanders stood on the north-east corner of the junction, twenty metres away from the wrecked motors. One of them was frantically making a call on his mobile. Another simply stood there, rubbernecking the scene. The other two had taken out their phones and were filming everything.

Three more civilians were rushing towards the Caravan. One of them raced towards the Explorer. The other two sprinted over to the minivan. They were fifteen metres away now and closing fast.

The Explorer, Street thought as his head cleared.

Of course.

The embassy must have been following me the whole time, he realised. Of course my friend Terry would look out for me. They must have seen Mohawk and the others lifting me from the car park and moved to intercept as soon as they could.

They've rescued me.

Thank God.

He glanced back at Mohawk and his two mates. Ring One had stirred and was coughing up shit from his lungs. Mohawk groaned. Ring Two still wasn't moving. They were disorientated but from the looks of them, they wouldn't be for much longer.

The car alarm continued to sound its distress note as Street unbuckled his seat belt. He leaned over and snatched up his jacket, blocking out the throbbing pain in his ribs. Then he half-turned towards the sliding door on the left side of the Caravan. Stopped, remembered the dossier and searched frantically around for it. He found it lying on the floor next to the middle row of seats. Street snatched it up, folded it in half at the waist and stashed it in the inside pocket of his jacket.

He placed his jacket over his wrists, hiding the plasticuffs. His pose looked slightly awkward, but it was the best he could do. Better than letting people see the cuffs and making all sorts of assumptions, none of which would be good for him.

The two civilians were less than five metres from the door now. There was no sign of his rescuers debussing from the Explorer. Street wondered what was taking them so long.

Up ahead, Mohawk winced with pain as he tried shifting his weight. Street figured he had only another couple of seconds before the pair of them realised what was going on. He shuffled forward, leaned over to the left-side door and tried popping it open. The panelling had been warped out of shape. It wouldn't budge.

Behind him, Ring One was making a deep keening sound in his throat as he stirred. Glass tinkled across the floor as the guy shook his head clear.

Street tried the door again.

Still nothing.

In the next moment the two civilians reached the side of the Caravan.

Street saw them through the window. A woman decked out in yoga leggings and a sweat-drenched halter top, and a heavyset black guy in loose-fitting jeans and a Washington Wizards basketball t-shirt.

The guy in the Wizards shirt stepped forward and wrenched open the sliding door from the outside with a mighty effort. Street did a quick check to make sure his plasticuffs were concealed under the jacket. Then he slid out of his seat and stumbled down to the blacktop. Wizards and Yoga Woman took an arm each and helped him away from the wreckage.

'Sir?' Yoga Woman said to Street. 'Can you hear me? Are you hurt?'

Street shook his head slowly. 'I'm okay, I think.'

'What about your friends, sir?'

He said nothing.

'One of them dudes don't look so good,' Wizards cut in, nodding at the wagon. 'That lady in the other ride neither.' Street looked over at the Explorer. The SUV had stopped in the middle of the junction box, at a right-angle to the Caravan. The front end looked as if a wrecking ball had taken a giant swing at it. The metal grille hung off the front, exposing a tangle of wires and pipes. Smoke hissed out from under the crumpled bonnet.

A woman was trapped behind the wheel. She was screaming for help, begging them to save her baby.

There was no one else in the car.

No embassy officials. No sign of Terry.

Not my rescuers.

Just a mother and her baby in the wrong place, at the wrong time.

A single thought screamed at Street above the ringing in his ears and the flaring pain in his chest.

You've got to get out of here.

Now.

'Someone's called for help, sir,' Yoga Woman said. 'An ambulance is on the way. They'll be here any minute.'

Street nodded, thinking fast. 'Stay here, will you? Help my friends.'

'You'll be okay, sir?'

'I'm fine,' Street lied. 'Just need to sit down. Don't worry about me.'

Yoga Woman and Wizards hurried back over to the Caravan like the dutiful citizens they were. Street watched them for a beat. Then he turned and hurried across the junction.

Dozens more bystanders had gathered at the side of the road, many of them taking out their phones to film the scene. Most of the bystanders had spilled out of the fashionable eateries and pubs lining Connecticut Avenue. They were in a well-to-do part of town. Brightly lit streets, with wide, clean sidewalks and quaint stores selling everything the blue bloods of the area needed. Another pair of good Samaritans rushed over to the Explorer.

They were trying to do their best to comfort the mother, but it was clear they couldn't get to her. Not with the Explorer badly bent out of shape.

Yoga Woman and Wizards were at the side of the Caravan, checking on the three toughs inside. Street quick-walked away from the crash, towards the crowd that had quickly formed outside one of the restaurants. A fancy-looking steak house on the corner of the junction, twenty-five metres south of the shattered vehicles. Street threaded his way through the crowd and continued past the bus shelter. Head down, avoiding eye contact. No one stopped him to ask if he was okay. Everyone was transfixed by the mother trapped in the Explorer, screaming for help. His muscles felt sore and stiff. There was a jarring sensation between his temples and every step caused shooting pains to flare up in his back. But Street forced himself to keep moving.

He knew he had to put some distance between himself and the toughs.

Any moment now they'll get their shit together.

Another step, and the throated growl of an engine reached his ears.

Street risked a glance over his shoulder. Beyond the crowd he glimpsed a dark blue Impala U-turning in the road, a hundred and fifty metres beyond the junction. The escort vehicle. The car Jogger Guy had been driving. He had swung the Impala around, presumably after seeing the accident in his rear-view. Now he was bombing south, moving at a fast clip towards the Caravan.

There was no chance of Jogger Guy spotting him from this distance, Street knew. The dense throng of bystanders outside the steak house was growing by the minute, shielding him from view.

But he couldn't afford to stick around.

Once the toughs were out of the Caravan, Yoga Woman and the others would inevitably point out the direction Street had gone. He was on a wide residential avenue, with no obvious alleys to escape down or cover to hide behind. As soon as his captors spotted him, he would become a target.

I need to get off the sidewalk.

He looked ahead. Fifty metres to the south there was a curved glass roof overhanging an escalator and steps leading down to a ticket hall. There was a signpost next to the escalator marked with an 'M'. The local metro station, Street realised.

It had been twenty years since he had used the DC metro. But he remembered the line that passed through here would take him far north, beyond the city limits.

Into Maryland, and safety.

Street quickened his stride. Forty metres to the station now.

Ahead of him a tight press of passengers was spilling out of the station entrance. Commuters, mainly. Men and women dressed in sharp suits. Lobbyists and government lawyers, returning to their expensive mid-town condos after a hard day at the office. Most of them were looking down at their phones. Several others were wearing huge designer headphones or small white earbuds, zoned out to the scene around them. They were utterly oblivious to the crash over at the junction.

Street kept moving.

Thirty metres to the station now.

Then he heard the screams. Glanced over his shoulder again.

The crowd outside the steak house was breaking up. People were diving for cover or rushing back inside the restaurant. Forty metres to the north, the two Samaritans were running across the junction. Then he saw why everyone was running. Ring One was staggering out of the Caravan, brandishing Ring Two's semi-automatic pistol in his right hand. Mohawk was a step behind. Street couldn't see Ring Two anywhere. He was still unconscious inside the wagon, Street guessed. Which wasn't a big surprise. He'd looked pretty fucked-up after the crash.

The Impala had skidded to a halt a couple of metres down-stream from the battered Caravan. Jogger Guy was launching himself out of the vehicle, looking from the Caravan to the Explorer. Mohawk was shouting at him and pointing furiously at the wagon. Jogger Guy rushed over to the Caravan to help out their friends.

As the crowd evaporated, Ring One caught sight of Street to the south of the steak house.

He raised his gun arm, aiming the muzzle at Street.

Then he squeezed the trigger.

The pistol jackhammered. A round exploded from the snout.

The round missed Street and thudded into the trunk of a tree a metre to his right, at his nine o'clock. Panicked cries erupted across the junction. People across the street bolted in every direction, diving into organic grocery shops or Polynesian restaurants. Anywhere that was still open at seven-thirty in the evening.

Street turned and ran.

He moved as fast as his tired legs could carry him. Which wasn't all that fast.

Twenty metres from the station now. The gunshot had snapped the commuters out of their phone-trance. Fear and confusion spread through the crowd. A few were quick to respond. Those who had caught sight of Ring One turned and hurried back down the escalators, shouting at the others that someone had a gun.

Others stopped just in front of the station entrance, wearing perplexed looks as they processed the scene in front of them. The fleeing civilians, the screams, the car crash to the north. The rest were taking out their phones and filming Ring One, seemingly unconcerned for their own safety.

Two more gunshots thunderclapped through the air.

The first bullet whipped past Street and struck one of the commuters in the neck. A guy in a pinstripe suit who'd been standing dumbly in front of the escalators, Beats by Dre headphones clamped around his head, his focus completely on his iPhone screen.

He spasmed and made a garbled noise in the back of his throat. Blood sprayed out of the exit wound before he flopped uselessly to the ground. A split second later the second round hit a woman in a pencil skirt, striking her in the calf as she ran for cover. She fell as if somebody had tripped her up, landing on her front outside a vegan food store. Her phone slipped from her grip, the screen shattering as it clunked against the sidewalk.

Street kept moving.

He dropped to a kind of crouch, shrinking low to make himself a smaller target. A fourth round glanced off the row of newspaper vending machines two or three metres short of the metro escalator, at Street's one o'clock.

A second passed.

Then two.

He heard no more gunshots.

Street was ten metres from the station entrance now. He crouched down by the bus shelter and looked back at the junction, his heart beating fast. The guy in the pinstripe suit was lying face-down on the concrete five metres away, blood pooling rapidly around his lifeless corpse. Still wearing his headphones. A couple of metres further along the woman in the pencil skirt was screaming in agony as she pawed at her rag-order leg.

In the distance, police sirens sounded. Ring One had stopped shooting. He stood next to Mohawk beside the Caravan, sixty metres away. The two of them appeared to be having a heated exchange. Mohawk gestured angrily at the pistol Ring One was gripping.

Jogger Guy was ignoring the argument. He was busy helping Ring Two out of the Caravan, his arm wrapped around the guy's waist.

The sirens grew louder.

Which told Street the cops were only a few blocks away now. Another thirty seconds until they hit the junction, he guessed. He suddenly understood why the toughs weren't giving chase. And why Mohawk was so pissed at Ring One. The guy had turned a T-bone crash into a homicide. They would have no choice but to clear off before the cops showed up in force. A foot pursuit was out of the question. There were witnesses who could identify Ring One as the shooter.

Getting off the grid was their priority now. Laying low. They were unlikely to know the city as well as Street, either. Mohawk and Ring One broke off their argument. Ring One hurried over to Jogger Guy, helping him walk Ring Two over to the Impala. Mohawk wrenched the rear passenger door open then stepped aside as Jogger Guy and Ring Two bundled their unconscious comrade into the back seat. Then Ring One rushed back over to the Caravan, dragged Soccer Mom out and shoved her into the back of the Impala alongside Ring Two. He climbed in after her while Jogger Guy dived behind the wheel.

Mohawk stopped beside the front of the Impala. Looked towards Street. Glaring at him as he stroked a finger across his neck in a throat-slitting gesture. As if to say, *This isn't over. You might have escaped today, but we'll find you again.*

Then Mohawk jumped into the front passenger seat.

Jogger Guy gunned the engine.

The Impala fishtailed, burning rubber as the toughs accelerated north on Connecticut Avenue. Heading away from the approaching police sirens.

Street watched them go, relief flooding through him.

Thank God, he thought. *I'm safe.*

For now, at least.

Ten seconds until the cops arrived.

He turned and hurried the last few metres to the metro station. All around him people were lying flat on the ground, hands over their heads. Others were still filming the action on their phones or making panicked calls. Nobody rushed over to the two victims. Street raced down the escalator leading to the station hall.

He had no intention of hanging around when the police showed up. Homicide detectives in the US were nothing if not thorough. They would take a long hard look at Street if they found him at the scene. They would wonder, inevitably, why a bunch of heavies had been chasing him. Had been so desperate to catch him that they had opened fire in the middle of a well-heeled DC neighbourhood. They might even find out about the dossier. And he wasn't about to let it fall into the hands of the Americans.

Through the fog clouding his brain a single thought stabbed at Street. The toughs had targeted him because of the dossier. They had made a point of retrieving it from his Corolla back when they'd lifted him at the car park. But he had been careful to keep the dossier a secret. Only a handful of people knew of its existence, including his friend . . .

Which could mean only one thing.

Someone had told Mohawk and his cronies about the dossier.

Right now I don't trust anyone.

There's only one thing for it, Street decided. He had to get off the grid.

A plan began to take shape in his head as he paced across the ticket hall, threading his way through the tight press of commuters. Lots of people were hunkered down in the hall, crowding the entrance as they peered anxiously up the escalator at street level.

One or two people gave Street curious looks as he brushed past. He glanced down and saw that one of the plasticuff ties was sticking out from beneath the folds of his jacket.

He carried on towards the northbound platform at a steady trot, intensely conscious of his appearance. The cuts and bruises on his head he couldn't do much about, but he would have to get rid of the plasticuffs as soon as possible. Apart from making him look conspicuous, they were digging painfully into his wrists.

He would find a hardware or general store somewhere over in Maryland. Ask the store owner to cut him free. He could explain that he was on a stag weekend and his friends had played a joke on him. With his English accent, Street thought, he might just be able to pull it off.

He tried to tell himself that things were going to be okay.

You've still got the dossier. More than one party is desperate to get their hands on it. Which could strengthen your bargaining position. You could demand more money. Perhaps insist on protection. A new identity, even.

There's still money to be made from this thing.

If I can stay alive that long.

But first, he needed a place to hide. His options were limited. He had no phone or passport. A grand total of eighty-seven bucks in his wallet plus change. Hardly enough for a cheap room for a night. Not in a place like DC. Using his credit or bank cards was out of the question, of course. The same for anywhere that required ID. Airports, hotels, car rental agencies. Anything that could be linked to his name. He couldn't risk leaving a trail. He'd been lucky to escape this time.

He would not make the same mistake twice.

What he needed was a hideout. Somewhere no one would think to look for him. A place his enemies wouldn't know about.

Street smiled with relief as he boarded the next train.

He knew exactly where to go.

SEVEN

Nine thousand miles to the east, ex-Regiment legend John Bald lifted the cold pint to his lips and took a long pull of his beer.

It tasted good.

Almost as good as the view he had of the Thai girl he was currently shagging.

Kamlai Divine sat on the stool to his left, rocking it in a red leather crop-top and a matching mini-skirt that showed off her stunning curves. Behind her, a projection screen across the back wall of the Drunken Monkey pub was showing the football. His beloved Scotland were playing in a World Cup qualifier, and they were one-nil up versus the Bulgarians.

Bald took another swig of his pint and grinned. Football on the telly, pint of Chang in his hand, and a girlfriend half his age with a cracking arse and small-but-perfectly-formed tits. Life really didn't get much better than this.

Moving to Bangkok, thought Bald.

Best bloody decision I ever made.

Kamlai set down her bottled beer on the counter and smiled suggestively at him. She had diamonds studded in her teeth. One of the reasons she'd caught Bald's eye at the club where she was working as a bargirl, seven weeks ago.

'You maybe want massage?' she said. 'Strong man like you need massage. All those big muscles.'

'Maybe later, love.'

Kamlai licked her lips and ran a hand up his leg until her fingers were lightly brushing against his crotch.

'We could go back to your flat,' she said in her sing-song voice. 'Kamlai show you good time.'

Bald shook his head. 'Not now, lass. Scotland are winning.'

The bargirl retracted her hand and pouted. 'Kamlai bored.'

'Have another drink. It'll be finished soon.' Bald winked at her. 'Then I'll show you a good time.'

'Kamlai don't want more drink.' She folded her arms and pulled a sad face. 'Kamlai want you to meet family. You made promise, remember. When you gonna meet?'

'Soon, love.'

'Always soon. Never happen.' Tears welled in her big, round eyes. 'Maybe you bored with Kamlai. You gonna leave me. Find new girl.'

A roar went up from the speakers either side of the screen. Bald looked over and saw the Bulgarians celebrating a late equaliser. A trio of English football fans sat at a table in one corner of the bar, cheering ironically. Bald gritted his teeth as he turned back to the bargirl.

'Next week, alright? We'll visit your family then. You can introduce me to your folks.'

'Then you make me honest woman?'

'Aye,' said Bald. 'Then that.'

That seemed to placate her. She nodded and wiped the tears from her eyes. 'Make sure ring nice and big. Kamlai no want cheap ring.'

Bald grinned. 'I've got something else nice and big for you, love.'

'You dirty man, Mr John.'

She flashed that diamond-studded smile at him again, and Bald felt a stirring in his loins. He'd had his way with plenty of bargirls since moving to Bangkok, but none of them had come close to matching Kamlai in the sack. The woman was out of this world. She did things that Bald had never heard of, much less experienced. And she was tough. Kamlai wasn't like the other girls he'd met. She'd lived a hard life and there was an edge to her that had impressed him. She wasn't desperately eager to please. She didn't put up with any shit. Bald respected that about her.

Which is why he'd agreed to marry Kamlai. That, and the crazy sex, of course. He was getting for free what every other punter was paying top whack for.

You wouldn't find a bird like this in Glasgow on a Friday night, that's for sure.

His luck had changed massively since his last major op for MI6 three years ago. Back then Bald had been tasked with infiltrating a rogue PMC outfit operating in Somalia, led by a delusional ex-soldier by the name of Kurt Pretorius. After the op, he'd planned on walking away from Six for good. But the suits at Vauxhall had other ideas. They'd stumbled upon evidence of Bald committing war crimes and persuaded him it would be in his best interests if he stayed on the payroll.

They gave Bald a simple choice. Work for Six, or spend the next fifteen years rotting in a cell at the Hague.

He chose the work.

Shortly after, he moved to Thailand.

He needed a change of scenery. He was tired of seeing the same old faces around Hereford, living in the same shoebox flat and drinking in the same pubs. Officially, he now worked for one of the biggest PMCs on the Circuit, Kliner Security. He took home a decent pay packet each month, far more than he'd ever pocketed in the Regiment, and in between his jobs he got to live like a king in the world's biggest fleshpot. Being at Six's beck and call was a small price to pay, Bald figured. And they hadn't reached out to him in months. Perhaps one day soon they'd cut their ties with him for ever.

Good fucking riddance.

Bald drained his pint, made the universal sign to the barman for another and stood up from his stool. He ducked into the toilets, emptied his bladder and returned just in time to see the Bulgarians score an injury-time winner.

When he looked over at the bar, he saw that someone else had taken his spot.

The guy sat with his back to Bald, nursing a fresh pint. Bald recognised him as one of the England fans who'd been cheering on the Bulgarians. His head was closely shaven, his arms were covered in naff tattoos and he wore a retro England shirt with SHEARER emblazoned across the back in big red lettering. The guy rested his free hand on Kamlai's thigh while he chatted her up. Kamlai pretended to laugh at something he said, then looked away.

The other two England fans were still engrossed in the footy. Bald tensed his muscles. Marched over to the bar.

Shearer was telling Kamlai a joke. Something about Muslims going sky-diving. Bald stopped beside him as he unloaded the punchline.

'. . . they had no idea why his snorkel and flippers didn't open.'

Kamlai smiled politely at him. Bald tapped the guy on the shoulder. Shearer ripped his gaze away from the bargirl and swivelled towards the ex–SAS man. He worked his ugly features into a scowl.

'What the fuck are you looking at, pal?' he said in a gruff voice that was part Essex, part forty-fags-a-day.

Bald stood his ground and nodded at Kamlai. 'This one's taken.'

'Yeah?' Shearer spat. 'Says who?'

'Me.'

'And who the fuck are you?'

'Someone you really don't want to piss off.'

Shearer's thin lips curled up into a wicked smile. He pointed to it. 'See this, sunshine? This is me looking fucking scared.'

Bald wasn't the biggest bloke who'd ever passed Selection. He stood a shade over five-nine and weighed exactly the same as the day he'd left 22 SAS, a trim seventy-five kilograms. A greyhound, rather than a mastiff. But what he lacked in size he more than made up for in strength and stamina and grim determination. Qualities that his instructors at Hereford had been quick to recognise. They had turned the angry kid from Dundee into an elite killer and a hero of the Regiment.

But Shearer didn't see any of that. He just saw a wiry, middle-aged Scot with greying hair, and figured he wasn't a threat.

Big mistake.

'Last chance,' Bald said calmly. 'Piss off now.'

'Or what?'

Bald looked him up and down. 'Know any more jokes?'

'Loads.' Shearer looked confused. 'Why?'

'You're about to become one. Once I've finished beating the shit out of you, your mates are going to be taking the piss for years.'

Shearer dropped the smile so fast Bald almost heard it hit the floor. He stood up from the stool and stepped into Bald's face, the vein on his forehead bulging. Behind him, the two other England fans had turned away from the game and slid out of their chairs. Fists balled, ready to wade in and help out their mate at the first sign of trouble.

For a second Bald thought Shearer was going to take a swing at him. Then his small black eyes slid across the bar as a new crowd of expats swaggered in through the door. They filed past Bald and Shearer, laughing and joking as they took up spots along the bar.

Shearer grudgingly relaxed his stance as he stepped back from Bald. He shot a look of contempt at Kamlai, then brushed past Bald and headed back to his mates.

'Scottish wanker,' he muttered.

Bald watched him shuffle away. He turned away from Shearer and his two mates, then pulled up a pew next to Kamlai. Over on the TV, the football match had ended. Two-one to Bulgaria. Another hard luck story for the Scots. The barman came over and put another Chang down in front of Bald. A commiseration pint. He took a long swig.

Better.

After ten minutes, the three England fans left.

Three more beers and a couple of slugs of Famous Grouse later, Bald stood up from his seat, settled his tab at the bar with a pair of thousand-bhat Thai notes, and made for the door. Kamlai dutifully followed at his side, whispering in his ear all the things she was going to do to him when they got back to his place.

They sounded good.

The Drunken Monkey was situated at the end of one of the many narrow alleys leading off the main strip on Sukhumvit Soi 11. In the distance, Bald could hear the repetitive thud of club music, the wild cheers and laughs of the partygoers on the nearby rooftop bar. The apartment Bald was renting was a twenty-minute stroll south along Sukhumvit Road, spitting distance from the Radisson. The night was cool, and he felt like walking back instead of flagging down a cab.

He turned right outside the bar and headed down the alley towards the main street sixty metres away. Chinese cars and vans lined both sides of the alley. Piles of stinking rubbish were piled high outside blocks of crumbling high-rise flats. A rat the size of a small cat scurried across the ground, dimly illuminated by the neon sign outside a massage parlour on the corner of the alleyway. At eleven o'clock at night the parlour was still open for business. The price list next to the sign offered hour-long massages for the equivalent of a tenner.

A soapy massage with a happy ending for less than the price of a cinema ticket, thought Bald. Not a bad deal, that. He briefly entertained the idea of popping into the parlour for a quick tug before the journey home. But then he looked across at Kamlai and changed his mind.

I've got an even better shag waiting for me when I get back.

He was twenty metres from the alley exit when Kamlai froze.

'What?' Bald said, stopping.

She held his arm tightly. 'Mr John.'

Kamlai nodded at the end of the alley. Bald looked in the same direction, his eyes adjusting to the semi-darkness. He saw them then. Three figures stepping out from behind a couple of old vans parked either side of the road.

Shearer and his mates.

EIGHT

Shearer stood in the middle of the trio, four metres ahead of Bald. The guys to his left and right immediately spread out on either side of the alley. The bloke on the left was squat and thickset, like a professional wrestler gone to seed. He wore a replica Wolverhampton Wanderers shirt that stretched like clingfilm across his huge beer belly. The guy to Bald's right wasn't wearing any kind of shirt at all. He had a polo t-shirt wrapped around his trunk, revealing a sunburnt chest with a St George's flag tattooed on his right shoulder. The jagged teeth of a broken beer bottle gleamed in his right hand.

Shearer grinned.

'Going somewhere, sunshine?'

'Home,' said Bald.

'Nah. I don't think so.'

Shearer took a step closer to Bald. Spat on the ground. 'You think you're fucking funny. You won't be smiling after me and the lads are finished with you.'

Bald glanced quickly at Wolves and Sunburn as the pair of them inched closer to him. Surrounding him on three fronts. They were both three metres away now. So was Shearer. Kamlai held tightly on to Bald. He could feel her long fingernails digging into his flesh. Bald slowly pulled her hand away from his. He stared firmly at her as he nodded in the direction of the Drunken Monkey.

'Go back to the bar, love. Tell them to call the cops. And an ambulance.'

She ran off back down the alley. Bald slanted his gaze back to Shearer. The bloke's grin widened, revealing a set of brown teeth, stained from decades of smoking.

'Hear that, lads?' he said, making a sideways glance at Wolves and Sunburn. 'Alan Hansen here is fucking bricking it.'

Wolves and Sunburn chuckled. Bald shook his head. 'Not really. But about five minutes from now, you're all going to need a visit to A and E.'

Shearer lost the grin. He dead-eyed Bald, curling his lips upward into a menacing snarl. His muscles bulged with pent-up aggression, and possibly sexual frustration.

Then he took a half-step towards Bald and took a swing at him. Which is just what Bald wanted.

Shearer was as wide as he was tall, with a neck as thick as a car tyre and arms the size of tower blocks. His fists were like a couple of racks of ham. Everything was buried under a layer of fat. There had been a lot of heavy lifting in the gym over the years, apparently. A lot of bench presses and bicep curls. All the work had been concentrated on the Hollywood muscle groups. Probably a lot of steroids and supplements, too. Shearer had obviously been aiming for mass, not definition. He wanted to get big. Probably a lifetime goal of his.

But all that weight slowed him down. It was called dumb muscle for a reason. Now Bald was going to make him pay for his lack of agility.

Shearer dropped his right shoulder in slow motion as he threw his punch. Like he was moving through treacle. Bald read the move easily. He was a half-second faster than his opponent. Which in fighting terms was an eternity. Like Real Madrid versus a pub football team.

He didn't wait for the punch. Bald got his counter-attack in first, shifting his weight to his right foot and stepping inside Shearer, simultaneously jacking his elbow back and balling his hand into a tight fist. The speed of his attack caught Shearer off-guard. The guy had no time to adjust his stance. No time to defend. He'd invested everything in the punch that he was half-way through unloading.

Bald slammed his fist into Shearer's midriff, drawing a gasp of shock from the guy as the bony ridge of the Scot's knuckles connected with his guts, driving the air from his lungs. Shearer jackknifed at the waist, forming a wide O with his slackened mouth. Bald followed through, grabbing Shearer by his shirt and bringing up his right knee in a sharp jerking movement. There was a dull crack as the hard surface of Bald's knee smashed into Shearer's face, doing all kind of damage to his nose and cheekbones. Shearer grunted in pain. Bald released his grip and let him fall away. The guy face-planted to the ground in front of Bald as if he'd spotted a £50 note lying in the gutter.

He didn't get back up.

Bald stepped back from Shearer, tensing his muscles. Wolves and Sunburn were already lunging at him from the flanks, looking to drop Bald before he could get an attack in. He saw them moving towards him in his peripheral vision. Wolves at his nine o'clock, his fist clenched as he shaped to launch a punch. Sunburn lunging at him from his three o'clock, gripping the broken beer bottle like it was a dagger.

Bald had a fraction of a second to react. He spun to his right. Towards Sunburn.

Deal with the biggest threat first.

Sunburn stabbed out at him with the bottle, aiming for Bald's face. Ready to cut him to pieces. He moved with the confidence of someone who assumed they held the advantage in a fight. Because he had a weapon, and Bald didn't. But the advantage was all in his head. Bald had his own weapon too: himself. He had eighteen years of Regiment training under his belt, plus another half a dozen years operating on the Circuit, and he'd spent thousands of hours training in combat, armed and unarmed. The guy with the bottle had probably been in a handful of fights in his life. He'd seen maybe half a dozen self-defence videos on YouTube.

No contest.

Bald parried the blow with a broad sweep of his left forearm, deflecting the beer bottle at an angle away from his face. Momentum carried Sunburn on half a step, bringing him into attacking range. He closed his eyes as if expecting Bald to slog him square in the face. Instead Bald sidestepped to the right, shoved Sunburn in the back and sent him flying in the direction of Wolves. Sunburn lost his balance, stumbled forward and crashed head-first into Wolves, knocking the latter off his feet before he could rush at Bald.

Wolves fell backwards, arms pinwheeling before he landed on a heap of bin bags dumped in the doorway of a closed shop. Some of the bags had split open down the sides, spilling rotten food, Red Bull cans and soiled nappies over the guy. Sunburn staggered on for a step before he spun back around to face Bald. He still had his right hand clasped around the neck of the beer bottle. His nostrils were flared. His shoulder muscles were pumping up and down with rage.

Bald glanced sideways at Shearer. He was still face-down in the middle of the alley space, kissing concrete. Wolves was lying on his back, covered in shit and flailing wildly.

For the moment, that left Sunburn.

The guy stood a metre in front of Bald, still gripping the neck of the beer bottle in his meaty right hand. He glanced uncertainly at his mates, as if worried he might suffer the same fate. Then male pride kicked in, mixed with animal hatred, and he charged again at Bald, slashing out at his face with the bottle.

His attack was ragged. Undisciplined. Sunburn hadn't expected to find himself one-on-one with his opponent. He didn't want to get dragged down into the trenches with Bald. Now he was rushing things, stabbing wildly in an attempt to land a quick killer blow and get the fight over with.

Bald easily ducked the thrust. He dropped to a crouching stance and left Sunburn thrusting out at dead air. Then Bald sprang up on the balls of his feet, moving inside his opponent. Sunburn had just enough time to register a look of surprise before Bald jerked his head forward and gave him an authentic Glasgow kiss, tucking his chin tight to his chest and headbutting Sunburn on the soft triangle in the middle of the face.

The blow stunned Sunburn. He groaned nasally. The bridge of his nose collapsed into a soup-like mush of shattered bone and cartilage. He stumbled backwards, then fell away, the beer bottle clattering to the ground as he pawed at his ruined face.

Bald kept his fists bunched as he spun around to face Shearer. The guy had scraped himself off the ground and he scowled at Bald from a safe distance. Blood streamed out of his nostrils, staining his teeth. His lips were purpled and swollen. Two of his front teeth had been knocked out. He looked all kinds of fucked-up.

Voices approached the alley from the direction of the main road. Shearer spat out a globule of blood and scurried over to Sunburn. Then he and Wolves hauled the guy to his feet before beating a hasty retreat out of the alley. As they hit the main road they bumped into a stag group out on the piss. Words were exchanged. Shearer shouted at them to move out of the fucking way. The stag group quickly parted. Bald watched the England fans disappear from sight, pleased with himself.

I've still got it, he thought.

Six years out of the Regiment, and I'm still razor-sharp.

Some of the guys who left the SAS let it all go after a while. They went soft. Took comfortable, low-paid security jobs to top up their military pensions and settled down to a life of mild contentment on Civvy Street. A life of Sunday BBQs, shopping trips and charity runs. But that was never Bald's style. He was a hard bastard, conditioned for violence. His whole life had been one giant war. Against the world, and himself.

Even now, I still need to feel the adrenaline of a fight.

He trooped back down the alley, stormed inside the Drunken Monkey and found Kamlai at a spare table messing about on her phone. He motioned for her to leave and they moved at a fast pace down the alley, merging with the crowd on the main street before the cops showed up.

They headed south down Sukhumvit Soi 11 for a quarter of a mile, passing a long line of hole-in-the-wall restaurants, youth hostels and garish nightclubs. They hung a left on Sukhumvit Road, ignoring the ladyboys touting for business as they continued south-east for another half a mile. A hundred metres before they hit the Radisson they turned off the main thoroughfare and approached the side entrance to Bald's apartment building.

As he dug his key card out from his trouser pocket, Bald could feel the hot stirring in his loins again. Beating the crap out of the England fans had put him in the mood. Bald wanted to celebrate.

He was looking forward to giving Kamlai the shag of her life.

Violence, thought Bald.

Better than Viagra, when it came to putting him in the mood.

Then his phone buzzed.

NINE

Eleven o'clock at night in Bangkok was five o'clock in London. Four minutes before he received the message, ex-SAS operator John Porter sat in a windowless basement, fighting a powerful urge to have a drink.

It was an urge he'd fought many times over the years.

One year, two hundred and nineteen days had passed since Porter had last touched a drop of the strong stuff. There had been moments when he was tempted to have a slug of Bell's, but Porter had resisted. After years of hitting the bottle, he was finally sober.

But he could never be completely free of his addiction. Whenever he was stressed or angry, the old thirst came back. The need to drink himself into oblivion.

And right now, Porter was feeling pissed off.

He turned away from the small TV fixed to the wall and glanced at the thickset bloke sitting across from him at the chipped kitchen table.

Derek Sinclair, like Porter, was ex-Regiment. The pair of them had been assigned by their PMC to house-sitting duties, providing round-the-clock security for the twelve-bedroom mansion overlooking Kensington Palace Gardens. They worked in twelve-hour shifts, slept in bunk beds in the bedroom adjoining the basement kitchen and had their meals fixed up for them by the housekeeping staff upstairs.

Nothing ever happened except when the owner, a minor member of the Qatari royal family, rolled into town. Which was almost never. The only entertainment on offer was the Freeview package on the TV, along with complimentary membership at the local gym. The job involved weeks of sitting around doing nothing, punctuated by the occasional visit from the Qatari royals.

There could be no duller or less demanding job for an ex-SAS man.

No stress. No danger.

Nobody shooting at you.

The job was just a placeholder. A way of keeping Porter in salaried work between ops for MI6. Several years had passed since he'd left the Regiment. Since then, Porter had been working for Six on a semi-regular basis. But Vauxhall wasn't in the charity business. They weren't able to offer him a steady income. Instead he'd been given a job with a British security contractor, run by someone with close ties to the intelligence services.

The arrangement was simple. Whenever MI6 needed Porter's talents, the PMC's directors would pull him off the gig and replace him with someone else. When the job was over, he'd return to work as if nothing had happened.

It was Six's way of keeping him on standby, without dipping into their pockets.

Porter didn't care.

He wanted dull.

Dull was good.

Dull meant he wasn't going to reach for the vodka bottle and go back down that dark, destructive path.

But after sharing a room with Derek Sinclair for two months, Porter was ready to snap.

At fifty-four, Sinclair was two years older than Porter. They were close in age, but miles apart in terms of personal hygiene. Sinclair was the dirtiest guy Porter had worked with. He rarely showered, and wore the same white shirt for three or four days in a row when on the job. He didn't even bother to change out of his gym kit after a running session, stinking out the cramped living quarters he and Porter shared.

Sinclair was also a professional bullshit merchant.

The guy was full of himself, despite the fact he'd been booted out of the Regiment for being a prize-winning dick. Whenever they were in the same room, he'd start bragging about previous ops he'd done or places he'd visited. He told the same old stories, over and over. Reliving the glory days of his time in the Regiment.

In Porter's experience, some blokes never moved on after they left the SAS. They spent their time looking back on their careers through rose-tinted glasses, shooting the shit about old COs and weaponry, and generally boring the life out of anyone in listening range.

Sinclair was one of those guys.

For the first few weeks Porter had done his best to ignore him and concentrate on the job. But now they had been cooped up inside the Qataris' mansion for two months. And Sinclair was really getting on his nerves.

A six-pack of Carling would help block this idiot out.

He took another sip of his coffee and tried to focus on the news channel. The main story was about a shootout in downtown Washington, DC. A lawyer in his early forties had been shot dead, and another victim had been wounded in the leg. The shooters had managed to flee the scene of the crime. Police were not treating the incident as a terrorist attack but the investigators said they were looking at all possible angles. The president had sent out a tweet suggesting whoever was responsible would be punished severely, along with anyone who'd assisted them.

Yeah, thought Porter. *Because there's nothing that criminals fear more than being threatened on Twitter.*

The news shifted to the next item. A story about the new president meeting with the Russian ambassador. There was an accompanying shot of them both, shaking hands for the cameras, grinning like a pair of wanking monkeys.

'This job is a bag of bollocks,' Sinclair moaned in his Brummie drawl.

Porter set down his coffee mug. Turned to Sinclair and shrugged.

'It's not so bad,' he said.

Sinclair made a face. 'Are you off your nut, mate? We've been sitting on our arses for weeks on end, doing sod-all except patrolling this gaff. What's so bloody great about that?'

'It's quiet,' Porter replied. 'Plenty of free time to stay fit. And the pay's steady. There's plenty of worse jobs.'

And I should know. I've done a fair few of them.

Sinclair snorted. 'Speak for yourself, mate. This work is doing my fucking head in.'

That makes two of us, Porter thought to himself.

He took another sip of his coffee, half-wishing that he'd laced it with a double-measure of whisky.

'I'm a fucking Regiment legend, me,' Sinclair droned on in his dull voice. 'I should be doing better than this. Thirty grand a year, for guarding this place? Do me a favour. I'm worth more than that.'

'If you say so,' Porter said through clenched teeth.

'I do, mate. I do. I mean, look at me.' Sinclair pointed to his flat stomach. 'Rock-hard abs, these. Have a feel, if you want.'

'I'm fine.'

'Suit yourself. But I'm telling you, I'm still in good nick. Better than half them lads over at Hereford these days. Reckon I could still pass Selection and all.'

Porter gave a dry laugh. 'Sure, mate.'

This guy's delusional. He'll be telling me he could storm the Iranian embassy single-handedly next.

Sinclair's expression hardened. 'I'm serious, Porter. You might be ready for the scrapheap, but I ain't. I've still got something to offer. I should be out in Syria making top whack, not pissing about here.'

Why don't you just fuck off then, Porter was tempted to reply. But he kept his mouth shut. He clenched his jaw, gripped by a sudden desire to punch Sinclair in the face. Another twelve weeks of this bollocks, he thought to himself as the blood boiled in his veins. Another three months of listening to this tosser bigging himself up, telling the same old tales and stinking out the basement with his dirty kit.

It's almost enough to make me want to go back to working for those backstabbing bastards at Six.

Almost.

His phone trilled urgently on the kitchen table.

New message.

Porter swiped to unlock and tapped the icon.

The message was from his daughter, Sandy. It said, 'Corey & me had a big fight. Kicked me out ... Now saying he won't pay maintenance. Don't know where else to go. Pls call me back. S xx.'

Porter felt another wave of anger surge up into his guts. Corey was Sandy's long-term waster of a boyfriend. The pair of them lived in a shoebox flat in Bromley and had been on and off more times than the light switches at a hotel full of OCD sufferers. Things between the two of them had become worse after Sandy announced she was pregnant. Now it seemed like Corey had made good on his threat to give her the boot.

He scooped up the phone, slipped on his jacket and stood up from the kitchen table. Sinclair looked up at him, a look of confusion playing out on his face.

'Where you off to, mate?'

'Out,' said Porter. 'For a stroll.'

'But you're on shift in twenty minutes.'

'Then I'll be back in nineteen.'

If I spend another minute in this basement, I'll end up nutting this twat.

Sinclair started to say something in reply but Porter was already stepping out of the living quarters. He passed the broom cupboards and utility rooms and private cinema, then climbed the ornate staircase leading up to the ground-floor reception room. Porter crossed the room, beat a path across the wide entrance hall and headed for the main doors. One of the Portuguese maids was busy dusting surfaces and she nodded quickly at Porter as he hit the doors and stepped outside.

The chill London air was a relief after the stuffy confines of the basement. Porter trotted down the pathway, slipped out of the gate and brought up Sandy's contact details on his phone. Hit Dial.

The phone rang. And rang.

No answer.

Porter tried again, then hung up without leaving a message.

Well, fuck it.

He turned right and marched south towards Kensington High Street. The gym he used was situated off the main street but Porter wasn't interested in smashing his personal best on the treadmill today. Without even thinking about it he found himself making his way towards one of the nearby boozers. Like any seasoned alcoholic Porter had scouted the area when first taking on the job and he knew where all the decent drinking holes were to be found. The place he had in mind was down a side street, sixty metres south of the main thoroughfare.

Porter had started drinking back in the Regiment. He'd been part of an op in Beirut that went disastrously wrong. Three Blades died that day, and although he'd been cleared of any wrongdoing, Porter had taken the blame for their deaths.

Shortly after, he turned to the bottle.

For a while, he'd managed to hide it from his superiors. But eventually the drinking cost him everything.

His career, his home.

His family.

Ten years ago, he'd been a dishevelled wreck, sleeping rough and drinking cans of K cider while he begged for pennies from the commuters outside Victoria station.

He'd worked hard to rebuild his life since then.

He'd cleaned up his act. Kicked the bottle. Taken up a job working as an asset with MI6. Porter had even patched things up with Sandy. For years she'd refused to have anything to do with him. Now they spoke once a week. Like a proper father and daughter.

Things were settled, but fragile.

The slightest stress or frustration could set him off, Porter knew. On those days, he struggled.

Today was one of those days.

He reached the pub in a few quick strides. An old-school place tucked away in the shadows, it had somehow avoided being transformed into an organic coffee house or a gluten-free pizzeria. It was the kind of place that still had a darts board on the wall and a one-armed bandit in the corner and a menu that hadn't been updated since the 1970s.

Porter stepped inside and made for the bar. A familiar pub smell lingered in the air. Eau de Fag Ash. The woman behind the bar looked fifty or thereabouts and shot him a bored look. Porter ran his eyes over the array of craft beers he'd never heard of.

Just one pint.

Something to take the edge off.

Porter knew he was making excuses. Classic alcoholic behaviour. *I need a drink because of X or Y.* But he was beyond caring. *I just want to have a bloody pint.*

'Yes, love?' the woman asked.

He was about to order when his phone trilled urgently in his jacket pocket.

Porter stepped away from the bar as he fished out the handset. He swiped to unlock. Glanced down at the phone.

A new text message.

But this one wasn't from Sandy.

The sender's number wasn't any of the paltry few in his Contacts list. It was just a long line of numbers that meant nothing to him. The message was just three short sentences, fourteen words long.

And seemingly innocuous.

Your mother wants to meet at the tea room. The usual place. Saturday. 12pm.

Porter knew what the message meant as soon as he read it. He'd received dozens of similar notes in the past, all framed in the same coded language.

Mother was his handler at Vauxhall. *Tea room* was the private suite at the Lancaster Hotel off Euston Road, regularly swept for bugs, and used by Six as a briefing room when meeting with their outside assets. The date was straightforward but to get the correct time you had to deduct three hours. So midday indicated the meeting was actually scheduled for nine o'clock in the morning.

Porter read the message through once more, then hit Delete.

He didn't know what Six wanted with him. There was no clue in the message about the job.

But I know one thing, Porter thought.

My boring life is over.

He cast a long, wistful glance at the bar.

Then he turned and left.

TEN

Thirty-nine hours after he got the message, Bald stepped out of the taxi in front of the Lancaster Hotel. He handed over a pair of twenties to the driver and took the change. The thick-bearded driver waited for a tip that never came and gave Bald the stink-eye before pulling out into the choked traffic of Euston Road in rush hour. Bald watched the guy for a few moments then made his way up the flagstoned taxi rank towards the hotel entrance. He was fourteen minutes early for the meeting.

He'd taken the first available flight out of Thailand, catching the eleven o'clock service to Heathrow direct from Bangkok International, on a creaking old Boeing 747 that served up cheap heated meals and overpriced cans of Belgian lager. Bald didn't much care, because he wasn't picking up the tab. Thirteen hours later, he touched down at Heathrow. Collected his brown leather holdall from the luggage carousel, grabbed a taxi from the long line outside the terminal. Fifty-seven minutes later he arrived outside a serviced apartment block in Aldgate, a quarter of a mile from Liverpool Street station.

Kliner Security owned the apartment, one of several they had scattered around the city. Paid for with the profits creamed from the decade-long wars in the Middle East, and the major security contracts handed out to private companies in the years since. The place had everything he needed, and a load of stuff he didn't. Designer coffee machine, a TV with more apps than channels, a fridge the approximate size of a meat locker.

By the time he'd checked in and unpacked his bag, it was ten o'clock in the evening. He awoke early the next morning, showered and fixed himself a pot of black coffee before catching another cab to the Lancaster. Bald didn't feel jetlagged. The opposite, in fact. He remembered reading in a magazine some-where that travelling east was always worse than travelling west. Some science bollocks.

Let's get this over and done with, Bald thought as he swept through the sliding glass doors into the lobby.

The hotel was a solid three-star job. Plain walls, cheap furniture that came in various shades of beige. Nothing spectacular. Evidence of the new accountability at Vauxhall. Six didn't go in for the lavish five-star places any more. Not with Whitehall pen-pushers scrutinising every invoice and receipt. Hotels like the Lancaster were cheaper, and more anonymous.

Bald scanned the lobby, searching for his usual handler. There was no sign of the guy, so he beat a path towards the bar located on the far side of the lobby. The place was half-empty. A few men and women in suits, sipping on flat whites while they crowded around laptop screens or chattered on their phones.

Apparently not an MI6 agent among them.

Bald knew the type. Stern, humourless, pretending to look casual while they studied their surroundings. They were unlikely to be staring hard at a PowerPoint presentation.

But he did see one familiar face in the bar.

The guy was sitting at a table in the far corner. Dressed in a dark short-sleeved shirt and a pair of beige combats, sipping a cup of black coffee while he people-watched through the window.

Not a businessperson.

Someone Bald recognised immediately.

He moved past the suits before drawing to a halt in front of the table. Nodded at the coffee cup and said, 'Shouldn't that be a pint of wine?'

John Porter looked up. He blinked, stood up from his chair and smiled at his old mucker.

'Jock. Jesus.'

'Expecting someone else, mate?'

'No one.' Porter creased his brow. 'What are you doing here?'

'I get a kick out of hanging out in crap London hotels. What the fuck do you think?'

Porter thought for a beat, nodded. 'Six reached out to you as well.'

'Aye.'

'They didn't say anything to me.'

'Does that surprise you?'

Porter shrugged. 'Nothing surprises me when it comes to those bastards.'

'Join the club. When it comes to hating Vauxhall, I'm a lifetime member.'

'You should order something,' Porter said. 'We're still early.'

Bald nodded. It would look suspicious if they didn't order any food or drink while they were waiting for their contact to show up. He took up the chair opposite Porter and browsed the menu. Settled on a glass of orange juice and gave his order to a dark-haired waitress with an impressive rack. Bald ogled her figure as she sauntered off towards the bar.

'One thing I miss about London,' he said. 'The tits. Thai women are a little on the small side, if you know what I mean.'

'I don't,' Porter said. 'Never been.'

'You're missing out, pal. Big-time.'

'You're still living in Bangkok, then?'

'Still living like a god, mate.'

'That's one way of putting it.'

'Is there any other?'

'Maybe not,' Porter said, thinking of his own problems. He caught Bald glancing at his coffee and grinned. 'There's no voddie in that. In case you were wondering.'

'Good,' Bald replied. 'Because if there was, I'd have to give you a fucking slap.'

The two former Blades shared an easy smile. Eight months had passed since they last worked together, leading a team of lads from the Regiment across the border into Syria to seize a vital dam. But Porter and Bald had known each other for much longer than that.

They'd served alongside one another in 22 SAS, more than twenty years earlier. Back then Porter had been a broken man, drinking heavily while on secondment to Training Wing, the unit in charge of Selection. Bald had been a promising young oper-ator, the youngest guy ever to join the Regiment, with a bright future ahead of him. Both were temporarily assigned to MI5 and

MI6 during their careers, hunting down murderous Serbian warlords and dodgy ex-generals.

But after leaving the Regiment, their lives had taken them in very different directions.

Bald had gone rogue on the Circuit. He'd got caught up in drug trafficking, blood diamonds. Murder. Until MI6 caught up with him, and made him an offer he couldn't refuse. Almost a decade later, he and Porter were now working together again.

They didn't always see eye to eye. But they'd saved each other's bacon more than once over the years, and they had a deep respect for each other in a way only old warriors could understand. Bald had also seen Porter struggle with his addiction, and he'd done more than most to help him get clean. They weren't like brothers or close friends, thought Bald. More like former teammates from a title-winning football side.

The waitress returned with Bald's orange juice, giving him another tantalising preview of her tits. Once she was out of earshot Porter looked over at his mucker and said, 'Do you have any idea what this is about?'

'None, mate. Whatever it is, they're keeping their lips sealed tighter than a nun's arsehole.'

'Could be another Syria op.'

'Could be,' said Bald, non-committally. 'One thing's for sure. They're definitely not fucking around.'

'What do you mean?'

'Setting up the meeting so soon. I barely had enough time to pack my bags. They're keen to get the ball rolling on this one.'

'Which means they're desperate.' Bald shrugged. 'As long as I get paid top whack, I don't give a toss what the mission is.'

'Your hooker fund running low?'

'Not hookers. Honeymoon fund.'

Porter almost spat out his coffee. 'You must be joking.'

'What's so funny about that, mate?'

Porter chose not to answer that question. 'Who's the lucky woman?'

'Kamlai,' Bald replied tetchily. 'She's a real woman. Not your usual Thai bride. Knows how to make a man happy, like. Soon as this is over, I'm going to marry her.'

'You're serious?'

'Why wouldn't I be?'

Porter shrugged. 'Just couldn't see you ever settling down. You're not the type to go soft.'

Bald shot him a look. 'Who said anything about going soft, you prick? I'm still hard as fuck. Anyway, you're not one to talk. The sad old cunt who hasn't had a shag since the Dark Ages.'

No, Porter thought to himself. Jock definitely hasn't softened up.

He thought about coming back with some lame joke, but surprised himself by actually being happy for his old mucker. Bald, the dirtiest bastard who'd ever set foot in the Regiment, getting hitched. The idea seemed ridiculous. But then again, there were no rules about happiness. People found whatever worked for them and just went with it. And if Bald's version of happiness was a five-foot-nothing Thai bird, who was Porter to judge?

He smiled. 'I'd say let's celebrate with a bottle of bubbly, but I'm still off the drink.'

'Aye. And it had better stay that way,' Bald replied.

Twenty seconds later a short, skinny guy in a bland suit swaggered over to their table.

He looked to be in his mid-twenties, with a prematurely receding hairline and a grey look on his face. Bald immediately made him as an MI6 lackey. Vauxhall was brimming with them these days, he knew. Posh cunts with PhDs who fancied themselves as super-agents. They resented guys like Bald and Porter: the assets who knew the streets, who could handle themselves in a fight. The ones who knew how to tail a suspect properly.

'Gentlemen,' Hairline said, wasting no time on introductions. 'Mother's upstairs. She's waiting for you.'

'About bloody time,' grumbled Bald.

Bald and Porter stood up, settled the bill and followed Hairline out of the bar and across the lobby towards the bank of lifts. They rode the lift to the fourth floor, and then Hairline led them down a series of corridors until they arrived outside a door with a brass plaque on it that said, 'Suite 406'. Hairline knocked twice, then stepped back.

The door opened and another suit answered the door. He looked broadly the same as Hairline, but older. The hair a little greyer and thinner, the bags under his eyes more prominent, the features a little more worn. The effects of a long-term position with Six. He gestured for Bald and Porter to step inside, with Hairline following close behind.

They entered a reception room with solid wood floors, art deco furniture and vintage canvas prints of New York City fixed to the walls. A door to the left of the reception led into the bedroom, with another door on the right leading to the bathroom. The windows on the far wall overlooked the bustling thoroughfare along Euston Road.

A sofa was arranged on one side of a coffee table in the middle of the reception room. There was a wooden breakfast tray on the table with a bunch of coffee cups, a French press, a bottle of sparkling water, plus a selection of croissants and pastries. Two matching grey chairs faced the sofa on the opposite side of the coffee table.

On the chair on the left sat a smooth-looking man in his late fifties wearing a dark blue suit and a purple waistcoat.

Nigel Moorcroft was Bald and Porter's handler at MI6. He looked like the kind of guy who had a lifetime membership at Queen's. Moorcroft was long and slim, with a full head of immaculate white hair on top of his head. Like a cigarette holder with a tab sticking out of the end. His legs were crossed, revealing a set of pink socks beneath his Savile Row suit. His one nod to ostentation.

Porter glanced at the person sitting next to Moorcroft.

Then he stopped dead.

Found himself looking at a face he hadn't seen in ten years.

ELEVEN

Dominique Tannon stood up to greet the two ex-Blades.

'John, Jock,' she said, nodding at them in turn. There was a hint of affection in the way she said the first name. Her eyes settled on Porter. 'Been a while, hasn't it?'

'Too long, love,' Porter said.

Bald was grinning wryly at his side.

Porter's mind drifted back to a mission they'd carried out, shortly before he'd quit the Regiment.

Freetown, Sierra Leone. An op to retrieve an ex-SAS major who'd gone missing in the middle of a violent coup. Tannon had been their contact at the British consulate at the time. She'd been trapped with Porter and Bald in the Ambassadors' hotel during the coup, along with hundreds of terrified expats, while out in the streets an army of bloodthirsty local rebels ran riot.

Porter had turned to the drink. The situation had been desperate. No one had thought they would make it out of there alive. He'd ended up sharing a bottle of vodka with Tannon one evening. A last drink before the battle. One thing had led to another. Somehow they'd ended up naked, on a bare mattress on the floor of Tannon's hotel room, while half a mile away hundreds of rebels prepared to lay siege to the hotel.

Later on, Tannon revealed that she'd been working with MI6. She was their boss at Six for several years after Sierra Leone, before being transferred to counter-intelligence operations. Porter had never seen or heard from her again.

Now she was standing in front of him.

He guesstimated Tannon must be in her mid-fifties by now, but she looked a decade younger. She had that healthy runner's glow to her. Her body fat was probably in the low single digits. The

shoulder-length hair was cut back to a soft pixie cut that emphasised her taut jawline, and the single-breasted jacket and trousers
she wore clung to her slender frame. Just looking at her made him
feel ancient.

Hard to believe I slept with her once.

Moorcroft remained in his chair, legs crossed.

'This is a fucking surprise,' Bald said at last. 'What is this,
Vauxhall's idea of a school reunion?'

'Nothing of the sort,' Tannon replied before nodding at
Hairline. 'You may leave us now, Nicholas.'

'Yes, ma'am.'

Hairline and the other suit stepped out of the suite, closing the
door behind them with a discreet click. Tannon waited until
they'd left, then turned to Porter and Bald.

'Please,' she said, indicating the sofa opposite. 'Have a seat.
Coffee? Water? Tea? Help yourself. You're both familiar with
Nigel, of course.'

Moorcroft smiled and nodded a greeting at Porter and Bald.

'Guys,' he said in a fake matey tone, an Etonian trying to pass
himself off as one of the boys. 'Good to see you both.'

'Yeah,' Bald deadpanned. 'Thrilled to be here. Not like you lot
were interrupting my downtime or anything.'

Porter eased himself down into the sofa next to his mucker
while Tannon poured herself a glass of water.

'What's going on?'

Porter directed the question at Moorcroft, but he didn't
answer. Instead he glanced over at Tannon and spread his hands,
as if deferring to her. Which implied that she was the one in
charge. And which also told him that Tannon had to be seriously
high up the Vauxhall food chain these days. Moorcroft was a
senior intelligence officer attached to the General Support
Branch, the secretive unit within MI6 that employed current
and former Regiment operators to do its dirty work. There
weren't many people above Moorcroft in the organisation.
There were even fewer who had been at Six for as long as him.

Tannon said, 'I never had the chance to properly thank you
both.'

'What for?'

'Saving my life. Back in Sierra Leone. If it hadn't been for you two, those rebels would surely have killed me. Along with every other person stuck inside that hotel.'

'Just doing our job, love. Any other Blade would've done the same.'

'Maybe. But I'm still grateful for what you did.' She looked both of them hard in the eye. 'I wanted you to know that. It's important.'

'Always happy to kill a few chogie bastards, lass,' said Bald.

'You're still at Six, then?' Porter asked Tannon.

Tannon gave a terse nod. 'I work with Nigel and his team.'

She offered no further explanation, but again Porter had the strong suspicion that regardless of her current job title at MI6, she was the one calling the shots. 'Dominique will be sitting in on the operation with us, guys,' Moorcroft said, trying to sound magnanimous. As if he was doing her a favour. 'Makes a pleasant change from the usual ugly fellows we have here, I think you'll agree.'

Tannon glanced sharply at him. Moorcroft, the old Etonian with the attitudes lifted straight out of the British Raj. She smiled, like a tolerant daughter listening to her racist old man.

'Nigel will remain your main point of contact here at GSB,' she said to Porter and Bald. 'But there are additional factors that make it a priority case.'

'What's the op?' asked Bald.

'Have either of you heard of a man called Charles Street?'

Bald and Porter exchanged blank looks.

'Doesn't ring a bell,' Porter said. 'Who is he?'

'Charles is one of ours. Or rather, he used to be.'

Tannon gestured to Moorcroft. Giving him the floor. Moorcroft uncrossed his legs, the cuffs of his trousers lowering over his bright-pink socks. He reached down into a black leather document bag and removed a thin file. He placed the file down on the coffee table and flipped it open.

Inside were a couple of blown-up A4 photographs. Porter studied them both closely. The first one showed a middle-aged man with a round, chubby face, dressed in a tuxedo at some kind of posh do. He had his arm around the shoulder of an attractive thirty-something brunette wearing a pearl necklace. The guy was all smiles. He looked like a hedge fund manager at a charity fund-raiser. Confident, relaxed. Happy.

The second snap was taken more recently. Same guy, but the worse for wear. The hair had thinned, the paunch had got bigger. His face was bloated and puffy. In place of the tux he wore a jacket that barely stretched across his front. The hedge fund manager, five minutes after the sub-prime mortgage market had crashed.

'Charles Street was one of our best field agents,' Moorcroft said. 'He joined the service after graduating from Merton College, Oxford in 1988. Charles specialised in Eurasian studies and quickly made a name for himself as an authority on all things Russian. Transferred to Moscow in the early nineties, shortly after the collapse of the Soviet Union.'

'Charles was in charge of Six's Russian operations through-out the Nineties,' Tannon added. 'It was a vital job. No one knew who was in charge, which way things would go. The situation on the ground was chaotic. We relied extensively on Charles for intelligence. He built up a wide network of contacts inside Russia. Criminals, oligarchs, politicians, FSB agents. Nothing happened in Moscow without Charles knowing about it. He became invaluable to us, basically.'

'You said he *was* one of your best,' Porter pointed out.

'Correct,' Tannon replied.

'So what happened?'

'What happens to every man, at one time or another. He got caught with his pants down.'

'Street was sleeping with an asset, old bean,' Moorcroft cut in. 'Daria Komova. Wife of a Kremlin official.'

'Hard to resist them Russian birds,' Bald said with a grin. 'They've got proper stamina, like.'

Tannon shot Bald a disgusted look. 'Two agents were killed shortly after Charles began his affair with the Komova woman. There were suspicions he may have passed on information that compromised the agents.'

'You think Street sold them out?' asked Porter.

'Nothing was proven. But at the very least, he was guilty of being reckless.'

'At least he got a good shag out of it,' said Bald.

Porter said, 'What has any of this got to do with us?'

Moorcroft glanced at Tannon before replying. 'After he left the security services, Street went private. He did work for various multinationals and government agencies, briefing them on the lay of the land in Russia. Corruption, that sort of thing. His last job was in DC. Producing reports for a security firm called Varangian Risk Assessment.'

'Never heard of them.'

'You wouldn't have. They're minuscule. We're talking two guys in a broom cupboard.'

'Bit of a comedown for one of your lot, that,' Bald commented.

'It's all Street could get, old bean.'

'Meaning?'

Moorcroft spread his hands. 'Charles has been out of the game for a long time now. Twelve years. That's practically an epoch in intelligence terms. He's yesterday's news.'

'Besides,' Tannon added, 'Charles doesn't have many contacts left. No one wants to buy what he's selling. There are even rumours he's taken to inventing claims, to help sell his reports.'

Porter shook his head. 'So this Street bloke was making stuff up for some two-bob outfit in Washington. What the fuck does that have to do with us?'

Tannon and Moorcroft swapped a look. Neither of them said anything for a beat. Then Tannon cleared her throat.

'Six days ago, Charles walked into the British embassy in Washington, DC and met with one of our officers working under diplomatic cover there. Terry Cooper.'

'I've heard of him,' Bald put in. 'He briefed us on a few ops while we were at Bagram, back in the day. Dresses like he's off to visit the Queen for afternoon tea.'

'That's the chap,' Moorcroft said.

'What was the meeting about?'

Tannon said, 'Charles said he'd found something while putting together his latest report. Something big. He said it was too important to take to Varangian. Charles wanted to get Cooper's take on it.'

'And he trusted this other guy, Cooper?'

'They're old friends. Cooper and Street go way back. They joined Vauxhall at roughly the same time and started out together as field agents in Washington. They've been close ever since.'

Porter nodded, visualising the scene. Two young agents, setting out on their new careers in the security services, the exhilaration and danger of operating abroad. Looking out for each other, watching each other's backs. A bond like that didn't break easily. If Street uncovered something big, his first port of call would surely be his old mate.

'What's in the dossier?' he asked.

'We'll come to that. The first thing you need to know is that Cooper considered the contents of the document important enough to fix up a meeting with an American contact of his. Bill Prosser. Ex-FBI.'

'What for?'

'To get a second opinion. On the value of its contents.'

'The meeting was set for three days ago,' Moorcroft explained. 'Wednesday night, at the American's private club.'

'And?'

'Charles never made it there.'

'What happened?'

Tannon sipped more water. Set down the glass. 'We don't have the full facts. You understand that we have to maintain low visibility on this one. Street isn't one of our own any more. He's an ex-agent, operating on his own remit.'

'So what *do* you know?'

Tannon bristled at Porter's tone. 'A snatch team tried to abduct Charles while he was en route to the meeting with Prosser. But the plan failed.'

'How?'

'There was some sort of accident. Their vehicle got T-boned. Charles managed to escape on foot. Shots were fired. One civilian was killed and another hospitalised. The abductors got away too.'

Porter listened, recalling the news report he'd seen on TV back at the Qataris' gaff in Kensington.

A violent incident in the middle of DC.

A wealthy lawyer in his forties, shot dead.

Another victim with a bullet to the leg.

75

Not being treated as terrorist-related.

He said, 'Where's Street now?'

Moorcroft shrugged. 'That's the problem. We don't know. But we can be sure the snatch team is actively looking for him. Which is where you two chaps come in.'

He looked towards Tannon. Porter and Bald stared quizzically at her.

'Charles is in trouble,' she said. 'We need you to get over to DC and RV with Cooper. You'll assist him in his efforts to locate Charles before the snatch squad does. Then you need to bring him home.'

TWELVE

Porter stayed quiet for several moments while he digested the int. A hundred questions jumped out at him, all at once.

'Who was on the snatch team?'

'We don't know,' Tannon replied. 'Not yet, at least.'

'But you must have some idea about why they targeted Street,' Bald said.

'We're not completely sure. But we have a working theory that it's because of what Charles discovered in the dossier.'

'Why?' Porter asked. 'What did he find?'

'I'm afraid we can't tell you any more than that,' Tannon replied curtly. 'That information's on a strictly need-to-know basis. And you don't need to know.'

'It might help us understand who's after your man Street. And what they're planning to do with him.'

Tannon looked quickly at Moorcroft. He shrugged. The two of them were having some sort of private conference. *Do we tell them this, or not?* Then Tannon sighed and said, 'Let's just say that what's included in the dossier is worse than your run-of-the-mill scandal. Far worse.'

'How bad are we talking?'

'If it ended up being made public, heads would roll. Lots of them.'

Porter said, 'So Street found out about this thing, put it in his intelligence report and now some snatch unit wants him dead?'

'Not dead,' Tannon corrected. 'We think whoever ordered Street to be lifted wants him alive.'

'Why?'

'To find out his sources.'

Tannon saw the puzzled looks on the faces of both operators and said, 'Charles masked the identities of the sources he

mentioned in the dossier. To protect them, he claimed. Cooper
tried to find out more at their initial meeting, but Charles was
reluctant to give them up. Extremely.'

'Why?'

'We think someone feared that Street was about to go public
with what he'd discovered,' Moorcroft explained. 'Then they took
action to intercept him. Find out who'd been talking to him.'

'Either way, this dossier's extremely hot,' Tannon cut in. 'The
contents could be used to extort the president, blackmail him, or
make all kinds of threats. It'd be more powerful than any conventional weapon.'

Bald said, 'How do we know Street isn't making it all up? You
said he's got previous when it comes to that shit.'

'We considered that. But his report is detailed, and as far as we
were able to, our people have fact-checked the claims contained
in the document.'

'And?'

'Everything checks out. Times, dates. Locations. We're confident that the contents of the dossier are authentic.'

'Besides,' Moorcroft added, 'Charles must have been on to
something. Otherwise why deploy the snatch squad? It makes no
sense unless his abductors had good reason to believe what's in
there is true.'

'And we really have no idea who tried to lift Street?'

Tannon and Moorcroft both shook their heads.

'Who else knows about this dossier?' asked Porter.

Tannon cleared her throat. 'Outside of this room, only a handful of people. Along with Cooper, and whoever was on the snatch
squad. But that might change very soon.'

'How so?'

'The police took Cooper in for questioning yesterday evening. They know he was the last person to speak with Charles
before he went missing. Which means they've already identified
Charles.'

'How'd they ID him?'

'We think they might have seen his face on videos of the incident filmed by members of the public,' Moorcroft explained.
'Facial recognition. The software the American intelligence

services use is highly sophisticated. They would have matched his face to their database almost immediately.'

'So what?' Bald cut in. 'As long as your man Cooper keeps his story straight, he's in the clear.'

Tannon shifted uncomfortably in her chair. She exchanged a furtive glance with Moorcroft. She said, 'It's a little more complicated than that.'

'The fuck is that supposed to mean?'

'If the police know about Street and Cooper, that will have raised a red flag over in Fort Worth. Someone's probably pulling their files as we speak. If they haven't done so already.'

Bald frowned deeply. 'The NSA have a file on Street?'

'He's ex-MI6. The NSA have a file on everybody in foreign intelligence. Same as ourselves. It's standard practice.'

Moorcroft said, 'Once the NSA realises that one of our own's been targeted on their turf, questions will be asked. They'll wonder why an ex-colleague of ours was caught up in a shootout in the middle of DC. They might even share that information with their friends at the FBI. Ask them to look into it.'

'Which is why it's vital we find Charles before they do,' Tannon added. 'We don't want the Americans getting their hands on a former agent and finding out about the dossier.'

A thought suddenly occurred to Porter. 'Whoever the blokes on the snatch team are, they must be professional operators. Or they had been once.'

'What makes you say that?'

'Two things. You said everyone on the squad escaped?'

'As far as we know.'

'That means whoever targeted Street must have had a solid plan in place, in case things got noisy. Otherwise they would've been given the silver bracelet treatment by now. The cops in DC aren't mugs.'

'And the second thing?'

'Their plan almost worked.'

'How do you mean?'

'Street's an ex-spy. He would have taken some basic anti-surveillance measures before the meeting.'

'Correct.'

'That would have been enough to throw off amateurs, but it didn't fool this lot. That means they had proper skills, love. And they're not the kind you learn on Civvy Street.'

Moorcroft smiled wanly. 'You see, that's why we need guys like you at Six. Rough men who know about the dark arts. We've got some wonderful people entering the service these days, great analysts, but they don't have the first clue about this stuff.'

As Moorcroft made the last remark he glanced at Tannon. There was a slight tension between the two Six officers, thought Porter. Moorcroft seemed irritated at having to defer to the younger woman.

'I don't get it,' Bald said, shaking his head. 'How did the snatch squad find out about the dossier in the first place?'

Tannon said, 'We have to assume Charles made multiple copies that even we don't know about. We're in the era of draft messages saved in anonymous email folders and air-gapped computers.'

Tannon saw the confused expression on Bald's face and said, 'A computer that's permanently offline. No better way to secure your data than by staying off the network completely.'

'But if the data's watertight, how did the snatch team get hold of it?'

'Charles may have got careless. He made the same mistake in Moscow, after all. Plus, he's old-school. When it comes to tech, he's not exactly Steve Jobs. One of the copies might have fallen into the wrong hands.'

'What about the Americans?'

'What about them?'

'How much do they know about what's in the document?'

'Only what Cooper told his ex-FBI contact,' she said. 'Which isn't much, apparently. He knows Street had stumbled on some-thing big, and of potential interest to our American friends, but that's all.'

Porter noticed Moorcroft staring at him.

'You don't think the Americans are behind the snatch attempt, do you?'

'It's not their MO. When the Yanks grab someone, they send in about a thousand FBI blokes in riot gear, armed to the teeth and trying to act rock-hard. Lifting a target off the street with a few guys isn't their style.'

'Then we can assume it's an outside operation.'

'That's my guess.'

'And if they haven't been caught, they're probably still looking for Street,' said Tannon. 'It's critical you get Charles out of there. Before *they* get to him. Or the Americans.'

'What's in it for you lot?' Bald interjected. 'Street's not one of your own, not any more. Do you give a toss what happens to him?'

'There's a certain political interest in what Charles has uncovered in the dossier. But there's more to it than that.'

'Like what?'

'Street is a talented former spy, armed with potentially compromising information on a key ally. We'd rather not have to go through the indignity of the media revealing that one of own has spent his retirement digging up dirt on our friends. The consequences could be damaging for all of us. Especially Downing Street.'

Bald puffed out his cheeks. 'Finding your man isn't going to be easy. Last time I checked, America was a fucking big country. He could be anywhere by now. Christ, he could be across the border in Mexico for all we know.'

'We have reason to believe otherwise.'

'How's that?'

'Charles is a lifelong spy. He helped recruit and train up dozens of agents and surveillance teams, and he handled his assets on a daily basis. He knows the standard operating procedures better than his own mother.'

Moorcroft said, 'As you both know, SOP in this situation for any field asset is to go off the grid. We believe Charles will have gone somewhere secure, where no one is likely to look for him. Somewhere that won't involve leaving a paper or electronic trail.'

'He could still be anywhere,' Porter said.

'You'll be working with Cooper,' Tannon replied. 'He has a couple of ideas about where Charles might be hiding.'

'Are we sure he'd know where to look?'

'They're old friends. They go back a long way. If anyone knows where to find Charles, it'll be him.'

Moorcroft said, 'This is what'll happen. You'll fly to DC and meet with Cooper. Then you'll search together for Street. Once you've located him, you'll ferry him out of the country.'

'Do we really need Cooper to tag along?' Bald asked. 'Our jobs would be easier if he just told us where to look.'

'Won't work. Charles is a naturally paranoid sort. If you two show up unannounced, it'll likely panic him. Cooper is the only one Charles trusts at the moment. Hence he needs to accompany you.'

Tannon seemed to be watching Bald and Porter carefully. 'You'll have to keep a low profile, of course. Make sure no one is watching you.'

'Don't worry about us, lass. Me and Porter are sharper than a pair of Savile Row suits. No one'll tail us.'

Porter said, 'When do we leave?'

'Tomorrow morning,' Moorcroft replied. 'We've booked you on the first flight out of Heathrow to Dulles International. Your ESTAs have already been authorised, so you're cleared for travel.'

'We'll need a cover story.'

'You're a couple of old army friends in town to check out the local tourist sites. We've drawn up an itinerary to match. You're booked in for five nights at a mid-range hotel, along with tickets for a guided tour of the Capitol and two passes for the International Spy Museum.'

Porter stared at the two MI6 officers. 'Is that Six's idea of a sense of humour?'

'It'll add to your cover. No one would suspect an MI6 asset of visiting a spy museum.'

Bald and Porter glanced at each other. Shrugged. Bald said, 'What about weapons?'

'You shouldn't need any, gents. Not for a straightforward exfil-tration job.'

'Yeah, well, forgive me for being cynical, but nothing's ever straightforward when it comes to you lot.'

Tannon crossed her legs and said, 'If you need guns, you'll have to forage locally. We can't give you any official assistance while you're over there. For obvious reasons.'

Porter nodded without replying. He and Bald had been playing the game long enough to know the rules. They'd be operating as *deniable* assets. Meaning if the op went sideways, HMG would deny any knowledge of Bald or Porter and their activities. Six would cut them off ruthlessly.

Hopefully this op will be simple. No complications. No weaponry.

I could do without the bloody stress.

'We'll need money,' Porter said. 'In case we run into trouble.'

'Already taken care of,' Moorcroft replied, checking his watch. 'You'll be given some walking-around money. Kliner also deposited a substantial bonus in each of your current accounts, approximately one hour ago.'

'How much?'

'Twelve thousand pounds each. That should be enough to deal with any unforeseen problems.'

Bald grinned broadly. 'I reckon so.'

'That's not a carte blanche for you to go wild,' Moorcroft cautioned. 'Don't spend a penny more than necessary. If you start raiding the mini-bar, that comes out of your own pocket. Understood?'

'Aye,' Bald replied sullenly.

Porter said, 'What happens after we get Street? We might not be able to stick him on a plane. Not if the NSA figure out what he was up to.'

'We've got a team over at GCHQ monitoring communications across the pond. If anything comes up about Street, we'll let you know.'

Tannon sat upright, pressed her hands together and looked at Porter and Bald in turn. 'Any other questions?'

'We haven't discussed pay,' Bald said.

Tannon smiled faintly. 'You already got paid. You're both on a retainer, with Kliner, remember?'

'That's just for having us on standby, lass. Not for going on an op. We're putting our balls on the line here. We should be getting a bonus. Danger money, like.'

'If you're hoping for big bucks, I'm afraid you're out of luck. Times are hard at the moment. Whitehall is having to fight for scraps with every other department.'

'Bollocks. You lot are at the front of the fucking queue when it comes to Downing Street handouts. Always bloody have been. So don't give us the sob story about how your chief is having to root for pennies down the back of the sofa.'

Tannon's smile disappeared. She folded her hands across her lap and sighed.

'Look, all we can promise is that you'll be allowed to keep the leftovers from your expenses funds. That's the best we can do. Anything more than that, it's out of our hands.'

Porter mulled over it for a few beats. Looked at Bald. Nodded. Turned back to Tannon. Nodded again. 'Works for me.'

'Good.'

Moorcroft tipped his head at Porter. 'You'll stay at the serviced apartment this evening. I'll swing by later this afternoon and hand over your itineraries.'

Tannon stood up, announcing the end of the briefing. 'Now, unless there's anything else?'

Bald made no move to get up. He fixed his gaze at Tannon and said, 'There's one other thing.'

Tannon looked at him funny. 'I'm listening.'

'After this op's finished, I'm done.'

'Done?'

'Yeah. Me and Six. It's over. I want out.'

Tannon stared at him. 'You're not serious.'

'I am, lass. Deadly.'

'You really don't get to decide that. Even if you did, I have no authority in this matter.'

'Then speak to someone who does.'

'It's not that easy, I'm afraid.'

Bald spread his hands. 'I'm not in the Regiment any more. Haven't been for a long fucking while now. And whatever leverage you've got over me, I've paid you back and then some.'

Tannon pressed her lips shut and exchanged a quick glance with Moorcroft. For the first time since they'd stepped into the hotel suite, she looked momentarily flustered.

'I've paid my way,' Bald continued. 'I did right by Vauxhall. Now you need to do the same for me.'

'Aren't you a patriot?'

'Me?' Bald laughed. 'Yeah, I am. But only in John Bald Land. I couldn't give a shit about your country.'

Tannon stared at him uncertainly, as if deciding whether or not Bald was joking. Then she saw the determined look on his face and nodded. 'Very well. Bring Street back safe and sound, and we'll talk about terminating your arrangement with us.'

'All I wanted to hear.'

They all stood up. Porter and Bald, then Tannon and Moorcroft. Moorcroft paced over to the window to field a private call. Tannon relaxed her features and smiled at Porter.

'It's good to see you again, John.'

'Likewise, love.'

'I read your file. All the drinking, living on the streets, the divorce. I'm sorry you had to go through all that.'

'Wasn't your fault.'

'No. But I wish there was something I could have done. If I'd known, I might have been able to help you.'

'Doesn't matter. I'm clean now.'

'Glad to hear it. You did well back in Sierra Leone. I'll never forget that. But I'm going to need you both to do even better now.'

'It's a routine extraction job,' Bald remarked. 'You said so yourself. How hard can it be?'

'Charles is a wanted man. What he's uncovered has made him a target. A big one, with a circle painted on his back.'

'We'll get him out of there,' Porter replied confidently.

'Make sure you do. Because if our enemies capture Street, they'll have their hands on an ex-spy who knows all the secrets. It'll be a national security disaster. And we'll be in a world of shit.'

THIRTEEN

'Are you serious, Jock?' Porter asked.

They were back at the serviced apartment owned by Kliner Security. After leaving the briefing at the Lancaster, Porter had returned to his pad in Wood Green to grab his things. Bald had spent the afternoon beasting himself in the basement gym. Most guys in their late forties were beginning to take it easy, but Bald only pushed himself harder with age. He considered himself fitter now than he'd been in his twenties. His muscles were like concrete. He had a six-pack most blokes would die for.

Bald towelled the sweat from his face. 'What about, mate?'

'Quitting Six.'

'Course I am. I've had enough of working with those wankers. Working for Vauxhall should come with a health warning.'

'What'll you do instead?'

'Settle down with my Doris on one of them Thai islands. Koh Samui, maybe. Build my own place, see out my days drinking, shagging and relaxing on the beach.'

'Sounds nice,' Porter said, feeling a twinge of envy.

'Better than doing Six's dirty work. Give me a beach and a pair of tits any day of the week. Might even open up my own bar.'

'How can you afford all that?'

'I've got some funds stashed away. My retirement pot.'

Porter stared at his mucker. He'd heard the stories that had been doing the rounds at Hereford a few years back. Stories about how Bald had gone over to the dark side. He'd got involved in everything from cocaine smuggling to diamond theft, and along the way he'd lined his own pockets.

No wonder Jock can afford an early retirement, thought Porter. *He's probably rolling in dodgy cash.*

'Soon as this op is over,' Bald said, 'This life is over for me. No more dealing with Vauxhall twats. I'll be getting pissed, getting my end tugged by a smashing Thai bird. Can't fucking wait.'

'You'll get bored.'

'Not as bored as you, you sad cunt. Look at you. Living in your crap digs, no cash, not even a decent bird on the go. The only action you're gonna get is a pity shag.'

Porter pulsed with anger. He looked down at the can of Diet Coke in his hand. Two years ago, that would have been a beer. *I'd be on my ninth or tenth drink of the day by now.*

'It's easy for you. You've got no ties. It's different for me. I can't just leave Six.'

'Why the fuck not? You've got no expenses. Ain't as if you're blowing your wad on the booze these days, is it?'

'It's Sandy. She needs my help.'

'That boyfriend of hers still taking the piss?'

'Something like that.'

Bald grunted. Porter had told him before about the problems Sandy was having.

Sandy had been at Porter's gaff when he'd returned earlier that afternoon to pack his bags. She hadn't wanted to talk about it at first, but had then admitted that Corey had kicked her out after their latest bust-up. With her mum, Porter's ex, and her stepdad now living abroad, Sandy had no one else to turn to. Porter had offered to let her stay with him until she sorted herself out. He'd spent the last few nights kipping on the sofa while his pregnant daughter took the bed.

'He says he doesn't want anything to do with the kid,' Porter said quietly.

'You should go round there, mate. Teach that streak of piss a lesson. If that was me, they'd be scraping his remains off the carpet after I'd finished with him.'

'Sandy doesn't want me to. She reckons I'd only make things worse.'

Bald shook his head. 'That's the problem with you southern pooftas. Too soft. Always better to go in hard, I say.'

'Is that what you tell Kamlai?'

'Piss off.'

They were interrupted by a knock at the front door. Two short, sharp raps. Not threatening. But not informal, either. Friendly, but businesslike. Porter set down his Coke, stood up from the breakfast table and approached the door while Bald grabbed a bottle of water from the fridge. Porter looked through the spyhole, saw Moorcroft and Hairline standing outside. Both of them wore stern looks on their faces. Like they were in training for the world frowning championship.

Moorcroft swept inside as soon as Porter cracked the door open, clutching his document bag and making his way over to the kitchen table. Hairline hung back by the door, hands behind his back, his gaze fixed at a spot on the far wall, as if he had a personal beef with it.

Porter, Bald and Moorcroft consolidated around the kitchen table in a loose semi-circle. The intelligence officer unzipped the document bag, took out two bulky white envelopes and set them down on the table.

'Your itineraries, gents,' Moorcroft said. 'Fifteen hundred dollars in walking-around money, plus two tickets for direct flights to DC from Heathrow, in economy plus. You'll note that the return portions are open-ended.'

'What about Street?' Porter asked.

'There's an open single ticket for him included in your pack, booked with the same airline. There's a replacement passport in there for him too. His current one was left in his hotel room.'

Bald noted all this and said, 'Where's the RV with Cooper?'

'That'll be up to him. Contact him as soon as you've hit the ground and checked in. He'll be expecting your call. The meeting time will be whatever he says, minus four hours. His number's stored in both your phones.'

Moorcroft rooted around in his bag again and pulled out a couple of slim, glossy paperbacks. Bald picked one up and glanced at the cover. He looked like someone had just handed him a turd.

'Guide books,' said Moorcroft.

'The fuck are we meant to do with these?'

'This might sound incredible to you, Jock, but try reading them.'

'What for?'

'You're going to Washington posing as tourists. You should at least know about the major sights, in case anyone with a Homeland Security badge starts asking questions. There are some maps of the surrounding area in there, too.'

Moorcroft took two more items out of his bag.

A couple of shiny black mobile phones.

And a slip of paper.

He gestured to the phones first. Porter picked one up to inspect it. It had a touchscreen, but that was about all that was modern about it. The phone felt brick-heavy compared to the swish new handsets he'd seen all the kids using. It had probably been cutting-edge, right around the time the *Titanic* sank.

Moorcroft pointed to them. 'Burner phones. You'll use these instead of your regular devices. They're unlocked so you can use them abroad, and both have been pre-loaded with a hundred dollars' worth of credit.'

Moorcroft pointed to the sheet of paper. It listed several long and seemingly random names.

'What the fuck are these?' Bald said.

'Twitter accounts. Someone will be monitoring them around the clock. If you need to get in urgent contact with us, follow the first account and we'll know you need to talk. The next time, use the second account. Then the third, and so on.'

Porter said, 'I'm not on Twitter.'

Bald said, 'Me neither.'

'You are now,' Moorcroft said. 'Check your phones. The boys over at GCHQ have created and populated accounts for both of you. They've also posted public messages on your Facebook accounts from your new fake friends, wishing you a great trip.'

Porter stared at the list and felt old. He looked up and noticed Moorcroft staring at him. 'What's the deal with you and Tannon, old bean?'

'We used to know each other. A long time ago now.'

'There's nothing else to it?'

Moorcroft was still staring at him. He didn't appear to notice Bald at his side, grinning slyly.

'We were in the shit together once,' Porter replied flatly. 'That's all there is to know. Why?'

'Nothing.' Moorcroft shrugged. 'It's just highly unusual to have someone in her position specifically request assets for a job like this.'

'Her position?' Porter repeated.

Bald stopped grinning. Moorcroft said, 'Didn't you hear? Tannon is Director of Operations now.'

Porter raised an eyebrow at that. D/O, he thought. That put her at one level below the current Chief of SIS. Tannon had done well for herself. She wasn't just Moorcroft's boss. She was even more senior than that. A resignation letter or a heart attack away from becoming the next head of Britain's secret service.

She's done a hell of a lot better than me.

Along with just about everyone else I know.

And then another thought hit Porter.

If someone as important as Tannon is involved, this op must be a big deal.

Bald shot Moorcroft a quizzical look. 'Hang about. Tannon is your boss? I thought she reported to you.'

Moorcroft snorted. 'Not for a long time now. She'll be even higher up the ladder before long. It's the worst-kept secret that Tannon is in the running to become the next chief.'

'Is she likely to get it?' Porter asked.

'It's a very short list, from what I hear.'

'Shouldn't you be in the running for that job? You've been around for long enough.'

The agent's voice turned bitter. 'They're not looking for someone like me to run the agency. They want someone young. Dynamic. Someone who's trained to deal with the emerging threats, cyber-hacking and non-linear warfare. Which means Tannon. Fellows like me, the ones who can speak Farsi and quote the Qur'an, are out of fashion.'

'Must be tough,' Porter said, pretending to give a toss.

Moorcroft waved off his concerns. 'I never wanted the job anyway,' he said, with the air of a man trying to maintain his dignity in the face of crushing disappointment. 'A year from now I'll collect my pension, retire to my cottage and catch up on a spot of reading. Others won't be so lucky. But you two are in a fortunate position.'

'The fuck are you talking about?'

'Don't you see? Tannon's relying on you to make sure this job goes smoothly. Pull this one off, and you'll have the future Chief of MI6 in your debt. Who knows? You might even get a pay rise at the end of this.'

Porter detected a hint of jealousy in the MI6 man's voice. Bald laughed and said, 'I don't want a pay rise. I already told you lot. Once this is over, I'm done.'

'You might change your mind.'

'I fucking doubt it.'

Moorcroft shrugged. 'Maybe not. But if you come out of this with a new job offer, you'll be doing a damn sight better than the rest of us.'

He straightened his back and nodded at the two operators in turn.

'Right, I'm off. I suggest you both get an early night. A car will arrive at half-three tomorrow morning to take you to the airport. After that, you're on your own.'

FOURTEEN

Their car arrived at 3.30am, just like Moorcroft had said. Porter was already showered and dressed when the text came through on his burner. *Your taxi is outside.*

The taxi turned out to be a grey Mercedes Benz C-class, several years old, with fifty thousand miles on the clock. Typical MI6 wheels, in Porter's experience. Nothing too flash or new. Nothing that would draw attention to the occupants.

Which also described the driver. He was heavily built, dressed in a flannel shirt and dark jeans, his cheeks threaded with veins either side of his ruddy nose. Early fifties, or thereabouts. Porter guessed he was Special Branch, maybe one of the blokes who ran the advanced driving course. He didn't talk. Which was understandable. He wouldn't have been briefed on who Bald or Porter were, or what their mission was.

The journey took them forty minutes. Traffic was non-existent. Even Londoners had to sleep occasionally, it seemed. They rocked up outside Heathrow Terminal Five in the faint light of pre-dawn, hauled their overnight bags and made a beeline for the check-in desk. Half an hour later, Bald and Porter were airside, giving their orders to a waitress at one of the chain restaurants while they killed time before their flight.

Bald went for a full English while Porter settled for a pot of black coffee. At the bar, a group of lads decked out in matching stag weekend t-shirts were getting well oiled before their flight, necking pints of Stella. Bald caught Porter staring wistfully at them.

'Feeling thirsty, mate?'

Porter shook his head. 'I told you already. I'm off the drink now.'

'Aye. And it had best stay that way.'

'What's that supposed to mean?'

'I know how you get. When you can't handle shit, you automatically reach for the bottle. You were a cunt hair away from falling off the wagon back in Syria.'

'That was different.' Porter felt his left hand instinctively clench into a tight fist underneath the table. 'It won't happen this time.'

'It had better not. Because if you get back on the drink, I'll fucking know about it. Then me and you'll have a problem.'

'I'll be fine. Seriously. Besides, this is a simple exfil job.'

'That depends.'

'On what?'

'Whether you believe what those wankers at Six told us.'

'You think they're lying to us?'

'I think they're being selective with the truth.'

'What makes you think that?'

'Experience. I've had my fingers burned in the past, listening to that mob. These days I don't believe a word that comes out of their fucking mouths.'

'Even Tannon?'

'Especially her. The higher up the ladder you go at Vauxhall, the better you get at lying through your teeth.'

'I don't know,' said Porter. 'She seems solid enough.'

'That's one way of putting it,' said Bald, grinning and making a lewd gesture with his hand.

Porter swung round to face his mucker. 'What d'you mean by that?'

'You think I don't know about what went on between you and Tannon, back in Sierra Leone? Come on, pal. I wasn't born yesterday.'

'It was a one-off,' Porter said, trying to downplay it. 'That's all.'

'I don't care what it was. Tannon was a real looker back then, and I would've done the same if I was in your boots. But you'd better not let your previous with her cloud your judgement.'

'That won't happen. You know me better than that, Jock.'

'Probably the last decent shag you had anyway,' Bald said. 'Fucking tragic, that.'

Porter looked away from his mucker, bristling with rage. Bald had always put himself first, looking out for Number One. But his spell in Thailand had seemingly made him dirtier and more cynical than ever. *That's the last thing I need right now,* he thought. *Jock tearing strips off me, pushing my buttons.*

His gaze drifted towards the TV in the far corner of the restaurant. Sky News was repeating the morning's headlines. There had been another suicide bombing in Russia. Pulkovo Airport at St Petersburg was the target this time. It was the latest in a spate of attacks carried out by suspected Chechen terrorists, according to the blonde newsreader.

Shoddy camera-phone footage showed civvies hurrying out of the airport, some of them covered in blood and dust. In Moscow, hardliners with swastika tattoos and shaved heads had taken to the streets to protest against the Chechens.

There was nothing further about the shooting in DC. Nothing about Street.

Porter looked back to Bald. 'What do you think's in the dossier?'

'Fuck knows,' Bald replied between mouthfuls of egg and bacon. 'Street's an old Russia hand, right?'

'That's what Tannon reckoned.'

'So he was probably selling int on agents who've been working for Russia on the sly. That's probably it.'

'Yeah, could be.'

Porter clenched his teeth in frustration. It was typical of Six to leave them out of the loop like this. They tell you everything you need to know, and nothing you don't. *And we're left fumbling around in the dark.*

'That still doesn't explain how the snatch squad found out about the dossier,' he said.

'Maybe Street got careless and bragged about it to someone over a G and T. Who gives a crap?'

'But this was a big deal, for Street. It could have made him for life. If I was in his boots, I would've been extra careful. I would've kept my bloody trap shut.'

'Listen, mate, I couldn't give a shit.' Bald shovelled more egg into his mouth. 'Our orders are to find Street and ferry him out of the country. That's it. Then I can tell Six where to shove it and head back to Thailand.'

'You'll miss it.'

'Nah. Trust me, I really fucking won't.'

Porter gave a weak smile. 'Maybe I'll pay you a visit. You could introduce me to your bird's sister.'

'I could. But she prefers blokes with a functioning cock. And a wallet that's got more than a fiver in it.'

'Bastard.'

'I'll take that as a compliment.'

Bald polished off the last chunk of sausage, set down his knife and fork. Looked thoughtfully at his old mucker.

'Tell you what, mate. If this goes to plan, we'll take the leftover cash and hit up the go-go bars in Phuket. Celebrate my early retirement.'

'Sounds good,' said Porter.

'Plenty of ladyboys in them places too,' said Bald. 'That's more your sort of thing.'

'Jock?'

'Aye?'

'Fuck off.'

Forty-two minutes later their flight was announced.

They breezed through the departure gate and squeezed into their seats near the front of the plane. They were booked on something called Economy Plus. Which meant they had about a quarter of an inch more legroom, and they got a personal USB charging point beneath their entertainment screens. The smile from the stewardess may have been friendlier too. Porter wasn't sure. Women didn't smile at him, as a general rule of thumb.

He took the window seat and gave Bald the aisle. A conscious decision. To put more distance between himself and the drinks trolley. Long-haul flights were one of his weak points. Hours of sitting around doing nothing, free booze being dangled in front of you by blonde stewardesses with massive tits. It was all too easy for Porter to give in to temptation and knock back a few miniatures.

People think once you're sober, that's the hard part over. But that's bollocks. Being sober is when the work really begins.

The plane taxied along the runway while one of the flight assistants went through the long, boring safety routine. No one was paying attention. People were still tapping out emails on their phones, fiddling with laptop cables and earbuds or wrapping up calls to their co-workers or partners. In the midst of all this organised chaos, Porter sat back and stared out the window. He thought about the mission.

A shootout in downtown Washington.

An ex-spy on the run, armed with a dossier that people were willing to kill for.

The dossier is worse than your run-of-the-mill scandal, Tannon had said at the briefing. *Far, far worse. If it ended up being made public, heads would roll.*

Lots of them.

The same questions stabbed away repeatedly at Porter, like a bunch of ice picks to the base of his skull.

Who found out about the dossier?

What was inside it?

And why were the guys on the snatch squad after it?

The third point was easier to answer than the first two. According to what Tannon and Moorcroft had told them, whoever was after the dossier wanted to intercept Street before he went public. To shut him down.

But why?

What could Street have found that was so important? Bald had suggested a list of double-agents working for the Kremlin. Perhaps it was really that simple.

I don't know, thought Porter. *But whatever's in that document, someone is taking a big risk trying to seize it.* They'd sent a team of professionals to DC, and they'd risked discharging their weapons in public in order to stop Street getting away.

The voice in the back of his head piped up again. The one that told him he was missing something.

Something big.

The engines roared. The plane lurched as it nosed up into the sky. Lights pinged and beeped. Porter thought some more about the op, without getting anywhere. Maybe Bald was right, the voice told him. Maybe it's none of our bloody business.

Just get in, find Street, and get the hell out again.

The rest is none of your concern.

He closed his eyes and settled into a troubled sleep.

FIFTEEN

They touched down in DC eight hours later. Ten-thirty in the morning, local time. Porter had slept shittily and intermittently. Bald had spent the flight watching crap action flicks on the tiny screen in front of him, in between flirting with the stewardess on the drinks trolley, a black woman with an arse the size of a drum kit. The woman wasn't biting, but Bald didn't take it personally. He just kicked back and enjoyed the view.

It took them twenty-four minutes to clear through immigration. Bald went first, followed by Porter. They were asked a ton of questions. Where they were staying, how much money they had on them, where they planned on travelling to while in the US. Then they were fingerprinted and digitally photographed and welcomed into the Land of the Free.

They needed wheels, so they skipped past the taxi rank and took the shuttle bus for the short hop to the cluster of car rental facilities located on Autopilot Drive. They made a beeline for the Enterprise desk and gave the booking details for the rental Six had arranged for them back in London. The over-enthusiastic assistant had them sign a bunch of forms then handed over the keys for a mid-size white Honda Civic, automatic. A small car by American standards. Practically a stretch limo, compared to the average British motor. But also the most popular vehicle in the US. It would allow Porter and Bald to blend in effectively with their environment.

Porter loaded up the built-in GPS system and punched in the address for the Hilton on Connecticut Avenue. The Civic had that new-car feel to it. Engine purring, all the new parts working in harmony as they bulleted along the freeway. The navigator guided them east along VA-267 and then onto I-66, past Arlington and Rosslyn, the outer satellites orbiting around the big hub of DC. After twenty miles they crossed the bridge over Roosevelt Island and headed east along Constitution Avenue, past the Lincoln Memorial and the Vietnam Veterans' Wall. They hung a left on 18th Street, got snarled in traffic and inch-crawled their way north through Dupont Circle. Twelve minutes later they steered the Civic into the Hilton underground car park.

They checked in at the reception desk, collected their room cards and dumped their bags in the twin room.

'Not bad,' Bald said as he cast an eye over the room. 'Better than the usual shithole Six puts us up in.'

Porter grinned. 'You're used to luxury these days, Jock?'

'Too bloody right. You should see my pad in Bangkok. Five-star living, that. Got our own spa and gym and everything.'

'How'd you afford it all? Kliner aren't paying us big money.'

'Thailand, mate. Cheap as fuck out there. Everyone knows that.'

'I thought that was just the women.'

Bald gave him the evil eye and ducked into the toilet for a piss. Porter fished out his burner phone from the side pocket on his cargo trousers. Fired it up, then tapped the Contacts icon and scrolled down to the names listed under 'C'. He found the number listed for T.C., and hit Dial. Then he pressed the handset to his ear.

Cooper answered on the second ring.

'Yes?' he said. 'Who's this?'

Porter gave his name. 'Dom sent us. We're friends of hers. We just arrived in town.'

'At long bloody last. It took them long enough to send someone.'

The guy didn't sound like the average MI6 agent, thought Porter. Not a posh twat. More like a barrow boy who'd worked his way up the corporate ladder. Maybe a grammar-school education, followed by a scholarship to Cambridge. There was still a trace of a northern accent there. Manchester, possibly. Porter had spent some time there as a kid, back when his family had moved over from Belfast. A brief stay in a rundown terrace, before they had moved south to Luton. Porter had been six years old at the time. The Northern Irish kid thrown into a rough school, forced to stand up for himself. These days, he didn't even have an accent.

He said, 'Where's the RV?'

Cooper said, 'Do you know the Dupont Hotel?'

Porter had studied a layout of DC and the surrounding terrain on Google Maps during his downtime back at the serviced apartment in London. 'I know the one.'

'There's a wine bar next to it. The Blue Room.' He added, 'I can give you a lift if you prefer?'

'No need,' Porter replied. 'We'll see you there. What time?'

'This evening. Six o'clock.'

Porter checked his G-Shock. 1156 hours.

The meeting time will be whatever Cooper says, minus four hours, Moorcroft had said back in London. So 1800 meant they'd be meeting at 1400 hours. A little over two hours from now.

'We'll be there,' Porter said.

Bald and Porter left the Hilton forty-nine minutes later. They'd showered and changed out of the clothes they'd travelled in, swapping their thick shirts for looser-fitting flannel shirts over their cargos. Both wore chukka boots, with Porter carrying one of the guide books Moorcroft had given them and Bald clutching a folded-up tourist map of DC he'd snagged from the hotel reception.

They both looked exactly like their cover suggested: a pair of middle-aged Brits on a sightseeing trip.

They took a long detour to the RV. Along the way they ran a few basic anti-surveillance measures, heading down the side streets, changing direction in the middle of the road and stopping in front of shop windows to see if anyone had eyes on them.

One hour before the meeting, they reached the RV.

The hotel was situated a hundred metres south of Dupont Circle, a grand old place with marble columns either side of the entrance and about a million American flags hanging from the portico above. To the right of the hotel stood the Blue Room wine bar. On the opposite side of the road, thirty metres away, Porter noticed a long row of shops. A Panera Bread bakery and a Wells Fargo and an organic coffee house.

They crossed the road, ducked inside the coffee house and found a table next to the window. From their position, Bald and

Porter had a clear view of the wine bar across the street as well as the main approaches north and south of the hotel. They would spend the next hour monitoring the RV, observing to see if anyone had eyes on the place or if Cooper showed up early. It was unlikely that the agent was playing games with them but it was SOP in the field to run surveillance on any RV ahead of a planned meeting.

Bald sipped at his black coffee. Porter had ordered a latte the size of a forty-gallon drum, topped with about an inch of cream.

'Don't go trying to sneak anything in there,' Bald said, nodding at his mucker's drink. 'You won't be having any Irish coffee on the job.'

'Like I said, I don't do that shit any more. I'm clean.'

'Aye. That's what every drunkard says.'

'You're a cynical bastard.'

'Maybe. But I'm a cynical bastard who's gonna get his dick sucked back in Thailand. That's more than you can say.'

They fell silent for a few moments while they OP'd the wine bar across the street. People came and went. Guys in suits entered, guys in suits left. Nobody was hanging around or looking out of place.

Porter took a swig of his epic coffee and said, 'You think this Cooper bloke will know where to find Street?'

'They're best mates, or so Tannon reckoned. He's got to have a good idea of where Street might have gone.'

'He might be wrong.'

Bald shrugged. 'This isn't a difficult op, mate. It'll be a few days here on Easy Street. We'll get our man, stick him on a plane and do the debrief. Then I'm on the next flight to Bangkok.'

Porter looked unconvinced. 'You really think Six will let you just walk away?'

'After everything I've done for those wankers, I should hope so.'

'This isn't like quitting a job at Tesco. This is the secret service. They've got leverage.'

'So have I.'

'What are you talking about?'

Bald grinned. 'All them years we've been working for Vauxhall and the Firm, I knew they'd try to shaft us one day. So I made plans. Hid a few things away, like.'

'What things?'

'My insurance policy,' Bald replied cryptically. 'Something that would make those fuckers think twice if they tried anything on.'

Porter stared at his mucker but Bald didn't elaborate. *Christ*, thought Porter.

Jock's even craftier than I reckoned.

He checked the clock on his burner.

1326 hours.

Thirty-four minutes until the meeting.

They watched.

And waited.

Thirty-three minutes later, a red-and-grey-striped taxi eased to a halt in front of the wine bar and a figure climbed out of the back seat.

Terry Cooper.

Porter recognised the agent from the recent snaps MI6 had included in their itineraries. Cooper looked just as smooth in real life as he did in the photos. Like a banker on the cusp of early retirement. The squash-playing physique, the hundred-buck haircut, the lantern jaw. Cooper was carrying a brown-leather attaché case, Porter noticed.

He straightened his back, adjusted his tie and made for the Blue Room. Porter and Bald observed him closely, watching his movements and his body language to see if anything was off. They were looking for tell-tale signs. A glance over the shoulder, indicating that someone knew or suspected they were being followed. Or a nod or visual acknowledgment of someone already in the immediate area. But Cooper didn't look suspicious. He simply moved at a steady pace towards the entrance, looking straight ahead. Then he yanked the door open and stepped inside.

Through the lightly tinted glass Porter saw Cooper briefly scan the faces seated around the bar. He drew a blank. Checked his watch, as if making sure he had the right time. Shook his head and then beat a path over to a booth in the far corner, away from the crowd of afternoon drinkers. Bald and Porter got up from their table and left the coffee house.

The Blue Room was a hipster's idea of a speakeasy. Hardwood floors, exposed brick walls, brass pendant lighting. A long line of beers on draught, cocktails served up in mason jars. Half a dozen trim guys in tailored suits sat around the bar, tapping out emails between taking swigs of their craft beers. Some sort of jazz music played over the sound system. There was no TV. It was that kind of joint.

Cooper had been given photos of Bald and Porter, evidently. Because he stood up to greet them as soon as they approached the booth at the far end of the bar.

'Terry Cooper,' he said. 'You must be the guys Dom sent.'

'Aye,' Bald said. 'That's us.'

They pumped hands. Cooper had a firm handshake, abrupt. 'You're right on time. That's good. I like punctuality. Please, take a seat. We should order something. Then we'll get down to brass tacks.'

A waitress came over and took their drink orders. Cooper went for a bottle of fifteen-dollar mineral water. Bald took a full-fat Coke. Porter's eyes lingered for a moment on the selection of bourbons on the menu. They had Wild Turkey 81 proof, Four Roses yellow label, Makers Mark, Woodford Reserve. All the good stuff. He thought about ordering a double. Imagined necking the booze, the warm feel of it as it slicked down his throat and flowed through his bloodstream, silencing the voices inside his head.

He looked up and saw Bald staring at him. There's no way I can order a drink while Jock's around, he thought. Porter reluctantly settled on a Diet Coke instead.

The waitress moved away. Cooper sized Porter and Bald up, as if examining cuts of meat at his local butcher. Porter glanced at the attaché case next to Cooper. It looked expensive. He guessed the guy had come to the RV straight from the British embassy.

'Dom tells me you're experts at this sort of thing,' Cooper said.

Porter nodded. 'Exfils. Yeah, you could say that.'

'I must say, you're a bit on the old side. I wasn't expecting Six to send a couple of pensioners.'

'Ant and Dec were all booked up,' Bald replied drily. 'So you've got us instead, mate.'

Cooper glared at him. 'Is this some sort of joke to you?'

'This is what we do for a living,' Porter insisted. 'That's all you need to know.'

The conviction in his voice seemed to satisfy Cooper. The guy eased back into his seat and folded his hands.

'Very well. I'll make this brief. There isn't much time, as you're probably aware, and I'm worried Charles is seriously out of his depth.'

Porter said, 'Six already filled us in on what happened.'

'How much did Dom tell you?'

'The basics. Everything we needed to know. Nothing we didn't.'

Cooper smiled like a proud father. 'That sounds like Dom. Very discreet. I taught her well, it seems.'

'You were her boss?'

'In a way. A long time ago. I was more of a mentor, you might say. I helped Dom, back when she was still finding her feet at Vauxhall. I can't take all the credit for her rise, though. Dom's done very well for herself.'

'She didn't mention you two had previous.'

'She wouldn't. But we know each other well. She's the reason you two are here, as a matter of fact.'

'How'd you mean?'

'Six was wary about getting involved with the disappearance of a disgraced former agent. Too much baggage for their liking. But as soon as Dom heard about the situation, she agreed to intervene. My name still carries weight around Vauxhall, it seems.'

Cooper flashed a smile full of fake modesty. His smile, his clothes, his accent: everything about Cooper suggested a guy who had worked very hard to pass himself off as old-school MI6. Porter could sense his patience wearing thin, and they'd had only been chatting for a few minutes.

'You and Street must be good mates,' he said.

'More than that. Charles is a very dear friend to me. He might not be with Six any more, but he didn't deserve everything that happened to him over the years.'

103

'You mean all the stuff about getting sacked for shagging that Russian?'

Cooper nodded. 'Charles is a bit of a maverick, I suppose. One of the last of the old school. He had a certain way of doing things, you might say. In the old days you could get away with that sort of thing, but not any more. The poor chap couldn't change.'

'But you did.'

'I'm adaptable. One of the reasons I've thrived in this job. But Charles is very much his own man. Always has been.'

The waitress brought over their drinks. Cooper unscrewed the cap on his bottle of water and tipped the contents into the glass. Porter didn't touch his drink.

'Dom told us you were lined up to meet some big-shot Yank,' he said. 'When the snatch happened.'

Cooper stared at his overpriced water for a long moment.

'The plan was to RV at the park and walk over to the private Georgetown club my contact frequents. Then we'd share the contents of the dossier with him, sound him out about a price. When Charles didn't show, I assumed he'd abandoned our meeting.'

'Why would he do that?'

'We agreed that if Charles suspected someone was watching him, he'd abort and we would reconvene the next day.'

'Was he worried about being followed?'

'We're spooks, old boy. Paranoia comes with the territory. I can't honestly recall the last time I took the same route to work two days in a row. That's the difference between us and you chaps. You can clock off at the end of the day and go down the pub. We can't.'

Porter ignored the dig. 'But Street wasn't being paranoid. Someone had his fucking number. They had eyes on him.'

'Unfortunately, yes.'

'What happened after you realised the meeting was blown?'

Cooper seemed irritated by the question. 'I don't see how that's relevant. You're here to follow orders. Not play detective.'

'We need to know about the fuckers on the snatch team. In case they try going after your mate again. If there's an MO they used, that might help to identify them.'

Cooper made a helpless gesture with his hands. 'Afraid I can't help you there. I was on the other side of the park when those bastards grabbed Charles. By the time I realised what had happened, it was too late. They were long gone.'

'What about the cops?' Porter asked.

'What about them?'

'Dom said they took you in for questioning.'

'More of a gentle chat, I'd say. There was no suspicion there. They simply knew I was an old friend of Charles's and wanted to know if I'd heard from him since he went missing.'

'What did you say?'

'Nothing incriminating. I knew they had Charles's phone, so I mentioned that he'd stopped by at the embassy a few days earlier. I told them it was just a catch-up between two old friends.'

'You didn't mention the dossier?'

'Of course not.'

'Did they have any idea who might have been behind the snatch?'

'They didn't. But one of the detectives showed me some sketches of the attackers, based on eyewitness testimony. They wanted to know if I'd seen any of their faces before.'

'What did you tell them?'

'The truth, of course. I didn't recognise any of them.'

'What did they look like?'

'They were white. Tough-looking.' Cooper regarded the ex-SAS men sitting opposite him. 'Like you two, I suppose. But younger. And with side-partings.'

'Probably not as good-looking,' said Bald.

Porter blanked his mucker and kept his gaze fixed on Cooper. 'Is there anything else? Some distinguishing feature? Anything that might help us.'

Cooper racked his brains. 'Nothing comes to mind. Sorry. I wish I could be of more help.'

'Did they have any marks? Scars?'

'One of them had a tattoo on the side of his neck, as I recall. But that's about it.'

'What was the tat?'

'It was quite striking. A skull on top of an oak tree branch, wearing a crown, I think. But I very much doubt it means anything to you two.'

Porter looked over at Bald, saw the troubled look on his face, the deep frown lines etching his brow.

'This skull,' Bald said. 'Was it smoking a cigar?'

Cooper stared curiously at Bald. 'Yes, I believe it was. Why?'

Bald hesitated before replying. 'I've seen it before.'

'Where?'

'On a yacht, in the south of France,' said Bald. 'It's a Russian mafia tattoo.'

SIXTEEN

Cooper sat very still. So did Porter.

'Are you sure?' Cooper asked Bald.

'A hundred fucking per cent,' Bald replied. 'I was doing close protection work for a Russian oligarch at the time. Couple of the lads on the BG team had the same tattoo, like.'

'But I've spent some time in Russia over the years. I've never seen that tattoo anywhere.'

'It's only used by one gang. They're based in Rostov. Most of them are ex–Spetsnaz operators. That's what the blokes on the yacht reckoned, when I asked them about it.'

Porter stared at Bald. *What was Jock doing on a yacht with a bunch of Russian oligarchs?* He thought again about the stories he'd heard about Bald, and wondered what other dark secrets his mucker was hiding from him. He shoved the thought aside, shifted his gaze back to Cooper.

'Why would the Russian mafia be after Street?'

Cooper steepled his fingers on the table. 'Because of what's contained in the dossier.'

'Why? What's in the report?'

'None of your damn business,' Cooper responded coldly. 'Last time I checked, neither of you are cleared for that particular conversation.'

'We need to know why your mate's in danger.'

'No. No, you don't. That information is Top Secret clearance only. You two dinosaurs are here to protect Charles and escort him home. Now I suggest you start doing your bloody job.'

Porter glanced over at his right. Bald was tightening his jaw, his anger building. They weren't going to get anything more out of Cooper about the contents of the document. That much was clear. Porter decided to move the conversation on. Before Bald got really pissed off.

'Dom told us you had an idea where Street might be hiding.'

Cooper nodded. 'There's a private retreat over in West Virginia. Down by Lake Fontaine.'

'Why would Street be hiding there?'

'Charles used to own a log cabin at the retreat. The two of us spent the weekends down by the lake, back when we were on our first assignment. We'd fish for trout, drink beer and talk about our plans for the future, as young men do.' Cooper smiled at the memory but his voice was tinged with sadness. 'Seems like a lifetime ago, now.'

'Street still owns the place, all these years later?'

Cooper shook his head. 'It belongs to his ex-wife now. She took it in the divorce. Charles was devastated, as I recall. I mean, that cabin meant a lot to him. But his ex lives down in Florida these days. She hardly uses it. The place is abandoned most of the year.'

'How far is it from here?'

'Four hours or so. Depending on traffic.'

'Does anyone else know about it?'

'I don't think so, no.'

'And Street hasn't tried to contact you since he went underground?'

Cooper smiled. 'Charles knows better than that. The rule is, once you're off the grid, you stay off. That means no phone calls. No Internet use. You avoid public places, or anywhere that requires ID or might have a security camera.'

'How would Street even get to the retreat?' Bald asked, rubbing his jaw. 'He's on foot. He couldn't rent a car or catch a plane.'

'There's a Greyhound bus that leaves from Union Station and goes west all the way to Morgantown. Charles could have hitched a ride from there. Or taken a local bus.'

'It's do-able,' Porter conceded.

'The log cabin is our best bet. It's the perfect hideout. There's no Internet, no cell towers. You could hide out there for weeks without anyone seeing you.'

Cooper threw up his hands and let out a frustrated sigh.

'Look, we've already wasted enough time here. Charles is in trouble. If the Russian mafia is after him, he's in even greater danger than I thought. We need to get over there and rescue him, before anyone gets there first.'

'That's assuming the Russians are still after Street,' said Bald. 'That's a big fucking if.'

'Jock's right,' Porter said. 'The Russians are wanted by the cops. Their mugs are all over the news. If I was in their boots, I'd be looking to lay low and get out of the country as soon as possible.'

Cooper went quiet for a moment. 'It's not just the snatch team we have to worry about.'

Bald glowered at him. 'What the fuck are you talking about?'

'We have reason to believe that other parties are actively searching for Charles.'

'Since when?'

'Since about four hours ago.' Cooper shifted. 'Didn't you know?'

'We've been stuck on a plane for the past eight hours. They haven't told us anything since the briefing yesterday afternoon, pal.'

'Then you're behind the curve.'

'We're used to that feeling,' Bald growled.

Cooper said, 'One of our local assets went down to Jacksonville, Florida, to speak to Charles's ex-wife, on a box-ticking exercise. It was unlikely he'd travelled down there, but we wanted to be sure.'

'And?' Porter prompted.

'She said two Americans in suits had already spoken to her. Asking questions about her ex-husband.'

'When?'

'First thing this morning.'

'Who were they?'

'We're not sure. Government, possibly. FBI. Or private investigators, working for a third party.'

'Or friends of the Russians,' Bald suggested.

'Possibly. But their accents suggest otherwise.'

Porter nodded.

'Do they know about the log cabin?' asked Bald.

'I doubt it. She didn't tell them anything, according to our people. But we need to get Charles out of there immediately. Before someone figures it out and gets there first.'

'What's the plan?'

Cooper said, 'Do you have a car?'

'Aye,' said Bald. 'A rental.'

'We'll use your wheels, then. It might draw less attention than my government-issue car. I very much doubt the Yanks have eyes on me, but in my line of work you can never be too careful.'

Porter said, 'When do we leave?'

'Now.' Cooper was already reaching into his jacket for his wallet. 'There's no time to lose.'

Cooper settled the bill. He left a miserly two-dollar tip, grabbed his attaché case and slid out of the booth. Bald and Porter followed him out of the wine bar. The light blinded them as they emerged before making their way north on Connecticut Avenue, heading back in the direction of the Hilton. Cooper waited in the hotel lobby, tapping out emails on his iPhone while the two operators hurried up to their room to collect their passports, return plane tickets, bank cards and the rest of the walk-around cash fund. Everything they would need in case the situation on the ground changed and they had to bug out of the country at short notice.

'This op's turning into a right pain in the arse,' Bald muttered as he gathered up his overnight bag.

'It's a four-hour drive into the country,' Porter said. 'Not a month-long stag in the jungle.'

'Aye, but that's not what Tannon told us. She said this would be an easy gig. A quick exfil. She didn't tell us anything about some trek into the middle of the fucking sticks. I haven't even had a chance to check out the local talent yet.'

'You're engaged, you dirty bastard.'

'Doesn't mean I can't look.'

Porter sighed. 'Do you think Cooper's right about his mate hiding at the cabin?'

'He'd better be. Otherwise I'll wring that old twat's neck for leading us on a wild goose chase.'

'You don't like him?'

'Cooper? I trust him about as far as I can spit.'

'He doesn't seem so bad to me.'

'He's with Vauxhall. They're all wankers, mate. I thought you'd have learned that by now.'

They slipped the Do Not Disturb card over the door handle. Returned to the lobby and RV'd with Cooper. The three of them rode the lift down to the underground car park. Four minutes later they were rolling out of the hotel garage, joining the wide lanes of traffic inching south down Connecticut Avenue.

Porter drove. Bald sat up front while Cooper took the rear passenger seat, his attaché case resting next to him. They motored south on 17th Street for a mile, past Lafayette Square and the heavy police presence around Pennsylvania Avenue. Crowds of tourists hogged the pavements, straining to catch a distant glimpse of the White House. At President's Park they made a right onto East Street. East took them west towards the Kennedy Center and the Watergate complex, then across Theodore Roosevelt Bridge. Then back past Rosslyn and Arlington and Fairfax, retracing the route they'd taken along I-66 earlier that day.

Porter kept the Civic under sixty-five miles per hour as cars weaved seemingly at random between the lanes ahead of him. Big electronic signs at the side of the road warned motorists not to text while they drove, but apparently no one was paying attention to them. For a country that spent most of its time behind the wheel, Americans were crap drivers, thought Porter. Periodically he glanced at the rear-view and wing mirrors but there was no sign of anyone following them.

The clock on the Civic dash read 1539 hours.

They'd been on the road for thirty-three minutes. Cooper had reckoned it would take them around four hours to hit the retreat down by Lake Fontaine.

Which meant an ETA at the log cabin around 1900 hours. If they made good time, thought Porter, they'd hit the retreat at least an hour before sunset. *The sooner this op is over, the sooner I can get back to my boring old life.*

And the less likely I am to want a drink.

'Can't you go any faster?' Cooper urged.

111

'Not without drawing attention to ourselves,' Porter responded. 'We're better off sticking to the speed limit.'

Bald said, 'You really think Street will be at this cabin?'

Cooper said, 'I'm certain of it. I know Charles better than anyone. Better than my own family, probably. I was best man at his wedding. We worked together for years. I know the way his mind works.'

'And if he isn't there?'

'Then we'll keep looking until we find him.'

'Great,' Bald moaned. 'Just what I wanted to hear.'

Cooper stared at him. 'Charles is one of my closest friends. I won't simply abandon him to his fate. I'm sure you two know what I'm talking about.'

Bald turned in his seat. 'What do you mean by that?'

'Dom showed me your files. You two have a long history. She told me you're old pals.'

'Something like that, yeah,' Porter replied tersely.

The truth was more complicated than that, he knew. Although their careers in the Regiment had overlapped, Bald and Porter had never been close during their time at Hereford. Bald hadn't really bought into the ethos of the SAS in the same way as Porter and the other lads. He'd been more concerned with looking out for number one, never playing it safe, always taking risks if there was an advantage to be had. Everyone in the Regiment took risks, that was the nature of the beast, but some guys pushed it further than the rest. None more so than Bald.

In the years since they had begun working for Six, a bond had developed between Porter and Bald. They had each other's backs, knew they could rely on one another in the field and had saved one another on more than one occasion. But there was still a distance there. *Jock doesn't give a shit about anything except himself,* thought Porter. *With a bloke like that, you never know what he's capable of.*

'It's vital that we get our hands on the dossier,' Cooper went on. 'Before anyone else does.'

Porter stole a glance at Cooper in the rear-view. 'How do you know Street has still got the document on him?'

'That report is Charles's golden ticket. The intelligence it contains is worth a small fortune. He won't have dared let it out of his sight.'

Porter nodded but said nothing.

Not for the first time, he wondered what was in that dossier that made it so valuable.

1601 hours.

Three hours to go.

SEVENTEEN

They drove on.

After a hundred miles Cooper directed them to a junction leading off the interstate. Porter eased off the gas, let the speedometer dial down to forty miles per, and followed the turn-off as the road corkscrewed through barren fields and gentle rolling hills, signposted by the occasional grain silo or farmhouse. They were two hours from DC now, but in a whole other country. Urban poor, rather than gentrified elite. The houses here were big clapboard structures, surrounded by acres of farmland, passed down from generation to generation, worth the equivalent of a one-bedroom crack den in the capital.

Fifteen miles later they crossed the state line into West Virginia. There was no big sign to welcome them to the Mountain State. They were in Virginia one moment and the next they were crossing into the eastern panhandle of the sister state. The landscape stayed the same. Rural, hilly, poor. The kind of place that had swept the new president into power, even though he'd probably never visited the state in his long and privileged life. They passed through tombstone towns, main streets lined with struggling mom-and-pop stores and shabby restaurants offering home-cooked food for ten dollars a plate. The stench of desperation hung in the air. And anger, thought Porter. Every other car they passed was a pickup truck with an NRA sticker displayed prominently on the rear bumper. Political slogans about draining the swamp cluttered front lawns. American flags hung from the porches of rundown homes.

'How much further?' asked Porter.

'Another two hours or so,' Cooper said. 'We'll get there before it gets dark.'

'What's the plan, once we get to the cabin?'

'We'll find Charles, then return to DC. I'll report back to Vauxhall on the secure line. Once I've spoken to Dom and received the all-clear, you'll take him back to London.'

'Assuming he's still at the log cabin,' Bald said. 'He might have pissed off. Someone might have spooked him.'

Cooper shook his head. 'Charles has nowhere else to go. He won't be in a hurry to leave.'

At 1754 hours they stopped for petrol at a nowhere place with a Sunoco and a diner and a motel. Lined up on Main Street in that order. Bald and Porter filled up the tank at the petrol station and loaded up on high-calorie snacks and energy drinks: their first bite to eat since stepping onto the tarmac at Dulles. They had settled the bill with the cashier and were pacing across the forecourt when Bald stopped and pointed towards the diner, fifty metres away.

Several pickup trucks were herded unevenly like cattle in front of the restaurant. Half a dozen good old boys were hanging out next to their wagons, hunting rifles slung over their shoulders. The windows on some of the trucks had been left lowered but the old boys appeared unconcerned as they stubbed out their cigarettes and headed inside the diner.

Bald said, 'What do you think, mate?'

'About what?'

'Nicking their guns. Those rednecks are bound to have left a few pieces in their wagons. Guarantee a couple of 'em won't have locked the doors either, like.'

Porter was about to laugh, then saw the look on Bald's face. 'You're serious?'

'Course I bloody am. We could sneak up while they're stuffing their faces, help ourselves to some firepower.'

'How do you know they've left anything in the wagons?'

'You know what those rednecks are like,' Bald said. 'They leave all kinds of shit in their cars. They'll have left a couple of pistols in the glove box at least. A rifle or two on the racks if we're lucky.'

'What if we get caught?'

'We'll be gone before they know what's happened.'

Porter studied the trucks for a moment, then shook his head. 'It's too risky. Even if we steal the guns, they'll go running to the police. The cops will have our description.'

'We're going up against the Russians. We're gonna need all the weapons we can get.'

'But if it goes wrong, our cover's blown, Jock. The mission will be shafted. It'll be on us.'

Bald turned fully towards his mucker. His features were screwed up in disgust. 'Aye, I should've known you wouldn't be up for it.'

'The fuck are you talking about?'

'You've lost your edge. You used to have a pair of balls on you. Now you're just a washed-up old cunt. Can't even hold your drink, for fuck's sake.'

A spark of anger flared up inside Porter. 'I'm not sabotaging this op. End of. Now get back in the fucking car.'

Bald stared at Porter for a moment. 'This is a mistake.'

'You won't be saying that if something goes wrong.'

Bald stepped into his mucker's face. 'Maybe. But if we run into the Russians, don't blame me when things start going pear-shaped.'

He turned away from Porter and stomped over to the Civic.

They continued west, the road winding through the Allegheny mountains. There were no more towns or thriving communities out here. Just mile after mile of tree-lined hills pockmarked by rundown farmsteads and steepled churches. After four hours behind the wheel, Porter was beginning to feel the strain. He'd hardly caught a moment's rest since setting out from London, almost twenty-four hours earlier, and the effects of the sugary snacks and caffeine were beginning to wear off.

He pushed on, determined to get to Street as soon as possible.

Questions bounced around inside his head. Who were the men in suits who'd gone sniffing around down in Florida? What did the Russian mafia want with the dossier? And how had they found out about it in the first place?

I don't know, Porter told himself. *But we're going to have some answers soon enough.*

Two hours later, at 1912 hours, they reached Lake Fontaine.

They almost missed the turn. It was a narrow dirt road leading deep into the woods, an hour or more from the nearest town. Fifty metres before the turn a rusted sign at the side of the road

116

announced: LAKE FONTAINE CABINS. There was a message below in smaller letters: *Private Property! No Trespassing!* Guests were instructed to report to the desk at the main office to collect their keys.

Fifty metres north of the dirt track, Porter spied a large cabin with a sign next to the door: OFFICE. Apricot light spilled out from a couple of windows on the ground floor. A dark green four-door Toyota Hilux with a Confederate flag was parked up next to the cabin.

Aside from the office, the landscape seemed empty. Abandoned. They hadn't passed another car in miles.

'What should we do?' Porter said as he slowed down on the approach.

'Ignore the sign. Take the turn. I'll give you directions to Charles's cabin.'

Porter hung a right onto the dirt road. The Civic shuddered up the winding, potholed track as they drove deeper into the woods. The road rose on a gentle incline for a hundred metres before it levelled out, revealing a wide shimmering lake flanked by thick forest.

Bald looked around, unimpressed. 'This is where you and Street would go at the weekends?'

'Once a month, or as often as our schedules allowed.'

'Looks deader than an old man's dick round here. Why would you spend your downtime in this dump?'

'Charles and I spent most of our lives in the DC bubble. This was somewhere we could go to get away from the hustle for a day or two. Somewhere to relax, enjoy our shared love of fishing. It's quite charming round here, actually. Especially in the autumn.'

'I'll take your word for it, mate,' Bald replied with a snort. 'Give me Las Vegas any day of the week.'

'Where now?' Porter asked.

'Circle round,' Cooper replied. 'Charles's cabin is on the far side of the lake. Slowly. We don't want to look suspicious.'

Porter veered to the right, following the track as it twisted through the forest. They passed a secluded log cabin with a wooden dock overlooking the lake, the kind of thing you saw in old horror films. There was a GMC Yukon Denali parked in the drive but Porter couldn't see any sign of the inhabitants. Enjoying the hot tub, maybe.

They continued for another hundred metres, passing two more log cabins similar in size to the one with the Denali parked out front. Both looked empty. A third cabin was under construction. The exterior walls had been partly raised, with a big pile of logs stacked to one side.

Bald took out the guide books from the glove box, along with a fold-out paper map of the area they'd purchased at the petrol station. If anyone stopped them they'd claim to be tourists looking for a nearby holiday resort. Their cover story might buy them some time, he reasoned. Enough to spring a surprise or make their escape.

Eighty metres past the construction site, Cooper leaned forward.

'There! That's it.'

Porter slowed down to ten miles per as he followed Cooper's pointing finger. Fifty metres beyond the Civic he could see a driveway to the left of the dirt road, leading down to the lake. Porter pulled over at the side of the dirt road with the Civic ahead. Then he looked out of his side window at the far end of the drive.

Twenty-five metres away stood a large log cabin with a tall sloping roof and a wide porch on the left, facing out towards a grassy area with a wooden picnic table and an outdoor grill. On the porch, two Adirondack chairs looked out towards the woods. Both were empty.

Then Porter saw something else.

And froze.

'Shit,' Bald said.

Parked at the edge of the cabin was a black Lincoln Town Car.

EIGHTEEN

'No one told us that Street had a set of wheels,' Porter said.

He had turned in his seat to face Cooper. The agent said nothing at first. The colour visibly drained from his face as he stared through the side window at the log cabin and the Lincoln.

'He doesn't. Not as far as I'm aware. Charles had a rental in DC, but he left it behind at the car park when the Russians tried to lift him. The cops found it.'

'Maybe he hired another one,' Bald suggested.

'Charles isn't that foolish. He'd know that renting a car would leave a paper trail.'

'So whose motor is that?'

Cooper said nothing.

'Maybe Street's ex,' Bald said.

Cooper shook his head. 'Charles said she never bothers coming up here. And he wouldn't have reached out to her for help. I know Charles. He wouldn't put her in that kind of danger.'

'Then who does the motor belong to?'

'The Russians. They must have followed us here.'

'No,' Porter replied. 'We'd have spotted them. Besides, how would they have gotten here ahead of us?'

'I don't know.'

Porter swung his gaze back to the cabin. Light spilled out of the window to the right of the porch. The Lincoln engine wasn't running. He couldn't see anyone inside the car. Which meant that whoever the car belonged to was inside the log cabin. 'What's the plan, mate?' asked Bald.

Before Porter could reply, the cabin light switched off.

The door swung open.

Three figures emerged.

Charles Street stepped out onto the porch first.

It took Porter a couple of beats to recognise the guy. Street's face was flecked with cuts and bruises. His clothes were dirty. He sported several days' worth of stubble, and his thinning hair was matted with blood. Some of the buttons on his shirt had been ripped off, Porter noticed, revealing a soft, pale beer belly.

The ex-spy was quickly followed by two guys in dark suits.

They looked like models for a Big & Tall menswear catalogue. The first guy out of the door had the build of a retired boxer and the face to match. His nose was smashed in. His hands were the size of shovels, and his eyes were slightly too wide apart, which gave him a dumb look. He had a burly frame, muscle hidden beneath the fat of comfortable middle age.

The second suit followed close behind. He was the tall model. He stood about seven inches taller than the guy with the smashed-in nose, and weighed about a hundred pounds lighter. Porter guessed he was six-five, six-six. He had silver hair, papery skin and eyes that were sunk crater-deep into his skull.

'Russian mafia?' Porter suggested.

Bald shook his head. 'They've not got any tats.'

Cooper shot forward in his seat. His eyes were wide with alarm.

'What the fuck are you two idiots waiting for? They've got Charles, for Chrissakes! You've got to stop them!'

The two suits didn't notice the Civic at first. They weren't facing the drive. Their attention was solely focused on marching Street down the porch, towards the Lincoln parked ten metres to the left of the cabin, in front of the grassy patch with the picnic table and outdoor grill. Street staggered along in front of the suits, his hands cuffed behind his back, his head hanging low. He looked like a condemned man.

There was no time to think. Porter grabbed one of the maps from the dash and unclipped his seat belt. He turned to Bald.

'Follow my lead. I'll distract these twats, you disable them.'

'With what?' Bald snapped. 'We don't even have a fucking pea shooter, thanks to you. I knew we should have robbed those hillbillies.'

Porter looked away and bit back on his anger. He hated it

when Bald was right. I fucked up, he thought. Back at the petrol station. *Maybe I am losing my edge.*

Just then Cooper reached over to his leather attaché case. He sprang open the locks, pulled out a small black object and handed it over to Bald.

'Here,' he said. 'Use this.'

Bald stared at the pistol Cooper had just given him. He'd handled dozens of different weapons during his time in the Regiment and this one was instantly familiar. A compact Heckler & Koch P30 semi-automatic. The SK model, with a shorter grip to make it easier to conceal. It looked like a regular-sized handgun that had shrunk in the wash. But it felt sturdy. It didn't rattle. It wasn't top-heavy. You could practically feel the German precision engineering as soon as you picked it up.

He thumbed the mag release, sliding out the clip. There was a full magazine inside, fifteen rounds of 9x19mm Parabellum brass. He inserted the clip back into the underside of the grip. Then he looked up at Cooper.

'You had this on you the whole time and you didn't think to tell us?'

'Never mind that, man!' Cooper's voice was increasingly urgent. 'Hurry up. Before they leave!'

Bald stuffed the P30 down the back of his cargos. Porter opened the map to the page showing the location of the private retreat. He was about to step out of the Civic when Cooper thrust out an arm.

'Make sure you take them alive. We'll need to question them. Find out who they're working for.'

'We know what we're doing. Wait here, and don't fucking move.'

'Fine. Now go!'

They climbed out of the Civic. Porter first, Bald a couple of steps behind him. Then they began moving down the driveway.

Twenty metres ahead of them, the two suits heard the thud of the car doors shutting and stopped in their tracks.

They were five metres from the Lincoln. Street was clearly distressed, pleading with his captors in a soft mumbling voice.

The tall guy with the silver hair looked up at the other end of the drive and saw Porter and Bald approaching. He turned to the big guy with the smashed-in nose. Pointed out the operators. They had some sort of private conference next to the porch. Then the guy with the smashed-in nose took hold of Street, half-dragged him over to the rear passenger side of the Lincoln and shoved him into the back seat, barking a command at the ex-spy before he slammed the door shut. Porter didn't catch the words.

But it sounded something like, *Keep your mouth shut.*

At the same time Silver Hair turned towards Porter and Bald, wearing a look of mild irritation. There was only one way in and out of the cabin, down the drive to the main track. Which was currently blocked by the Civic. Which meant Silver Hair and his mate couldn't simply drive off. They would have to deal with this nuisance before checking out of the retreat.

The guy with the smashed-in nose padded back over to Silver Hair in front of the porch. Porter could see the bulges in their jackets from their shoulder-holstered weapons, but neither of them reached for guns. Dressed in their civvies and clutching the fold-out map, Bald and Porter didn't look threatening. But Silver Hair and his mate weren't relaxed either. Their stance was neutral, stiff. Cautious.

It was Porter's job to make them lower their guard.

Six metres now.

'Leave the talking to me,' he whispered.

'Sounds about right,' Bald muttered. 'You talk shit while I get stuff done.'

Porter blanked him, waving the map at Silver Hair as he drew closer.

'Mate, can you help us?'

Silver Hair made no reply. The guy with the smashed-in face took a step towards Porter.

'Sir, you need to walk away.'

Porter ignored his advice. The guy had an American accent. Not local. Gruff, north-eastern. From one of the big cities on the eastern seaboard. New York, possibly. Or Philadelphia.

Not Russian.

He remembered what Cooper had said about the guys who had paid a visit to Street's ex-wife. *Two Americans in suits. Asking questions about her ex-husband.*

He wondered, Are these the same guys?

Porter shrugged off the thought and tapped a finger on the map, hamming up his accent.

'Easy, mate. We're just asking for directions. Been looking for this Sunshine Springs resort but the GPS is on the blink and we can't find the place anywhere.'

He remembered seeing the Sunshine Springs Golf Resort advertised on several road signs some miles further up the road. He didn't know where it was, but a golf resort sounded like exactly the kind of place a couple of Brits might head to for a few days on their hols.

Silver Hair kept on staring at Porter. But his posture relaxed slightly.

'You need to head on back up the road, bud,' he said. 'Try the gas station up the road. We can't help you. We're not from around here.'

'We tried them already. The bloke there was useless.'

Porter took a step closer to the suits. He held out the map towards Silver Hair. Like a peace offering.

'Come on, mate. We just need a bit of help, that's all. Then we'll be on our way. Help us out.'

Silver Hair hesitated. Then his eyes lowered to the map. The guy with the smashed-in nose moved in closer, tilting his head to get a better look at the layout. Both of them had crucially shifted their focus away from the two operators. Towards the map right in front of them.

Neither of them saw Bald reaching for the concealed P30.

The attack happened very very fast.

In the first half of the next second, Bald brought up the pistol, whipping it out from his cargos. He hadn't chambered a round in the snout, but his intention wasn't to kill. He just wanted to put the guy in the suit down. Preferably for a long time.

In the next half-second, Bald went for the guy with the smashed-in nose. Sticking to the first rule of hand-to-hand combat.

Deal with the biggest threat first.

The suit saw the attack coming a fraction too late. He glimpsed the movement at his side and looked up just as Bald struck him in the face with eight hundred dollars' worth of gun.

There was a dull crack as the cold-hammer forged barrel smashed into the guy's face, shattering his already fucked-up nose. The guy grunted as he stumbled back in shock, his arms doing a good impression of a couple of windmills. His nose looked like a piece of gristle from a slab of meat.

In the next second, Silver Hair looked up from the map.

The expression on his face shifted from confusion to horror as he saw Bald clubbing his mate over the head with the P30. Silver Hair was still holding the map with his left hand. But his right hand was free. He had some sort of basic training, evidently. Because his instincts kicked in. He spun back to face Porter, thrusting his spare hand into his jacket for his holstered weapon.

Porter gave away five inches in height to Silver Hair. Didn't matter. Height and reach were only effective if you could keep your opponent at long range. Porter made that factor irrelevant by stepping into the guy's face. In a lightning motion, he dropped his right shoulder and punched up at an angle with the palm of his hand.

It wasn't a clean strike. But Porter wasn't getting points for artistic flair. He just wanted to put the guy out of the equation as quickly as possible. Which meant fighting fast and dirty.

There was a sickening crunch as the heel of his palm struck Silver Hair on the chin, snapping his neck back. The guy went floppy. His right arm fell away from his holster. Then Porter followed through with an upward jerk of his right leg, striking his opponent hard in the balls. Like a rugby player kicking for a penalty.

Silver Hair let out a pained groan.

He doubled over, gasping.

Which was when Porter struck him on the temple, using his clenched fist as a hammer, like an angry executive at a boardroom meeting, slamming his fist down on the conference table.

Silver Hair's legs gave way. He collapsed to Mother Earth a few inches in front of Porter. He didn't look like he had any fight left in him, but Porter wasn't taking any chances. Not when the fucker had a weapon on him. He delivered a couple of swift kicks to the guy's side, very little backlift, but hard enough to crack a rib or two.

After three more blows, Silver Hair went limp.

From start to finish, the fight had lasted no more than four or five seconds.

Porter dropped down next to Silver Hair and reached into his jacket. He could hear the guy's shallow breathing as he snatched the weapon out of his holster.

A Glock 22, chambered for the .40 S&W round. The kind of weapon favoured by federal law enforcement.

Porter stretched to his full height, keeping the Glock trained on Silver Hair while he looked across to see how Bald was getting on.

Bald stood over his floored opponent, legs wide apart, his arms lowered by his sides. Blood and tissue glistened on the muzzle of the P30. Bald had a wild look in his eyes. Porter knew it well. He'd seen it before on ops they had been on together.

The look of uncontrolled rage.

The guy with the smashed-in nose lay in front of Bald.

His skull had split open at the dome. Blood pumped out of the wound, pooling around his limp body. His face had been pulverised beyond recognition. It didn't look like the kind of damage caused by a couple of pistol-whips, Porter thought.

More like the result of a sustained, violent beating.

The guy's right leg twitched a couple of times, then stopped. Porter stared in horror at his mucker. 'Jesus, Jock. What the fuck did you do?'

'Nothing. I just hit the bastard a couple of times, that's all.'

The sound of a car door opening and closing drew Porter's attention away. He snapped his gaze towards the driveway and saw Cooper hurrying towards them from the direction of the Civic.

From inside the Lincoln, Porter could hear Street's muffled cries for help. He turned to Bald. 'Get Street out of there,' he said, pointing to the car. 'I'll check on this one.'

Bald jolted out of his stupor and swung around to the side of the Lincoln. Porter left Silver Hair groaning on the dirt, then knelt down beside the guy with the smashed-in face. He was careful to avoid treading in the widening puddle of blood. Porter pressed his index and middle fingers to the side of the guy's throat, feeling for a pulse.

A second passed.

Then another.

Nothing. Blood everywhere. Cooper rushed over to the Lincoln as Bald helped Street out of the rear passenger seat.

'Charles!' Cooper said, breathlessly. 'Good God! Are you all right?'

Street managed a kind-of nod.

'Fine,' he groaned.

He looked relieved to see his old friend. But also weary. Bald rested him against the side of the Lincoln, letting the guy catch his breath. Cooper lowered his eyes to the two suits. Silver Hair was well out of it. He was lying on his back on the dirt, making a strangled groaning noise in the back of his throat. The guy looked like the victim of a hit-and-run.

Then Cooper saw the guy with the caved-in skull.

He stiffened.

'Is he—'

'Dead?' Porter nodded. 'Yeah.'

'Jesus. 'What the hell happened?'

'I only nutted him once or twice,' Bald protested.

Porter looked up at his mucker and felt a cold chill run down his spine. He knew that Bald had a temper on him. An animal rage that boiled under the surface. *Was this an accident, or did Bald mean to do this?*

'You bloody fool.' Cooper glowered at Bald. 'I told you *not* to kill them.'

Bald offered no response. Cooper turned to Porter and said, 'Don't bloody stand there, man! Check his pockets.'

Porter patted down the dead guy and pulled out a dark-brown billfold from the breast pocket of his jacket. He found a couple of credit cards inside, plus a membership card for a gym in Arlington and a driving licence, all in the name of Clay T. Kennard.

He handed the billfold to Cooper. Rooted around some more. Found a set of keys, including one with a long shank fastened to a steel loop that Porter guessed was the handcuff key.

Then he found something else.

A wallet badge, roughly the size of a passport holder.

Porter took it out.

Flipped it open.

The right side of the wallet had a laminated pass inside it with a barcode at the bottom. The kind of thing you use to swipe through the turnstiles at the entrance to an office. There was a photograph of the dead guy at the bottom-right corner, along with his name and signature.

On the left side of the wallet was a gleaming gold badge with an eagle at the top and embossed lettering below. Two words at the bottom of the badge: *Special Agent.*

Above it, three more.

Department of Justice.

Porter felt his stomach muscles constrict with dread.

'What is it?' Cooper demanded.

'These guys aren't Russian,' Porter said, handing over the badge. 'They're with the fucking FBI.'

NINETEEN

Cooper stared at the badge for longer than a little while. Porter rose to his feet and took a step back from the guy with the caved-in skull. Bald stood next to him, watching the blood disgorge from the deep wound to the guy's head.

'You idiot!' Cooper exploded as he rounded on Bald. 'Do you realise what you've just done? You've killed a federal agent.'

Bald's expression tightened. 'Don't blame me. It's not my fault this prick's head was made of mush.'

'You beat him to death, you stupid bastard!'

'What's the big problem? You've got your man.'

Cooper looked apoplectic. His eyes were so wide they threatened to burst out of their sockets.

'What do you think will happen once the FBI realise one of their agents has been murdered?' he said, arms flapping. 'They'll put all their resources into searching for us. You've just put the entire mission in jeopardy.'

'Fuck off. We just saved your mate. If it wasn't for us they would have gotten away.'

Porter glanced sideways at Street. He was leaning against the side of the Lincoln Town Car, staring at the dead agent a few metres away. The relief on his face crumbling away, replaced by a look of shock and fear.

Porter thought, Lincoln Town Car.

Men in suits.

Government-issue Glock 22s.

I should have known.

First the Russian mafia.

Now the FBI.

This is getting serious.

'How did the Bureau find this place?' he asked.

'Perhaps they followed us.'

Porter shook his head. 'If anyone had been tailing us, we would have seen them. Besides, there's only one road leading here. How did they manage to get ahead of us?'

Cooper thought quickly, then said, 'Property taxes. Charles's ex would still be paying them on the cabin. The NSA must have searched her records and tipped off their friends at the Bureau.'

'You think these were the same guys who were sent down to Florida, to speak to Street's ex-wife?'

'Had to be. This is standard practice for the Bureau. You want to find someone, you look at their close friends and family. They must have suspected she was holding something back from them. Hence the property tax search. Now pass me the damn keys.'

Porter chucked them at Cooper. The latter selected the one with the long shank and hurriedly unlocked Street's handcuffs. Street winced in pain as he touched his swollen wrists.

'Thanks,' he croaked. 'Thought I was done for back there.'

'Forget it. I'm just glad you're okay.'

'How did you know where to find me?'

'Call it a lucky guess. And the memory of that big catfish.'

Street tried to smile, then grimaced in pain.

'Are you hurt?' Cooper asked.

'The accident. Think I broke a rib.'

'We'll get you checked out, as soon as we're clear of this place. Don't worry, old boy. It's going to be okay.'

Street nodded slowly. The guy looked scruffy bordering on homeless. He had a week's worth of stubble, several oval-shaped bruises on his temple and jaw. Cuts to his face that had recently scabbed over. There was a wild look to his eyes. Seven days on the run, his head was probably all over the place, thought Porter.

He glanced warily at the operators.

'Who are they?'

Cooper slid over to Street, putting an arm around his back. 'It's alright, old boy.' He gestured at Bald and Porter. 'These chaps are working with Vauxhall. I sent for them. They're going to help get you out of here.'

Street lifted his head. 'Vauxhall? Then they know—'

'About the dossier?' Cooper nodded. 'I had no choice but to tell my superiors. The situation was critical. They needed to be in the loop. You understand.'

'The men who ambushed me, Terry. Back in Washington. They were Russians. Mafia. I recognised the tattoos.'

'We know.'

'Someone told them about the dossier. They knew about it.'

Cooper said, 'Where is it now, Charles?'

'In the cabin. I hid it. In case anyone showed up.'

'Where?'

'Bathroom. Loose panel. Next to the sink.'

Cooper walked his friend over to one of the Adirondack chairs on the front porch, to the left of the cabin door. Street sat down and relaxed slightly, forced a smile. 'Sorry, Terry.'

'For what?'

'Getting you involved. I didn't mean for this to happen.'

'Nonsense. You weren't to know that things would turn out as they did. Now wait here.'

He turned to leave. Stopped, then looked back at his friend. 'The FBI. Did they ask you about the dossier just now?'

Street shook his head slowly, trying to clear the fog inside his head. 'They wanted to ask me some questions. About the shooting.'

'What did you tell them?'

'I said I didn't know anything. They didn't believe me. That's when they threatened to take me in.'

'That's good. They can't know about the tape.'

'No.'

Bald and Porter looked at one another in puzzlement.

'What tape?' Bald demanded.

Cooper pursed his lips.

'We just put our necks on the line to get your mate back,' Bald went on. 'It's about time you levelled with us. We're all in the shit here.'

An uneasy look flashed across Cooper's face. Then he sighed. 'Very well. I'll explain everything, once we've cleaned up this mess.'

Bald shook his head. 'I'm not lifting a finger until you tell us what's going on.'

'Don't be a fool, man. We can't stay here for a moment longer than necessary. Once the FBI realises these two are missing, they'll send out a search team to look for their chums.'

'He's right,' said Porter. 'We've got to bug out of here.'

'And go where?' Bald countered. 'The original plan's blown. We can't stick your man on a commercial flight now. Not with the FBI on the lookout for him.'

'What about heading to the embassy?'

Cooper shook his head. 'The Bureau might be watching it. If they're looking for Charles, they'll have eyes on anywhere he might go. Which means we can't leave any sort of trail for them, either.'

Porter thought for a moment. 'We're gonna need a place to lie low for a while. Somewhere we can reach out to Six and figure out how to get out of this fucking mess.'

'There's a few safe houses along the east coast,' Cooper said. 'We could try one of those.'

Of course, thought Porter. *The safe houses.*

Vauxhall owned hundreds of properties around the world for their assets to use whenever needed. Some of the houses were left empty and served as temporary holding cells for suspects. Others were manned by resident housekeepers, equipped with secure comms lines and state-of-the-art defences. None of the buildings could ever be traced back to Six. They were registered in the names of their housekeepers, or owned by shell companies registered in the Virgin Islands.

Porter said, 'Where's the nearest house?'

'I don't have that information to hand. Dom will know.'

'We'll have to clean this shit up before we start making any calls,' said Bald. 'I reckon we've got about four hours until the backup team shows.'

'How can you be sure?' asked Cooper.

Bald pointed to the Lincoln. 'Those are Pennsylvania plates. These lads must have driven down from one of the big cities. Pittsburgh, or Harrisburg. It'll take them a couple of hours before they realise something's wrong, and two more hours for the second team to get here.'

Cooper waved a hand at the two FBI agents. 'Take these two inside while I fetch the dossier.'

'What do you want us to do with this one?' Porter gestured towards Silver Hair.

'We could slot him,' Bald said.

Cooper stared at him in disbelief. 'Christ, man. Are you mad?'

'Easier that way. No witnesses.'

'Absolutely not.'

'His mate's dead. If we get caught we'll get Death Row anyway. Might as well double-tap this fucker and cover our tracks properly, like.'

'They're with the FBI, for fuck's sake. We're supposed to be on the same team.'

'So?'

Cooper's eyes bulged. 'If you think I'm about to authorise the execution of a federal agent, you're even thicker than I thought. Killing people may be how you solve problems in the Regiment, but this is the real world. The rules are different.'

'But he might identify us. He's seen our faces.'

It took all of Cooper's power of self-control to calm himself down. He closed his eyes, took a deep breath and gritted his teeth. Then he met Bald's gaze.

'If we're questioned, we'll say it was an act of self-defence. The agent drew his weapon on Porter when you approached to identify yourselves. His finger was on the trigger and you feared for your friend's life. A struggle ensued, resulting in the accidental death of a federal agent. I'll back up your version of events. It'll be three witnesses versus one.'

'I don't like it.'

'Perhaps you should have thought of that before you bashed his brains in. Now get a move on and shift those bodies before anyone else comes along. That's an order.'

Cooper left Street sitting on the chair to the left of the door and disappeared inside the cabin. Bald sighed before turning to Porter.

'Fuck it. Let's get this done.' Silver Hair was slowly coming around, groaning as he writhed around on the dirt. He caught sight of his dead partner and began shaking uncontrollably.

'You sons of bitches. You killed Clay. Goddamn beat him to death.'

'Get up,' Porter growled. 'Unless you want to join him.'

'Fuck you.'

Porter grabbed hold of Silver Hair by the lapel of his jacket and hauled him to his feet. In the same move Porter spun the agent around so that he was facing the porch and nudged him in the small of the back with the Glock.

'Get moving, or I'll fucking drop you.' Silver Hair trudged towards the porch. Porter followed close behind, his weapon trained on his target's centre mass. Bald brought up the rear, two steps further back.

They climbed the porch and swept through the cabin door, into the front room.

The cabin had the lived-in look. There were empty tin cans on the kitchen counter, opened boxes of cereal. Street's diet for the past week had apparently consisted of spam, chicken soup and Lucky Charms. There was a chintzy sofa, an old box-style TV, threadbare carpeting. Porter couldn't see Cooper anywhere but he heard the guy rooting around in the bathroom as he searched for the dossier.

He forced Silver Hair to his knees in front of the wood-burning stove. Then he took out the handcuffs from the nylon pouch attached to the agent's duty belt. Bald stood guard next to the breakfast counter with the P30 while Porter slapped one of the stainless-steel bracelets around Silver Hair's left wrist. He took the other bracelet and fastened it around one of the stove's iron legs.

'You're fucking dead,' Silver Hair said, rattling his cuffed wrist against the stove leg. 'All you assholes. You messed with the wrong team. Just you wait and see.'

Porter ignored his threats. He detoured into the kitchen and found what he was looking for in the cabinet under the sink. A filthy rag. Silver Hair was still yelling threats.

'You hear me? You'll fucking pay for this. My buddies will find you. Count on it!'

Porter hurried back over to the stove. Then he stuffed the rag in Silver Hair's mouth, gagging him.

There was no point interrogating the guy. It would take hours to prise any int out of a trained agent, and they didn't have the luxury of time. Torturing him would only add to their list of problems. Better to leave him there, a present for the backup team. With luck, they would be out of the country before the Bureau sketch artist could get to work.

They left the FBI agent screaming into the rag and stepped out of the cabin. Onto the second part of their clean-up op. The dead guy.

Porter wrapped his hands around the dead agent's broad chest in a clinch. Bald took the feet. Then they rose together, lugging the guy towards the cabin. Like carrying a piece of furniture. It was hard work. There was a lot of muscle, buried under even more fat. By the time they'd carried him up the steps and through the door, Porter and Bald were both drenched in sweat.

They dumped the body on the kitchen floor. No need to handcuff this one. He was all the way gone. Porter retrieved the dead man's service pistol, ammo and BlackBerry phone. He prised open the case, flipped out the battery and SIM card, then crushed the card using the butt of the Glock.

Bald did the same with the other BlackBerry. With the phones disabled, there would be no way for Silver Hair to reach out and alert his buddies, even if he somehow managed to break free of his shackles. Which Porter considered highly unlikely.

When they'd finished cleaning up the scene, Porter unlocked the home screen on his burner phone. He swiped left, tapped on the Twitter icon. Tapped again on the search bar at the top of the screen. Then Porter entered the first Twitter handle from the list Moorcroft had given them.

A generic account picture of a thirty-something woman appeared at the top of the search results, along with a few lines listing her hobbies and interests. Porter hit *Follow*, then closed the app.

Fifty seconds later, his burner rang.

Unknown Number.

Porter answered.

The voice on the other end of the line belonged to Moorcroft.

'John? Where the devil are you?'

Moorcroft sounded hoarse. Irritable. Tired. Porter checked the time. 1927 hours. Which meant it was past midnight in London.

'West Virginia,' Porter replied. 'Cooper's with us.'

There was a sudden urgency to Moorcroft's voice. 'Do you have the package?'

'We've got it.'

'Good.'

'But there's a problem.'

There was a long pause.

'What sort of problem, exactly?'

'We ran into some trouble. It went noisy. People are down.'

'Who?'

'Friendlies. Law enforcement.'

Moorcroft muttered something under his breath that Porter didn't quite catch. 'For fuck's sake, man! Can't you two fools do anything right?'

'We weren't the only ones looking for the package.'

'Don't say anything more on the phone, for God's sake,' Moorcroft snapped. Porter gripped the phone tightly as he waited for Moorcroft to calm down. On the other side of the cabin Cooper emerged from the bathroom clutching a thick brown A4 envelope. The dossier, presumably.

'Listen carefully,' Moorcroft continued. 'You need to get off the grid. We can't afford to let the Americans get hold of the package.'

'Just tell us where to go.'

'There's a safe house over in Monroe, Virginia. I'll send you the housekeeper's details. He'll give you directions.'

'Who is he?'

'Peter Stillman. Call him an hour from now to sort out the details. He'll be expecting to hear from you. We'll talk more, once you've arrived.'

Click.

The line went dead. Porter listened to the dead air for a beat.

'Well?' Cooper said.

'Moorcroft's going to send through the details for a safe house in Virginia. We'll call the housekeeper once we're on the road.'

'Fine. Let's get moving.'

Cooper crossed the room and made for the door. The guy looked composed. Which surprised Porter. Most of the senior staff at Vauxhall were desk jockeys. They spent the majority of their days in open-plan offices, sipping flat whites and staring at computer screens. Not dealing with slotted federal agents. Any other officer in this situation would be bricking it.

Maybe he's been in this sort of situation before, thought Porter. *Or maybe he's really fucking good at hiding his emotions.*

As he approached the cabin door his burner vibrated. He opened the encrypted messaging app that had been pre-downloaded to the phone. Two new messages flashed up, both from an unidentified UK number. The first was a simple text listing a phone number for Peter Stillman, the housekeeper.

The second message included a photo attachment. A profile shot of Stillman, so they knew who to look for. He had a forgettable face, late middle age, with more miles on the clock than he had road ahead of him. Sagging jowls, thinning hair shaped into a widow's peak, small blue eyes, the irises faded to the colour of worn denim.

Porter closed the app. Stuffed the burner in his back pocket, with the Glock concealed at the back of his cargos. Bald wiped down the P30, handed it back to Cooper and shoved the other Glock down the waistband of his trousers. Cooper inspected it, then stashed the pistol in his jacket pocket.

The agent followed Porter and Bald through the door. He darted to the right as he stepped out onto the porch and made his way over to Street. The ex-spy was still resting on the Adirondack chair to the side of the porch, head lowered, staring at his hands.

Porter had taken three paces outside when he saw a snarling blur of movement at his nine o'clock. He spun to his left and looked out across the driveway, squinting in the gathering dusk.

Then he saw the dog.

From a distance of twenty metres it looked like an Alsatian, but skinnier. Medium-build and short-haired, with a tan coat and black-tipped ears. Teeth bared. Confederate bandana tied around its neck.

Tearing straight towards him.

TWENTY

Porter knew the breed just by looking at it. A Belgian Malinois. Herding dogs. Pure muscle. Killing machines, fast and intelligent and ferociously loyal. Often used on ops by the Regiment and Yank SF to detect IEDS or take down suspects.

The Malinois was galloping down the drive at a frightening speed. Ten metres away from Porter now. A second or two until it pounced on him.

Bald had followed Porter out onto the porch. He had stopped to the right of his mucker and looked in the same direction. Saw the Malinois rushing towards them from the driveway.

There was no time to reach for his Glock, Porter knew. The dog would rip him apart before he could line up his sights and loose off a round. Instead Porter threw up his left arm, bending it at the elbow and presenting his forearm to the Malinois. An irresistible target, to an animal whose natural aggressive instincts were to chase and bite its prey.

The Malinois leapt up on its hind legs. A burning pain shot through Porter as the dog clamped its jaws around his forearm and bit down, tearing through the fabric of his flannel shirt, teeth sinking into his flesh, drawing blood. The dog wrenching its neck from side to side in an effort to drag him to the ground.

'Help us!' Porter yelled at Bald. 'Put this fucking thing down!'

It was impossible to try and shake the Malinois off. Once that dog had a firm grip on its victim, it wouldn't let go. There was only one way to stop that fucker. By working as a pair.

Bald swung around Porter, grabbing the dog with both hands as it hung from Porter's forearm, rocking from side to side. Then

Porter and Bald both went down, clinching the dog between them as they dropped to the porch, like a couple of guys wrestling over a sack of gold coins. They landed on top of the Malinois and pressed down with the combined weight of their bodies, crushing the animal beneath them.

The dog thrashed wildly, snarling and kicking out with its hind legs. Its teeth sank deeper into Porter's left arm, tightening its grip on him. Cooper and Street were on the other side of the porch, staying back from the animal, hypnotised by the sheer ferocity of its attack.

Bald kept the Malinois pinned down with his left arm while he reached around and retrieved the Glock from the back of his cargos. Now he shoved the muzzle against the underside of the dog's chest, aiming just below the front legs. Right on the spot where he knew the heart was located.

The dog flinched as Bald emptied a round into its chest. It made a light yelping noise, then went limp.

A voice at the far end of the drive screamed hysterically. 'Cato! Those sumbitches killed Cato!'

'Shit,' Cooper said as he turned towards the drive.

Porter tugged his arm free. The wound stung like fuck. He looked up at the driveway and saw that a pickup truck had drawn to a halt on the dirt track, several metres back from the Civic.

Toyota Hilux. Dark green, with a Dixie flag.

The same one they' had seen parked outside the main office.

Three rednecks were swarming forward from the truck now. They had already reached the driveway and were twenty metres away from the cabin. And they were armed.

Two of them had their guns raised at Bald and Porter. The third guy was skinnier and younger-looking. He was running a metre behind the others, tears streaming down his eyes as he pointed at the dog bleeding out on the steps of the porch.

The two guys with the guns were wiry and weathered, as if they'd been worn down to the nub. The one on the left was five-nine, dressed in a plaid shirt with the sleeves rolled up to the elbows, a pair of muddied jeans and a watch cap. His gaunt face was the texture of petrified wood. The guy on the left was the same build, with the same slow-witted inbred look. He wore a pair of faded overalls and gave away four or five inches in height.

Both the old-timers were gripping rifles. Long steel barrels with brown laminate stocks and rifle scopes mounted above the receivers.

Porter recognised them as Remington 798s. Bolt-action rifles, chambered for the .300 Winchester Magnum. Good hunting weapons. The kind of thing rednecks took on camping weekends to shoot elk or moose. Effective up to a range of at least six hundred metres.

'You'd best lose that piece, boy,' the guy in the watch cap slow-drawled. 'Else you're gonna git got.'

Bald slowly set down the Glock. At his side, Porter stood still. So did Cooper and Street. All four kept their hands by their sides, not wanting to give the rednecks any encouragement. Even a hillbilly would struggle to miss a target from fifteen metres away. Especially when they were packing something as heavy as a Remington 798.

'Look what those bitches did, Uncle!' the younger guy shouted. 'They killed Cato!'

'I heard you the first time!' Watch Cap snapped. 'Now quit your hollerin'.'

The younger guy fell into a moody silence, evil-eyeing Bald and Porter. He looked like the runt of the litter. He was dressed in a pair of baggy combats and scuffed military boots, with a Kid Rock t-shirt underneath an army surplus jacket and a baseball cap with the words DON'T TREAD ON ME etched across the front.

Kid Rock had some sort of revolver stuffed down the front of his combats. The hardwood grip and stainless-steel cylinder were sticking out above the waistline. One of the big Smith & Wesson double-action variants, Porter guessed. A 686, maybe. A grizzly bear-killer, with the extra-long barrel. To compensate for erectile dysfunction, presumably. With his man boobs and bumfluff moustache, Kid Rock looked like the sort of bloke who had problems downstairs.

The guy in the watch cap took a couple of steps forward. He

kept his hunting rifle trained on Porter while the old-timer in the overalls cautiously eyed Bald. Kid Rock hung back a couple of paces, his body trembling, his eyes welled-up. He didn't make any move to draw his revolver. Maybe he liked the feel of the steel against his balls, thought Porter.

'What in the name of fuck are you boys doing here?' Watch Cap snarled.

He spoke in a dull, slow voice. A combination of cheap beer, several generations of inbreeding and the gaps in his front teeth. It sounded more like *Wad in de name of fud are ew boys duin?*

Porter said nothing.

The old-timers took another step towards the two operators. They were ten metres away now. Watch Cap spat out a wad of chewing tobacco before he went on.

'Can't you boys read? Like the sign says, this here is private property. No trespassin'. You ain't the rightful owners of this hut. And you sure as hell ain't renting no place else, or Billy Bob here would know about it.'

He cocked his head at the guy in the overalls.

'Which means you boys are intrudin' on private property. And you just killed Tucker's dog, which is gettin' him all kinds of worked up.'

He nodded at Kid Rock, then took a step closer to Porter, keeping his Remington pointed at the latter.

'Now, you boys have got three seconds to tell me what the fuck you're doin'. Otherwise we're gonna git all Hiroshima on your asses.'

Watch Cap waited for an answer. He was the leader of the gang, Porter decided. Or at least the one capable of fully formed sentences. Porter raised his arms.

'Mate, we're not looking for any trouble here.'

'Could have fooled me, son.'

'We're friends of the owner.'

'What's her name?'

'Linda,' Street croaked. 'Linda Kenny. My ex-wife. She's letting us stay here for a few days.'

'Bullshit.'

'It's the truth,' Porter insisted.

'Son, us Claytons have been running this place for forty years. Our daddy ran it before us, and our granddaddy before him. We've heard just about every excuse you care to name. So don't get wise with me.'

'We're not lying.'

'Says you. Miss Kenny didn't say nothing to me about no guests.'

'She probably forgot,' said Porter.

'Ain't like Miss Kenny to forget nothing. Ain't like her to go letting strangers stay at her place, neither.'

Kid Rock thrust an accusing finger at the Brits. 'They're lying, Uncle Wilbur! I knows it! I say we kick their fucking asses! Teach 'em a lesson for killin' Cato!'

Wilbur, aka Watch Cap, glanced over at Kid Rock. 'Shut your damn trap, Tucker! Ain't nobody getting nothing kicked yet. Leastways not till we get some answers.'

Tucker went quiet. Wilbur slid his gaze back to Porter, his facial muscles twitching with rage. At his side Billy Bob evidently noticed something by the Lincoln. He nodded at it.

'Heck, Wilbur. That there's blood.'

Wilbur caught sight of the bloodied pool near the Lincoln's rear wheels and tensed. Porter could sense the atmosphere about to turn even uglier. Like a pub on a Friday night, moments before it all kicked off.

Wilbur looked back towards Porter. His eyes narrowed to mean slits. 'You care to explain that too, boy?'

Porter kept his arms raised. 'We had an accident. That's all.'

'Don't look like no accident to me, Wilbur,' Billy Bob remarked.

Porter didn't reply.

Wilbur took a step closer to the Brits. 'Step aside from the door.'

Porter didn't move. Neither did Bald. Cooper and Street remained standing next to the Adirondack chairs.

At his six o'clock, Porter could just about hear the strangulated cries of Silver Hair coming from inside the cabin. A faint noise, barely perceptible. The kind that you had to really focus on. Wilbur and his mates showed no indication that they'd heard

141

Silver Hair yet. But if they drew much closer, they'd soon notice it.

Wilbur tightened his bony finger on the Remington trigger, white-knuckling it. He was ten metres away from Porter now. Another quarter-inch of pressure and he would blow a hole in Porter's chest big enough to sink a bowling ball into.

'Boy, I ain't gonna ask again. Move away from that door, or I swear to Jesus I'll drop you like a bad habit.'

Porter scanned the driveway, searching for some way of distracting the good ole boys. Nothing. They were boxed in, with two weapons trained on them at point-blank range, by men who were dumb enough and angry enough to use them. A dangerous combination.

We're trapped.

He slowly stepped away from the door, making no sudden movements. The rednecks looked jumpy. Porter didn't want to do anything that might result in an accidental discharge. He shifted to the right of the porch, with Bald sliding along next to him.

Kid Rock dug out the giant Smith & Wesson 686 and waved the muzzle at Cooper and Street, at a distance of about eight metres. 'You two stay right where you are,' he snarled. 'Don't try nuthin', now, or I'll pop you. Same way you popped Cato.'

Street and Cooper said nothing but stayed rooted to the spot beside the Adirondack chairs, a few metres to the left of the cabin door. On the right side of the porch, Billy Bob stood guard over Bald and Porter. The black mouth of the hunting rifle eyefucking them. Wilbur nodded, satisfied that he had the situation under control. He rearranged his balls with his spare hand, then cocked his head at Billy Bob and Kid Rock.

'Wait here,' he said.

Then he approached the door.

Stopped.

Realisation flickered across Wilbur's face, telling Porter that the guy had heard the muffled cry from inside the cabin. The old-timer yanked the wrought-iron handle.

He stepped inside.

From his position three metres to the right of the porch, Porter could see Wilbur through the sash window. The redneck took three steps into the living area then stopped cold in his tracks when he caught sight of Silver Hair cuffed to the stove-top.

'Uncle?' Kid Rock called out.

'Stay put, boy, unless you're itchin' for a whuppin',' came the stringent reply from inside the cabin.

Through the window, Porter saw Silver Hair gesticulating furiously at Wilbur, jerking his head in the direction of the kitchen. Trying to tell him something. *In there.* Wilbur took the hint and stepped deeper into the cabin, the floorboards groaning under his mud-caked boots. He reached the kitchen and stopped cold, and Porter knew then that he'd discovered the dead FBI agent.

Shit. Three or four seconds passed. Then Wilbur swept back out through the door, his face looking as grey as parchment. He flashed an anxious glance at Porter and Bald before he turned towards Kid Rock.

'Tucker, go get my phone out of the truck. Call Sheriff Tatum. Tell him he needs to haul his fat ass over here, right this fuckin' minute.'

'Why, uncle? What's in there?'

'Dammit, boy, just do as I say!'

Kid Rock got the message. He spun away, giving his back to Cooper and Street as he set off up the gravel path towards the Hilux.

Billy Bob still had the Remington sighted on Bald and Porter. Eight metres between the operators and the redneck. Wilbur stood on the porch, his rat-like gaze fixed on Kid Rock.

We're fucked, Porter told himself.

As soon as the sheriff arrived, they could forget about any hope of escape. Porter could see it all playing out in front of him. Arrest for the murder and kidnap of two federal agents. Life sentences in a super-max prison, if they were lucky.

Death by lethal injection, if they weren't.

Shafted by a bunch of gap-toothed hillbillies.

Kid Rock was five metres up the drive now. Fifteen metres from the pickup. From inside the cabin, Silver Hair screamed again.

'Stay here,' Wilbur said to Billy Bob. 'I'm gonna check the rest of the rooms. Make sure there ain't no more nasty surprises.'

'Sure thing, Wilbur.'

The old-timer nodded. Turned back towards the door.

Then his head exploded.

TWENTY-ONE

Porter was three metres from Wilbur when he heard the gunshot.

In his peripheral vision he saw Cooper standing five metres away, on the opposite side of the porch. P30 in his right hand.

Billy Bob had been focused on Bald and Porter. The obvious threats. Kid Rock had turned away from the porch. Wilbur had stepped towards the cabin door, giving his back to the others. There had been no eyes on Cooper or Street for a split second. Long enough for Cooper to draw his weapon and squeeze off a round at the nearest redneck.

The 9x19mm Parabellum round smashed into the side of Wilbur's head and exited somewhere out of the base of his skull. Bone and brain matter pebble-dashed the cabin door. Porter felt the splash-back, warm drops of blood spattering his face as Wilbur dropped to the porch, loose and heavy and fast.

Billy Bob didn't react at first. He just stood dumbly on the spot. Which didn't surprise Porter. The guy was suffering from sensory overload. His brain was trying to process the cold hard fact of his brother's sudden death, along with a load of other information. It took a second for the lizard part of his brain to engage. Billions of years of evolution kicked in, telling him he had an urgent threat to his existence to deal with. It took another second for him to identify the shooter as Cooper, and a third to arc the Remington rifle towards the new target.

Three whole seconds.

By which time Porter had whipped out the Glock 22 from the back of his cargo trousers.

Billy Bob had no time to adjust to the new threat. He was still bringing the hunting rifle to bear on Cooper when he glimpsed the gun in Porter's right hand. Then he froze.

Billy Bob's face was a picture of indecision, his eyes flicking between Porter and Cooper. *Do I shoot this guy, or do I shoot that guy?* He looked like an audience member at a magic show, trying to decide which cup the ball was under, left or right.

He needn't have worried about it.

Porter squeezed the trigger and made the decision for him.

The Glock 22 barked. A tongue of flame licked out of the snout, an instant before the .40 S&W round thumped into Billy Bob's chest, just above the right pectoral. There was a lot of vital plumbing in there. Heart, lungs, plus several major blood vessels. The force of the impact spun Billy Bob away from Porter. He did a kind of drunken pirouette and then tumbled to the dirt. In the next moment, Porter heard a series of shots ringing out. Three of them in quick succession.

Half a metre away at his three o'clock, the cabin window shattered. Another bullet thwacked into the timbers below the window, showering Cooper and Street with wooden splinters as they dived to the floor.

He didn't see where the third shot hit.

Porter automatically ducked low, then glanced up. He saw Kid Rock in the middle of the drive, fifteen metres away, holding the Smith & Wesson in a crap single-handed shooting stance as he emptied rounds at the Brits. Bald hit the deck in the same instant as Kid Rock unloaded another two rounds at them. The bullets whipped over Bald's head and thudded into the open doorframe over Bald's head, missing him by a matter of inches.

The kid turned and made a run for the Hilux.

Porter's training instincts took over. Every muscle in his body was working in cooperation, ingrained with decades of fighting experience. He remembered reading somewhere that you needed to practise something for ten thousand hours before you became good at it. Porter had spent many more hours than that in the Regiment, down the shooting ranges and on ops.

This is what I'm good at.

Killing.

He took up a kneeling firing position. Elevated the Glock, drawing it level with Kid Rock. The young redneck was

146

scrambling towards the Hilux, arms and legs pumping. Porter estimated the distance between Kid Rock and the pickup at ten metres.

Beside him, Bald had also drawn his Glock.

Porter didn't panic. He lined up Kid Rock's slender back between the front sight post and notched rear sight. Kept the target focused, kept his trigger arm firm but relaxed.

Eight metres now. Seven metres. Six.

Porter took a breath, then fired on the exhale.

Kid Rock was five metres from the pickup when the round slammed into his upper back. He jolted and went down as if someone had hit him with a sledgehammer. The Smith & Wesson clattered to the dirt a few inches to his right.

The kid rolled onto his front, coughing up blood. Some sort of primal instinct made him reach for the revolver. Then Porter heard a double-bark from Bald's Glock as the latter emptied a pair of rounds at Kid Rock.

The rounds nailed Kid Rock in the back and neck.

The kid stopped moving.

Silence descended over the cabin, broken only by the wet sucking noise coming from the hole in Billy Bob's chest. Porter looked over at the others. Bald had moved forward, side-footing the Remington away from Billy Bob's grasp.

Cooper was on his feet, rushing over to Street. The latter was lying face down on the porch, his hands placed over his head, his body trembling. Cooper bent down, checking him for injuries.

'It's alright,' he said. 'You're okay, Charles.'

Bald glanced at his mucker with puffed-out cheeks. 'Jesus, mate. That was fucking hairy. Thought we'd had it for a moment.' Porter nodded then looked towards Cooper. 'What the fuck were you doing back there?'

Cooper swung around to face the operators. 'Someone had to take action.'

'Bollocks,' Bald snarled. 'You almost got us fucking killed. If that prick in the overalls had been any quicker, he'd have slotted me and Porter.'

'If I hadn't stepped in, those inbred thugs were going to jeopardise the entire mission.'

'You should have left it to us. We had it under control.'

'Really? Because from where I was standing, it looked very much like you were out of options. Honestly, you should be thanking me for saving your lives.'

Bald looked away, bristling with anger. Street was still lying on the front porch beside the Adirondack chairs, now curled up in a foetal ball, knees hugged tight to his chest. Porter caught sight of Wilbur lying on the cabin porch. Blood was gushing out of the huge hole in the side of his head. He turned back to Cooper.

'Where'd you learn to use a weapon properly, anyway?'

'I took a firearms training course when I joined counter-intelligence.'

'You didn't look rusty when you were blowing his head off.'

'What can I say?' He shrugged.

Porter stared at Cooper but didn't say anything more. Thought, There aren't many Vauxhall types who have got the skills to execute a guy in cold blood. Even fewer with the balls to pull the trigger.

Maybe there's more to this bloke than I realised.

Bald scanned the bodies sprawled in front of the cabin. 'These pricks might have done us a favour.'

'How'd you mean?'

'We can fix it to make it look as if these twats got into a bullet-pissing contest with the FBI. When their mates show up, they'll think it was the hillbillies who slotted them, not us.'

Cooper stroked his chin, deep in thought. 'That might actually work. It could buy us some more time to get to the safe house.'

'But only if there were no witnesses,' Porter said, thinking of Silver Hair.

Bald spread his hands and made a helpless gesture. 'We're committed, mate. We're already deep in the shit. At least this way we've got a chance of getting away.'

'I agree,' said Cooper.

Porter shook his head. 'Even if we made it look like the hillbillies got into a shootout with the Bureau, their investigators won't buy it. They'll figure out what happened soon enough. The ballistics won't match.'

Cooper said, 'We're not trying to persuade a jury. We just need to muddy the investigative waters, long enough for us to get to the safe house.'

'We don't have time to piss around. The locals will have heard those rounds going off. They might already be on the way over.'

'You're forgetting where we are. Hunting is practically a way of life in West Virginia. A few gunshots won't have alarmed the locals We've got time to clean this scene up.'

From inside the cabin Porter could hear Silver Hair's gagged cries.

'Of course,' Cooper went on, 'one of you will have to put that chap out of his misery.'

Bald and Porter looked at each other. Both thinking the same thing. *Not me.* They were seasoned operators. They had no problem with killing those who had it coming. But there was no honour in slotting a bloke who was supposedly on the same side as them. Especially when he was unarmed and handcuffed to a stove-top.

'I'll do it,' Bald said at last.

'Good man. I'll take Charles over to the car. He needs to rest.'

Cooper smiled. He stooped down beside Street, slipped an arm around his back and slowly helped the ex-spy to his feet. The pair of them slow-walked up the drive towards the Civic, giving a wide berth to the dead kid with the Kid Rock t-shirt and the slotted Malinois.

Porter turned back to Bald. 'You don't have to do this.'

'One of us has got to drop the bastard. Might as well be me.'

'You sure about this?'

Bald shrugged. 'What choice do we have?'

He didn't wait for an answer. Bald stepped towards the porch, picked up the Remington 798 lying beside Wilbur's dead body and yanked open the cabin door. Porter caught a glimpse of Silver Hair inside. The FBI agent went white with fear as he saw Bald moving towards him with the hunting rifle. Then the door swung shut.

Silver Hair screamed. As loud as a man could when he had a soiled rag stuffed into his mouth.

The Remington *ca-racked.*

A couple of beats passed. Then Bald stepped back outside. He nodded at Porter but avoided making eye contact. Porter tried to think of something to say to comfort his mucker, but there were no words. He just stood there in numb, cold silence.

'Let's do this,' Bald said quietly.

The first priority was to move the bodies. Before they set to work, Porter tore the other sleeve off his shirt and wrapped it around the wound on his left forearm to help stem the bleeding. Once he'd secured the emergency dressing, he and Bald got to work.

They dragged Kid Rock over to the cabin and dumped him on the porch, a few paces from Wilbur and Billy Bob. Then they hefted up the FBI agent Bald had clubbed to death and carried him over to the door, using his dead mass to wedge it open. Porter took the agent's Glock, wiped it down for prints using a floral tea towel he'd taken from one of the kitchen drawers, then placed the gun in the guy's hand. He dumped the Smith & Wesson next to Kid Rock then emptied the last round into the front of the cabin.

Bald took the other Glock belonging to Silver Hair and dropped low beside Billy Bob, checking his pulse to make sure he was dead. Then he opened the redneck's right hand, spreading out the fingers. Took the butt of the Glock 22 and brought it crashing down on Billy Bob's hand, crushing the digits until all that was left was a gristly patty of knuckle and tendon.

When he was done, Bald manoeuvured across the room, positioning himself directly behind Silver Hair. He fired three rounds at Billy Bob with the agent's Glock. Wiped down the weapon with the same floral-print tea towel. Planted the gun in Silver Hair's stiff, cold grip. Patiently wiped down every surface they'd touched.

It was hard, hot work. Seven-thirty in the evening, the temperature outside was in the high twenties, the air in the cabin was thick with cordite and the hot stink of blood. At 1938 hours, they finally stepped out to the porch to survey their handiwork. Twenty-six minutes had passed since they had first arrived at the cabin.

Bald said, 'Two FBI agents were searching the cabin for a

suspect. The retreat owners showed up after suspecting a possible break-in. They confronted the agents on the front porch. An argument broke out.'

Porter said, 'The lad with the baseball cap lost his nerve and opened fire, missing his targets. Special Agent Clay Kennard, after shooting the kid, was attacked by Billy Bob, who clubbed him in the face. Kennard's partner shot and killed Billy Bob. In retaliation, Wilbur turned his weapon on the agent and slotted him.'

'Who killed Wilbur?'

'Special Agent Kennard turned his weapon on Wilbur, killing him before he lost consciousness. Died of his head injuries.'

'Sounds good to me, Jock.'

Bald fumed through his nostrils. 'This was meant to be a routine exfil.'

'When was anything straightforward when it comes to Six?'

'Aye. But I didn't expect to have to slot that cunt.'

'Don't blame yourself. We had no choice.'

'Maybe.' Bald shook his head. 'Fuck it. A few doubles of Famous Grouse and I'll be fine. One thing's for sure, though. This is the last time I lift a finger for those tossers at Vauxhall. Telling that lot to fuck off is the best decision I ever made.'

Porter studied his mucker for a beat. On the one hand, he understood where Bald was coming from. They had been doing Six's dirty work for years now, risking their lives on the ground while Moorcroft and others like him kept their hands clean and stayed safely behind their desks. That setup would test anyone's patience, and Bald's relationship with MI6 could be described as frosty at best. He had his reasons to quit, and that was fair enough.

But there was something coldly cynical about Bald's decision as well. Bald had never been a team player, even during his years at Hereford. Fighting for his country, for his mates, none of that meant anything to him. The guy was in it purely for himself. *Jock's never happy lifting a finger for anyone else.*

'We should get going,' Porter said at last.

'Aye. I need that fucking drink. You'll have to get that shit checked out, too.'

Bald nodded at Porter's left arm. The sleeve of his flannel shirt had been ripped to shreds by the Malinois. Blood stained the emergency dressing he'd applied to the wound. There was no severe damage but Porter knew he would have to get it cleaned and properly dressed as soon as possible.

'I'll get it sorted once we hit the safe house,' he said. 'Let's go.'

They marched up the driveway towards the Civic. Darkness had begun to settle over the land. Crickets chirped in the woods. As they moved on Porter heard the old familiar voice in his head. The one scratching at the base of his skull, telling him that he needed a drink.

Something strong.

He would never be free of that voice, Porter knew. It had stalked him remorselessly for most of his life, but his struggles with the demon drink had really begun after he'd left the Regiment. Without the discipline and routine of life in the SAS, Porter had started hitting the bottle big-time. Half a dozen pints and a few whiskies down the pub became a bottle of Jim Beam every day. He'd gone from being a part-time drinker to a full-blown alcoholic.

Porter had worked hard to keep that voice under control. To lower the volume. But it was still there, every day, making its presence felt. Whispering in his ear, telling him to get a drink in. Now, as he felt the stress of the mission building in his chest, Porter could hear the voice getting louder again. The old temptation was beginning to come back.

He refocused on the voice. Shoved it aside, forcing it back into the mental box inside his head. Porter put the lid on it, and carried on towards the Civic.

Street was sitting in the back seat, one hand clutching his side, the other resting on top of the brown envelope on his lap. As if he was afraid someone might snatch it from him.

Cooper sat in the front passenger seat. He stepped out of the vehicle as Porter and Bald approached.

'Well?' he asked. 'Is everything taken care of?'

'It's done,' Porter said.

Bald stayed quiet. Cooper stared at him for a beat.

'What are you waiting for, then? Come on.'

'Where are we going?' Street asked.

'Somewhere safe, Charles,' Cooper replied. 'Somewhere the Russians won't be able to find us.'

That didn't seem to put Street at ease. He shook his head frantically. 'There's no such place. We have to get out of the country, Terry. The Russians. They're still out there.'

'They won't get you now. You'll be safe with us.'

Street slumped deeper into his seat, looking down at the envelope on his lap. The guy looked like a broken man. I know the feeling, Porter thought. He pointed to the Hilux.

'Jock will take the pickup. We'll take the Civic. We'll have to stop on the way, find somewhere to dump the Civic. Make it harder for anyone to trace the vehicle.'

'There's a salvage yard about fifty miles from here,' Cooper said. 'Near a small town called Wheeler. Charles and I used to stock up on supplies before hitting the retreat. We can leave the car there.'

'Fine.' Porter nodded at Bald. 'We'll lead the way. Follow us. We'll switch to the truck once we've got rid of the motor.'

'Roger that.'

Bald headed over to the Hilux and climbed into the front cab. The beat-up old pickup sputtered into life. Bald backed it up out of the drive, headlamps burning in the semi-darkness. Then Porter got behind the Civic's wheel. He K-turned in the driveway, shunted into Drive and motored down the dirt track ahead of Bald, steering towards the entrance at the front of the retreat.

Three minutes later they were turning back onto the main road.

Porter said, 'How far is the safe house from here?'

Cooper consulted the map he'd taken from the glove box. They were going to have to navigate the old-fashioned way. Using the map apps on their phones meant activating the GPS functionality. Which could theoretically alert anyone to their location.

'Two hundred and twenty miles, roughly.'

We'll have to watch our speed, thought Porter. The last thing they needed was to get pulled over by some jumped-up highway patrol officer. Say, an average speed of sixty miles an hour. Four hours to their destination, Porter calculated. In light traffic, they could reach the safe house by midnight.

'Think Dom will be able to help us get out of the country?' he asked.

'She's the future Chief of Six. If she can't help us, no one can. Just get us to the safe house, and I'll take care of the rest.'

'We'll get you there. Don't worry about that. Then you're going to tell us what the fuck is going on.'

TWENTY-TWO

Forty-nine minutes later they reached the town Cooper had described. A one-road place with a petrol station, army surplus store and Days Inn motel. They passed a long line of decaying houses until Cooper directed them down a potholed back road leading towards a salvage yard set in a wide gravel lot with a chain-link fence. Porter parked the Civic in the middle row of rusted old wagons. He dumped the keys in the boot of an Oldsmobile Aurora with the side doors missing, wiped down the steering wheel and door handle, then climbed into the front of the Hilux cab along-side Bald. Street and Cooper took the back seats.

Porter dug out his burner, opened the encrypted messaging app and dialled the number for the housekeeper. It rang four times before the person on the other end picked up.

'Stillman,' the voice said. 'Who's this?'

'It's your uncle and aunt,' said Porter, using the pre-arranged code they'd been instructed to use by Vauxhall. 'We're on our way now. We've got two packages with us.'

'How far away are you, fella?'

The guy had a matey English accent. Not posh, but not Cockney either.

'Three hours,' Porter replied. 'How do we get to the safe house?'

'I'll come and meet you, fella. Safer that way.'

'Where?'

'Head to the junction between Belcher Street and Jackson Drive. It's a mile north of the parkway. There's a strip mall to the right of the junction. I'll be parked in front of the dog shelter in a white Tahoe with a licence plate ending in 86L.'

Porter made a mental note of the directions, then gave Stillman a brief description of the truck they were driving.

'Is the truck yours?' the housekeeper asked.

'Borrowed. Why?'

Stillman clicked his tongue. 'We'll have to hide it in the garage. Safer that way. Don't want anyone passing by and seeing your wheels in front of the house.'

'Whatever you think needs doing.'

He killed the call.

Cooper said, 'You should turn your phones off now.'

'What for?'

'In case the FBI is watching us. Or their colleagues at the NSA.'

'Why the fuck would they be doing that?' Bald said as he turned in his seat. 'We covered our tracks back at the retreat. They won't have linked us to what happened there yet.'

'No. But the FBI is still looking for Charles, remember? They'll know he's missing once the backup team gets to the cabin.'

'So?'

'The FBI already know that Charles and I met shortly before the Russian mafia tried to abduct him. It's logical to assume that they'll be monitoring my communications now.'

'Yours, maybe. But they don't know about me and Porter.'

Cooper stared at Bald with raised eyebrows. 'Two former SAS operators, entering the country several days after a former British spy went on the run? You're already on a list, I'd imagine.'

Bald glared at him, 'You didn't think to tell us that before?' Cooper merely nodded at Porter's burner. 'Those phones are basically portable GPS devices. We can't risk them giving away our location. Turn them off. Now.'

Porter sighed and switched off his burner, holding down the power button for a few seconds. The burner display faded to a black screen. Bald took out his handset and shut it down too. Cooper and Street just sat in the back.

'Neither of you have phones?' Porter asked them.

'The Russians took mine,' Street explained.

'What about you?' Porter said, looking towards Cooper.

'Mine's dead. I forgot to charge it up last night. The battery died on the way to the cabin.'

Porter turned in his seat and nodded at Bald. 'Get us moving.'

'About fucking time.'

Bald kickstarted the Hilux. He navigated out of the salvage yard, then turned back onto Route 219, heading east towards the state line.

Towards Monroe and the safe house.

They crossed the state line two hours later. They rode the interstate east until they hit Gainesville, then veered south onto the parkway, heading in the direction of the sprawling Virginia suburbs. Street sat quietly in the back, gazing out of the side window, clutching the envelope on his lap. Cooper stared ahead, keeping his eyes on the road, helping Porter and Bald out with directions. He'd dated a woman in one of the towns some years ago, Cooper explained, back when he first moved to the US. He knew the area well. All the shortcuts.

After ten miles they hung a left onto Belcher Street, following the directions Stillman had given them. They continued on for another mile, passing a Jiffy Lube and a local armoury. The land was low and green and suburban. Billboards flanked the road, advertising unmissable real-estate opportunities.

Fifty metres further on, Bald hit the junction with Jackson Drive and turned into the car park in front of the modest strip mall.

The mall was deserted. At 2346 hours, every shop was closed. The only light came from the glowing neon signs in some of the store windows, advertising dry cleaning services or discounts on electrical items. Porter spotted the dog shelter at the opposite end of the mall, next to a closed-down Guatemalan restaurant. A white Chevrolet Tahoe was parked in front of the shelter.

'Virginia plates,' said Porter. 'Ending in 86L. That's his car.'

'What now?' asked Bald.

'We wait for him to lead us to the safe house.'

'Let's hope it's not far. I'm gasping for a fucking drink.'

Me too, Porter thought. *Me too.* The voice was needling him again, prodding at the base of his skull. Getting louder and more insistent with every passing minute. Soon the voice would be irresistible. Porter knew what he'd do once they reached the safe house. Scope out the rooms. Look for the booze. Find a way of getting a drink in without his mucker noticing. Then drink, until he'd passed out and the voice went quiet again.

Bald nosed the Hilux into a spot opposite the Tahoe. Stillman must have been alert, because he fired up the Tahoe almost as soon as Bald had shifted the pickup down into Park.

They followed Stillman out of the car park, back onto Belcher Street. Motored north for half a mile until they hit Hillcrest Road, then made a left down a quiet residential street. They eased along at thirty-five miles per, rolling past quaint stone houses and tall deciduous trees, black against the stained-glass blue of the night.

After five hundred metres Stillman hooked a right. Took them down a winding country lane that snaked past several large clapboard houses, each one built on a parcel of land the size of a football pitch. They were on the outskirts of the town now, Porter realised. Bigger homes. Cheaper, but more isolated. He could imagine would-be buyers weighing up the decision. More square foot per buck, versus the inconvenience of having to drive everywhere, and the unsettling sense of being cut off.

They drove on for another three miles. Out of the suburbs, into the country. There were no homes out here. Just mile after mile of unlit road, winding through dark tree-lined hills.

After another quarter of a mile they turned down a gravel path that led to a two-storey stone house, set fifty metres back from the road.

The house was pure American backwater. Green mailbox to the left of the gravel path. Wide driveway leading to a double garage big enough to fit a couple of tanks. To the left of the property Porter could see a path leading around to the rear of the house. A hundred metres beyond, the land dipped down towards a gloomy lake, black as an oil spill.

Stillman pulled up to the left of the driveway. He debussed, then hobbled around to the rear of the Tahoe and pointed towards the garage doors. As if to say, *Park her in there*.

The garage door on the right whirred open as Bald steered towards it. He stowed the Hilux inside, killed the engine. Then the four occupants stepped out and exited the garage.

Stillman was waiting for them beside the Tahoe. His appearance matched the picture Six had given them. Medium height, medium build, widow's peak. The guy wore a dark short-sleeved shirt one size too big, maybe in an attempt to cover his beer gut. Loose grey trousers, pair of tattered sneakers. Porter caught a whiff of Stillman's gin-breath as he pumped the guy's hand. He recognised the glazed look of a fellow drinker.

'Name's Peter,' he said. 'Everyone calls me Pete. At your service.'

His accent had been harder to place on the phone, but in the flesh Porter detected a definite South London gruffness. The guy was bubbling with excitement. This was obviously a big thrill for Stillman, Porter figured. An MI6-sponsored safe house, out in the middle of Virginia, he wouldn't have many guests. They were probably the first guests Stillman had hosted in months.

'This is your gaff?' Bald asked as he glanced around the isolated plot. Woodland flanked both sides of the house. There wasn't another house in sight.

Stillman nodded. 'It's mine, but Six helped with the additional security features and so on. Anything you fellas need while you're here, anything at all, you just let me know. You need something fixed or sorted, I'm your man.'

'Thanks,' Porter replied flatly.

He'd stayed in enough safe houses in his time and he knew Stillman's game. The guy was trying to ingratiate himself with his new guests, to get them to lower their guard and perhaps share some Six gossip with him. As a housekeeper, he would be kept out of the loop on all but the most basic operational details.

Stillman glanced briefly at Street. 'You lads had a long journey?'

'Something like that, mate,' Porter said in a polite but firm tone, indicating to their host that they wouldn't be revealing anything about their mission.

'Anyone follow you? Anything I need to know about?'

'No, mate. It's all gravy. Let's just get inside, yeah?'

'No worries. This way, lads. I'll give you the grand tour.'

'Can't fucking wait,' Bald muttered under his breath.

Stillman set off in the direction of the front door. A sudden wave of exhaustion hit Porter just then. It had been more than twenty-four hours since they'd flown out of London, but it felt more like a month. They'd covered a lot of ground. DC, then the log cabin. Now a safe house in the middle of the Virginia sticks. He was running on fumes.

I need calories, he thought, and some kip. A drink would be nice as well.

But more than anything, I need some fucking answers.

Cooper turned to follow the housekeeper across the front drive. Porter placed a hand on the agent's shoulder before he could move away. He looked Cooper hard in the eye. 'We're here now. When are you gonna tell us what's going on with this dossier?'

'Soon,' Cooper replied. 'We need to reach out to Vauxhall first. Tell them what's happened. Then I'll explain everything.'

'You'd better,' Bald warned. 'I've had enough of being messed around by you and your mates.'

Cooper shrugged off Porter's hand and walked Street over to the front door. Stillman was chatting away to them, slurring his words. Bald sighed and shook his head.

'Just our bloody luck. We're in the middle of nowhere, stuck with this chatty prick for fuck knows how long. Six had better hurry up and sort something out for us.'

'Dom will take care of it,' Porter responded. 'She won't let us down.'

'I hope you're right,' Bald said. 'Because unless she's got a plan up her sleeve, we're well and truly fucked.'

TWENTY-THREE

Stillman led them inside the safe house. The entrance opened out into a spacious foyer with a tiled floor and wood-panelled walls lined with landscape paintings. A winding staircase in the middle of the room led up to the first-floor landing. Past the stairs the hallway continued down towards the kitchen.

An alarm inside the foyer made a pulsating wail. Stillman punched in a four-digit code on a keypad on the wall to the right of the front door, disabling the alarm.

'Infra-red beam sensors,' he said. 'There's one at the front of the drive. Any object over three foot tall crosses the beams, the alarm goes off.'

'What about the back?' asked Bald.

'Same deal, fella. Alarm covering the footpath. Got security cameras overlooking the front and rear of the property as well. Take it from me, no one can get within fifty metres of this place without me knowing about it.'

They followed Stillman as he moved down the hallway, pointing out the various rooms as he went. Dining room and master bedroom off to the left. Living room to the right, with another door leading into the ground-floor study. Three guest bedrooms upstairs, two en-suites and a third separate bathroom.

They reached the kitchen at the rear of the ground floor. The décor was vintage American diner. Fifties-style round table and chairs, black-and-white floor tiles. Breakfast bar to the left with a pair of swivel barstools. A Wurlitzer jukebox had pride of place to the right. French doors at the back faced out towards the tree-lined garden. There was a wooden pool deck the size of a tennis court, with a path leading down from the deck around the side of the house.

'You'll have to excuse the mess,' Stillman said. 'Didn't have much time to prepare. Six only gave me a few hours' notice. Called me right out of the blue.'

Porter glanced over at the breakfast bar. Amid an assortment of dirty glasses and takeaway cartons he counted four half-empty bottles of Beefeater gin and Wild Turkey bourbon. The voice in his head made a mental note of them.

You'll be wanting some of that later.

'Still, it's good to have some company,' the housekeeper went on. 'Gets a bit lonely out here, you know. Ever since my Gemma died.'

'Gemma?' Porter repeated.

Stillman nodded again. 'My missus. She passed away seven years ago. Three years to the day after we bought this place, believe it or not. Not the same without her, you know?'

'Sure,' Porter said, feigning interest.

He wasn't really listening. Porter was already sizing up the defences with his keen operator's eye. The obvious weak points were the sliding French doors at the back of the safe house, along with the multiple windows in the rooms either side of the foyer. A lot of potential entry points to cover, if someone managed to breach the perimeter. Any assaulting team might just as easily attack from the rear of the property as the front.

'What about guns?' Bald asked.

Stillman grinned. 'In the strong room. This way, fellas.'

They followed him back down the hallway. Stillman turned right at the staircase and led them through the bedroom, towards a heavy-duty security door on the right side of the king-size bed, painted the same colour as the surrounding walls to help it blend into the scenery. The door was open, Porter noticed.

'Everything's in here,' Stillman explained.

Porter was familiar with the setup. Strong rooms were a big hit with rural homeowners. Anyone who was paranoid about home intruders, or who needed somewhere bigger to store their valuables than your average home safe. A room-within-a-room, constructed out of rectangular breeze blocks, reinforced with steel rods. To withstand a barrage of enemy fire. Put down a sustained burst from a heavy machine gun on a standard brick wall and it would crumble apart. But the rods held the breeze blocks together, like meshes on a fishing net. No bullet could pass through that structure. In addition the walls were lined with galvanised sheet metal, and the door was fitted with a high-security multi-point locking system, along with a pair of hinge bolts for an extra layer of protection. No one could break into that thing.

Keys clanged on a chain as Stillman unlocked the strong room door. He yanked the brass handle and ushered Bald and Porter inside. The room wasn't big enough for all of them so Cooper and Street elected to hang back in the bedroom.

Inside the strong room, Porter spied a large gun safe against the far wall, the approximate size of a Smeg fridge. Stillman punched in the entry code on the electronic lock and there was a loud beep, followed by the clanking of moving metal parts as the bolts released.

Inside the safe was a stash of sleek-looking guns.

Several rifles were arranged vertically in the main storage compartment, like snooker cues on a rack. Porter counted a pair of Colt AR-15 semi-automatic rifles, plus three Smith & Wesson M&P15s and a Mossberg 500 Tactical pump-action shotgun. A collection of rail attachments and scopes gathered dust on the top shelf above the weapons. Spare clips and boxes of ammo on the smaller shelves to the right. Half a dozen handguns were stored in nylon pouches on the inside of the safe door. Porter ID'd three of them from the logos stamped down the side of the grips. Two FN Five-Seven pistols, named after the 5.7x28mm round they were chambered for, plus a Glock 17 semi-automatic. Three revolvers in the pouches below, plus several multi-tools, Gerber combat knives and Armex flashlights.

Jesus, thought Porter.

There's enough firepower in here to start a bloody war.

'They're untraceable, of course,' Stillman said. 'All bought at gun shows down in North Carolina. Plenty of ammo there too.'

Bald grinned at the array of weaponry. Stillman pointed to one of the pistols. A Glock 17 semi-automatic.

'You're familiar with this one, lad? It's my latest addition.'

Before Bald could answer, Stillman snatched the Glock from the door pouch, wrapping his hand around the textured rubber grip. Bald looked on in bemusement as the housekeeper pointed out the various details on the weapon. Like a teacher instructing a first-timer in gun safety.

'We used these all the time when I was in the firearms unit. It's fairly straightforward. Mag release button here, next to the trigger guard. Insert your clip, manually pull back the slider and release to load a round in the chamber. Like so.'

He demonstrated to Bald. The guy's movements were slow and clumsy, and Porter started to wonder how much Stillman had had to drink that evening already.

'I always find that a two-handed stance is best for the Glock,' Stillman went on. 'Feet shoulder-width apart, arms extended into a triangle, knees flexed slightly to give yourself a solid firing platform.'

Stillman took up the stance, aiming the Glock at an imaginary target on the bedroom wall. Bald stared darkly at the housekeeper, and Porter could sense his mucker getting angrier by the minute. He looked like he might punch Stillman in the face at any moment.

This bloke is really pushing Jock's buttons.

'We've seen enough here,' Porter said, cutting the demo short. 'Why don't you show us the comms kit.'

'Sorry, fella. You're in a hurry to speak to your handler?'

'Just show us where everything's set up.'

Stillman replaced the Glock in the pouch and closed the safe door. He trudged out of the bedroom and made his way across the foyer, stopping in front of a door opposite the study.

'It's all down there in the basement. Comms kit, encrypted mobile phone, the works.'

Porter nodded and turned to Cooper. 'Me and Jock will head down. Make the call.'

'Actually, I think I'll come with you.'

'What for? So you can listen to us getting bollocked by your mates?'

'I'm good friends with both Nigel and Dom. I know how to deal with them. You're going to want me in the room when you put in that call.'

'What about him?'

Bald pointed with his eyes at Street. The ex-spy had been quiet for most of the journey to the safe house. Now he just looked knackered. Which was understandable, thought Porter. Street had spent the past seven days on the run, watching his back. Right now, he was probably experiencing the world's biggest comedown.

'I'll be alright,' Street said. 'Just a bit worn out, Terry.' Cooper half-smiled at his friend. 'That's an understatement. Look, why don't you wait in the lounge while we're dealing with the chaps over at Vauxhall? I'll brief you as soon as we're off the phone.'

'I could talk to them? I might be able to help fill in the blanks.'

'No need. We've got this covered. Just put your feet up for now, old boy.'

Street nodded uneasily. Cooper led him off to the living room. He emerged several beats later and hurried back over to join the others in front of the basement door.

'Is your mate okay?' Stillman asked.

'He'll be fine. He's just had a long day.'

'So have we all,' Bald said.

Stillman led them through the basement door. Down a creaking wooden staircase, into a brightly lit space with beige carpet and bare grey walls. They passed a recreation room cluttered with free weights and various exercise machines. None of the equipment looked as if it had been used in a long time. Which didn't surprise Porter. Stillman didn't look like the kind of bloke who regularly broke into a sweat.

At the far end of the basement they reached a small office. An oak corner desk took up most of the room, with a pair of budget ergonomic chairs parked in front of it. There was a whole bunch of computer equipment on the desk, and underneath it. Wires, monitors, keyboards, printers. Two flat-screen monitors, both in screensaver mode. A separate bank of TV screens ran a live feed of the security cameras overlooking the grounds of the house.

'This is it,' Stillman said, patting the top of a shiny black box on the desk.

The box resembled a clunky old DVD player. Blue lights

flashed on the front and several long cables snaked out the back of the unit, connecting it to a regular landline phone. Next to the landline was a standard-looking BlackBerry mobile. Stillman nodded when he saw Porter eyeballing it.

'Ghost phone. It's installed with military-grade encryption. You can use it to make calls, send messages or use the Internet, without anyone knowing about it.'

Bald pointed to the black box. 'How does this thing work?'

'It's a voice-encryption system. You just make a call like normal, using the landline. The box encrypts your chatter, and another box at Six's end does the same. Means no one can listen in to your call.'

'Is it secure?'

'When it works. It can be a bit volatile.'

Bald planted himself down in one of the chairs. Porter took the other one. Cooper leaned against the side of the desk while Porter retrieved the contact number he'd been given from his burner phone. He was conscious of Stillman hovering in the office doorway.

'Do you need anything else, fellas?'

'Not at the moment,' Bald said. 'We'll take it from here.'

Stillman lingered for a moment, then tipped his head at the wound on Porter's left arm. 'Can I get you something for that?'

Porter lowered his eyes to the temporary dressing he'd applied to the wound. In the rush to reach the safe house, he'd temporarily forgotten about the souvenir the Malinois had given him. The torn sleeve was stained with blood and his forearm throbbed dully.

'A sterile dressing, if you've got one,' he said. 'Some painkillers. Whatever you've got.'

'Right you are. I'll be upstairs. Just give us a shout when you're done.'

Stillman turned and left, closing the door behind him.

'Thank fuck for that,' Bald muttered. 'We've only been here five minutes, and he's already getting on my tits.'

Once the housekeeper's footsteps had faded away Porter pressed the speakerphone button on the landline and tapped out the UK number he'd memorised from his burner. It took several moments for the call to connect. Then someone picked up on the other end.

'John?' Moorcroft said. 'Is that you?'

'Yeah,' Porter responded. 'It's me. We're at the safehouse. We just arrived a few minutes ago.'

'Took you long enough. Jesus. I was beginning to wonder when you'd call.'

Porter noted the time on the wall clock. 0026 hours. Almost five-thirty in the morning in London. 'Don't you ever sleep?'

'Not when you idiots are fucking everything up. Are you alone?'

'Street's upstairs with the housekeeper. Jock's here with me, and Cooper. You're on loudspeaker.'

'Perhaps you can begin by telling me exactly what the hell happened this evening.'

Porter gave him the abbreviated version of events. Told him about how they'd identified the snatch squad as Russian mafia. About the retreat, the discovery of the FBI agents at the scene, the run-in with the good ole boys. The subsequent firefight, the diligent covering up of their tracks. He left out the part about Bald smashing the FBI agent's brains in.

'Well, that's wonderful,' Moorcroft said once Porter had finished talking. 'Instead of carrying out a simple exfiltration, you fuckwits have killed a pair of federal agents, not to mention three rednecks who are probably on first-name terms with their local sheriff, no doubt prompting a state-wide manhunt.'

'It wasn't our fault,' Bald protested. 'Things got out of control. We did the best we could.'

Moorcroft snorted down the line. 'If that's your best, I'd really hate to see your fucking worst.'

Out of the corner of his eye, Porter noticed Bald staring at the phone with balled fists. As if he might smash it to pieces.

'What about the package?' Moorcroft went on. 'Is he okay?'

Cooper said, 'He's badly shaken, but it's nothing a good night's sleep and a stiff drink or three won't fix.'

'He still has the dossier, I take it?'

'Holding onto it as we speak.'

'Do we think the Americans know about what's inside?'

'Charles doesn't seem to think so. He thinks the FBI just wanted to speak to him about the incident with the Russians. They suspect foul play, but they don't know any more than that.'

'Good. We need to keep it that way.'

'What's the plan for getting us out of here?' asked Bald.

'That's still to be decided. We're weighing up various factors.'

'We don't have time for you to sit around debating shite. The longer we're here, the more likely it is the cops will link us to the murders.'

'I understand your concerns. But this is a delicate situation. We can't be seen to be doing anything that might hint at our knowledge of this operation. If the Americans find out we've been tampering with a live investigation that resulted in the deaths of two of their agents, all hell will break loose.'

'But you need to get us out of here,' Porter said.

'And we will. You have my word. But there are implications that need to be discussed before we can give the green light.'

'Who's "we"?'

'Myself, Dom, the Chief, plus various other senior personnel. There's a meeting taking place later this morning to discuss next steps. We should know more after that.'

'When is this meeting happening?'

'Nine o'clock, our time. But if you're expecting the cavalry to come riding to your rescue, I wouldn't get your hopes up.'

'What the fuck does that mean?' Bald demanded.

'All I can tell you at the moment is that it's very likely you'll be heading to Canada. Once you're safely across the border, we can put you on a private flight out of the country.'

Porter said, 'Canada? How are we supposed to get there?'

'That's yet to be decided. Our chaps are still looking at all the angles. As I said, I'll know more after the briefing.'

Nine o'clock, thought Porter. Four o'clock in the morning on the east coast.

Three-and-a-half hours until the briefing.

'Can't you make it any earlier?'

'I'm afraid that's not possible. You two aren't the only crisis on our radar, you know.'

Bald said, 'If we need to leg it across to Canada, we'll have to leave as soon as possible. Once the FBI identifies us, we won't stand a fucking chance.'

'Nine o'clock is fine, Nigel,' Cooper said quickly, before Moorcroft could reply. 'We can hold on till then.'

'We'll reach you on the encrypted mobile,' Moorcroft said. 'Keep it on you at all times. One of us will be in touch as soon as the meeting's over.'

'How long will that take?' asked Bald.

'I can't say for sure. It depends how the meeting goes. For now, just sit tight and try to stay calm.'

'Easy for you to say. You're not the one with a target on your back.'

'That's where you're wrong. We're all in this together. If Street falls into the hands of the Americans, my career will be on the line. So will Dom's. We'll get you out of there soon. Just don't let anything happen to him before then.'

TWENTY-FOUR

The line went dead.

Porter leaned over and switched off the loudspeaker. He stared at the phone for a cold moment, his stomach muscles twisting with anxiety, tying his bowels into vicious figure-of-eight knots.

First the clusterfuck at the log cabin. Then the run-in with the good ole boys, and the narrow escape. Now the extraction plan has gone pear-shaped too, Porter thought. This op is several kinds of fucked-up.

I could really use a drink.

'What was all that about?' Bald snapped, rounding on Cooper. 'Telling Moorcroft that we're happy to sit on our arses for the next four hours?'

Cooper sighed. 'We can't rush them into a decision. That's not how Six works. They'll make up their minds in their own time. Or would you prefer them to cook up a half-arsed plan that lands us all in even deeper shit?'

'I'd prefer not to be in this situation, full stop. I'd prefer not to have anything more to do with you and your mates at Six ever again.'

'Calm down, man. We'll be out of here soon enough.'

'You're not the one whose neck is on the line here.'

'I've got just as much at stake as you, actually.'

'Bollocks. If you get caught, you'll just claim diplomatic immunity. The worst the Yanks can do is kick you out of the country. If they arrest us, it's fucking curtains.'

'That won't happen. We're going to get out of this.'

Cooper spoke with a relaxed voice that Porter found puzzling. Again he cast his mind back to the log cabin, recalling the agent's cool demeanour, moments after he'd shot the redneck dead on the porch. Again he wondered about Cooper's background.

Bald snatched the military-grade BlackBerry from the desk and stashed it in the side pocket on his cargo trousers. Then the three of them left the basement office and climbed the stairs to the grand foyer.

Street was waiting for them in the living room. He sat on the sofa with his shoulders elevated and pulled tight, as if frozen in mid-shrug. His eyes were alert-wide, as if he expected the enemy to come crashing through the window at any moment. Fear and stress were consuming the guy, Porter thought, the stress of the past week catching up with him.

The dossier rested on the cushion next to Street. A glass of water sat untouched on the coffee table while he absently watched the fifty-inch TV mounted to the wall. On the screen, a pair of photogenic news anchors with disturbingly white teeth were recapping the day's main stories. Stillman was nowhere to be seen, although Porter could hear movement upstairs, floorboards groaning underfoot.

'He's getting the rooms ready,' Street said, by way of explanation. He fiddled with the remote, putting the Ken and Barbie newsreaders on mute. 'What did Six say?'

Cooper said, 'They're having a meeting later this morning to discuss our options. They'll call us back as soon as they've reached a decision.'

'When will that be?'

'A few hours. The meeting is at four in the morning, our time.'

Street went pale. His shoulders pulled tighter with fear. 'Why can't we just leave now?'

'It's not that simple, Charles. Six can't have their fingerprints on this thing. They need to make sure the escape plan is airtight. They won't give us the go-ahead until they're confident they've examined every option.'

He flashed a reassuring smile at his friend.

'There's nothing to worry about. I've got every faith in Nigel and Dom. Trust me. Twenty-four hours from now, we'll be back in London and cracking open the bubbly.'

He spoke in a soothing voice but Street obviously remained

uneasy. *I thought these two were supposed to be best mates*, thought Porter. *If that's true, they've got a funny way of showing it.*

Street said, 'What will happen? Once I'm out of the country, I mean.'

'We shouldn't get ahead of ourselves. But assuming all goes to plan, I imagine Six will want to debrief you. Probably at one of their domestic safe houses. They'll want you to keep a low profile until this thing blows over.'

'What about my report?'

'Six will pay you a finder's fee for bringing it to them, I expect. Although it won't be anywhere near as much as we might have got from Bill Prosser.'

Street's eyes drifted down to the envelope. 'Better than nothing, I suppose.'

'That's the spirit, old boy.' Cooper smiled again. 'This is a win for you. It could have been a lot worse.'

Street nodded slowly as heavy footsteps approached the living room. Stillman waded through the door, carrying a roll of self-adhesive sterile dressing wrapped in clear plastic, a pack of alcohol-free wipes and a bottle of Advil. He offered them to Porter.

'This stuff any good?' he asked. 'For the wound?'

'That'll do fine, thanks.'

'Guest rooms are ready,' Stillman said to the others in the room. 'There's fresh towels, toiletries. All the basics.'

Cooper looked towards Street. The guy didn't appear to have heard Stillman. He was staring absently at the TV, his eyelids drooping with tiredness. Adrenaline giving way to exhaustion.

Cooper said, 'You should get some rest, Charles. We've got a long day ahead of us tomorrow. I'll let you know as soon as we've heard back from London.'

Street nodded again. 'Okay.'

He pushed himself up from the sofa and turned to leave the room. Cooper spotted the dossier lying on the spare cushion and scooped it up. 'Here. You forgot this.'

Street raised a weak smile. 'Thanks, Terry.'

He turned and followed Stillman across the hallway. Up the winding staircase, towards the guest bedrooms. Porter left Bald and Cooper in the living room watching the news while he headed for the downstairs bathroom.

He shut the door, ran the sink tap and gently peeled back the makeshift dressing from his left forearm. The bite marks weren't deep but they had broken the skin and he needed to keep the wound cleaned and sealed to ward off infection. He tested the water temperature and placed his forearm under the tap. The warm water stung as it flowed over the wound, washing out dirt and traces of fabric from the punctures.

Porter kept his arm in place for one minute. Then he took an alcohol-free wipe from the packet and applied it to the bite marks. He tore the sterile dressing free from its plastic wrap and bound it over the wound several times, making sure that it was tight without restricting the blood flow. He popped a couple of pain-killers into his mouth, washed them down with a gulp of cold water. Tossed the bloodstained shirt sleeve into the bin along with the swab packet and plastic wrapping.

When he returned to the living room, he almost ran into Cooper. The guy was moving towards the living room doorway. Bald was sitting on the far end of the sofa, channel-hopping.

'You off to bed as well?' said Porter.

Cooper patted his jacket pocket. 'Popping outside. For a cigarette.'

'You're a smoker? You kept that bloody quiet.'

'Only the occasional tab. Just when I'm stressed. Helps to clear my head. Excuse me.'

He stepped past Porter and left the room, pacing down the hallway towards the kitchen. Porter watched him step through the French doors into the garden, then turned to Bald. 'What's the deal with him, do you think?'

'Cooper?' Bald shrugged. 'What about him?'

'He seems more streetwise than your average Six handler.'

'Maybe he's got some hands-on experience. He was probably a field agent, back in the day.'

'Maybe.'

Bald channel-flicked back to the news station and tossed the remote aside. 'Who cares, anyway? At least he's not a whining twat, like some of his mates at Vauxhall.'

Something else occurred to Porter. 'How do you think Six will get us across to Canada?'

'Fuck knows, mate. But Moorcroft and his pals had better make up their minds toot-sweet. Because if the FBI links us to those murders, we're done for.'

'They'll sort something out before then. Dom won't leave us in the lurch. She wouldn't do that to us.'

Bald stared archly at his mucker. 'Sure that's not your manhood talking?'

Footsteps padded towards them from across the hallway. Porter looked towards the door, expecting to see Cooper return from his fag break. Instead, Stillman stepped into the living room. He glanced around, noticing the empty seat on the sofa next to Bald.

'Where's your mate gone?' he asked.

'Out the back,' Bald said. 'Fag break.'

Porter said, 'How's the other one?'

'Sound asleep. Passed out as soon as his head hit the pillow. I left some water and painkillers on the side table for him.'

Stillman narrowed his eyes.

'What happened to him, if you don't mind my asking? He looks like he's been through the wars.'

Here we go, thought Porter as he gritted his teeth. A bored housekeeper, poking his nose into our situation.

'Something like that,' he said, in a flat tone of voice that implied it wasn't up for discussion.

Stillman held up his hands like he was directing traffic.

'Say no more, lads. I know my place. Now then, how about a drink? There's coffee, Coke. I've got a drinks cabinet in the dining room if you're in the mood for anything stronger.'

'Whisky,' said Bald. 'Famous Grouse, if you've got it. Make it a big one.'

'Got it.' Stillman nodded at Porter. 'What about you, fella?'

Porter was tempted to ask for a double vodka. The voice inside his head was impossibly loud now. Repeating the same persuasive argument at him, over and over. Demanding that he give in.

Just the one drink. A livener.

Something to get you through the night.

You know you want it.

174

He noticed Bald glaring at him. The booze would have to wait, Porter realised bitterly. He knew that Bald would tear a strip out of him if he asked for a drink.

'Give us a Coke,' he said. 'Diet.'

'Anything else I can get you?'

'A laptop, if you've got one to hand. We need to check out a few things online.'

'No problem. There's one in the study. Be right back.'

He turned and left. Bald and Porter made themselves comfortable on the sofa. There had been some sort of summit meeting in Paris, according to the Ken and Barbie lookalikes on TV. All the major heads of state were in attendance. Crowds of protestors were gathered in the streets outside, hurling bricks at riot police. The screen cut to the world leaders, smiling for the cameras.

The world's going to shit, thought Porter, and all these wankers care about is a photo opportunity.

A minute later Stillman returned with their drinks. Can of Diet Coke for Porter. Tumbler glass for Bald, topped up with two fingers of whisky, neat, with ice. Bald gave Porter a cheerful grin and a thumbs-up as he took a sip of his Famous Grouse.

Porter stared forlornly at his Coke. Stillman ducked out of the room again, returning a short while later with a clunky old laptop wedged under his arm. Like one of the Beach Boys lugging a surfboard. He placed the laptop on the coffee table, flipped open the screen and tapped in a password on the prompt screen.

'Is that everything, lads?'

Bald nodded. 'That's it. You can go to sleep, if you want. We'll be on stag throughout the night. We'll be sure to keep the noise down, like.'

'Don't worry about that, lads. Truth is, I hardly sleep these days. Ever since my Gemma passed on, bless her.'

Bald set down his glass and glowered at the housekeeper. 'Look, mate. We're grateful for the hospitality. But do you mind giving us a bit of space, like?'

Stillman looked disappointed. He seemed to make a heroic attempt to mask his feelings before admitting defeat.

'I'll be in the kitchen if you need anything else.'

Porter and Bald spent the next few minutes browsing local

175

news sites for West Virginia, searching for any information on the log cabin shootings. The first four sites they visited carried no news of the firefight. There were reports of an escaped inmate drowning in a river, a fire destroying a home in Huntington, a woman severely injured in a hit-and-run. A big feature on the opioid crisis. But nothing about the deaths of Wilbur and his mates.

Which Porter thought was odd.

'Maybe it's too early,' Bald suggested. 'They've probably only just discovered the bodies.'

They searched some more sites. Three minutes later, Cooper swept back into the living room, reeking of cigarette smoke. Bald glanced up at him.

'Call that a fag break? You were gone for ages.'

'Couldn't find my Zippo. Had to fetch the cigarette lighter from the truck.' He collapsed into the La-Z-Boy recliner opposite the sofa, tipped his head at the laptop. 'Find anything?'

'Not yet.'

Bald gave up and closed the screen lid. Stillman poked his head through the door, checking to see if Cooper wanted a drink. He asked for a gin and tonic, long on the tonic and short on the gin. Stillman fetched his drink and retreated back to the kitchen.

Porter watched the others sip their drinks and felt thirsty.

The voice grew louder inside his head.

On the TV, Ken and Barbie were still recapping the day's news. The images of the masked protestors had been replaced by footage of the new president on a stage, standing next to his Russian counterpart. They were pumping hands, grinning for the cameras. Two guys in silk suits, with ten thousand nuclear warheads between them. The handshake lasted about a minute. Both sides seemed keen to keep it going for as long as possible. As if they were competing to establish dominance. Eventually they unclasped their hands and retracted them, both claiming victory. The president began fielding questions from the gaggle of journalists.

Cooper laughed. 'If only they knew what was really going on, they'd soon roast him.'

Bald searched the agent's face. 'Knew what?'

Cooper said nothing.

Porter said, 'What the fuck's going on?'

'It's complicated. Not to mention dangerous to know.'

'I don't give a shit. We had a deal. Back at the cabin. You said you'd tell us what was in that dossier once we'd delivered you and your mate to the safe house. So start talking.'

'I can't see what good it will do. Why do you even care about what's in the report?'

'Whatever's in there, people are willing to kill for it. The Russians already tried to lift your mate once. They might come for him again. Or someone else might try and nab him. We need to know what we're up against here.'

Cooper considered this for a moment while he sipped at his drink. 'Fine. But what I'm about to tell you doesn't leave this room.'

'We used to be in the Regiment,' Bald said. 'We know how to keep our gobs shut. But you need to level with us.'

Cooper let out a long sigh. He drained half his glass, then lifted his gaze to Bald and Porter.

'Charles contacted me seven days ago, claiming he'd uncovered something massive in a report he'd put together. At the time, I was surprised to hear from him. We hadn't spoken in quite some time.'

'How long?' Porter asked.

'Six years.'

'I thought you two were old mates.'

'You know how it is. An old friend leaves a job. You promise to keep in touch, but you drift apart. Before you know it, years have passed.'

'Go on.'

'Charles was desperate to meet up. He thought the information he'd uncovered might be worth something. I was apprehensive, but I agreed to take a look. So I invited him to my office. He brought along the dossier. I offered to show it to some contacts of mine, but he flat out refused. However, he agreed to show it to me.'

Porter said, 'What was in the report?'

'Lots of things. It was standard fare, for the most part. Russian bribery, state corruption, corporate raiding. Nothing out of the ordinary. But one thing stood out. A claim made by one of Charles's sources.'

177

'I thought he didn't have any sources left,' Porter said, recalling what Tannon had told him at the op briefing.

No one wants to buy what he's selling.

He's taken to inventing stuff.

'He still has a few good sources,' Cooper said. 'They tend to be of the more unsavoury variety. Organised criminals, gang leaders, right-wing militia leaders. The kind of characters most respectable agents would stay clear of. Which is probably why none of us had heard about it.'

'Heard about what?'

'The report mentioned the existence of a tape. Specifically, a sex tape the Russian mafia had managed to obtain.'

'That's what this is all about?' Bald said. 'Some dodgy footage of a celeb getting his end away?'

Cooper shook his head. 'Not a celebrity.'

'Who, then?'

Cooper looked down at his drink.

'The President of the United States,' he said.

TWENTY-FIVE

No one said anything for a few seconds.

Bald watched Cooper intently. On the TV, the president gave the thumbs-up sign to the cameras before marching off the stage, cheerfully slapping the Russian president on the back.

Porter craved a drink. Like nothing he'd ever craved before.

He tried to shut out the voice and refocused on the agent. 'That's what Street found out?' he said. 'That the Russians have got a dodgy sex tape on the president?'

'That's what Charles's source claimed.'

'Fuck me,' Bald said. 'He must be knocking back the Viagra like Smarties, bloke his age. Ain't as if he's a model of health, either.'

'I wouldn't know. I haven't seen the tape. Neither has Charles.'

'If that's the case,' Porter said, 'how can you be sure it even exists?'

'There've been rumours floating around DC for months. Everyone in the intelligence community has heard them.'

'What rumours?'

'Claims that the Russians have got incriminating material on the new man in the White House. Everyone's been looking hard. The president's enemies at the FBI and CIA included. But no one could produce any tangible proof. Not until Charles's source came forward with his claims.'

'Who is he?'

'Charles won't reveal his name. But he's a high-ranking Russian criminal who fell out of favour with the Kremlin after they seized his assets. He knows all the dark secrets.'

'He might be bullshitting.'

'He might. But his story adds up.'

Bald said, 'How did the Russian mafia get their hands on the tape in the first place?'

Cooper said, 'According to the dossier, the president made several trips to Moscow four years ago, before the election. His various businesses were in trouble, and one of his associates had agreed to introduce him to potential new investors. Among them were several key figures in the Russian criminal underworld.'

'Why would the president risk going into business with Russian crime bosses?' Porter asked.

'He didn't have a choice. The recession had hit his businesses hard. He lost a lot of money. He was sitting on a lot of devalued real-estate and construction projects with spiralling budgets, and the banks wouldn't lend a penny.'

'But he must have known taking money from the mafia would look bad.'

'The money was hidden. No one would ever know about it. It was acid-washed and fronted by shell corporations and private foundations.'

Cooper took a sip of his gin and tonic before he continued. 'According to the dossier, while the president was being wined and dined in Moscow, the mafia learned about his addiction to prostitutes.'

'The president's got a thing for hookers?' Porter asked.

Bald grinned. 'Can't say I'm surprised.'

Cooper said, 'Charles's source reckons this was common knowledge among the Russians. Every time the president flew in to Moscow, the crime bosses would set him up in a plush apart-ment, a penthouse just off Red Square. Then they'd supply him with the girls.'

'Why would he agree to that arrangement?'

'For reasons of secrecy.'

Porter nodded at that. It was well known that the Russian security services had sources inside every major hotel in the country, tipping them off about the activity of any high-profile guests. He could see why the future president wouldn't want to risk checking into a hotel under his own name.

'What he didn't realise,' Cooper went on, 'was that the bosses had rigged the entire penthouse with hidden cameras. They were secretly recording everything that went on.'

'Didn't he search the place for bugs?'

'Apparently not. Otherwise the president wouldn't have made repeat visits to the penthouse.'

'Or he might have failed to pick them up,' said Bald. 'The Russian mob have access to all the equipment the blokes in the FSB use. They could have hidden those cameras well enough so that they wouldn't get picked up by a detector.'

'It's possible. But either way, the crime bosses are now in possession of video footage of the most powerful man in the world shagging a nineteen-year-old prostitute.'

Something troubled Porter. 'You said this happened a few years ago?'

'Four years, to be precise. Why?'

'This was before the guy was even being talked about as president. Why would the Russian mafia go to all this trouble over a Yank businessman?'

'Standard practice for these guys. They collect compromising material on almost every wealthy foreigner who has business dealings in the country. Then they store it away, in case it ever becomes useful. Or perhaps they foresaw he would go on to become the next president.'

'I don't think anyone could have predicted that twat's rise,' said Bald.

Porter said, 'What are the Russians planning to do with the tape?'

'The dossier doesn't specify. But I presume the aim is to blackmail the president. Pay up what he owes, or they'll release the tape to the world's media.'

'The president's in debt to the fucking mob?'

'Heavily. The mafia invested in several foreign ventures over the past few years. Casinos, hotels, luxury apartments. Primarily they saw it as an opportunity to launder their dirty money by reinvesting the profits. When the projects failed to produce the expected returns, the bosses lost big.'

'How much?'

'Hard to say. But at a conservative estimate, they're out of pocket by a hundred million dollars. Perhaps more.'

Bald scratched his cheek. 'So now that the bloke is sitting pretty in the White House, the bosses figure they can blackmail him into coughing up the cash?'

Cooper nodded. 'It wouldn't be a straight transaction, of course. That would be impossible without drawing attention to it. But they might demand that the president invests in their projects to absorb the cost. Or pay him via one of his children's companies.'

'The president would agree to that?'

'He's fighting for his political life. His approval ratings are historically low. He'd do anything to stop that tape from coming to light.'

Something puzzled Porter. 'Could a sex tape bring him down, though? We're talking about the president here, not the Pope. The bloke's done far worse.'

Bald said, 'You know what some of those Yanks are like, mate. They see a flash of nipple on TV and they lose their collective shit. If it was damaging, the president would do anything to stop people finding out about it.'

Porter shook his head. 'If the Russian mafia have the dossier, who were the guys on the snatch squad?'

'Mob foot-soldiers.'

Cooper said, 'Why would they want to lift Street?'

'To suppress the dossier. If Charles went public with his findings, the bosses would lose any leverage they have over the new president. Blackmailing the man won't work if the rest of the world knows his dirty secrets,' Cooper added in a condescending tone.

'But why go to the trouble of lifting him at all? Why not just kill the guy instead? Problem solved.'

'The mob needs to question Charles. Make sure they get hold of every copy of the report he might have made. It would be pointless to knock him on the head, only for someone to get access to the document through a misplaced USB key.'

Porter sat back, processing the int. Thoughts buzzed around inside his head.

This dossier is extremely hot, Tannon had said. *The contents could be used to blackmail the president.*

It'd be more powerful than any conventional weapon.

A sex tape of the president.

A Russian mafia blackmail plot.

One hundred million dollars.

His eyes wandered back to the drinks Bald and Street were holding. The voice was telling him to think up an excuse. Sneak off to raid the drinks cabinet. He imagined the booze juicing his bloodstream. Another voice piped up in his head. Quieter than the first one. The voice that Porter listened to, when he wasn't feeling stressed. It told him to fight the urge.

Don't give in.

He turned back to Cooper. 'How did the Russian mob find out about the dossier? Dom reckoned only a handful of people know about it.'

'That's what I've been trying to find out. My best guess is, it came from the source Charles spoke to.'

'The exiled criminal? Why would he spill his guts?'

'Perhaps he was bragging to someone about it. One of his old associates, maybe. The Russian criminal underworld is incestuous. Everyone knows everyone else.'

'And you're sure the dossier is accurate?'

'One hundred per cent,' Cooper responded haughtily. 'Other people may have had their doubts about the veracity of Charles's work over the years, but I've never for a moment had anything less than the greatest respect for the man. He was a first-class agent in his day. I should know. I worked alongside him in Russia.'

Bald pulled a look of surprise. 'You were based in Moscow as well?'

'For a couple of years. Charles was the undoubted golden boy of MI6 at the time. The rest of us had our moments, but he was something else. That's why I trust his judgement on this one. Charles knows Russia, and Russians, better than almost anyone.'

Porter glanced at the clock on the wall to the left of the TV. 0104 hours. Less than three hours until the meeting at Vauxhall. Cooper finished his drink, set down his empty glass on the coffee table and rose from the La-Z-Boy recliner.

'We should take the opportunity to get some sleep. There's nothing else we can do until we hear back from London.'

Bald said, 'We'll stag on and off through the night. Me and Porter. In case Six needs to reach us.'

'I'll take the first stag,' Porter offered.

Bald stared at him, one eyebrow cocked. 'You sure? I don't mind staying up, mate.'

'Get your head down. I'll wake you up three hours from now.'

Bald continued to stare hard at his mucker. They both knew what Porter was planning. It was one of the oldest tricks in the Regiment book. Take the first stag on an op, while your body is still wired with adrenaline and sleep almost impossible. Use the time to relax, while the other bloke tosses and turns in his bed, trying in vain to get some shuteye.

And I can finally help myself to a drink at the same time, thought Porter. Bald knew what he was thinking. Porter could see it on his mug. *There's fuck-all he can do to stop me.*

Bald necked the dregs of his whisky, the ice clinking at the bottom of the glass as he put it down.

'Three hours, then. Not a minute longer. Give us a shout if you hear from Six before then. Tell us what the plan is.'

Porter turned to Cooper. 'You reckon your mates at Six will reach a decision at this meeting?'

'I expect so. Retrieving Charles is a priority right now. There will be considerable pressure from above to move fast.'

Bald said, 'Whatever they do, they'd better make it quick. We can't hang around here for long. Not with the FBI involved.'

'How long do you reckon we've got?' asked Porter. 'Until they link us to the murders?'

'They'll be pouring every available resource into the investigation. Every field agent will want to be involved. But they'll have a lot of ground to cover. They'll need to rule out the rednecks from their inquiries before anything else. Sift through any traffic the NSA picks up. We might have twenty-four hours, max.'

Porter shook the surprise from his face. 'You think they'll identify us that soon?'

'Put it this way,' Bald said as he looked up from his glass. 'If we're still sitting on our arses twelve hours from now, we're gonna have to bug out of this place. Plan or no fucking plan.'

TWENTY-SIX

Cooper left first. He trudged out of the living room and made his way upstairs, a weary traveller at the end of a long journey. Bald lingered for a few beats in the living room while he handed Porter the ghost phone. The voice inside Porter's head counted down the seconds until Bald and Cooper had both disappeared into their guest rooms. Then he got to his feet and moved quietly across the foyer, making for the kitchen.

He couldn't shut the voice out any longer. The stress of the op had been brewing inside him and the voice was insistent now. Overwhelming. *You need a drink.* Porter couldn't focus on anything else at that moment except getting some booze into his system.

I don't care what Jock says.

After the day I've had, I bloody deserve something stronger than a Coke.

He found Stillman in the kitchen. The housekeeper was sitting on a retro stool at the breakfast bar, nursing a drink while he watched some sort of NRA commercial on his iPad. Porter saw a flagon of Beefeater gin on the counter. The bottle was three-quarters empty. Which told Porter that he wasn't the only piss-head at the safe house.

Stillman looked up from the tablet.

'Just having a nightcap. Join me?'

'Fuck it. Why not.'

A sly grin crept out of the corner of Stillman's mouth. 'What's your poison?'

'I could murder a double measure of Bell's.'

'Coming right up, lad.'

Stillman put the iPad to sleep, slid off the stool and disappeared into the dining room. He returned a few moments later clutching a bottle of Bell's in one hand and a short whisky glass in the other.

Porter looked on as Stillman set the glass down on the granite counter, unscrewed the cap on the whisky bottle and poured the golden liquid into the glass, filling it to the brim.

Jesus, thought Porter. There's enough booze in there to knock out an elephant.

This guy must be an even bigger alcoholic than I realised.

'Drink up,' Stillman said as he handed Porter the drink. 'Plenty more where that came from.'

Porter raised the glass to his lips. The logical part of his brain told him he shouldn't be drinking. He knew nothing good ever happened when it came to the booze. He wasn't the kind of bloke who could have a glass of pinot grigio with his evening meal. When Porter drank, he had only one aim. To blot out the demons.

Drink, the voice told him.

Porter took a swig of whisky.

The booze burned the back of his throat. He felt an instant warm glow spread through his chest as the alcohol flowed through his veins, working its magic.

Better.

'Long day?' Stillman asked.

'You could say that, yeah.'

Stillman topped up his own drink and took a hit. 'I was in the game myself once, you know.'

'Is that right?'

Porter took a long swig of his triple measure of Bell's, secretly hoping Stillman would shut up and leave him in peace.

'I did twenty years in West Midlands police,' he went on without encouragement. 'Ten years in the firearms unit, plus a stint on secondment to Diplomatic Protection. I saw plenty of action back then.'

'I can imagine.'

'Fella, I could tell you some stories. We dealt with all sorts. Crack dens, gang violence, organised crime. Real frontline stuff.'

Stillman helped himself to another gulp of his drink.

'The SAS might steal all the glory, but our boys are the real deal as well. Our team responded to more than a thousand incidents during my time in charge, as a matter of fact.'

Porter almost did a spit-take on his whisky. He knew what was going on here. Stillman was bragging about his service, trying to bolster his rep. Put himself on the same level as his house guests. Porter decided to change the subject.

'How long have you been in the US?'

'Ten years now. Moved here after I left the job. Did my ankle falling down a flight of stairs on the job. Had to retire early. Took my pension, sold up the house in Walsall and bought this place.'

'How did you end up working for Six?'

'It was after my Gemma passed away. I'd been running a few surveillance courses, private investigations, that sort of thing. Someone from Vauxhall approached me through my business connections. Said they were looking for trusted UK nationals who'd be willing to let their place be used as a safe house. I signed up on the spot, before they even mentioned money.'

'Don't they pay you?'

'I'm on a retainer, plus security expenses. It's a decent whack. All the money's routed through private accounts, off-shore, so there's nothing to officially tie to me to Six. But I'm not doing this for the wonga.'

'Why, then?'

Stillman looked puzzled by the question. 'Loyalty, mate. I'm serving my country. Same as you.'

Porter smiled at that. Loyalty, he thought. There's a word that Six doesn't know the meaning of. He and Bald didn't see eye-to-eye on many things, but they both shared a deep mistrust of Vauxhall. Maybe Jock is right to be getting out after this, he thought. *Maybe I should quit too.*

'What about you?' asked Stillman. 'How long have you and your mate been involved with Six?'

He spoke in a jovial tone of voice. Two lads, trading old war stories over a few drinks. But Porter saw a glint in the house-keeper's eyes. Porter wondered if this was mere idle curiosity, wanting to be in with the crowd, or something more sinister. Right now, he thought, I don't know who to trust.

'I was in military intelligence,' he replied lamely. 'I got recruited while I was in Iraq. That's how it happened.'

'You've been working for them for a while, then?'

'A few years, yeah.'

187

'What sort of jobs have they got you doing?'

'This and that. But it's mostly menial work. Nothing very interesting.'

'What happened to your fingers?' Stillman nodded at the two stumps on Porter's left hand.

'Training accident,' Porter lied.

The stumps were a permanent reminder of the Beirut op. The one that had left three good SAS men dead, and Porter's Regiment career in tatters. He'd been shot in the hand by one of the Lebanese gunmen holding a British national hostage. Whenever he tried to forget about the deaths of his muckers, the stumps brought the memories rushing back. Only one thing helped to shut out the nightmares . . .

He took another long swig.

Stillman's gruff voice cut through the booze-fog building up inside Porter's head. 'Where are you based?'

'England, most of the time.'

Stillman said, 'I'm a Croydon lad myself. Moved up to Brum in my twenties, but Croydon's home for me. I miss it sometimes. Whereabouts are you from?'

'Hereford,' said Porter, sticking to the cover story they'd been given by Moorcroft.

'Fuck me, I've got a mate in Hereford. He lives on that road where the football stadium is. What's the name of that street again?'

'Edgar Street.'

'That's the one. What's the supermarket next to the stadium again?'

The guy is trying to catch me out, thought Porter. Poking holes in my story. He wondered again if Stillman was working to a secret agenda. Or perhaps he was simply another old copper who couldn't shake the habit. Porter set down his drink and shot a cold, hard look at the housekeeper.

'Look here, pal. Do us a favour and lay off the bullshit psychology. It won't work with us, alright? Have a drink if you want, but leave your profession behind.'

Stillman raised his hands in a gesture of apology. 'Sorry. I didn't mean to pry. An old habit of mine from my police days.'

'That's fine. Just keep the conversation neutral from now on. You know what I mean.'

Stillman nodded. In the bright lights of the kitchen Porter could see that his eyes were glassy and heavily-lidded. He looked drunk, and tired.

'You can call it a night, if you want,' Porter said, secretly hoping he would piss off. 'I'll be keeping watch.'

'What for? No one knows about this place except me, my handler at Vauxhall and the local postman.'

'You sure about that?'

'This place is safe as it gets,' Stillman insisted. 'We're miles from anywhere. That's one of the reasons Six cut me the deal. They wanted somewhere off the grid. Trust me, we won't be getting any visitors.'

The conversation petered out. They drank in silence for a while. Stillman polished off the rest of his G and &T in one long gulp and rose clumsily to his feet.

'I'm turning in, mate. What time are you expecting to hear from Six tomorrow?'

'Some time after four o'clock. We'll try to be quiet.'

'Don't worry about me. I'll be up long before then, I'm sure.'

He shuffled out of the kitchen, crossing the foyer to the ground-floor master bedroom. Porter watched him go. He knocked back the rest of his drink, grabbed the bottle of Bell's and retreated to the living room. The voice at the base of his skull told him that he shouldn't drink any more, but Porter wasn't in the mood to listen.

Tomorrow I might be arrested for the murder of an FBI agent. *Might as well enjoy a drink tonight.*

He sank into the sofa and poured more whisky down his throat. Placating that old voice inside his head. On the coffee table, amid the empty glasses, he noticed a coaster from the last presidential election. A laminated graphic of the new president beamed at Porter from the coaster, grinning while he gave his trademark thumbs-up.

Porter felt a leaden, dense fog settle behind his eyes. He suddenly felt very tired. His eyelids were heavy, as if someone had sewn a couple of hockey pucks into them. He was dimly aware of the time on the wall clock.

0126 hours.

Two-and-a-half hours until the meeting in London.

Nothing to do now but wait.

And pray that Six can get us out of here alive.

He pressed the whisky bottle to his lips and took another long gulp. Thirty minutes later, the darkness closed around him.

He woke to a vicious pounding in his head and a sharp trilling noise in the side pocket of his cargos.

The sound jolted him out of his sleep. He sat upright on the sofa, the fog inside his head slowly clearing. His mouth was dry. There was a distinct pain behind his eyes, as if someone was stabbing at the backs of his pupils with an ice pick. His eyes focused on the empty bottle of Bell's on the coffee table. The TV was still turned on. Ken and Barbie had been replaced by an ad for some sort of weight-loss supplement.

Porter glanced at his watch.

0511 hours.

Shit.

The trilling repeated. Porter dimly remembered the encrypted BlackBerry. The ghost phone. He reached down to his side pocket, pulled out the phone. Squinted at the display while he tried to ignore the savage thumping inside his skull. The screen displayed an unknown number, prefixed by the international dialling code for the UK.

He killed the sound on the TV.

Hit the Call button.

'Yeah?'

Moorcroft's voice came down the line loud and angry, like a hiss of steam.

'Where the fuck have you been, man? I've been trying to reach you for the past twenty minutes.'

'I was in the shower. Didn't hear the phone ringing.'

'I told you to be ready to pick up the phone at all times. Christ, can't you do anything right?'

The hangover pounded relentlessly between Porter's temples. A wave of nausea surged in his guts and tickled the back of his throat. He fought a sudden urge to hurl the ghost phone across the room. 'Did you and Dom have your meeting?'

'It finished half an hour ago.' Moorcroft exhaled. The anger in his voice dialled down to a mild annoyance. 'We've reached a decision. I've been trying you every minute since.'

'Let's hear it.'

'We're in agreement that the only realistic option is a ground exfiltration to Canada. Given your location and the critical nature of your situation, your best hope is to attempt a crossing at Buffalo.'

'Go through a border checkpoint crawling with armed guards? That's your bright idea?' —

Moorcroft said, 'The crossing at Buffalo is the busiest along the Canadian border. Thousands of people cross through every day to go to work, or to visit friends or family. Which means the officials will be too busy to check your documents thoroughly.'

'You're forgetting Street is wanted by the FBI. The guards will stop us the moment they identify him.'

'He's a person of interest, not a suspect.'

'That won't make a difference. As soon as the guards run his name through the system, we'll be taken aside. We'd never make it across to the Canadian side.'

Moorcroft let out a deep breath. 'Look, you've only got to avoid the American border guards. The Canadian side won't be a problem. They won't have access to the same information as their American counterparts.'

'It's not gonna be easy.'

'No one said it would be. But I'm sure you'll find a way.'

'Yeah, well. I'd feel a fuck of a lot better if you just stuck us on a private jet.'

'That's not an option. The feeling is we can't do anything that implies British state knowledge of this matter. I've explained this already.'

'I don't give a toss.' Rage pulsed inside Porter's chest. 'You told us to find your man and get him to safety. We've done our job. How about you start doing yours for a fucking change.'

'We're doing our best, John.'

'Yeah? It doesn't look like that from where I'm sitting.'

'Our hands are tied on this one. It's impossible to provide you with direct assistance without alerting our American friends. If they rumbled us, it would get very uncomfortable.'

Porter sighed. There was nothing to be gained by arguing for an alternative extraction plan. Once the brains trust at MI6 had made up their minds, they were utterly inflexible.

'What happens once we make it across?'

'Someone will meet you on the Canadian side. You'll be debriefed and then escorted to a private airfield for immediate extraction to London. I'll send you a number to call once you're on the road.'

In the rough map of North America in his head, Porter knew that Buffalo was roughly four hundred miles from the safe house. A seven-to-eight-hour drive, depending on traffic and the route taken. Maybe another hour to cross the border and hit the RV.

Nine hours total.

'We'll have to leave soon,' he said.

'That's your problem. Not mine.'

'What about Cooper?'

'What about him?'

'Are we bringing him with us?'

'I don't think we have any other choice. It's too dangerous to leave him in play. He'll accompany you across the border. We've already notified the embassy.'

'It might look suspicious. Him making a quick exit.'

'That's a risk we'll have to take. In the meantime, I suggest you make the necessary preparations for your journey. Stillman will assist you with any requirements you may have.'

Moorcroft clicked off. MI6 handlers weren't big on goodbyes.

Porter heard footsteps across the foyer. He looked up as Cooper stepped into the room, dressed in his crisp suit, mug of coffee in his right hand with the Crystal Palace badge on the side. Cooper jerked his chin at the ghost phone in Porter's hand. 'I heard voices. Was that London?'

'What are you doing up so early?'

'Couldn't sleep. Too wired, I suppose.'

'Where's everyone else?'

'Your friend's asleep. So is Charles. Stillman's in the kitchen. There's a pot of coffee on the go.'

Porter said, 'I just got off the blower with Moorcroft.'

'What did he say?'

'Wake the others,' Porter said. 'Then I'll explain. We've got work to do.'

TWENTY-SEVEN

They held the conference in the kitchen. Porter, Bald, Cooper, Street and Stillman were all gathered around the breakfast bar. Bald stared daggers at Porter while Stillman put on a fresh pot of coffee. Then he dished out steaming hot mugs while Porter briefed them on the plan. He left out any details Stillman didn't need to know about.

'Your handler's right about one thing,' Stillman said after Porter had finished. 'Getting across the border will be the easy part.'

Porter turned to him. 'How well do you know it?'

'Well enough. Crossed there a few times on my way up to Toronto.'

'Can we expect any problems?'

'As long as you look the part, you should be fine. The guards won't check your documents too closely. They'll ask you a few questions. Reason for your trip, where you're staying.'

'We should book somewhere on the Canadian side,' Bald suggested. 'Make it look legit.'

Porter shook his head. 'We can't risk the paper trail.'

'You could say you're going over to the casinos,' said Stillman. 'Plenty of tourists head over to those resorts and come back the same evening. That wouldn't raise any questions.'

Porter nodded. 'You'll need to tell us where security is lax. Any hotspots along the border that we need to avoid.'

'We've also got to figure out what to do about him.' Bald gave a cursory nod at Street. 'The Yanks will be all over us the minute they run his ID through the computer.'

'We could hide him in the boot,' said Porter.

'But if the Canadians did a routine check on the car, we'd be fucked.'

'What if we smuggle him in the boot before we pass through the American side? Then get him out before we reach the Canadian checkpoint.'

'That could work,' Stillman said. 'The checkpoints are at opposite ends of the Peace Bridge. Which is about half a mile long. If you make the journey in one of them cars with folding back seats, your friend could crawl in and out of the boot without you lads needing to pull over.'

Cooper cleared his throat. 'How long until we leave?'

Porter said, 'Two hours, at least. We've got to plan the route, sort out a hire car and get a change of clothes.'

'What's wrong with the clothes you've got on?'

'When we cross that border, we need to look professional. We can't rock up to the checkpoint looking like a bunch of tramps. The guards will definitely take an interest in us then.'

'He's gonna need some new clobber too,' Bald added, running his eyes over Street's bloodstained shirt and trousers.

Stillman said, 'There's a Walmart at the mall in the next town over. A big twenty-four-hour store. We can pick up some threads there.'

'That'll do. As I said, we'll need you to sort us out a hire car as well. One with folding back seats. There's no way we can risk running that truck up to the border.'

'That's going to be a problem. The local rental place doesn't open until later.'

'When?'

'Ten o'clock.'

Bald shook his head. 'That's too late. We need to be out of the country twenty-four hours after last night's incident. Anything longer than that and we risk being identified.'

Stillman said, 'We could try Dulles. The rental desks at the airport are open twenty-four seven.'

'How long will it take to get there and back?'

'Half hour each way. Plus time to stop off at the Walmart. I reckon we're looking at a ninety-minute round trip.'

'We should leave now, then,' said Bald.

'I'll need to get rid of that truck before you leave, lads. Can't have that thing sitting in my garage.'

'Have you got somewhere you can dump it?'

'I know a place. There's a wooded area three miles south of here. But I'll need one of you lads to come with me. Drive the truck to the woods, then drive the rental back from the airport.'

Porter knew he wasn't in any fit state to drive. He felt as if someone had scraped out the inside of his guts. The nausea rose higher in his throat. He thought he might puke. 'Jock will go with you. I'll stay here and watch the others.'

'How much cash have you got on your, right now?' Stillman asked. Porter remembered the walk-around money they'd been given. They'd dropped just short of three hundred dollars at the car rental desk at the airport. Plus sixty bucks at the petrol station en route to the log cabin, on gas and sugary snacks. Which left them with around eleven hundred and fifty dollars in the walk-around fund.

'A grand, or thereabouts.'

'You're gonna need at least that when you hit the border. Especially if you're telling them you're planning to hit the casinos.' Stillman indicated the master bedroom. 'There's ten thousand in the safe. The money belongs to Six. Take as much as you need, just make sure you sign for it. They're a bit funny about people dipping into the fund.'

'No worries.'

'Right, we'd best get moving. I'll show you lads how to work the sensor, in case the alarm goes off.'

Stillman left the kitchen and moved off down the hallway. Cooper intercepted Bald and Porter as they turned to follow him. 'Anything we can do to help?'

'Just sit tight,' Bald said. 'And sort him out.'

He tipped his head at Street. The guy looked edgy. His right leg was bouncing up and down with nervous energy. He held onto the dossier like it was a security blanket.

'What's his problem?' Porter asked quietly.

'He's just anxious about the plan,' Cooper replied in a low voice, so Street wouldn't overhear. 'Charles doesn't know where his head's at.'

'I don't give a toss,' Bald said. 'You need to calm him down before we leave. If he's a bag of nerves when we hit the border, the guards might get suspicious.'

'He'll be fine. I'll make sure of it.'

'Do that.'

Bald gave his back to Cooper and marched down the hallway towards the front door. Porter moved after him, pain splitting his skull. Stillman lingered by the front door at the far end of the foyer. He punched a series of buttons on the keypad, demonstrating how to disable the infra-red alarm. Once they'd committed it to memory, Stillman stepped out into the pre-dawn light. Bald turned to follow him, then stopped in the doorway and abruptly rounded on his mucker.

'What was all that about earlier? You were supposed to wake me up at four. That was the fucking deal.'

Porter said, 'I thought I'd let you sleep in.'

Bald laughed. 'You're a shit liar, mate. I can smell your breath from a mile away. You've been on the piss.'

'I had a couple of drinks, that's all. There's no harm in that.'

'It was more than a couple. You murdered a bottle of whisky. You and the housekeeper. I heard you two chatting away downstairs.'

Porter clenched his hands into fists at his side. 'I didn't see you saying no to a beer last night.'

'The difference is, I can stop when I need to. You can't. You're an alcoholic, for fuck's sake.'

Porter clenched his jaws. 'I needed a straightener. It's no big deal.'

'It is when you can't perform. When are you gonna learn your lesson and give that shit up?'

Another flare of anger surged up inside Porter, burning through his veins. Bald's needling comments were really beginning to get to him. 'Leave it off. It's none of your business. What the fuck do you care if I have a few drinks?'

Bald took a step closer, his features contorted into a scowl. 'I couldn't give a toss about you, or that knackered liver of yours. But if you don't get yourself clean soon, you're gonna get us both clipped.'

'It won't happen again.'

Bald eyed him for a moment longer. 'What about this plan Six has cooked up? Think it'll work?'

'It has to. Moorcroft's right. There's no other way out.'

'If the FBI connects us to them murders at the retreat, we won't stand a chance of getting across the border.'

'There's nothing we can do about that. All we can do is focus on getting out as fast as we can.'

Bald grunted. 'I hope Tannon and Moorcroft know what they're doing.'

I hope so too, thought Porter.

They left the safe house a minute later. Stillman drove off in the Tahoe, Bald trailing him in the Hilux. Porter watched them depart through the blinds in the ground-floor bedroom. The hangover had migrated to the sides of his head now. Drilling directly into his temporal lobes, pain clawing away at his temples. His stomach heaved. He stumbled into the downstairs bathroom and just about made it to the toilet before he vomited. Porter gripped the bowl, retching until he had nothing more left in his guts. He flushed and spat the acid taste out of his mouth.

Christ, he felt like shit.

You know what you need, the voice said.

Another drink. Sort you out.

He pushed the voice aside and shuffled back down the hallway to the kitchen. Cooper and Street had set themselves up in the living room, passing the time in front of the TV. Porter could hear the sound of canned laughter as he ran the faucet and guzzled down three straight glasses of cold water. He waited for the nausea to pass, fixed himself a fresh cup of coffee. Settled down in front of the laptop.

He spent the next ninety minutes chasing down painkillers with his coffee and checking West Virginia news sites for any mention of the log cabin shootings. After a solid hour of fruitless searches, he began to think they might have got away with the murders after all.

After the fifth cup of coffee, his appetite returned. Porter found a pack of protein bars in the pantry. He still felt rank but he forced down two of the bars. The sickness had passed but the hangover kept on niggling away at him, rapping its knuckles against the sides of his skull.

Twenty-two minutes later, the sensor alarm shrieked.

Porter traipsed back down the hallway. Cooper stepped out of the living room, looking on as Porter punched in the combination on the keypad next to the front door. The alarm cut out, and he opened the door as Stillman's Tahoe eased to a halt in front of the garage. A dark-blue Chevrolet Cruze pulled in behind the Tahoe. Bald emerged from the Cruze while Stillman retrieved four large carrier bags from the back seat of the SUV.

'Everything sorted?' Porter asked as Bald and Stillman approached.

'Aye,' Bald replied. 'It's all taken care of.'

Stillman held up the carrier bags. They were Walmart-branded, stuffed with clothes. 'Shirts and trousers. Hope they fit.'

'As long as they don't make us look like a pair of cunts, they'll do fine.'

Bald said, 'Any news from West Virginia?'

'Nothing.'

'Still?'

'Maybe we're in the clear. Our luck could be changing.'

Bald pulled a look as if Porter had told him a crap joke. 'The way things have gone for us lately, I wouldn't count on it.'

'How long until we leave?'

The question came from Cooper. The guy had been frowning at his watch, Porter had observed. 'Half an hour or so. Once we've changed and sorted out the route to Buffalo, we'll get going.'

Cooper stole a glance at the alarm keypad. 'That reminds me,' he said, addressing Stillman. 'It might be nothing, but I heard the comms equipment downstairs making a strange noise earlier.'

Stillman let out a frustrated sigh. 'Bastard thing's probably on the blink again. I'll take a look at it.'

'What were you doing down in the basement?' Bald asked Cooper.

'Looking for my Zippo. I thought I might have left it down there.'

They split up. Porter, Bald and Street headed for the stairs, each carrying a shopping bag. Stillman disappeared into the basement while Cooper made for the kitchen to check again on the news sites.

A folded cotton towel was laid out on the unused double bed in Porter's room, with a set of travel-size toiletries arranged on the bedside table. Hospitality, MI6-style. He emptied the contents of the shopping bag, stripped off and stuffed the dirty clothes into the empty bag. Then he took a brief, scalding shower in the en-suite bathroom, the water stabbing at him as it washed away the blood and the dirt. He brushed his teeth, shaved, deodorised and stepped out of the bathroom feeling borderline human again. Not great. But better than an hour ago.

After he'd applied a new dressing to his wound, Porter tore open the clothes package and dressed. The shirt was a long-sleeved white Oxford with a front breast pocket. It was snug around the neck and an inch short on the arms, but otherwise fitted okay. The trousers were what Americans referred to as dress pants. Long and shapeless and functional. But comfortable, with a lot of spare real estate to fill out.

When he'd finished dressing, he inspected himself in the mirror. He looked reasonably smart, without being too formal. Like a holidaymaker heading for a night at the casino.

At seven-thirty, Porter left the guest room and headed downstairs to the kitchen.

He found Bald and Cooper gathered around the breakfast bar. They were staring at the laptop screen, scrolling through news reports. Bald had another cup of coffee on the go. Cooper periodically glanced at his watch. The guy looked agitated. Perhaps he's just desperate to get out of here, thought Porter.

That makes two of us.

He said, 'Where are the others?'

Bald said, 'Stillman's in the basement, testing the comms kit.'

'Street?'

'Getting changed.' He added: 'You all need to see this.'

The three of them crowded around the breakfast bar, Porter leaning in for a closer look at the laptop screen. The browser was open at a local news site. Half the page was populated by banner ads for fashion labels and discount furniture stores. Porter mentally screened it out as his eyes drifted to the header at the top of the page. It carried the name of a regional newspaper.

Charleston Herald. West Virginia's Leading News Source Since 1962!

Below the header was a breaking news story about a shooting in Lewis County, W. Va. Porter felt a growing sense of dread as he skimmed through the article.

He finished reading.

The pounding in his head worsened.

'Shit,' he said.

They've found the bodies.

'The police are calling it a gangland shooting,' Bald said. 'They're portraying the rednecks as some sort of local criminal element, possibly involved in the crystal meth trade.'

'Why would they put out a statement so soon? Even the cops don't usually jump to conclusions that quick.' 'The FBI must have figured out what went down. They've put out this bullshit cover story to make it look as if they've drawn a line under the case.'

Porter tried to hide his alarm. 'You think they've rumbled us? If that's the case, why haven't they got our mugs all over the news?'

'They might not know who's behind the attack. But their backup team would have rocked up hours ago. They would have had enough time to form a rough idea of what happened, put out the gangland story.'

'But why bother with the fake news?'

'They want us to think we got away with it, mate. They want us to get fucking sloppy.'

Porter nodded, grasping the implications. Dozens of FBI agents were probably combing the crime scene at that very moment. Sooner or later they would turn up something linking them to the killings. An eyewitness in the woods or one of the neighbouring cabins. A piece of forensic evidence they'd missed. Security footage. Anything. 'We've got to hit that border as soon as possible,' he said.

'Aye.'

'Get Stillman. Now. We need him to point out the route.'

Bald hurried out of the room and disappeared into the basement. Several moments later he emerged with the housekeeper. Stillman swept into the kitchen, shaking his head.

'Sorry, lads. Comms unit is working fine now. Bloody thing's always playing up. Move over, I'll get the route up.'

Porter shuffled along, giving Stillman the floor. The guy opened a new browser window, accessed Google Maps and started tapping keys and swiping on the trackpad. Over by the French doors, Cooper had nervously plucked a fag from his pack and stepped outside. He stood on the patio steps, smoking his cigarette, checking his watch.

That's the third time Cooper has done that, Porter thought.

His phone suddenly buzzed.

He dug the ghost phone out of his back pocket. Bald and Stillman were focused on the laptop screen. Stillman was zooming in on an area of Buffalo, pointing out the Peace Bridge.

A number flashed up on the ghost phone display. Porter vaguely recognised it. The same number Moorcroft had used when calling him a few hours earlier. He tapped the screen and answered.

Moorcroft's voice came down the line, urgent and serious.

'John? Can you talk?'

Porter said, 'I'm here.'

'Where are you?'

'At the safe house. We're leaving soon.'

'Listen to me very carefully. You need to get out of there right now.'

'Why? What's going on?'

'Your location has been compromised. The Russians know where you are.'

The blood instantly turned to ice in Porter's veins. On the other side of the breakfast counter, Bald looked a question at him. Cooper had stepped back inside the kitchen, a faint smell of cigarette smoke wafting across the room. Porter shut everything else out and focused on the voice on the other end of the line.

'How the fuck did they find us? How do you know?'

'The chaps over at GCHQ picked up chatter in Moscow,' Moorcroft said. 'A Kremlin officer with known underworld links just mentioned your address on the phone. Someone told the Russians where to find you. They're sending people over there now.'

Porter felt his stomach muscles constrict. He stared at Bald and Cooper in turn, dread seeping into his guts.

Someone sold us out.

'The safe house is blown,' Moorcroft said. 'Get out of there, man!'

Porter was about to reply when he heard another noise.

Coming from beyond the house.

The roar of an approaching car.

TWENTY-EIGHT

The engine roar grew louder.

Stillman glanced over his shoulder at the front door, twenty metres away from the kitchen, at the other end of the long hallway. 'That's weird. The alarm didn't go off.'

'You expecting someone?' Bald asked.

'No.'

Bald swung around to face Porter. They didn't need to say anything to one another. It was all right there on Porter's face. They both heard the motors barrelling up the driveway and instantly realised what was happening.

Unexpected visitors.

A safe house no one else knows about.

We're under attack.

They knew what they had to do. There was no messing about. No valuable seconds lost debating their plan. They just reacted to the situation, trusting in their decades of training.

Bald turned to Stillman. 'What's the code to the gun safe?'

Stillman didn't hear him at first. He was staring with a puzzled look at the front door at the other end of the hallway, a kid trying to work out how to solve a Rubik's cube.

'*The code*,' Porter repeated.

Stillman snapped out of his trance. 'Three-seven-two-nine-five.'

Bald repeated the code and sprinted out of the kitchen. He raced down the hallway, towards the ground-floor bedroom to the right of the staircase. Porter moved after him, grabbing Cooper by the shoulder and shoving him into the corridor. 'Into the strong room. Now.'

'What the hell's going on?' Cooper rasped.

'There's no time. Move yourself.'

Cooper saw the look on Porter's face and got moving, running ahead of Porter as they scrambled out of the kitchen. Ahead of them Stillman was moving towards the front door, scratching his head. Porter and Cooper were eight metres from the bedroom now.

The roar outside became deafening. At this distance he could hear at least two individual motors. More than that, possibly. There was the clatter of loose gravel being flung about as the vehicles skidded to a halt in front of the safe house, before the engines abruptly cut out.

They've arrived, thought Porter.

We've only got a few seconds to get our shit together.

Four metres ahead of him, Bald ducked into the master bedroom. Cooper was a couple of steps behind.

Porter was about to dart into the room when he glimpsed a figure at his ten o'clock. He stopped in front of the bedroom door and glanced over his shoulder at the staircase.

Street stood at the foot of the stairs, dressed in the same long-sleeved shirt and trousers as Bald and Porter, his body stiff with terror as he looked towards the front door.

'In the strong room, now!' Porter shouted.

'Four cars here, lads,' Stillman called out from the entrance. 'Bloody loads of 'em.'

Porter spun towards him. Stillman had stopped at the window to the left of the front door, fifteen metres away. He cracked open the blind between his thumb and forefinger, peeking through the gap as the cars rocketed up the front drive.

'Some of them are going around the back, by the looks of it,' Stillman went on.

'Get away from there!' Porter thundered. 'NOW!'

Stillman started to turn towards him.

Which was when the bullet took his face off.

The round shattered the glass, whacking into the housekeeper's left eyeball and punching out of the back of his skull an inch or so above the nape of his neck. Blood and grey matter sprayed across the magnolia wall. Instant death. Like someone had yanked out the power cord.

Street looked on, body tensing with horror, as Stillman melted to the floor. Mouth gaping, a moist black hole where his left eye used to be.

'Jesus, no,' whispered Street. 'Oh, God.'

There was no time to waste. Porter rushed over to the stairs, clamped a hand around Street's arm and pulled him towards the master bedroom as two more bullets pierced the window, thudding into the wall to the right of the stairs, a metre away from where Street had been standing.

Another pair of cracks rang out as they scurried across the hallway. Behind him, Porter heard glass shattering as the rounds smacked into one of the paintings on the wall, putting holes in the frame. More bullets thudded into an antique cabinet, ripping through the wood.

They hit the bedroom before the next shots rang out. Porter found Bald crouching inside the strong room, working the gunsafe keypad. Cooper hung back by the security door, casting nervous glances in the direction of the hallway. Porter swept past him and joined Bald, his heart drumming erratically.

Four cars, Stillman had said. Maximum of five guys per motor. Which meant they could be up against anything from four to twenty X-rays.

The Russians must really want to get their hands on that dossier.

Porter heard a distinct beep as the gun-safe keypad unlocked. Then Bald wrenched the safe door open.

'Grab us a couple of longs,' Porter said.

'Where's Stillman?'

'Dead.'

'The fuck—'

'There's no time. Hurry.'

Bald reached in and seized two of the Colt AR-15s from the vertical rack. He chucked one of the rifles at Porter, took the other for himself and plundered the bottom shelf for ammo. Grabbed half a dozen clips of 5.56x45mm NATO rounds and passed three of them to Porter. They were the box mag type, with a twenty-round capacity. All the clips were full.

Beyond the foyer, Porter heard voices. Thick, guttural accents. Eastern European. They were shouting at one another with the urgency of professionals who knew they were against the clock.

Porter tried to put himself in the enemy's boots. They wouldn't want to get bogged down in a prolonged firefight. If he was attacking the safe house, he'd look to go in hard and fast. Use the element of surprise to overwhelm the defenders before they had time to get organised. They would be looking to attack multiple entry points, using their superior numbers to press home their advantage. The French doors at the back of the kitchen and the windows at the front and sides of the stronghold were the obvious weak points. All of them would need to be defended.

Some of them are going around the back, Stillman had said.

His hangover faded to a dull ache as he turned to Bald, adrenaline taking over. 'We're gonna have to cover the front and back approaches. I'll take the front. You cover the kitchen.'

'What sort of hardware do you think them lot are packing?'

'If they're Russian mafia, it'll be gun-show kit. Pistols, submachine guns. Grenades. Fucking everything.'

'What about us?' Cooper asked, anxiously glancing at the hallway.

'Stay here in the strong room. Keep your heads down and for fuck's sake don't move until we come get you.'

'It's them, isn't it?' Street said, stiffening with fear. 'It's the Russians. They've found me.'

'Get in,' Porter ordered. 'Unless you want to get fucking dropped.'

Fear of death was a wonderful thing. Cooper and Street hustled into the strong room. The surrounding breeze-block walls and reinforced steel door would protect them from any stray rounds coming through the windows and walls. Locking it would have given them an added layer of protection, but there was no time to retrieve the key from Stillman's body. They would just have to hope they could keep the enemy pinned down outside the house.

If the X-rays breach the entry points, Porter told himself, we won't stand a chance.

He nodded at Bald and stepped out of the strong room, the spare twenty-round mags tucked into his back trouser pockets. Porter inserted the other clip into the underside of the AR-15 mag well. He depressed the release on the side of the receiver. Pulled the charging handle all the way back and let it shunt forward, chambering the first round of 5.56 brass.

He didn't even think about it. Muscle memory. A decade of training in the Regiment. It never leaves you.

The voices outside gave way to a loud splintering thud. Coming from the far end of the foyer. Fuckers are kicking in the door, Porter realised. *They'll be crashing inside any second.* 'Stay here in the strong room. Keep your heads down and for fuck's sake don't move until we come get you.'

Bald emerged from the strong room gripping the other Colt long. He smiled grimly at Porter. They both knew the score. They were trapped in the safe house, surrounded by an unknown number of X-rays, with weak points at both sides of the safe house. If they were going to stand any chance of survival, they would have to fight like madmen.

'Let's fucking do this,' Bald said.

They charged out into the hallway.

TWENTY-NINE

They moved fast.

Bald peeled off to the left, setting off in the direction of the kitchen with his Colt long, ready to slot the X-rays manoeuvring around to the rear of the safe house. Porter gave his back to his mucker. He sprinted past the staircase, heading towards the foyer, fifteen metres downstream from the bedroom doorway.

He was twelve metres from the foyer when a loud crack split the air. The front door crashed open, swinging back on its hinges as a pair of figures burst inside.

The first guy bulled through the door. He was a fat fuck, as wide as he was tall, wearing a dark black t-shirt, black trousers and matching boots. He looked like a bruised testicle. He held a Heckler & Koch HK416 assault rifle in a two-handed grip. The Bin Laden killer. A SEAL Team favourite, chambered for the same 5.56 round as the rifle Porter was using.

The second X-ray swept into view a half-step behind Testicle. Also armed with the same HK416 rifle. He was a foot taller than his mate, with the jacked upper torso of someone who had taken way too many steroids. He was decked out in a light blue track-suit, with a white vest underneath and a gold chain draped like a garland around his neck.

Porter reacted to the threat sluggishly. The alcohol in his system slowing him down. As if he was moving through treacle. His muscles felt heavy and weak as he dropped to a knee, making himself a smaller visual target. With his left hand gripping the underside of the barrel, Porter thumbed the fire selector on the side of the rifle, moving it from SAFE to FIRE. By the time the first shooters had both feet inside the foyer, Porter had lined up the target.

Testicle was ten metres away now. A better shooter would have raised his weapon before breaching the door, scanning the entrance for targets. But Testicle had charged inside without bringing his weapon to bear. Which was a mistake. He looked like he was in a big hurry to get inside the safe house, full of misplaced confidence, still mentally celebrating his head-shot on Stillman. Thinking he'd won the battle all by himself.

Then Testicle realised his error and started to heft up his weapon. Porter depressed the trigger before the guy could finish raising it.

The Colt rifle made a satisfying crack. The gunshot boomed inside the foyer. Like a million car engines backfiring.

Porter's shot was off-target. He'd been aiming for the chest but the round struck low, nailing Testicle in the thigh. The guy grunted in pain as he staggered forward, bent at the waist.

Porter fired again. The second round went where he intended it to go, smashing into Testicle's forehead. The guy's rifle clattered to the tiled floor as he fell away, slumping down beside Stillman's lifeless corpse.

Tracksuit was next through the door.

He stepped around his dying mate, bringing his weapon to chest height. He was determined not to repeat his friend's mistake, clearly. From his assured grip Porter could tell the guy had received some basic military training. Stock tucked against his shoulder, eyes locked on the target. Finger tensing on the trigger.

Tracksuit squeezed off a round before Porter could zero in. He felt a streak of hot air grazing his cheek as the bullet whipped past his face two or three inches to the left, embedding itself in the banister post at the foot of the staircase, spitting out wood.

Tracksuit adjusted his aim. Porter had a second to get his shot off. Plenty of time for a seasoned Regiment operator, aiming at a human-sized target nine metres away. But not for an ex-Blade nursing a killer hangover. Porter fought off the pain in his head as he lined up the Colt long with Tracksuit, focusing on the guy's overdeveloped upper body, aiming for mass over any specific point. He pulled the trigger half a second before Tracksuit could loose off another shot.

The Colt barked.

The round missed.

It struck high and wide, slamming into the door next to Tracksuit. A piss-poor shot. Like a striker missing an open goal. Tracksuit half-flinched, momentarily throwing his aim off. Then he drew the HK416 level with Porter's head. A smile crept spider-like out of the corner of his mouth.

Porter rolled to the right as the muzzle flashed, a desperate last-ditch manoeuvre. He heard the crack of the rifle as the bullet discharged. It took a chunk out of the floor, ricocheting off the tiling as Porter came up into a kneeling stance a metre to the right of the stairs.

Tracksuit was swivelling towards him. There was no time to aim properly. Porter centred the muzzle on Tracksuit, pushed aside the hangover and fired again. Two rounds in a controlled burst. The first one missed completely, thudding into the door. But the next one did the damage. It slammed into the guy's left shoulder, exploding his joint in a shower of blood and tendon and bone. Tracksuit howled in agony as he jerked back a step, teeth clenched as his left arm flopped uselessly by his side. The rifle fell from his limp grip. Porter depressed the trigger again, sending him over to the dark side with a bullet to the throat. He landed on his back next to his fallen mate.

Porter took a breath as he stared at Tracksuit. Two rounds out of four had missed their target. If the guy had been sharper, or if Porter had failed to roll out of the line of fire, he would be dead by now. The X-rays would have swept inside the foyer and surrounded Bald.

Christ, he thought. I nearly lost it there, because of the booze. *I've got to raise my fucking game.*

He glanced back at his six o'clock. Bald had dropped low beside the jukebox in the kitchen, ten metres back from where Porter was kneeling, his rifle pointed at the rear entry point. The French doors facing out to the patio were open, and Porter realised Cooper must have forgotten to shut them when returning from his fag break.

Twenty metres beyond the open doors he glimpsed a couple of figures racing across the garden towards the patio. A guy in a Ducati motorcycle jacket, and a second figure in a Spartak

Moscow replica shirt. Both of them were gripping the same Heckler & Koch assault rifle as the two dead X-rays in the foyer.

They ran fast, like two sprinters competing in a race. Ducati had the lead. He was on the pool deck. Spartak was a few metres behind, racing up the steps to the patio.

Ducati was fifteen metres from the doors as Bald put down a three-round burst at them. Flames lashed out of the rifle snout, lighting up the room. The brass jackets dinked on the kitchen floor. The first round glanced off a stone water feature to the right of Ducati. The next two bullets nailed him in the upper chest in a close grouping and sent him belly-flopping into the pool, spilling chlorinated water across the deck.

Spartak had a choice. Shoot, or dive for cover. He went for the first option, unloading four wild rounds at Bald. Two of the bullets spiderwebbed the glass frame next to the patio door. The others struck the jukebox immediately to Bald's left.

Bald stayed perfectly still as he emptied another burst. The shots struck Spartak in the head with surgical precision. The guy plummeted like Bear Stearns stock. He was dead before he even hit the pool deck.

The rifle report was still echoing through the house as Porter heard more voices outside. One of them did most of the talking. Several other voices came back with single-syllable responses. An order being given, acknowledged by the subordinates. Then the heavy thudding of footsteps to the west of the house. More attackers were sweeping around to the back garden, Porter realised. Following the same route Ducati and Spartak had taken. They'd be sweeping into view any moment.

'More X-rays moving towards your position!' he shouted at Bald.

'Fuck's sake!' Bald hissed. 'How many of these bastards are there?'

I don't know, Porter thought. *But they're committing a lot of firepower over a fucking sex tape.*

He heard a crash at his twelve o'clock and swung back to the foyer as another attacker swept through the front door.

The metal clicker inside Porter's head told him that he had expended six rounds on Testicle and Tracksuit. Which left him with fourteen rounds in the AR-15 clip, plus the forty in the two spare box mags.

He trained his attention on the X-ray bursting into the foyer. The guy was built like a powerlifter, clad in a digi-cam top and combats, with a tactical grenade belt strapped around his sizeable waist. Half a dozen hand grenades were held in place by elastic loops, secured with Velcro flaps over the top.

Powerlifter blasted from the hip as he swept inside the foyer, pissing bullets across the hallway, blasting chunks out of the wall as he stepped around the lake of blood spreading across the floor. He was panicking at the sight of his dead mates, firing more out of hope than anything else.

Porter blocked out his hangover. He shut out the voice in his head and focused solely on lining up Powerlifter's torso. Gave the guy a three-round burst to the stomach, stitching his gut with bullets. Powerlifter made a tangled cry in his throat before he collapsed to the floor in a ragged heap.

Eleven rounds left.

At his six o'clock he heard Bald discharging rounds at the attackers sweeping across the ground to the rear. The two operators were working in tandem, like a well-oiled machine. They'd never lived in each other's pockets but they both knew they could rely on one another in the heat and chaos of a firefight.

Porter knew what the Russians were trying to do. Push them both back inside the house, so that they could establish a foothold at the front and rear entry points. Once they'd breached the stronghold, they could gradually advance until Porter and Bald had nowhere left to run.

If that happens, we'll be fucked.

And Street will be taken.

'Fuckers throwing the kitchen sink at us!' Bald yelled during a brief lull in the gunfire. 'Three more coming this way.'

Five dead so far, Porter thought. With perhaps as many as fifteen more targets converging on their position. But there had been only five Russians in total on the snatch squad that had targeted Street, according to their briefing. 'Where the fuck did the rest of them come from?'

'Bastards must have sent for reinforcements,' Bald shouted back.

Which made sense, Porter thought. The Russian mafia had a presence in every major city on the east coast. The snatch squad could have sent for backup from as far south as Charlotte, or Columbus or Cincinnati to the west. To the east there was Baltimore and New Jersey. Anywhere within a four-hundred-mile radius.

'Keep them pinned down,' Porter called out. 'Don't let the fuckers get inside.'

'Doing my best here, mate.'

Just then Porter heard a flurry of noise from across the hallway. The sound of fracturing glass, coming from one of the rooms on the left side of the foyer. He looked across at his nine o'clock, at the ground-floor study on the other side of the foyer.

The door was ajar.

Through the gap he spied two figures breaking through the window above the computer desk, on the wall backing onto the east side of the safe house. Two guys in matching grey trousers and dark t-shirts, both wielding Benelli tactical twelve-gauge shotguns.

The first attacker jumped down from the shattered window. He had a thick, squat frame, a shaven head and a handlebar moustache. Broken glass crackled like ice beneath his Timberland boots. The second guy was clambering through the opening after his mate, swinging up his left knee onto the window frame. The less athletic of the two. The first guy had stopped and turned to help his mate climb through.

Porter sprang into action. He rushed over to Powerlifter's corpse, almost slipped on the puddled blood and snatched one of the hand grenades from the elastic loop. Then he raced over to the study and dropped to a knee beside the door. He set down his Colt AR-15, pulled the firing pin and tossed the grenade inside the study.

Someone screamed in panic.

The grenade detonated.

The scream was drowned out by the tremendous crashing boom of the explosion. Porter felt the shudder in his bones as the shockwave ripped through the hallway like rolling thunder. There were anguished cries inside the room as smoke gushed through the opening, spewing out debris and bits of broken glass.

In the next instant Porter grabbed his rifle and swung round into the doorway. The blast would have killed anyone in a five-metre radius but he didn't want to take any chances.

The room was hot with smoke and debris. The air stank of burnt flesh, incinerated fabric. Chunks had been ripped out of the ceiling. The walls were lacquered with blood. Handlebar lay on the ground in the middle of the room, his guts hanging out of a wide gash in his stomach in a glistening red coil. The other guy was slumped below the window. Both his legs had been blown off below the knee. His hands and face were pitted with shrapnel.

Through the clearing smoke Porter glimpsed a third guy attempting to climb through the window. Porter fired a two-round burst, hitting him in the chest. The guy buckled and lost his grip on the window, blood arcing out of his upturned mouth as he fell away.

Two more rounds used.

Nine left.

From the other side of the foyer came the sound of breaking glass. A cold sick dread twisted through Porter's guts as he realised that the attackers were swarming through more entry points across the house. What the Americans called a full-court press. He burst into movement, the blood rushing in his ears as he made for the study door.

Porter estimated that the firefight had lasted sixty seconds so far. The Russians wouldn't want to stick around for more than five minutes. Any longer carried the risk of running into the police. They were a mile from the nearest house but there was always a chance of a passer-by hearing the gunshots. And the sound of a rifle discharge travelled further on a clear night than during the daytime, when there was less ambient sound to cancel it out.

We've got another four minutes to hold out against the enemy, he thought.

It's going to be tough to last that long.

He bulleted through the door, his shirt heavy with sweat. Porter glanced over at his three o'clock at the kitchen, ten metres south of his position. Bald was crouching beside the jukebox, loading the second clip into his rifle mag feed as three more targets swarmed across the garden towards the patio doors. Spent brass littered the floor around him.

Porter swivelled his gaze across to the foyer.

A guy stood outside the dining room, a metre to the right of the front door. Twelve metres from where Porter stood. He wore ball-hugging jeans with a leather jacket over a white tank top and a huge gold crucifix around his fat neck.

Porter glimpsed the broken window frame in the room behind Crucifix. Two more attackers were pouring through the breach, desperate to press home their advantage. But Porter wasn't focusing on those guys.

His eyes were locked on Crucifix. On the HK416 in his grip.

Aimed directly at Porter.

THIRTY

Porter waited to die.

He had no time to react. It would take him a whole second to raise his weapon and empty a shot at Crucifix. By which time the guy would have cut him in half with a burst from the rifle. He was out of options, and time.

Then a crack exploded at the far end of the hallway. From the direction of the kitchen. A bullet slapped into the wall three inches to the right of Crucifix, spitting out masonry.

Crucifix arced his HK416 away from Porter and turned towards the new threat at the other end of the hall. It took him an age to turn. All that fat and muscle, slowing him down. In the same instant Bald surged into view at Porter's right, sweeping forward from the kitchen as he emptied three more rounds at Crucifix.

The bullets thumped into Crucifix, punching holes in his chest and jaw. The lower half of his face disintegrated in a claret mist, fragments of shattered teeth and jawbone splashing down his leather jacket as he dropped to the floor. He wouldn't be needing a filling any time soon.

Bald looked briefly in Porter's direction. Porter nodded at his mucker. There was no time to thank him as more shouts came from inside the living room, directly opposite the dining room. A guy in a Boston Red Sox baseball cap swept around the doorway, glass shards sprinkled across his shoulders from where he'd obviously crashed through the window. Red Sox let out a throated cry as Bald gave him a two-round burst to the chest. He did the dead man's dance and flopped to the floor amid the tangle of limbs and brass.

'Cover my six,' Bald boomed at Porter, his voice barely audible above the shouts from the other attackers storming the safe house. 'I'll keep these cunts busy.'

There was no time to reply. Porter gave him a brief nod of acknowledgement and charged towards the kitchen, eight metres to the south of the staircase. Ninety seconds had passed since the Russians had opened fire, he figured.

Another three-and-a-half minutes to hold out.

He looked ahead and saw that the three guys who had been tearing across the garden had almost reached the pool deck. Two of them were in the lead, athletic guys decked out in puffer jackets and Adidas tracksuit bottoms. They were twenty-five metres away.

Porter ran on towards the kitchen with renewed determination. He dropped to a knee next to the jukebox, in the same spot where Bald had set himself up. His hangover had gone now, fear and adrenaline taking hold, smothering the voice in his head.

I'm not going to lose to these pricks.

Not today.

Porter levelled the Colt sights with the nearest of the Puffer Brothers. Put down a three-round burst as they swept around the swimming pool. The rounds didn't hit the targets, but Porter didn't need them to. Not at this range. He just needed to put the brakes on the enemy's advance. Puffer One and Two dived behind the shed to the right of the swimming pool, narrowly avoiding the stream of incoming rounds.

The third guy continued running towards the patio. A lanky bloke, with a goatee and skin the colour of milk. Porter arced his sights over to the guy.

Then he spied the gun Goatee was holding.

It was the same type of HK416 that Crucifix and the others had been using. But with one major difference.

Instead of the usual box mag, a pair of cylinder mags had been inserted into the feed assembly on the underside of the receiver. The drums had a hundred-round capacity, Porter knew. In the Regiment, the guys called them street sweepers. Because when the selector was set to full auto, the rate of fire could clear a room all by itself.

At a range of twenty metres, the street sweeper was lethal.

Goatee fired. Porter shrank behind the jukebox as the street sweeper raked the kitchen with several booming staccato bursts. Round after round of hot lead chugged out of the modded rifle, decimating the tiled walls and taking chunks out of the breakfast bar, punching fist-sized holes in the cabinets, shattering the plates and glasses inside. Three rounds struck the jukebox above the coin chute. The plastic tubes glowed into life, in a rainbow of bright colours, as Starship's 'Nothing's Gonna Stop Us Now' filled the air.

Porter waited for a lull in the fire. Past the jukebox, he glimpsed Puffer One and Two scrambling towards the patio door. They had used the covering fire of the street sweeper to push forward. Now they were eight metres from the entry point, loosing off rounds as they moved. Bullets glanced off the floor a metre to the right of the jukebox, chewing up the tiles. Goatee was six metres behind the Puffer Brothers, inserting a new cylinder mag into the street sweeper.

I can't stay here, Porter thought to himself. I don't stand a chance against that fucking thing.

Get moving.

Now.

Mickey Thomas and Grace Slick were singing about building dreams together as Porter stepped out from behind cover and fired a two-round burst at the Puffer Brothers, forcing them to hit the deck. Porter turned and sprinted back down the hallway towards Bald as Goatee let rip with the street sweeper once again. Bullets riddled the jukebox, reducing the song to a jittery warble.

Porter regrouped alongside Bald in the hallway. Bald was still concentrating his efforts on the front of the safe house, putting down suppressive fire on the doorways either side of the foyer. Porter dropped down beside him and trained his sights at the kitchen. The two of them were fighting back-to-back now, making their stand at the foot of the stairs.

Thirteen metres to the south of the staircase, Puffer One and Two were storming through the patio door, into the kitchen. Goatee had almost reached the sliding door too.

Porter gave them a burst from the AR-15, putting the brakes on their advance. The rounds smashed like fists into the tiled wall to the right of the door and sent Puffer One and Two diving for cover behind the bullet-riddled jukebox. Goatee scrambled to the side of the patio, out of sight.

Two minutes since the firefight started.

Three more to survive.

The clicker in his head told Porter that he had two bullets left in the magazine. Plus the two spare twenty-round clips. Which gave him forty-two rounds, total.

We won't be able to keep these fuckers nailed down for much longer.

Bald emptied another burst at the front of the safe house. 'More X-rays coming through the living room window. Bastards are getting closer.'

'Shit!' Porter hissed.

They were in serious danger of being overrun now. The Russians wouldn't spare them once they'd cleared the safe house. That wasn't their MO. They would slot everyone apart from Street.

There's nothing for it but to stand our ground.

And hope the cops show up before we run out of ammo.

In the next instant Goatee stepped out from behind cover, ready to spray the hallway with 5.56mm brass. Porter aimed a two-round burst in the guy's direction, nailing him in the ankle. Goatee crumpled to the ground in the kitchen doorway, screaming. Porter went to finish him off and got the dead man's click as he reached the end of the clip. He thumbed the mag release and fished out one of the spare mags from his trouser pocket.

Inserted it into the mag feed.

Looked up.

One of the Puffer Brothers briefly edged into view from behind the damaged jukebox. The guy had something in his right hand, Porter noticed.

Grenade.

His breath trapped in his throat as he watched the guy roll the hand grenade down the hallway before shrinking back behind the cover of the jukebox.

Porter unfroze.

'GRENADE!' he roared at Bald as he shot to his feet, spinning away from the kitchen. 'FUCKING MOVE!'

Bald was on his feet before Porter had even finished shouting at him. Porter instantly saw why. One of the attackers at the front of the house had also chucked a grenade down the hallway. A simultaneous attack, coordinated to ensure maximum damage. The grenade rumbled towards Bald and bumped against the basement door, where it stopped dead.

The grenades were F1 types. Soviet-issue. Four-second fuse. Effective blast radius of thirty metres.

Four seconds to get to cover. Bald and Porter were at the bottom of the staircase, at the mid-point of the main hallway. There was no cover in sight around them. Nothing that would shield them from the grenade blast. The nearest room was the master bedroom, six metres away.

Too far.

For the first time that morning, Porter was thinking with a clear mind. He instantly gauged the situation and knew what they had to do. 'Upstairs!' he yelled.

Bald, grasped his intention. He turned and vaulted up the stairs to the first-floor landing. Porter ran after him, clearing the treads two at a time. On three seconds, Bald hit the first-floor landing. He careened to the right, diving towards the nearest guest bedroom.

Porter was two steps from the landing when the grenades detonated.

A blast of incinerating air surged up behind him, roaring inside his eardrums, scorching the skin on his back as the explosion ripped through the hallway. He heard the thwack of shrapnel studding the walls, the blasting of glass. Tendrils of smoke swept upwards, showering the stairs with debris and nicking the flesh on Porter's hands and face.

He was stunned for half a second. Then the lizard part of his brain took over. He shook his head clear and crawled over to Bald in front of the guest-room door, six metres further down the landing. Ears ringing, lungs burning. Fumes stinging his eyes.

'That was fucking close,' Porter said, gasping for air as he took up a firing position opposite Bald.

'It's not over yet, mate.'

Both operators kept their AR-15s pointed at the top of the

stairs. Their index fingers resting on the rifle triggers, ready to brass up anyone who charged up to the first floor.

This is it, thought Porter as he waited for the first X-ray to pop into view. No way out. We're cornered on the first floor of the safe house, with at least half a dozen shooters downstairs armed to the teeth. It'll take a miracle to survive this.

All we can do now is take down as many of these fuckers as possible.

Six seconds passed.

Then seven.

Then eight.

No one charged up the stairs.

'Where are they?' he wondered.

'Maybe they've fucked off,' Bald said.

'Why would they do that?'

Bald shrugged.

Porter pricked his ears, listening for any noise coming from the ground floor. He couldn't hear a thing. There was only the urgent bleating of a smoke alarm, the dull constant ringing in his ears. On the jukebox, 'Africa' by Toto was blaring out.

After fifteen seconds he signalled to Bald. 'I'm going to check it out. Watch my back.'

'Roger that.'

Bald kept his rifle focused on the uppermost tread as Porter edged forwards. He stopped by the side of the banister at the top of the stairs, then inched around to the right. Peering down the Colt's front and rear sighting posts as he scanned the stairs below.

Empty.

Where the fuck did the Russians go? Porter asked himself again. If I was in their boots, I would have been rushing up the stairs as soon as those bangs went off. Toss up a few more grenades, then finish off the job with a couple of long bursts from the street sweeper. I definitely wouldn't have given my enemies a chance to regroup.

So where are they?

He motioned for Bald, indicating that the area was clear. Bald slowly crept towards the stairs as Porter moved down the treads, listening for the slightest movement coming from the ground floor.

Still he heard nothing. Just the background noise of eighties soft rock and the beeping of the smoke alarm.

As he rounded the corner at the mid-point of the stairs, Porter heard an abrupt noise. The familiar clunk of a car door shutting, followed by the stammering sputter of a car engine cranking into life, the mechanical growl of motors picking up speed. The chorus to 'Africa' kicked in as Porter turned at the corner and moved down the stairs, quickening his pace. He hit the bottom and hurried down the hallway.

Dead bodies littered the floor. There was a blackened patch in the middle of the hallway where the grenades had detonated. Shrapnel studded the walls. The floor was strewn with spent jackets and blood splatter and broken glass. A couple of the dead Russians had the same tattoos on their necks as the guys on the snatch squad, Porter noticed. The skull resting on top of the oak tree branch, smoking a chubby cigar.

He looked towards the front door, twelve metres away. The door was wide open, giving him an unobstructed view of the driveway and the adjacent garage. Stillman's Hilux was there, along with the rental Cruze.

No sign of any other cars.

Bald bulled down the stairs after Porter, eyes sweeping the foyer. He drew up alongside his mucker, caught sight of the front drive and stopped dead in his tracks.

'Shit,' he said as he lowered his weapon. 'The motors.'

'Bastards must have legged it,' Porter said.

As he looked on a cold chill clamped around his neck. There was only one explanation for the enemy's sudden departure. He spun away from the foyer and hurried back down the hallway, his chest swirling with unease.

Porter knew what he would find inside the master bedroom. He'd known in his guts as soon as the enemy had gone silent. Their hasty retreat from the safe house had merely confirmed his suspicions.

He barged through the bedroom door ahead of Bald, his heart pounding. Cooper stood just outside the strong room, his arms raised above his head, surrendering to an enemy that had already disappeared. Porter gave him the briefest of glances before he swung around the bed, beating a path over to the strong room.

The strong-room door was open.

He took a step into the room. Stopped.

No. Bald caught up with him, breathing hard. He looked inside the strong room.

'Fuck,' he said.

Street wasn't there.

THIRTY-ONE

Porter stared at the empty space for a long, cold beat. The thumping in his head came back with a vengeance. A jarring pain, pulsating behind his eye sockets.

The Russians. They've taken Street.

He spun away from the strong room and looked towards Cooper. The agent looked momentarily surprised to see Bald and Porter. Then he lowered his hands to his sides as he peered out into the hallway.

'Are they gone?' he asked.

Bald nodded. 'They just fucked off. What happened?'

'Two of them burst in. They grabbed Charles and took him away. There was nothing I could do.'

'What about the dossier?'

'They took that too.'

'Shit.'

Porter looked again at the empty strong room, gritting his teeth in bitter frustration. He understood now why the Russians hadn't bothered wiping them out when they had been trapped upstairs.

Because they didn't need to slot us. We weren't the target. They just needed me and Jock out of the way for long enough to grab Street. Now the bastards have taken him.

We've failed.

He turned back to Cooper. 'Why didn't they slot you?'

'I hid under the bed. After I heard the grenades go off. I knew the Russians would reach the bedroom and find us. I tried to tell Charles to hide but he refused to move.'

Bald said, 'Didn't they look for you?'

Cooper shook his head. 'They sounded as if they were in a hurry. They just grabbed Charles and left.'

224

Porter said, 'Must have bugged out as soon as they heard us two coming downstairs.'

A puzzled expression played out on Bald's face, 'How did the Russians find us? No fuckers were supposed to know about this place.'

Porter said nothing. A troubling thought needled him as he stared at Cooper. One that had been forming in the back of his mind ever since they arrived at the safe house. First the snatch attempt in DC. Now the attack on the safe house. Two incidents that only a handful of people knew about.

And somehow the Russian mafia had known where to find Street on both occasions.

'Someone sold us out,' he said. 'Someone told the Russians.'

'You think there's a leak inside Six?'

'Not over there. It had to be someone inside the house. The same person who disabled that front alarm. They knew the Russians were coming and wanted to stop us from being warned.'

His gaze stayed focused on Cooper. The agent read the accusing look on Porter's face and laughed nervously. 'Don't be ridiculous. You actually think I had something to do with this?'

'There's only five people in this house who could have disabled that sensor,' said Porter. 'One of them is dead. The other was just taken. That leaves me, Jock and you.'

Cooper bristled with indignation. 'Have you lost your mind? I've been trying my hardest to protect Charles, for Christ's sake. Not hand him over to the mafia.'

'Yeah, and you've been doing a crap job of it. Every time he asks for your help, he ends up getting attacked.'

Cooper shot him an icy glare. 'You forget who you're talking to. I'm the senior intelligence officer for our North American operations. One word from me and you'll go back into the hole you crawled out of.'

'I don't give a toss. Someone set us up, and you're the only one who could have done it.'

'What about him?' Cooper jabbed a finger at Bald. 'He's worked in Russia. He's got contacts over there, I imagine. He could just as easily have been the one who told them where to find us.'

'Jock wouldn't do that. He can be a mean bastard, but he wouldn't stab us in the back.'

Cooper glowered at Porter. 'Have you lost your fucking mind, man? We should be getting out of here before the police show up, not throwing around baseless accusations.'

'We're not going anywhere until you level with us.'

'I've heard enough. Out of my way.'

Cooper shaped to barge his way past, lashing out at Porter with his elbows. Something inside Porter snapped. He shoved Cooper back, engaging his core and leg muscles, throwing all his weight into the move. The force of the blow sent Cooper stumbling backwards, arms flailing as he went off-balance. He gave out a grunt as he fell back, crashing against the bedside table, knocking off the lamp and a framed picture of Stillman's dead wife.

'You idiot!' Cooper hissed. 'You'll pay for that. Insubordination. Your career is finished. I'll make fucking sure of it.'

But Porter wasn't listening.

He stared at the object lying on the carpet next to Cooper. It had tumbled out of the guy's trouser pocket when he'd fallen backwards.

A mobile phone. Similar to the two burners that Porter and Bald had been issued back in London. Some cheap knock-off brand with a rudimentary touchscreen.

Bald had noticed it too.

It wasn't Cooper's regular phone. Porter distinctly recalled Cooper using an iPhone several times in DC, and on the drive to West Virginia. This one was different.

Cooper looked over to his side. When he saw what had seized Bald and Porter's attention, his face went white. He reached for the phone but Porter reacted faster, snatching it up. The handset was turned on, running some older version of Android. A plain digital clock face glowed brightly on the display.

Porter lowered his gaze to Cooper. The agent was slumped on the floor, back pressed up against the wall, lips pressed tight. Eyes darting between the two operators. 'What the fuck are you doing with a burner?' said Porter.

'Nothing,' Cooper replied defensively. 'It's just a backup, that's all. In case my main phone runs out of battery.'

'Bollocks. None of us were supposed to have our phones switched on at the safe house. You didn't say nothing about a backup phone.'

Cooper said nothing. Porter could see his eyes shifting left and right, as if looking for a way out.

No chance.

He grabbed the agent by the lapel of his jacket and hauled him to his feet.

'I've had enough of your shit. You've been playing us from the word go. Now tell us what's going on.'

'I don't know what you're talking about.' 'Bullshit! Who were you reaching out to on that phone?'

'No one, I swear!'

'We need to leave, mate,' Bald cut in. The cops will be showing up soon.'

Porter kept on eyeballing Cooper but the stopwatch in his head told him that six or seven minutes had passed since the Russians had attacked. Although they were out in the sticks, someone was bound to have heard the barrage of rifle reports and explosions. A distant neighbour, or a person out walking their dog. Police response times in rural districts were slower than in major towns and cities, but not much.

We've got about ten minutes until the first patrol car rocks up, Porter guessed. *Perhaps less.*

'We've got to go,' Bald continued. 'Now.'

'Listen to your friend,' Cooper said, his voice cracking with fear. 'We can't stay here, man!'

Porter scrolled through their options in his mind. They would have to get rid of anything inside the house that connected Stillman to MI6 before they left. Hard drives, computers, documents, encryption kit. There simply wasn't enough time to rough Cooper up now. They'd have to wait until they were well clear of the safe house.

He released his grip on Cooper and jerked his head at Bald.

'Take him out to the car. We'll question him once we're on the road. I'll get this place cleaned up.'

'Roger that.'

Porter swung his gaze back to Cooper. 'We're not done with

you. Make a fucking move, try to leg it, and I'll put one right between your eyes. Don't test us.'

Cooper looked terrified. His lips parted but no sound came out of his mouth. Bald manhandled him out of the bedroom and dragged him outside to the Cruze while Porter sprinted over to the basement door.

He retrieved the voice-encryption box from the basement office, along with the stack of portable hard drives Stillman used to store the footage from the security cameras. Anything that might reveal the housekeeper's links to Six had to go. Porter stashed the hard drives in a gym bag he found next to the exercise equipment and lugged the kit upstairs.

He ignored the bodies sprawled across the floor. There was no time to clean up the scene properly. They just had to hope that they made it across the border, four hundred miles to the north, before the cops figured out what had happened. It would take them a while, Porter reasoned. Once they discovered that the house belonged to a British ex-copper, the police would focus their attention on Stillman. They would naturally wonder why he had a load of dead Russians on his property. Crime-scene investigators would canvas the scene. Bullet casings would be painstakingly marked and photographed and bagged. Forensics taken.

Porter rushed back into the master bedroom and made a quick scan of the gun safe to see if Stillman had left any incriminating documents inside. He found two white envelopes in the pouches below the handguns, each containing five thousand dollars in clean bills. He snagged the cash, took one of the FN Five-Seven pistols and a single twenty-round clip of 5.7x28mm brass in case they ran into any trouble en route to the border. A handgun was easier to conceal than one of the Colt rifles. And easier to dispose of.

He left the rest of the weapons in the gun safe. They were untraceable, Stillman had said when he'd given them the grand tour. Bought at gun shows, without records of sale or background checks. Nothing illegal. Nothing to make the cops suspicious.

Porter wiped down the two Colt longs they had used and left them in the safe with the other weapons. He grabbed the envelopes stuffed with cash, the Five-Seven and the gym bag, and jogged across the hallway to the front door.

Bodies littered the foyer. Five of them either side of the entrance. Plus the three guys Porter had taken out in the study, and the three Bald had slotted in the garden. Eleven dead, in total.

A bloodbath.

Something doesn't make sense here, thought Porter.

A disturbing thought calcified inside his head.

If what Cooper had told them was true, the Russian mob had been willing to commit serious resources to the op in order to retrieve a dossier that briefly mentioned a sex tape.

Maybe I'm wrong, Porter told himself.

But it seems like overkill.

Bald was waiting for him by the Cruze. Cooper was in the back seat. Porter dumped the encryption box in the boot, along with the gym bag filled with hard drives. He held on to the Five-Seven and kept the ghost phone in his side pocket. They'd need to reach out to Moorcroft once they'd had put some serious mileage between themselves and the safe house.

'That's everything?' asked Bald.

'That's the lot. The place is clean.'

Bald slammed the boot shut. 'What now?'

'We'll get clear of this place and rough up this twat,' Porter said, cocking his head at Cooper in the rear passenger seat. 'Find out what he knows.'

'What about the escape plan?' 'We still need to get out of the country. Can't be hanging around here, mate.'

'The plan stands. We'll head to the border, as soon as we're done questioning Cooper.'

'We should call Six. Tell them what the fuck is going on.'

'Not until we get some answers out of that cunt first.'

Porter gestured at the contents of the boot.

'We'll have to stop somewhere along the way too. Get rid of this shit.'

Get yourself cleaned up too. You look fucking homeless.'

Porter glanced down at his hands. They were blackened with a greasy film of lead particles. His new shirt was smeared with sweat patches and dirt. There were grazes on his hands and face from the grenade blast. His clothes reeked of cordite.

'Thanks, mucker,' he said, looking up at Bald.

'What for?'

'Saving my arse back there. That bastard with the crucifix would have put a hole in my nut if it wasn't for you.'

'Thank me later. We've still got to get out of the country first.'

Porter half-smiled. Jock might be a hard bastard with a savage tongue on him, he thought, but he's also a top operator. He gets the job done. You can count on him when you're in the shit.

If it hadn't been for him, we would never have survived that assault.

'Reckon we'll make it across?' he asked. 'Unless the local cops are geniuses, it'll take them a while to piece together what happened here. Longer than it'll take us to reach the checkpoint, anyway. As long as there's nothing in that house to connect that housekeeper to Six, we're in the clear.'

'I hope you're right.'

Bald studied his mucker carefully, as if trying to read his mind. 'You think Cooper's working for that lot? The Russians?'

'I don't know,' Porter said back. 'But we're gonna find out, one way or another.'

THIRTY-TWO

Porter dived into the back seat next to Cooper. Bald took the wheel. He knew the roads around the safe house, having made the journey to Dulles airport and back with Stillman earlier that morning. They pulled out of the driveway, tyres chirping as they turned on to the private road. Bald floored the gas, taking them away from Monroe, sticking to the directions Stillman had laid out for them on Google Maps. Five minutes before a Russian mobster had put a hole in his head.

The quickest route to Buffalo was north through West Virginia and Pennsylvania, Stillman had explained, avoiding the rush-hour traffic around DC and the suburbs. Once they reached Pennsylvania the interstate would ferry them north through the Alleghenies, all the way to Buffalo and the border crossing at the Peace Bridge. Total estimated journey time of around eight hours.

Cooper protested his innocence as they motored north on a dilapidated county road. Porter threatened to kill the guy unless he shut up and for the next three miles Cooper sat with his hands in his lap, a despondent look plastered across his mug.

The road ploughed through the Virginia plains, taking them past low rolling hills, sprawling vineyards and cattle ranches. The sun was fully up now, a white-hot orb suspended in the clear sky. When they were five miles clear of the house, Porter turned to Cooper and pressed the Five-Seven against his ribs.

'Start fucking talking,' he said.

'I told you already. I don't know anything, I swear.'

Porter simmered with rage. He shoved the Five-Seven harder against Cooper's ribcage. The agent winced, squirming in his seat as the hammer-forged tip dug into his flesh.

'Tell me,' Porter growled. 'Or I'll put one through your chest. Your choice.'

He didn't want to let off a round in the car. The Five-Seven had a louder report and brighter muzzle flash than a standard nine-milli pistol. If he fired a bullet inside the Cruze, the handful of other motorists on the road would see and hear it. But Cooper didn't know that.

'Please,' Cooper said. 'Please, don't do this.'

Porter's index finger tightened a quarter of an inch around the Five-Seven trigger. 'Last chance. Tell us what the fuck is going on, or you can join your Russian mates.'

'I had no choice!' Cooper blurted. 'They were going to kill my family unless I agreed to help them!'

Porter kept the Five-Seven digging into Cooper's side. 'Who?'

'The Russians.'

'You led them to the safe house?'

Cooper nodded. 'My contact gave me a burner. I had orders to call them as soon as we'd located Charles.'

Bald scowled at him in the rear-view mirror. 'That's why you kept taking them cigarette breaks. You weren't gasping for a crafty fag. You were reaching out to your Russian mates.'

'I couldn't make the call in the car. Not with you two listening in. I knew that no one else in the house was a smoker. It was the only way I could get a few minutes alone.'

Porter now understood why Cooper had been on edge for most of the night. Constantly checking the time, pacing up and down. At the time, he'd simply assumed the MI6 man was eager to get on the road. But that hadn't been the case at all.

The bastard was just waiting for the Russians to show up.

He understood something else too. 'That bullshit about the comms unit acting up. That was just so you could get Stillman out of sight and disable the alarm.'

Cooper lowered his gaze to his feet. 'Yes.'

'Who's your contact?'

'An agent, over at the Russian embassy. We knew each other from my time working in Moscow.'

Porter said, 'You're working for the Kremlin?'

'You don't understand,' Cooper said, his voice quivering with fear. 'You can't say no to these people. They were threatening to kill my wife and kids unless I cooperated.'

'I thought the Russian mob was behind the snatch squad,' Bald said. 'The ones with the tats.'

Cooper shook his head. 'They're working for the Kremlin. They outsourced the job to one of the crime bosses. A man named Artem Zhirkov.'

Porter listened in silence. He'd heard the stories about the Russian security services hiring mafia bosses to do their dirty work. Overseas assassinations, cyber-hacking, selling arms to Russia's friends abroad. In return, the mobsters were free to carry out their criminal activities unchecked.

He said, 'If Zhirkov's working for the Kremlin, who has the sex tape?'

'The FSB. They've been waiting for the right moment to use the tape against the new president.'

'So the Russian mafia aren't the ones behind the blackmail plot?'

'No.'

'You fucking lied to us,' Bald said. 'Back at the safe house.'

'I just told you what was in the dossier,' Cooper protested. 'Which is mostly true. There' is a sex tape of the president, and the Russians are planning to use it against him.'

'Where are Zhirkov's mob taking Street now?' Porter demanded.

'I don't know.'

Cooper averted his gaze as he replied. It was obvious to Porter that he was lying through his teeth. He shoved the barrel into the side of Cooper's cheek and curled his finger tighter around the trigger.

'Tell me, or I'll end your shit excuse of a life.'

The agent's eyes widened with fear. Drops of sweat trickled down his cheeks, staining the Five-Seven barrel. Porter kept the gun in place as Bald held the Cruze to a steady forty miles per hour on the single-lane road. Porter glanced up, checking that both sides of the road were clear of traffic. Rush-hour in rural Virginia.

'Where are they taking Street?' he snapped. 'Tell me!'

'All I was told was that they were smuggling Charles out of the country. To a mansion outside Moscow, owned by Zhirkov.'

'Why take him there?'

'Zhirkov has got a secret torture chamber there. They're going to interrogate Charles.'

'What the fuck for?'

'The Russians want the sex tape to remain a secret. They need to know how many copies Charles made of his dossier. Where to find them. The passwords to his computers. Everything. They want to make sure that his report stays buried forever.'

From behind the wheel, Bald sucked the air between his teeth. 'Street won't hold out long against those henchmen.'

Porter pressed the Five-Seven harder against Cooper's cheek. 'Where is this mobster's place?'

'If I tell you now, you'll just kill me.'

'We'll slot you if you don't.'

Cooper said nothing.

'We don't need this cunt,' Bald said. 'We've got the mobster's name. Six can tell us where his gaff is.'

'They won't know where to find it,' Cooper replied. 'That hideout is a well-kept secret. There's nothing in the deeds, nothing to trace it back to Zhirkov. Only a handful of people know it even exists. I'm the only one who can lead you there.'

Bald met Porter's gaze in the rear-view. 'Bastard's lying. He'd say anything to save his own arse. We should pull over. Drop this wanker.'

Cooper said, 'You can't kill me. Do that, and you'll never get Charles back.'

'Maybe not. But we'd get a kick out of blowing your fucking brains out.'

Cooper was still trembling but Porter noted a defiant gleam in his eyes. *He's got us by the balls and he knows it.* 'How do we know you're telling the truth?' he asked.

'You don't. But it's your only option.'

Porter felt a shiver run through him as he remembered what Tannon had said at the briefing.

If our enemies capture Street, they'll have an ex-spy who knows all the secrets.

It'll be a national security disaster.

And we'll be in a world of shit.

234

'Even if what this twat says is true,' Bald argued, 'how are we going to rescue Street from the Russians? He'll be heavily guarded by the mobster's toughs.'

'I've been to Zhirkov's mansion before,' Cooper said. 'Several times, in fact. I know the layout. There are ways around his security ring.'

Bald shook his head furiously. 'We can't trust this twat. He betrayed us, mate. He got Stillman killed. Almost got the pair of us slotted too.'

Porter held the gun up for a moment. He was sorely tempted to put a round through the guy's skull. But he knew he couldn't do it. If he killed Cooper, they could forget about locating Street.

He relaxed his finger slightly on the trigger.

Lowered the gun.

'The fuck are you doing?' Bald said.

'He's right. Cooper. We need him alive.'

Cooper exhaled in relief. Porter turned to him in the back seat. Shot him a long, hard look.

'We'll get you across the border,' he said. 'Then you're gonna lead us to that mobster's pad. But if you try and escape, by the time we're done with you, you'll wish you were fucking dead.'

THIRTY-THREE

They drove on through wine country. Cooper went quiet, his gaze lowered to his feet, shoulders hunched. Porter rested the Five-Seven on his lap and took out the ghost phone. He drew up the list of recent calls from the menu and thumbed the trackball over the latest entry. Then he tapped the call icon and dialled Moorcroft's number.

The line took a few seconds to patch through. Longer than a regular call. Something to do with the encryption, he guessed. Moorcroft picked up on the fourth buzz.

'Well? Are you out of there?'

Porter said, 'The Russians hit us before we could leave. A bunch of those fuckers stormed the safe house. The housekeeper's dead.'

There was a sharp intake of breath on the other end of the line. Porter had never seen Moorcroft look flustered, but he imagined that was what he looked like right about now.

'What about Street?' he asked.

'They've taken him. They got away before we could stop them.'

Moorcroft muttered a curse. 'How the hell could you let this happen? I told you idiots to get out of there immediately.'

'There was no time. The Russians were all over us before we could get our shit together. Me and Jock held out for as long as we could, but the bastards kept coming.'

'What about Cooper?'

'He's here with us in the car.' Porter hesitated. 'He sold us out. He's the one who led the Russians to the safe house.'

'Cooper? Impossible. He's one of our most experienced agents.'

'We found a burner on him. Cooper used it to call his man over at the Russian embassy and direct the Russians to our location.'

'Are you sure?'

'He confessed after we roughed him up. Told us everything. Says he's been working for the Russians the whole time. He told them about the dossier Street had put together. Cooper set him up.'

'Terry's working for the Russian mafia?' Moorcroft sounded dubious.

'It wasn't my fault!' Cooper had turned towards Porter and was shouting at the ghost phone glued to his ear, arguing his case. 'I had to do what they told me!'

'Shut up!' Porter snapped at him. A swift gesture with the Five-Seven emphasised the point. Cooper got the message and abruptly clamped his mouth shut.

'He's not with the mob,' Porter said, refocusing on the conversation with Moorcroft. 'Cooper says he's working for the Russian security services. They co-opted one of the crime bosses into doing their dirty work. Some bloke called Artem Zhirkov.'

Moorcroft said nothing for several beats. Porter heard the drumming of fingers down the line. 'Do we know where Street is being taken now?'

'Zhirkov's got a hideout, in the middle of nowhere. Cooper reckons the henchmen are gonna take Street there and rough him up.'

'Why?'

'To find out where the other copies of the dossier are. The Kremlin want the sex tape to remain secret.'

Moorcroft was quiet for a moment. 'How do you know about the tape?'

'Cooper told us everything. The blackmail attempt, the hundred million dollars.'

'I see.' Moorcroft steepled his fingers again, as if tapping out a thought. 'What's the address for the mobster boss's place?'

'Cooper won't tell us. Not until we've got him out of the country and into Russia.'

'You should have consulted us first.'

'There was no time. We had to bug out of the safe house before the cops showed up. But if you've got a better idea for getting Street out of Russia, I'd love to hear it.'

Moorcroft's silence said everything. 'If you're going to smuggle Cooper across the border, you'll have to be careful not to alert our American friends.'

'Why?'

'Their agents are monitoring the embassy in DC. We think they've made the connection between Terry and Charles and are sniffing around, seeing what comes up. But if Cooper tries to get through on his passport, they'll pull him aside.'

'What about the Canadians?'

'They won't have access to that information. Not for a while.'

Porter clenched the ghost phone tight in his hand. This fucking op. *It doesn't get any easier.*

'Did you clean out the house, at least?' Moorcroft asked.

'We've got the electronics. Hard drives, the encryption kit. Plus the security camera footage. Stillman's laptop got shot to pieces when the Russians attacked.'

'None of that stuff is to survive. If the police somehow find out that Stillman was working for us, it could lead to some very awkward conversations.'

'We'll take care of it.'

'Good.' Moorcroft cleared his throat. 'What's your ETA?'

'We're on the road now. Should make the border in about eight hours.'

'I'll let Tannon know. She'll meet you on the other side.'

Porter sat upright. 'Dom's meeting with us?'

'She wanted to handle the debrief herself. Especially after she learned about the Russian involvement. She's in the air now but I'll update her on the situation once she's landed.'

Porter furrowed his brow. He'd worked for Six for long enough to know that someone as high up as Tannon didn't get involved in field duties. Not unless it was a big fucking deal. 'We're going to need some help once we're on the other side. We can't just hop on a plane to Russia.'

'Dom will take care of all that. She's carrying a burner. I'll send through her number after this call. Contact her as soon as you're safely across the border.'

Moorcroft clicked off the call. Porter put the ghost phone to sleep and stared out of the window.

Questions bit away at him. He thought again about the bodies in the safe house.

Eleven dead.

Something that didn't make sense.

He put away the phone and looked over at Cooper. The guy stared vacantly ahead, watching the road but not really watching it. A kind of calm had settled over his face. A defendant on the wrong end of a guilty verdict, waiting to be sentenced. 'Why are the Russians so desperate to stop this dossier from being made public?' Porter asked.

Cooper continued to stare ahead as he replied. 'I'd have thought that was obvious. Blackmail.'

'But this is the Kremlin we're talking about. They're not exactly short of a few quid.'

Cooper shook his head. 'The security services aren't interested in cash. They're playing a longer game. They believe they can use the sex tape to make the president do their bidding.'

'How so?'

'I don't know. I'm not privy to their plans. But I suspect they'll want to use it to advance Russia's interests. They could force the president to drop sanctions, for example. Or persuade him to withdraw from NATO, forcing the entire thing to collapse.'

'Over a skin tape?'

'Whoever has that tape can force the president to do their bidding. He'd do anything to avoid it coming to light. Which is why the Russians are so determined to stop Charles going public.'

Bald grunted. 'Sounds like a lot of fuss over a tape of some old bloke shagging a hooker.'

Cooper shot a withering look. 'You Hereford types wouldn't understand. They train you to kill the enemy. You don't see the bigger picture here.'

'At least we don't go around stabbing each other in the back.'

'You're referring to Charles, I presume.'

'Who the fuck else?'

'Charles put himself in danger long before I did.'

'How? By doing his job?'

'By threatening to go public with his findings.'

'You could have helped him. You didn't need to sell him out to your Russian chums.'

'If I'd said nothing and the dossier came to light, the Russians would have realised I'd withheld vital information from them. They would have executed me, as well as my family. I had no choice.'

'So you betrayed Street to the Kremlin instead?'

'What else could I have done? Gone to Six? They couldn't have protected Charles from the Russians. No one is safe from them. Even someone as thick as you must surely see that.'

'I can see that you're a backstabbing twat. That's clear as fuck.'

Porter said, 'How long have you been working for the Kremlin?'

'Long enough. Fifteen years.'

'What did they offer you? Money?'

Cooper hung his head low.

'I had gambling debts. Back when I was working at the embassy in Russia. Some of the people I owed money to, they made the average loan shark look respectable. They were making all kinds of threats. I didn't know where to go. Then one night this guy approaches me in one of the bars off Red Square. An FSB agent. Said he'd heard about my problems and wanted to offer me a way out. That's how they suck you in. They find a weak point, and exploit it.'

'Why didn't you go to your boss and ask for help?'

'I couldn't. Don't you see? If I'd gone to my superior and said I was in financial difficulty, that would have been the end of my career at MI6. Officers in the intelligence service can't have money problems. It would leave them open to blackmail.'

'Yeah, and you just fucking proved it,' Bald snapped from the front seat.

'I didn't see the harm,' Cooper said. 'It was just the occasional piece of intelligence. Nothing more than that. Later on, they started making more serious demands. Tampering with documents. Spreading misinformation. Tipping them off about British operations.'

Porter said, 'You sold out your mates, over a few quid you owed to some dodgy bookies?'

'It was more than a few quid. I'd racked up serious debts. We're

240

talking tens of thousands. My wife was threatening to leave, because of the drinking. I wasn't thinking right. If I could go back now, I would have done things differently. But I didn't.'

'Why did you keep working for them, after your debts were paid off?'

'I tried. But whenever I told them I'd had enough, they threatened to release video footage of me. They had me on tape, accepting a bag of money from a Russian associate. Twenty grand. It would have been the ruin of me.'

'All these years, no one suspected you?' Cooper wet his lips. 'I was careful. Covered my tracks. But two of our agents in Moscow had their suspicions. I had to get rid of them.'

Porter felt a spark of rage flaring inside him. 'Those agents who got killed in Russia. The ones your mate Street took the blame for all those years ago. That was you?'

'I didn't kill them. Just told my contact about the problem. They said they'd take care of it. I didn't know what they'd do.'

'Bullshit,' Bald said with a scowl. 'You signed their death warrants.'

'They had to be stopped. They were going to report their suspicions to my boss. I was getting my life back on track. I'd cut out the drinking. Anna was pregnant with our first child. They would have destroyed me.'

This bloke sounds just like my old Rupert, thought Porter. They don't care about the job, or doing the right thing. All they care about is covering their own arses.

'So instead of coming clean, you let a couple of agents get executed and sold Street up the river?'

His words seemed to hit a nerve. Cooper glanced up at him, a fire burning behind his eyes.

'Charles was the golden boy. He passed every test with flying colours, outperformed the rest of us. I respected him, but everything came easier to Charles. He came from a privileged background. Public school, Oxford, old money. Everything was handed to him on a plate. Me, I had to fight and scrap to get to where I am today. Charles was my friend, but there was part of me that resented him. I'm sorry for what happened, but in this world, you do what you can to survive.'

'Except you screwed him over twice. Once in Moscow, then again now.'

'I didn't mean for him to get hurt. After he showed up with that dossier, I thought the Russians would simply want a copy of it. When they ordered me to help trap Charles, I told them I wanted no part of it. He'd suffered enough.'

'But you went ahead with it anyway.'

'They sent pictures to me of Anna and the boys. The implication was clear. Either I helped them snatch Charles, or they'd make my family suffer. I didn't know what else to do.'

'You betrayed your country,' Porter said, anger burning in his guts. 'Your mates.'

'I'm not proud of what I did. But my family was at stake. My career. Everything I'd worked so hard to achieve. Anyone else would have done the same.'

'No. You're wrong. Most people wouldn't have sold out their mates in the first place.'

That's the difference between the Regiment and Vauxhall, Porter thought. The guys at Hereford don't always get along. But there's a bond that exists between operators that can never be broken.

I might not go out for a drink with Jock, but I'd never betray him to our enemies.

Cooper lowered his head again and fell silent. Porter closed his eyes, questions buzzing around inside his skull. He was knackered. More tired than he'd ever been in his life. He pushed it aside and looked up at the road ahead.

This isn't over yet, Porter reminded himself. We've still got to get out of the country.

Find this mobster's secret hideout. Rescue Street.

So much for a simple extraction op.

Six hours to go until they hit the border.

THIRTY-FOUR

They raced up the eastern panhandle of West Virginia and crossed into Maryland at the narrowest point of the state. Two miles, north to south. Ten minutes later they were driving through central Pennsylvania. Abandoned steel plants and paper mills jutted out like gravestones against the horizon. The effects of thirty years of automation, right there. Cooper stared out of the window, not saying a word. Bald had the radio tuned in to the news stations, checking for any reports on the bodies at the safe house. There were reports of a shooting, multiple dead bodies. But details were scant. No mention of the Russians.

Every so often Porter glanced at his watch. They had bugged out of the safe house at 0743 hours. Which meant they would reach the border crossing at around five o'clock that evening, including rest-stops. Which was ideal, from their point of view. There would be lots of traffic. Lots of commuters travelling back from work, eager to get home for the evening. Everyone in a hurry, the border guards under pressure to keep the line moving. They'd be less likely to stop and ask too many questions, Porter figured.

They stopped at a rest stop north of Altoona. Porter and Bald took it in turns to clean up in the restroom while the other kept watch over Cooper to make sure he didn't make a run for it. They stocked up on bottled water, energy drinks and snacks to keep themselves from flagging during the rest of the journey.

After another sixty miles, they turned off I-80 onto the state highway, following the road north through a desolate sprawl of woodland. Three miles further on, Bald pulled over into a lay-by at the side of the road, backing directly onto the wooded area. He kept the engine running while Porter climbed out and grabbed the hardware from the boot.

He took the encryption box, carried it over to the treeline and dumped it beside a narrow ditch. He returned to the boot, grabbed the stack of hard drives containing the footage from Stillman's security cameras and lugged them over to the same spot beyond the treeline. Porter threw the drives to the ground, then stomped on them repeatedly until they were smashed to bits. Then he tossed the broken drives and the box into the ditch, covering them over with leaves and loose soil.

The chances of anyone stumbling across the electronics were slim. Even if they did, the water and physical damage would have corrupted the data. Once he was finished, Porter released the clip from the Five-Seven, buried the gun in a neighbouring ditch and chucked the clip into a bin at the side of the road. Making the last leg of the journey unarmed was a risk, but he didn't want to waste valuable time driving around Buffalo looking for somewhere to dispose of the weapon.

Job done, he hurried back to the Cruze.

'What's the plan once we hit Buffalo?' Bald asked as he steered out of the lay-by and continued north.

Porter said, 'We'll drop the back seats when we're two miles out from the Yank checkpoint. Cooper can crawl through the gap into the boot. Once we're past that side, he'll climb back out before we hit the Canadian checkpoint, on the other side of the bridge.'

'We won't have much time to smuggle him back out. Stillman reckoned that bridge is less than half a mile long.'

'There's no choice. It's the only way of getting him through.'

Bald cocked his head at Cooper in the rear-view mirror. 'Why don't we just leave this cunt in the boot until we're past both checkpoints? Surely that's easier.'

'Too risky,' Porter replied. 'The Canadian guards might pull us over. Random vehicle search. If they found Cooper hiding in the boot, we'd be shafted. All we need to do is keep him out of sight from the Yanks.'

'Won't his name be on the Canadian database too?'

'Moorcroft doesn't think so. Says the FBI won't have shared that int with the Canadians yet.'

Bald gripped the wheel tightly. 'Moorcroft had better be fucking right about that,' he said. 'Otherwise we're never making it across that border.'

An hour later they crossed through the Alleghenies and hit New York State. Ninety minutes to the border. Seventy miles to go.

Almost there.

Porter's hangover began to clear somewhere north of the state line. The drilling pain in his skull settled down to a mild, dull throb. His bowels felt as if they'd been scraped out. He thought about how close he'd come to getting slotted back at the safe house. Tracksuit standing nine metres away, the muzzle staring him in the face. Only the Russian's piss-poor aim had saved his bacon.

You got away with it this time. But you won't get that lucky again.

At 1709 hours, they reached Buffalo. The place looked depressing. A bleak skyline of dated office blocks and crumbling civic buildings, a picture of industrial decline. Bald pulled over so that Porter could switch to the front passenger seat. One guy in the front of the Cruze and another in the back would look more unusual than a couple of blokes riding up front. They drove on towards the Peace Bridge, sticking to the route Stillman had laid out for them. The bridge was the main crossing point between Buffalo and Fort Erie, extending east to west across the Niagara River. The American checkpoint was located on the eastern approach, with the Canadian border on the western side of the river.

When they were two miles out from the US crossing, Bald signalled to Porter. 'It's time.'

Porter leaned over to the rear passenger seat and nodded at Cooper. 'Get that backrest lowered and get in the boot. Make a fucking sound and I'll kill you.'

Cooper twisted in his seat and operated the release button on the back seat, folding the backrest forward. He wriggled through the narrow opening into the Cruze boot. Once he was fully inside the space Porter reached over and flipped the backrest into the upright position so that it clicked into place, concealing Cooper from view.

'Ready, mucker,' he said to Bald.

They turned off the Niagara Thruway, taking the exit for the Peace Bridge and Fort Erie. Ahead of them was the US side of the border crossing. The first of two obstacles.

The road veered round to the right, past a cluster of lorries awaiting inspection in a parking bay. Teams of customs officers and sniffer dogs were diligently searching through the contents of each vehicle while the drivers looked on. A handful of armed agents patrolled the area on foot but none of them gave the Cruze a second glance. They seemed more concerned about what was coming into the country than anything going the other way.

The road straightened out, past a duty-free shop, and suddenly they were crossing the Peace Bridge.

One obstacle down, thought Porter.

One to go.

Bald jerked his head at the back seats as they joined the flow of traffic rolling west towards the Canadian checkpoint. 'Get him out of there. Hurry, mate.'

Porter reached around and flipped the release button on the back seat, tugging the backrest forward. Cooper struggled through the gap between the boot and the rear passenger seats, crawling out legs first. A glance over his shoulder told Porter that they were less than four hundred metres from the Canadian side now. They had twenty seconds to get Cooper out and close up the opening.

Porter grabbed Cooper by his shirt, yanking him through the opening. The guy tumbled out and rolled off the seat, tumbling into the rear passenger footwell and striking his head against the back of Bald's seat. He crawled forward, slammed the backrest into the upright position and buckled himself in with mere seconds to spare.

'Moment of truth,' Bald muttered. He eased off the gas as they headed towards the Canadian checkpoint.

Ahead of them was a sea of blacktop with lanes on either side of a central building, with a maple leaf flag fluttering from a brass pole out front. Signs in front of the sentry huts read: *Stop! Arret!* Bald nosed the Cruze into one of the lanes marked AUTO on the right side of the main building. 'Let's hope this works,' he said.

Porter turned to Cooper. 'Got your ID?'

'Driver's licence.' Cooper patted his breast pocket. 'In my wallet.'

'When the border guard asks for it, hand it over. Keep your mouth shut and leave the talking to us.'

'What if they start asking me questions?'

'Give them straight, simple answers. If they ask you what we're doing in Canada, we're three guys on a holiday trip who are going over to lay down a few quid at the casinos.'

Cooper nodded his understanding. They inched further along the queue. Porter counted four vehicles ahead of them. Three crossover SUVs, and a Toyota Camry. The Camry had stopped next to the sentry hut. The border guard stepped out of his hut, a plump guy wearing a pair of Ray-Bans and a baseball cap. He stood beside the Camry, speaking to the driver through the lowered window. His body language wasn't threatening, but it wasn't friendly either.

The Camry trundled off. The first of three SUVs rolled forward.

'What happens if they stop us?' Porter asked.

'We'll have to floor it. Smash through the barrier. No other option.'

'They'd shoot us before we could get away.'

'Stillman reckoned the guards are only packing nine-millis. We'd be gone before they could brass us up.'

'We'd still have to deal with the cops,' Porter said. 'Soon as we crash through that barrier, we'll have every fucker in the area after us.'

'Better than the alternative. I don't know about you, mate, but I'm not spending the rest of my life rotting in a Yank prison.'

They edged forward. Two SUVs remained before their turn at the sentry. Ray-Ban didn't spend long on each vehicle. It was a well-rehearsed performance. A quick glance at each passenger's ID document, seven or eight seconds spent cross-checking their names against the computer. Which was linked to the Canadian criminal database. Then the step out of the shack, the returning of the documents, a word or two to the onward travellers, and the wave at the next vehicle, motioning for them to approach.

The third SUV stopped in front of the hut.

'We're next in line,' Bald said.

Porter thought, Either we make it through to Canada, or we're going to be in the papers tomorrow.

Bald dug out his passport from the go-bag containing their personal items in the front seat. He handed the other passport to Porter. Cooper flipped open his wallet and plucked out his driver's licence.

The driver of the SUV ahead of them fanned his ID at Ray-Ban. The guard casually inspected the document, stepped into his hut. Popped back out again, handed the licence over to the driver. Nodded at the guy. The SUV moved off towards the toll booths, a hundred and fifty metres due west of the checkpoint. Then Ray-Ban turned towards the Cruze and waved them over.

'We're up,' Bald said.

He lightly tapped the gas, rolled forward a dozen or so metres and then stopped. Behind them a long line of cars had formed, twelve deep. A glance at his left and right told Porter that the other lanes were equally busy. There was no turning back now.

We're boxed in.

Bald buzzed down his window. Ray-Ban scanned the three faces inside the Cruze from behind his shades. Switched his attention to Bald. His face gave nothing away. He had the same humourless demeanour as border guards the world over.

'How are you today, sir?' he asked tonelessly.

'Fine, thanks.'

Bald had been through this situation plenty of times. He knew what to do. Play it straight. Don't be over-friendly, or the guards will get suspicious. Keep it neutral.

'See some ID, please.'

'Aye,' said Bald.

Porter and Cooper handed him their documents. Bald passed them to the guard, along with his own passport. The guy studied them each for a long moment, checking them against the faces in the car. He didn't hand them back. Not immediately.

'Where are you guys from?' he asked Bald.

'England, mate. We're on holiday.'

'Reason for your trip?'

'We're heading over to the Lakeview Casino.'

'You or your buddies staying the night?'

Bald shook his head. 'We'll be coming back later. Just a few drinks and bets on the old roulette wheel.'

'Bringing anything into the country, sir? Guns? Knives?'

'No, mate,' Bald replied. 'Nothing like that.'

The guard stared at him again with the same rigid expression. Then he glanced at Cooper and Porter in the back seats. Noted the cuts on Porter's hands and face before turning his gaze back to Bald.

'You guys look a little worse for wear.'

'We've been paintballing, mate. Got a bit scrappy, like.'

'Paintball?' Ray-Ban's expression cracked a little at the edges. 'In New York? I thought they only use real guns over there.'

Bald laughed. 'Me too.'

Ray-Ban took a step back from the window and retreated to the hut, still holding onto their passports and Cooper's driver's licence. He scanned the documents, tapped a few keys on the computer.

Porter expected the guard to return their IDs and wish them a safe journey. But he didn't do that. Instead, he picked up the phone. Spoke a few words into the receiver while he squinted at something on his computer screen.

'Shit,' Bald muttered. 'They're on to us. We should have kept that twat in the boot. I fucking knew it.'

'We don't know that,' Porter whispered. 'Stay cool.'

The three of them sat rigid inside the Cruze as the seconds ticked by. Bald rested his right foot over the gas pedal, ready to mash the accelerator if the guard suddenly ordered them out of the car.

Fifteen seconds passed. Porter glanced over at the hut. Ray-Ban was still holding the receiver. The guard was doing most of the talking. The voice on the other end of the phone didn't say much. Questions were being asked, presumably. Information being cross-checked.

Ray-Ban kept staring at the Cruze.

He hung up the phone.

Stepped back out of the shack.

For a cold moment Porter feared their names had been flagged up on the computer system. We're done for, he thought. We're gonna have to make a run for it.

Bald's right foot hovered over the gas pedal. Preparing to floor it.

Then the guard was handing over their documents and nodding at them. 'You're free to go. Have a good evening.'

There was no smile. Border hospitality didn't extend that far. Porter didn't care. A wave of relief flooded through him as Bald hit the gas and drove on towards the toll booths. He pulled up at the nearest free booth, slipped the operator a ten-dollar bill and got seven singles in change.

The exit barrier lifted.

Bald arrowed the Cruze through.

We're in.

They continued west along Queen Elizabeth Way. At some point in the next day or so, the NSA would pick up on the fact that a man by the name of Terence Cooper had crossed the Peace Bridge into Canada at 1734 hours, accompanied by two UK nationals. That information would be passed on to the FBI, who would in turn notify the Canadian authorities. Arrest warrants would be swiftly issued for all three men.

But by then, Porter and Bald would be long gone. When they were a mile clear of the checkpoint Porter took out the ghost phone and opened the text message Moorcroft had sent him seven hours earlier. The message containing the number for Tannon's burner.

The BlackBerry went through the same performance when Porter dialled through. First the long pause, followed by a series of faint clicks. Then the unusual tone, like making a call to a foreign country. Tannon picked up midway through the first beep. As if she'd been sitting by the phone in a hotel room somewhere, waiting for the call.

Tannon said, 'Yes?'

'It's Porter. We're through.'

'Any problems?'

Her voice was stiff and formal, but Porter knew there was more to Tannon than that. He'd seen her soft side all those years ago in Sierra Leone, and a warm feeling spread through him at the thought of seeing her again. They hadn't had a chance to talk privately at the briefing in London, but he wondered if things might be different now. Conflicting emotions swirled inside his chest. Seventeen years had passed since Freetown. They were different people now. Different lives.

Perhaps she doesn't even remember that night, thought Porter.

'Nothing we couldn't handle,' he said.

'Have you still got the package?'

Porter glanced at Cooper. 'Looking at it as we speak.'

'Good. Where are you now?'

'We just cleared the border a couple of miles ago.'

'You'll need to stay on the road for another hour or so. Do you have GPS?'

'Not in this model, love.'

Stillman had deliberately asked for a rental that didn't include GPS. The chances of anyone tracking the Cruze were slim. But they'd decided not to risk it.

'Then listen carefully. Stay on Queen Elizabeth Way, following the signs to Toronto. Once you hit Mississauga, you'll see a sign for Exit 124, onto Winston Churchill Boulevard. I'll be five hundred metres up from the exit on the hard shoulder, in a blue Volkswagen Jetta with my hazard lights on. Pull in directly behind me. Have you got all that?'

'Exit 124. Blue VW Jetta. Got it.'

'Meet me there,' said Tannon. 'Then we'll talk.'

THIRTY-FIVE

It took them seventy-four minutes to reach the RV. Traffic was heavy. Which was to be expected. Porter had read somewhere that Queen Elizabeth Way was one of the busiest stretches of road in Canada. The highway curved like a horseshoe around the western shore of Lake Ontario, past St Catherine's, and the port at Hamilton. Then across the canal and north-east through Burlington and Oakville, weaving through the lanes as they closed in on the RV.

Three miles past Oakville, Porter spotted the sign for the exit onto Winston Churchill Boulevard. Bald passed the slip road, sticking to the lanes on the left-hand side of the highway. Five hundred metres beyond the slip road, Porter saw the Jetta parked on the hard shoulder, in the shadow of a concrete flyover, hazard lights blinking in the evening gloom. The bonnet was popped open, to make it look as if the car had broken down.

Standing alongside the Jetta was Dominique Tannon.

She was dressed in a buttoned-up grey trouser suit, white blouse and heels, with a brown-leather messenger bag slung across her shoulder. Her arms were folded as she stood next to the guard rail at the side of the road, staring into the middle distance, playing the part of a broken-down motorist to perfection. She looked just the right combination of bored and frustrated.

Bald whistled appreciatively. 'She might be getting on, but I'd love to have a crack at that.' He shook his head at Porter. 'I still can't believe you managed to shag her.'

'It was a long time ago,' Porter mumbled as he watched Tannon. That warm feeling spread through him again, like a hot breath on the back of his neck.

Bald slapped the hazards on, dropped his speed and nudged the

Cruze into the space behind Tannon. To the drivers on the main road, they looked like a few mates arriving to help a friend who'd broken down. More importantly, arranging to meet on the highway meant no one could follow them. Anyone pursuing either vehicle would have to call off their surveillance as soon as they reached the RV. They couldn't pull up on the hard shoulder without drawing attention to themselves.

Tannon's got good instincts, Porter thought. She's always thinking ahead.

No wonder she rose so quickly through the ranks at Six.

Bald tore the keys out of the ignition and climbed out of the Cruze. Porter popped his seat belt and half-turned to face Cooper. 'Wait here. Try anything, and I'll break every bone in your fucking body.'

'You don't have to threaten me. I've got as much interest in getting out of here as you two. Besides, look around you. Where would I go?'

Cooper looked supernaturally calm again, Porter noticed. The guy didn't look like someone who was facing a long stretch in prison. *Maybe he's just relieved we didn't slot him, back at the safe house.*

He popped the side door and stepped out onto the hard shoulder. Traffic blasted past the operators in a windswept roar as they approached Tannon. She stepped forward from the Jetta and met them halfway.

'Where's Cooper?' she asked.

Porter jerked a thumb at the Cruze. 'Stewing in the back. Want us to get him, love?'

'That won't be necessary. I have to make this quick. We don't have much time.'

Porter watched her for a beat, waiting for a smile that never came. He'd expected a personal touch of some kind. A few words, a private joke. Something that hinted at what they had once shared. But Tannon gave away nothing. She kept up the same businesslike façade he'd heard on the phone. As if that night in Sierra Leone had never happened.

At his side, Porter noticed Bald smiling wryly. Tannon didn't appear to have noticed. Her eyes were still fixed on Porter. He swallowed his disappointment and moved the conversation on.

'Did Moorcroft tell you what went down at the safe house?'

'He filled me in shortly after I landed. It's chaos back at Vauxhall right now, as you can probably imagine. A lot of uncomfortable questions are being asked. Everyone's running around, trying to figure out how we missed something this big.'

'None of your lot suspected Cooper of anything?'

'Never. His record was spotless. If there had been the slightest doubt, we would never have involved him in the operation.'

'He almost had us fooled too,' Bald cut in. 'He's a slippery bastard. That's for sure.'

Tannon nodded and said, 'I understand that Cooper is willing to cooperate with us.'

'He had a change of heart, aye. Right after we threatened to blow his brains out.'

Tannon turned to Porter. 'Nigel outlined your plan to me. The Russia thing. Are you sure we can trust him?'

'Cooper? Fuck knows. He sounded convincing enough. But there's only one way to find out.'

'I agree. Nigel has his reservations, but I don't think we have any choice but to go along with the plan. Just as long as you're aware of the risks. You'll be entering an extremely hostile environment. If you run into trouble, we can't help you.'

'Why can't you lot send in some local assets to rescue Street?' Bald asked. 'That's got to be easier than sending us halfway round the fucking world.'

'We don't have anyone we can call on over there. Not at this short notice. Even if we could, the Chief wouldn't sign off on it. Too much risk of something going wrong.'

'So we're having to get our hands dirty because your bosses are worried about getting caught?'

'If you want to put it like that, yes.'

Bald shook his head. 'If you're so worried about the Kremlin having this sex tape, you should just tell the Yanks. Get them to take care of it. It's their fucking problem, not ours.'

Tannon stared at him. 'Are you having second thoughts?'

'Just saying. It's not our fault one of your own turned out to be a lying snake.'

'We need to get Charles back,' Tannon replied sternly. 'That's non-negotiable. Even if he didn't have the dossier, rescuing him would still be our number one priority.'

Porter said, 'We'll do the job, love. But we might not get there in time. The Russians have got a ten-hour start over us. Street might give up what he knows before we can get to him.'

'Charles won't break easily. He's trained in resistance-to-interrogation. Same as the rest of our field agents.'

'That would have been a long time ago,' Bald pointed out.

'True. But a good agent doesn't forget the techniques. And Charles was one of the best.'

'Even so, he won't stand a chance against Zhirkov's henchmen. I've heard stories about his mob. They're savages.'

Tannon sighed. 'Regardless of what Charles does or doesn't tell his abductors, we need him back alive. The Russians capturing one of our own is unprecedented. Not to mention hugely damaging to our reputation.'

'Street isn't with the service any more. How damaging could it be?'

'Worse than you can imagine. Charles is a senior former spy with a lifetime of secrets inside his head. They could find out anything from him. Who knows? The FSB might even parade Charles on Russian state TV, try and make us look like fools.'

'You don't need a camera for that,' Bald said.

Tannon stared at him. 'It's vital we get Charles back. If you manage to rescue him before he tells Zhirkov's mob what he knows, then great. But either way, we can't abandon him. That is not an option.'

Porter said, 'Whatever we do, we'd better fucking hurry. Street won't last long once those mobsters break out the thumbscrews.'

'Agreed.'

'We'll need new documents as well. The Russians aren't gonna let us stroll through security at their end.'

'I've already taken care of that. This way.'

Tannon led them over to the Jetta. She flipped open the boot, revealing a black nylon gym bag stowed inside. Tannon worked the zip on the side compartment, pulling out a thick padded envelope.

'Passports, bank cards and drivers' licences,' she said, handing the package over to Porter. 'You'll be flying to Moscow under assumed identities. I'll hang on to your genuine documents until the mission is over.'

Porter took out one of the passports to examine it. The coat of arms on the front had been scuffed, to make it look older. Brand-new documents made border officials suspicious. A Russian tourist visa had been stickered to one of the inside pages. Porter's photo stared out at him from the back page. The passport gave his name as Gary Hutton and his place of birth as Enfield. The date of birth was the same as his real one.

'How did you get these at such short notice?'

'We didn't. We sourced four sets of identities, originally. As a precaution, in the event that you two, Cooper and Street, needed to make a rapid exit from the US.'

'What happens once we've grabbed Street?'

'You'll head to the British embassy in Moscow and await further orders. I've already notified our station chief. He'll be expecting you.'

'Let's hope your man in Moscow isn't as bent as Cooper,' said Bald.

'He's been vetted thoroughly. The guy is so straight you could use him to paint lines on a road.'

'When do we leave?' Porter asked.

'Tonight. You're booked in on the red-eye flight from Toronto to Moscow. You'll arrive tomorrow evening, around seven o'clock.'

'Itineraries?'

'Also included in the packet. We've booked you in for one twin room and a single at the Marriott Grand Hotel.'

'Swanky.' Bald grinned. 'My kind of place.'

'You won't be staying there, of course. But the reservations will help with your cover story as tourists. That reminds me.'

Tannon reached into the boot and unzipped the main compartment of the gym bag. Porter leaned in and peeked inside. Saw a bunch of glossy books nestled in the bag, along with a couple of Nikon SLR digital cameras.

'Moscow guide books,' she went on. 'You know the drill. Read up on a few sights around the city. Museums and so on. In case you get pulled aside at the airport.'

'Expanding my cultural knowledge,' Bald said as he browsed through one of the guide books. 'Just what I signed up to Six for, that.'

Porter said, 'What's the plan once we've landed?'

'Someone from the embassy will RV with you when you land. One of our drivers. He knows what you look like, what flight you're on. The basics. His photo is in the envelope, so you know who to look out for.'

'Where do we meet him?'

'The terminal car park. Third floor. He'll be waiting there for you.'

'What about kit?'

'Our guy will have everything you need for the mission. Car, weapons, money. Plus any other equipment you deem appropriate, within reason.'

'We'll need kit to break into the mansion,' Porter said. 'Bolt-cutters, snap gun, head torches. And a change of clothes. We can't go sneaking around Zhirkov's gaff dressed like this.'

'I'll send a list.' Tannon nodded at the Cruze. 'I presume Cooper will need a new change of clothes as well?'

'He's got to come with us, love. He's the only one who knows the layout of Zhirkov's mansion.'

'What'll happen to that wanker?' Bald asked. 'Once we've nabbed Street?'

'You'll escort him back to the embassy with Charles. A team will be waiting there to receive him. We'll question him. Find out who his contacts are over at the Kremlin, who else they've turned.'

'And if he cooperates?'

Tannon shrugged. 'I imagine we'll come to some sort of arrangement.'

'What the fuck does that mean?'

'The general feeling at Six is that we need to keep this thing as quiet as possible. The Chief would prefer to cut a deal with Cooper. Information, in exchange for avoiding prison.'

Bald's face twisted with rage. 'That's a load of bollocks. Cooper set us up. He almost got us killed, for fuck's sake.'

'Believe me, if it was my call then Cooper would be spending the rest of his days rotting in a cell. But the Chief is determined to avoid any unnecessary exposure. There are issues of trust at stake. He's worried about how this would look to our allies.'

'Who gives a shit? The bloke's a traitor.'

'Cooper will still lose his job, and his pension. He'll be discredited. He won't be coming out of this smelling of roses.'

'He shouldn't be coming out of it at all.'

'As I said, it's not my decision.' Tannon stole a glance at her watch, signalling the end of the briefing. 'Now, you should get going. Your flight leaves in four hours.'

Bald hefted up the gym bag and marched over to the Cruze, dumping it in the back next to Cooper. Porter turned to leave. Tannon stepped across his path before he could walk away. He caught a whiff of her perfumed neck as she moved closer to him, searching his eyes with hers.

'Can I ask you something?'

'Sure,' said Porter. 'Anything.'

'Do you really think you can rescue Charles?'

'We'll do our best, love. But I can't make any promises. We're talking about the Russian mob here.'

'You know why I chose you for this mission?'

'Because of our good looks and sense of humour?'

'Because you always get the job done, no matter what. What you did for me in Freetown, for all of us, I won't ever forget, John.'

There was a tenderness to her voice, a softness in her eyes. Porter felt that familiar warmth rise up through him once more. A vivid memory seared across his brain. Sierra Leone, seventeen years ago. The Ambassadors Hotel. Lying on the mattress next to Tannon, her head resting on his chest, the sound of gunfire cracking and popping in the distance.

For the briefest moment, the distance between them melted away.

'You saved us back then,' Tannon continued. 'I'm counting on you again now. We can't lose on this one. We need you to bring Charles home. Whatever it takes.'

THIRTY-SIX

Toronto Pearson Airport was a twenty-minute drive from the meeting point. They left the Cruze in a parking garage a short hop from the terminal. Porter took out the ghost phone, snapped off the casing, flipped out the battery and crushed the SIM card under his boot. Like grinding a cigarette. He chucked the battery and SIM card fragments into one bin and tossed the handset into another. Did the same with the two burners they'd carried. Bald ushered Cooper out of the Cruze, left the keys under the front wheel, and the three of them made for the terminal entrance.

They checked in at one of the Lufthansa kiosks, using the same credit card the flights had been booked with. Porter swiped the card through and punched in the flight number on the screen. Then they took turns to place their new passports down on the machine reader. There was an anxious wait while the computer processed their documents. Then the kiosk whirred and printed out three business-class tickets, and they headed for security.

It took them twenty-five minutes to get airside. Most of which was spent waiting in line. They had no luggage to speak of. Nothing on them except for some loose change, their wallets and passports, plus the guide books and SLR cameras. Porter had worried that their lack of baggage might draw attention. But no one seemed to notice. Plenty of other businesspeople were travelling light.

They had a couple of hours to kill before their flight was announced, so they hit the duty-free shopping and paid cash for three embroidered baseball caps from a Ralph Lauren outlet, each one a different colour. The caps would conceal their faces from surveillance cameras when they entered Russia. Whether they liked it or not, they were going to be on camera. Nothing they could do about that. Concealing their faces was the next best option.

They found a bar with a free table, pulled up three chairs and loaded up on black coffee, pulled pork burgers and sweet potato fries. Their first cooked meal since they'd arrived in the US.

Porter popped some fries in his mouth and said, "Tell us about the mobster's gaff."

Cooper shook his head. 'That wasn't part of the deal. I said I'll take you there once we land. I'm not saying any more until then.'

'Not good enough. We need to know what we're dealing with. Security details, guards, the works. If we go in blind, we won't stand a chance of rescuing Street.'

'Or we can call the whole thing off now,' Bald threatened. 'Hand you back to Six. Whatever deal they're offering you will be off the table once we tell them you're refusing to cooperate.'

Cooper pondered this while he stared at his burger. 'How much do you know about Zhirkov?'

'He's a crime boss,' said Bald. 'Rich as fuck, and a complete nutter.'

'He's not just any old criminal,' Cooper replied. 'Zhirkov is the most powerful mobster in the country. He made his money by offering protection to the oligarchs during the aluminium wars. He guaranteed their safety, in exchange for shares in their companies.'

'Nice work if you can get it.'

'But also very dangerous. Most of the other bosses from that time are either dead or in exile. Zhirkov is the last survivor.'

'How'd he manage that?'

'By being cautious, and keeping a low profile. The other bosses splashed their cash, bought up football teams and New York penthouses, but that was never Zhirkov's style. He preferred to stay under the radar. Hardly anyone even knows what he looks like.'

Porter said, 'Where's the mansion?'

'North of his hometown. A speck on a map, two hours north of Moscow. He bought the land years ago and registered the property under the name of his sister-in-law.'

'Why build it in the middle of nowhere? I thought all those rich Russians lived in Moscow.'

'They do. But it's not Zhirkov's usual residence. He had the place constructed as a private retreat. Somewhere all the top guys in his criminal empire could meet up. He held lavish parties there from time to time as well. Very exclusive. All the Russian elite were invited. The place is legendary, in the criminal underworld.'

'What about security?'

'There's a permanent detail at the estate. They patrol the grounds in shifts.'

'How many guys?'

'A four-man team.'

'Do they carry?'

'A couple of them, I think. Zhirkov only trusts his most loyal guards with weapons. The others won't be armed.'

'Shotguns? Longs?'

'Handguns. Nothing bigger than a nine-millimetre. You won't be coming up against any serious firepower.'

'Guard dogs?'

'Not any more.'

'The mobster used to have them?'

Cooper nodded. 'The first time I went there, he had a pack of German shepherds. Vicious things. The second time, the dogs weren't there. Apparently one of them got away and attacked his daughter. Scarred her for life. After that, Zhirkov ditched the dogs.'

Porter said, 'What about the mansion itself?'

'There's a perimeter fence around the house, and an earthen rampart surrounding it. Like you get at old castles. To stop anyone firing RPGs at the property.'

'Sounds like Zhirkov's got a lot of enemies.'

'He's a crime boss. In Russia. You don't stay alive for long in his world unless you're extremely careful. The place was designed to be impenetrable.'

Bald wiped his mouth with the back of his hand and said, 'How are we going to get inside if Zhirkov's got the place on lockdown?'

'You won't need to break into the house itself. There's a garden at the back, with a boathouse backing on to the lakefront. That's where they'll be holding Charles.'

'You're sure?'

'Zhirkov had the boathouse converted into a torture cell when he bought the place. To question friends and enemies.'

Porter stared at Cooper, 'How do you know the place so well?'

'Like I said, Zhirkov used to host private parties at the estate. I happened to be invited there on a couple of occasions, back when I was working at the embassy in Moscow.'

There was a definite note of pride in his voice. 'Was this before or after you fucked over your best mate?'

Cooper stared back. 'You think I'm not sorry about what happened to Charles? He was my friend, for Chrissakes.'

'Some friend, letting him take the blame for those two agents who got murdered.'

'You don't know what it's like. To live in someone else's shadow. Charles was the star young agent, destined for great things. Me? I was just another name. I had a chance to make something of myself. Charles was in the way. It's as simple as that.'

'You shafted his career.'

'It was twenty years ago. I can't be blamed for everything that happened to him since. Charles has had plenty of opportunities to pick himself up.'

'Yeah,' Bald said. 'Just long enough for you to screw him all over again with the dossier.'

Cooper glowered at Bald but made no reply.

Porter checked the time on the departures screen. 2052 hours. Thirteen hours since the Russians had taken Street from the safe house. He figured it would have taken them a couple of hours to get to the nearest airfield, cover their tracks and leave the country. Say, thirteen hours to fly to the mansion. With a stopover somewhere for fuel, probably. A fourteen-hour flight, plus the travel time at the other end.

Seventeen hours, total.

Which meant the foot soldiers would get to Zhirkov's place for around 0800 hours tomorrow, local time.

Our flight gets in at 1925, Porter thought. That gives the Russians a head-start of eleven hours.

We'll have to leg it there as fast as possible.

'How long will they keep Street at the mansion?' he asked Cooper.

'As long as it takes to find out what he knows. All the state secrets and missions that Six has carried out. Anything that might be of use to Zhirkov's paymasters over at the Kremlin.'

'What happens after that?'

Cooper stared at his half-eaten burger. 'Once Charles has told them all his secrets, they'll want to get rid of the evidence. They'll execute him.'

Porter looked over at the electronic board. A gate number had flashed up, next to their flight number. He shovelled the rest of the chips into his mouth, polished off his Coke and stood up.

'Come on,' he said to the others. 'Let's go.'

They boarded the Boeing 777 and settled into their business-class seats. There was less legroom than Porter remembered. Or perhaps he was just getting bigger. I'm not in the shape I used to be, he thought. Maybe it's time to call it a day after this. Get myself a job on Civvy Street. See my daughter more often. Find a woman.

If we make it out of Russia alive.

Bald and Porter took the seats on the right side of the aisle. Cooper had the seat opposite. He sat upright, with his eyes closed, his hands resting in his lap. Looking relaxed. Untroubled. A cool character.

'Why's he so chilled?' he wondered.

Bald shrugged. 'What do you expect? That twat's getting off lightly.'

'Not that lightly. His career's over. He'll lose everything.'

'Aye. But he's avoided jail. Someone'll give him a job after the dust has settled. On the Circuit, or in the City.'

'You reckon?'

'Until yesterday, he was a big deal at MI6. Bloke like him, he's got a contacts list as long as a horse's dick. All he's getting from Six is a slap on the wrist. He's got plenty of reasons to smile, mate.'

Porter nodded and said, 'How long do you think we've got? Until Street spills his guts?'

'Not long. Zhirkov's toughs will have been trained up by the FSB. They'll know all the interrogation techniques. The Russians are world-class when it comes to torturing suspects.'

'Twenty-four hours?'

'If he lasts that long, it'll be a fucking miracle.'

Porter sat back, resting his head against the cushion. If every-thing went to plan, they'd arrive at Zhirkov's mansion thirteen hours after the Russians. There was nothing else they could do now, except get there as soon as possible once they'd landed.

And hope Street hadn't forgotten all of his interrogation training.

The cabin doors closed. Announcements were made as the plane started to taxi. A video played on the entertainment screens, a soothing voice telling the passengers to buckle up and turn off their electronic devices, though nobody seemed to be paying any attention. Twelve minutes later they were climbing into the sky. The seat belt signs flicked off. The lights dimmed.

Porter waited until Bald was fast asleep, then stood up from his seat and paced down the aisle. He snagged a few miniatures from the drinks trolley and got a funny look from the German stew-ardess with the school matron build. Porter didn't care. He stuffed the miniatures into his pockets and slipped into the vacant toilet. Locked the door, and tore off the cap from one of the miniature bottles of vodka.

The stress of the op was beginning to get to him. In four-teen hours we'll be landing in Russia, the voice in his head told him. Surrounded by enemies, with no way out if things go Pete Tong.

I just need a drink to take the edge off. Deal with the stress I'm feeling.

He was about to tip the voddie down his throat when he caught sight of himself in the bathroom mirror.

The face of a drunk stared back at him. His eyes were blood-shot. His skin was puffy and bloated. He looked like shit.

I slipped up once at the safe house, thought Porter. I can't afford to go down that same route again. Not when I'm going up against the Russian mob.

He remembered the promise he'd made to Bald.

To Sandy.

Well, fuck.

He re-screwed the cap on the voddie bottle. Tossed it into the bin, along with the rest of the miniatures. Pushed the voice aside, shoving it back into the dim, dark recesses of his mind.

Then he stepped out of the toilet. Bald was still snoring away.

Porter sank into the seat next to his mucker, closed his eyes and settled into a restless sleep.

They kipped through most of the flight. Following one of the oldest rules in the Regiment. Sleep when you can, because you never know when you'll next have the chance. There was no need to keep a close eye on Cooper. At forty thousand feet, he wasn't going anywhere. They landed at Munich at 1210 the following day. Had a three-hour stopover, which they spent refuelling with toasted sandwiches and coffee at the airport Starbucks. Cooper sipped at his latté while Porter and Bald browsed through the guide books, committing a few of the major tourist sights to memory.

At 1535 they boarded their connecting flight to Moscow Sheremetyevo, on an Aeroflot Airbus A321. The final leg of their journey. Bald kipped some more, but Porter couldn't rest. His mind was racing ahead of him, working the angles. If Cooper was right, once they'd passed through security and RV'd with the driver, it would take them around two hours to reach Zhirkov's mansion. Which gave them an ETA of around 2230 hours.

Fourteen hours after the Russians would have reached their mobster boss's hideout.

Fourteen hours to torture Street.

Nightmare scenarios played out in Porter's mind.

If Street gave up what he knew, the Kremlin would have their hands on a sex tape they could use against the new American president. They would be in a position to make him do whatever they wanted. They could force him to drop sanctions, Cooper had said. Persuade him to withdraw from NATO. Anything.

That can't happen. I'm not gonna let the Russians win.

Three hours later, they touched down at Sheremetyevo airport.

THIRTY-SEVEN

They were first off the plane, along with the handful of passengers in first-class. Porter moved ahead, followed by Cooper, with Bald as the tail-end Charlie. They shuffled down the jet bridge, rested but still weary, heavy-legged from half a day spent in the air. Porter handed his passport to a bored-looking officer at the security booth. The guy glanced at his visa for about a second before waving Porter through. Bald and Cooper went through the same routine. Then the three of them donned their Ralph Lauren baseball caps, concealing their faces from the surveillance cameras as they swept past the luggage carousel into the arrivals hall.

Security was tight at the airport. Police officers in ballistic vests patrolled the area, wielding PP-2000 submachine guns. Porter counted at least a dozen of them. He recalled the news report he'd seen on the TV at Heathrow.

The suicide bombing at St Petersburg airport.

Chechen terrorists. Blood and dust and broken glass.

The Russians were beefing up their security in the wake of the latest attack. That much was clear.

They bought coffee from a sour-faced woman at a drab-looking café. Sat down at one of the tables and sipped their shit coffee, scanning the hall to see if anyone had eyes on them. The cops didn't give them a second glance. They were on the lookout for nervous-looking Eurasians, dressed in unseasonably hot outerwear. Not middle-aged white blokes in suits.

When they were sure no one was watching them, they ditched their paper cups and beat a path across the hall, following the signs for the multi-storey car park. Announcements pinged out in Russian and English as they rode the escalator to the second floor and took the emergency stairs to the third floor of the multi-storey.

Most airport car parks were rigged with CCTV cameras, so Porter, Bald and Cooper kept their heads lowered as they swept out of the fire doors. They hung back by the lift, heads low. Ten seconds later a bloke in a slate-grey suit debussed from a black Mercedes G-Class wagon parked in the opposite corner and marched over.

The driver matched the description Tannon had included in their itineraries. Short and stocky, with a buzz cut and squinting eyes the size of pinpricks. As if someone had just kicked sand in his face. He looked to be in his mid-forties, and he moved at a brisk pace, eyes casually taking in every detail. Ex-military, Porter guessed. Probably a background in army intelligence. A four-year stretch in Northern Ireland, working surveillance. Then the tap on the shoulder by one of his handlers, the offer of a career in the secret service. The foreign posting to Russia.

That's how they suck you in.

Buzz Cut carried an A4 envelope in his right hand. He cocked his head at Porter.

'Gary Hutton?' he asked. There was a trace of Geordie to his accent, watered down by the years spent working for MI6. Porter nodded.

'That's me.'

'Anyone follow you here?'

'No one's watching us,' Bald said. 'We're clear, mate.'

Buzz Cut nodded. 'Your car's over here. Follow me, lads.'

He turned on his heels and strode past the banks of silent motors towards the Mercedes G-Class. Vehicle of choice for the well-heeled in the new Russia. He waved a hand at it.

'Tank's full. Documents are in the glove box. All the paperwork is made out in the name of Gary Hutton.'

Bald gave the motor the once-over and nodded his approval. 'Decent wheels for a change,' he said. 'Not like the knackered old bangers Six usually sets us up with.'

'Where's the kit?' Porter asked.

'In here.'

Buzz Cut circled around to the boot. He'd parked so that the back of the G-wagon was facing the exterior wall, away from the multi-storey CCTV cameras. The exterior wall was about a metre high, a block of smooth concrete overlooking the open-air car park directly to the east. Four hundred metres away stood the Park Inn hotel. Too far away for anyone inside the hotel to make out what was in the back of the G-wagon.

Buzz Cut popped the boot. Inside was a black leather bag. Bald unzipped it and rummaged through the contents. The bag contained a pair of thirty-six-inch Neiko bolt cutters, two Petzl Tactikka head torches, black gloves, a Klom snap gun with a set of blades and a tension tool, and two sets of Asp tri-fold plastic restraints. More flexible than standard plasticuffs, which meant Bald and Porter could fold the restraints and carry them in their pockets instead of hanging them from a belt-loop.

Also included in the bag: two burner phones, virtually identical to the ones Porter and Bald used in DC, and a Garmin Montana handheld GPS unit with a car charging kit. Everything they'd need to break into the mansion, retrieve Street and deliver him to the British embassy.

'Clothes are in the back,' Buzz Cut said. 'Dark jeans, t-shirts, waterproof jackets, trainers. Three pairs of each. Everything's in your sizes, as you requested.'

Porter nodded. They would have to find somewhere to change before they made their assault on Zhirkov's mansion. Buzz Cut handed him the envelope. 'Cash. Clean, untraceable notes. In case of emergencies.'

Porter dipped a hand into the envelope. He pulled out a slim band of five-thousand-rouble notes. Fifty notes to the band. There were four wads in total inside the envelope. Two million roubles. Equivalent to a couple of grand in UK pounds.

'What about weapons?' Bald asked.

'Glove box,' Buzz Cut replied. 'Two MP-443 Grachs.'

Porter recognised the weapon brand. Semi-automatics chambered for the 7N21, the Russian version of the 9x19mm Parabellum round. Nicknamed the YaP. The Yarygin Pistol. After the guy who'd designed it.

'Ammunition?'

'One box. Fifty rounds.'

'What if we need anything meatier?'

'That's all we could get at this short notice, lads. Anything else would've taken more time.'

Bald clicked his tongue. 'Fuck it. We'll have to make do.'

Buzz Cut handed Porter the keys to the G-wagon. 'There's a car waiting to pick me up as you leave the airport. I'll direct you. After that, you're on your own.'

Porter snatched the keys. Buzz Cut wandered around to the rear passenger side and climbed inside. Then Porter turned to Cooper and said, 'Do you know how to get to Zhirkov's place from here?'

'I spent seven years working in Moscow,' Cooper replied snootily. 'I worked the streets more than any other agent at Six in that time. So yes, I think I know my way around.'

'Get in the back. You'll show us the route as soon as we've dropped this guy off.'

Bald glowered at Cooper as the latter ducked into the front passenger seat and slammed the door shut. 'This twat is really starting to piss me off.'

'We'll be rid of him soon enough,' Porter replied. 'Soon as we've got Street.'

'The quicker the better. Otherwise I'll end up slotting the cunt. No matter what Tannon says.'

The sun was sinking towards the horizon as they pulled out of the multi-storey. Eight-thirty in the evening, the last light of the day coating the clear Moscow sky in brushstrokes of orange and pink. Porter took the wheel, Cooper riding shotgun, with Bald sat in the back with Buzz Cut. The latter gave directions to the airport exit. After five hundred metres they passed the Radisson Hotel and continued south. Four hundred metres later Buzz Cut pointed out a wide gravel parking lot to the right of the exit road.

'This is it,' he said. 'Stop here.'

Porter slowed the G-wagon down to a crawl as he steered over to the side of the road. He stopped but kept the engine running as Buzz Cut dived out of the back of the wagon. The driver hurried across the lot to a white BMW X3 parked up in the far corner and hopped into the front passenger seat. As Porter pulled away he could see the BMW reversing out of the parking lot. Porter knew the routine. The second car would ferry Buzz Cut back to the British embassy on Smolenskaya

Street, on the eastern bank of the Moscow River. The exchange meant Bald and Porter didn't have to set foot anywhere near the embassy.

And if we're caught, Six can deny they had anything to do with the mission.

'Which way now?' he asked Cooper.

'Take the M11 south. We'll take the ring road across the city. It's always busy, but it's the quickest way to get where we're going.'

'You'd better be right. If I find out you're lying to us, Jock here will put a hole in the back of your head.'

'There's no need for that tone. I'm well aware of your threats against me.'

'Twat,' Bald said under his breath.

They took the next junction and rolled onto the motorway. At the toll booth Bald handed over a fistful of roubles. Then they headed south across the canal until they hit the Moscow ring road. Which was when they ran into their first obstacle of the mission: Russian roads, and Russian drivers. A lethal combination, made worse by Russian traffic cops. Everyone in Moscow was terrified of getting a speeding ticket, it seemed. No one dared edge over fifty miles per.

The AC was working overtime as they made slow progress on the ring road, circling around the northern edge of the city. The Moscow evening was hot and sticky. Smell of distant peat fires slithered in through the air vents. High-rise blocks stretched out across the skyline, the balconies piled high with rubbish. Porter glanced down at the clock on the dash.

2044 hours.

Seventy minutes since they'd landed at Sheremetyevo. In another two hours they would reach Zhirkov's stronghold.

They stuck to the ring road, passing several exits. President Gabulov's smirking face beamed out at them from roadside election posters. At nine o'clock the sun finally dipped down below the horizon, a band of gold that glowed beyond the high-rises. Cooper directed Porter to the next exit and they slingshot northeast on the M8, leaving Moscow's orbit.

Porter said, 'How long to the mansion from here?'

Cooper said, 'Ninety minutes.'

The dash clock read 2104. We'll get to the mansion at around 2230 hours, Porter realised.

Fourteen hours after the Russians.

'What's the plan once we get there?' Bald asked.

Porter rubbed his jaw. 'We'll OP the estate and the surrounding grounds. Find the optimum point of entry. Deal with the guards at the boathouse and get Street out of there.'

Bald considered. 'We'll have to watch for cameras. Sensors. If the mobster's got any thermal or infra-red kit, we won't stand a fucking chance of getting inside without alerting them.'

'Zhirkov doesn't have anything like that,' Cooper said.

'Why not? He's rich enough to afford it.'

'He's a personal friend of the president. That gives him a certain level of protection. Better than any security contract could buy.'

'What about cameras?'

'I know where they are,' Cooper responded. 'Zhirkov can't stand the smell of cigarette smoke, so I spent a lot of time out in the garden when he hosted his parties. I know all the dead spots.'

Porter stared at Cooper for several moments. Questions reverberated inside his skull. *Twenty-four hours ago Cooper was selling his old mate out to the Russians. Now the bloke wants to help rescue Street. He's changed tack.*

He put this to the back of his mind. Gripped the wheel and refocused on the road ahead. Eighty miles to the mansion.

A few hours from now, if everything went to plan, the op would be over. I'll be back home, Porter thought. Back to my boring, stress-free life.

The one where I'm not tempted to hit the bottle every day.

They drove on.

Into the darkening Russian night.

THIRTY-EIGHT

North of Moscow the road turned into one massive construction site. Mounds of excavated soil and digging equipment lined the sides of the motorway. Apartment blocks and shopping malls and office complexes were cropping up everywhere. Porter had the sense of a sleeping giant awakening after a long slump. Flush with money, ready to reassert itself.

After eleven miles they passed Pushkino and the landscape shifted again. Long stretches of dense woodland, interrupted by rolling fields of wheat and sugar beet, faintly illuminated by the light of the crescent moon. Flat terrain, rugged and poor, marked by the occasional ramshackle village or closed-down garage.

Darkness closed in around the land as they continued north. Stars specked the coal-black sky, the temperature on the dashboard plummeting to a cool fourteen degrees. They passed the city of Sergiev Posad, the G-wagon juddering as it rumbled along the worn-down tarmac. Ten minutes later they were crossing the district line into Vladimir Oblast.

'How much further to go?' Porter asked. Cooper didn't reply. He was gazing out of the side window at the gloomy vista, looking wide-eyed at the black nothing, a man lost in his troubled thoughts. Porter nudged him with his elbow.

'I said, how long to the stronghold?'

Cooper blinked at the road ahead. 'Half an hour. No more than that.'

The guy resumed his staring-out-of-the-window thing. He looked pale. Like a convict coming out of a long stretch in solitary. Cooper was feeling the strain, thought Porter.

No wonder. His balls are on the line here.

Same as ours.

At 2231 hours Cooper broke his silence and told Porter to take the next left off the main road. Porter made the turn and arrowed the G-wagon down a potholed country lane for two miles, plunging deeper into the Russian countryside. They hit the end of the lane, hung a left and carried on for another mile. Past an old army barracks that looked as if it was abandoned long ago.

'You weren't joking,' said Bald. 'This mansion really is in the fucking middle of nowhere.'

They took the next right and rolled on for another half-mile. Thick forest flanked the sides of the road. After five hundred metres Cooper said, 'It's the next left. Zhirkov's place is down there.'

Porter switched off the headlamps, driving on with just his sidelights to make the G-wagon less visible to any sentries guarding the approach. He downshifted through the gears, slowing the motor down to ten miles per hour as he took the turn.

The approach road curved slightly before opening up, revealing a single-lane road that extended towards the distant lakefront. Pine forest to the left and right of the road. At the far end stood a huge estate surrounded by a tall earthen rampart. Cooper pointed at it through the windscreen. 'That's it. That's the place.'

Porter peered at the estate through the windscreen, three hundred metres away at the opposite end of the approach road. The rooftop of the main building was visible above the top of the rampart, a Chinese-style pagoda with turrets at each corner. Like a medieval castle. An imposing gate faced out from the front of the estate.

'This Zhirkov bloke must be fucking minted,' Bald observed, admiration creeping into his voice. 'This place is massive.'

'He's richer than you can imagine,' said Cooper.

Porter said, 'What now, Jock?'

'We'll have to pull over. Make our way on foot. This road's too exposed.'

Porter nudged the G-wagon off to the left, veering towards a footpath at the side of the road. He nosed the wagon down the footpath for several metres until it was hidden from view by the surrounding foliage. Then he killed the engine.

'What now?' Bald asked.

'We'll move closer. Recce the defences. Find a way past the

perimeter. Once we're in, we'll OP the boathouse. Wait for an opportunity to hit the guards and nab Street.'

'Works for me, mate.'

'What about me?' Cooper asked.

'We could plasticuff the fucker,' Bald suggested to Porter. 'Stuff him in the boot, like.'

Cooper shook his head. 'You can't leave me here. I'm the only one who knows the layout.'

'Bollocks. You're not trained. You'll be a liability.'

'I handled myself at the cabin.'

'Bastard's right,' Porter grumbled. 'We need his knowledge. We need to know the optimum point of entry. Where the cameras are located. All that shit.'

Bald grunted. 'Fine. But if he tries anything, we drop him. No ifs or buts.'

They stepped out of the wagon, jumping down to the dry, crusted earth. The temperature was still somewhere in the low teens, the stars studding the black expanse above. Grasshoppers chirped in the woods as they changed out of their white shirts, dress pants and shoes into the dark clothes and sneakers Buzz Cut had left for them in the back seat.

They dumped their old threads in the back seat. Then Bald retrieved the two Yarygin pistols from the glove box while Porter fetched the kit from the leather bag in the boot. He took out the Petzl head torches, the flexible plastic restraints, the Klom snap gun, gloves and bolt cutters, plus the two burners.

All three of them were carrying their travel documents. Porter also had the wad of rouble notes tucked in his back pocket. Everything they would need if they had to make an emergency exit.

Porter left the two digital cameras in the boot, along with the heap of Moscow guide books. They wouldn't be needing tips on art museums where they were going tonight.

He slammed the boot shut and remote-locked the G-wagon. Passed the snap gun and bolt cutters to Cooper, then took one of the Yarygin pistols from Bald. Porter rested the head torches and gloves on top of the wagon, released the empty clip from the underside of the Yarygin mag feed and began thumbing in rounds from the box of ammo. Bald did the same with his weapon, the pair of them loading the clips. Eighteen rounds to a mag. Thirty-six rounds between them. Not much, thought Porter. *But it'll have to do.*

They divided up the spare rounds left in the ammo box. Fourteen bullets. Seven apiece. Then they distributed the rest of the kit, Bald taking one of the head torches, a pair of gloves and the plasticuffs, along with one of the emergency burners. When they'd finished checking through all their kit, Porter looked over at Bald.

'Ready, mucker?'

'Aye. Let's go.'

Before they set off, Porter turned to Cooper. 'Follow our lead. Do exactly as we say. Make a sound and I'll nut you.'

'I'll need a weapon?'

'Forget it. They only gave us two guns. And we're not about to give you a fucking piece.'

'But how am I supposed to defend myself, if we're attacked?'

'Look hard.'

They headed off into the forest.

Porter led the way. He set off at a quick trot towards the mansion, following a route parallel to the approach road. Bald moved along a couple of paces further back, with Cooper at his six o'clock.

Standard operating procedure in the Regiment dictated that the best approach to an enemy stronghold was usually the dirtiest. Which meant having to make their way towards the rampart through the pine forest. They'd head for the section of the rampart closest to the boathouse, then observe the ground before making their next move.

Cooper had told them Zhirkov didn't have any electronic surveillance but Porter figured his int might be out of date. If they found any advanced kit, they'd have no choice but to call the attack off.

We'll probably have trekked all this way for nothing.

Street will be a dead man.

After a couple of minutes his natural night vision kicked in. Peering between the gaps in the trees he saw they were just over two hundred metres from Zhirkov's estate now. At this distance Porter could make out the wrought-iron gate. Gold eagles were mounted on the posts either side of the gate.

He stopped and jerked his head at Cooper. 'Which way?'

The agent pointed to a section of the rampart due east of the main gate, at their eleven o'clock. 'The boathouse is on the south-east corner. We should approach from that direction.'

'Any cameras over there?'

'None. They're all at the front gate.'

Porter gave his back to Cooper and ventured deeper into the pine forest, picking his way through the undergrowth as he moved stealthily towards the estate. They carried on for another two hundred metres until they reached the southern edge of the pine forest, facing the south-eastern corner of the estate. Porter stopped a metre short of the treeline and crouched down as he scanned the area immediately in front of him.

Beyond the treeline a narrow gravel path ran west to east, parallel to the earthen rampart. An access road, Porter guessed. Six metres away from him, on the far side of the gravel path, stood the defensive mound of earth enclosing the mansion.

The rampart was taller than Porter had expected. It rose steeply for two metres, the soil tightly compacted, presumably to absorb the blast of a rocket or mortar round. At the summit the ground had been flattened. From his point of view Porter couldn't see beyond the mound of earth but he knew from Cooper's description of the estate that a wire fence lurked on the other side.

Bald and Cooper silently dropped low either side of Porter. Cooper stayed still while the operators began observing the rampart, searching the ground for hidden sensors and cameras.

'Can't see anything,' Bald whispered after a couple of minutes. 'Looks clear enough to me.'

Porter lifted his gaze to the top of the mound. 'Over there,' he whispered. 'Guards approaching. Two of them.'

Bald chased his mucker's line of sight, looking to the east as a barrel-chested guy in a black t-shirt, matching slacks and boots paced along the crude walkway on top of the rampart. He carried a torch in his left hand and a walkie-talkie in his right. A holstered pistol was clipped to his belt, jutting out from underneath his black shirt.

In the faint light of the moon Porter saw a second guard in a beanie hat approaching, fifty metres behind the first guy. The tail-end Charlie. A regular patrol tactic. One guard leads, with the second man sweeping the ground immediately behind the first guard. If anyone tried to cross the perimeter after the first bloke had moved on, they would be caught by the tail-end Charlie. An effective tactic, for catching amateur intruders.

But it wouldn't work against two ex-Blades.

'Move back,' Porter said quietly.

They retreated a couple of steps further from the treeline, then settled down to OP the rampart through the sporadic gaps in the foliage. Bursts of static carried across the night air as the first guard passed by on his patrol. Porter watched him move on.

Twenty seconds later, the second guard walked past.

Bald and Porter both stayed very still, waiting until both guards had carried on to the next section of the rampart and were out of earshot. Then they crept back over to their positions at the tree-line and continued observing the routine. Porter checked the time on his G-Shock.

2256 hours.

He set his stopwatch. Watched, and waited.

Twenty minutes passed. Then twenty-five.

On thirty minutes, the guard in the loose-hanging black shirt reappeared as he made his next sweep of the grounds. He went through the same routine, sweeping his torch beam over the gravel path directly beneath the rampart, occasionally pausing to speak into his walkie talkie.

He moved on.

Twenty seconds passed.

Right on cue, the guy in the beanie hat appeared.

Porter waited for the guard to move on. Then he turned to Bald. 'Come on. We've got half an hour until those guards are back.'

They crept out of the treeline, crouching low to reduce their visual signature, their dark clothes helping them to blend in to the grainy blackness. Cooper followed Bald and Porter as they picked their way across the gravel path towards the nearest section of the rampart. Every so often they stopped to scan the terrain ahead of them, listening for any hint of the approaching guards or the bleat of a triggered alarm. But there was nothing except the sound of their own breathing, the soft crunch of gravel shifting beneath their boots.

They reached the rampart in half a dozen steps. Paused again. Then Porter gave the signal and they dropped to their fronts, chests pressed flat against the dirt as they belly-crawled up the side of the mound.

Porter went first. The mound was reinforced with stones and he felt his elbows scraping against the sharp edges of several rocks as he inched towards the summit. Twice he had to stop when his movement dislodged loose material from the mound and sent rocks and soil tumbling down the side. But the guard had moved too far away to hear and in another few seconds he had reached the summit.

Porter caught his breath for a moment. Then he crawled along the top of the mound and scaled down to the opposite side, Bald and Cooper close behind at his six. The mound dipped down into a shallow ditch on the far side. Two metres past the ditch was a sturdy chain-link fence, twelve feet high, with barbed spikes running along the top rail to prevent anyone from climbing over.

Beyond the fence was a row of thick fir and spruce trees, three deep, lining the edge of the garden. Shrubbery extended out from the treeline, blocking his view of the rest of the estate.

Porter signalled for the others to wait at the bottom of the rampart. Then he crawled up through the ditch, the dank water soaking his shirt and dress pants. He stopped at the top of the ditch, straining his eyes in the pitch black as he scanned the length of the fence, looking for any sign of security cameras or motion detectors mounted atop the posts. When he was confident the area was clear, he beckoned Bald and Cooper over.

They joined him at the foot of the chain-link fence and padded along the edge until they located a point where two sections of mesh fencing had been woven together to create a longer section. Then Porter stopped and nodded at Bald.

'Get this fucker open.'

Bald slipped on the gloves from his back pocket. Then he crept over, lugging the bolt cutters in his right hand. He clamped the cutter jaws around one of the woven steel wires a few inches up from the ground. There was a sharp metallic ring as the cutters sliced through the mesh.

'Keep it quiet,' Porter hissed.

'Doing my best here, mate.'

Bald worked quickly but calmly, cutting apart the vertical section of the woven fence He made four cuts, each a foot or so higher than the last. Then he set down the bolt cutters and pulled back on the severed wires with his gloved hands. The two sections of mesh separated at the bottom. Like flies unzipping on a pair of jeans.

Porter dropped to all fours and crept through the four-foot gap in the fence. He shifted to the left of the opening, sticking to the shadows behind the trees at the edge of the garden. Cooper was next, wriggling head-first through the gap, Porter whispering at him to stay low. Bald went last. He crawled through, stooped low by the fence and sealed up the gap, weaving the mesh back together so the guards wouldn't notice the breach on their next patrol.

Then he nodded at Porter as if to say, *Job done*.

They were in.

THIRTY-NINE

Porter edged forward from the chain link fence, surveying the ground ahead. In front of him, directly west of their position, was the main building.

Zhirkov's mansion.

The place was huge, and garish. Like an imperial palace from feudal Japan, given a makeover by a Mexican drug dealer. It stood three storeys tall, with whitewashed walls and a solid gold front door. A pair of Bentley Bentayga SUVs were parked in the front drive, with all the pimp trimmings. Exotic plants and Buddha statues dotted the porch. Two guards stood outside the front door, decked out in the same gear as the two guards patrolling the rampart. At this distance Porter couldn't tell if they were armed or not.

To the rear of the mansion he spotted a tennis court and a timber-clad sauna, with a guest house built off to the side. A stone path led from the rear of the mansion, down towards the lake at the far end of the garden, eighty metres due south of Porter.

At the edge of the lake stood the boathouse.

The timber structure extended out across the lake on a purpose-built floating deck. Like a ship moored at anchor. Wooden steps led up from the lakefront to the living quarters on the first floor of the boathouse. Storage area below. For the mobster's collection of boats, Porter supposed.

Lights glowed inside the two first-floor windows.

'Someone's home,' Bald said quietly as he drew alongside his mucker.

Porter nodded at Cooper. 'Looks like you were telling us the truth.'

'For a fucking change,' Bald murmured.

The two operators observed the boathouse for a few moments longer, squinting in the darkness. 'What now?' asked Bald.

'We'll have to get closer.'

Bald passed the message along to Cooper, speaking to him in a low, hissing voice. There was a threat in there too, which Cooper acknowledged with a cold, hard stare. Then Porter waved for the others to follow him as he set off towards the lake.

They edged cautiously forward, sticking close to the ground and using the available cover to conceal their presence. As far as Porter could see there were no more guards patrolling the garden at the rear of the mansion. Just the two guys at the front and the other pair doing the rounds of the rampart. Plus however many guys were watching over Street.

Every few steps Porter stopped in his tracks, scanning the area ahead. He wasn't expecting any more guards, but they were inside the perimeter of a ruthless Russian mobster. *We don't want any nasty surprises.*

They edged closer to the boathouse.

Forty metres now.

Bronze statues of wolves and stags dotted the garden. Above them the crescent moon shone starkly, pale light reflecting like sword points off the surface of the lake. There was no sound coming from the house, and Porter felt the tension pulling like a band across his chest as he picked his way through the vegetation.

We're close now.

Almost there.

They moved on for another twenty metres, until they reached a point where the tangle of trees and shrubs ended. Beyond, a stretch of exposed ground led down towards the lakefront.

Porter halted near the edge of the shrubbery and raised his hand, signalling for Bald and Cooper to stop. All three of them crouched low, making sure they were hidden from view.

Directly beyond the bushes stood a rockery. Twenty metres further to the south was the boathouse.

They settled down to OP the target area to the south. At this distance Porter could hear at least two separate voices coming from inside the boathouse. One guy sounded as if he was laughing. Another was shouting in a thick foreign tongue. There was a beat of silence. Then an agonised scream pierced the night air.

Then more laughter.

'Fuckers *are* torturing him,' Bald murmured.

Porter nodded. 'Got to be three blokes in there.'

'At least.'

'Why aren't you two getting over there?' Cooper barely whispered.

'We don't know how many guys are inside, what the setup is,' said Porter. 'If we go steaming in and it kicks off, the rest of the guards will be alerted.'

'What are we going to do?'

'Wait. Whoever's inside will have to change over at some point. Or they might get sloppy. Or take a break. Until then, we stay fucking put.'

Cooper shut up. Porter wondered again about the guy's change in attitude. His sudden concern for his old mate.

The interrogation carried on. The guy with the angry voice asking the questions, followed by the whimpering pleas from Street. Which in itself was a good sign, Porter decided. Because it meant the Russians hadn't finished with him. Street was still holding out. He hadn't given all his secrets up.

Not yet.

Charles won't break easily, Tannon had said. *A good agent doesn't forget his training.*

They continued to OP the area. Dividing their attention between the boathouse and the surrounding estate.

Watching.

Waiting.

They didn't have to wait long.

Eleven minutes later, Bald pointed towards the rear of the mansion.

'Movement,' he whispered.

Porter looked across at his two o'clock as a pair of figures emerged from the tall patio doors facing out across the garden. Two guys with shaven heads and jacked physiques. Like twins who'd been raised on human growth hormone instead of breast milk.

'Must be the changeover guards,' Bald said.

The HGH twins strode purposefully down the path towards the boathouse, forty metres to the south of the mansion. As they drew closer, Porter saw that they were kitted out with the same walkie talkies and holstered pistols as the guards patrolling the rampart. They climbed the steps to the first floor, and then one of the twins knocked on the boathouse door.

The screaming stopped.

The door opened.

Two more figures stepped outside.

A younger-looking bloke wearing all black, with a high-and-tight haircut and a face like a rat. Small and thin and pointed.

Next to him was the biggest guy Porter had ever seen. He had the build of a heavyweight brawler, but with about a hundred pounds extra in fat. His legs were like marble columns in a Greek temple, his hands hanging like bags of cement from his meaty arms. His eyes were the only small thing about him. They were narrow and wide, like slashes of a knife across a car tyre, either side of his bulbous nose. He had a gold chain around his neck. Rings gleamed on each of his huge fingers.

The four of them had a mini-reunion on the steps. Words were exchanged. Cigarettes shared around and lit up. Gold Chain and Rat Face looked relieved to be clocking off for the night. They were laughing and grinning broadly, looking forward to catching some rest after several gruelling hours on the job.

They were halfway through their cigarettes when a fifth bloke appeared in the boathouse doorway. Solidly-built, with a beer gut and a shark-fin Mohawk, gripping a cattle prod in his right hand.

Mohawk addressed the HGH twins, gesturing at the mansion with the cattle prod. Porter guessed he was the guy in charge of the interrogation. He spoke in a loud, deep voice that carried clearly across the estate. The mood among the guards shifted. The twins seemed unhappy about something. They made a half-hearted protest to Mohawk, gesticulating at Gold Chain and Rat Face. Mohawk simply shrugged, as if to say, *What can you do?*

The argument went on for a few moments, before the twins finally admitted defeat. They turned away and headed back down the steps, shaking their heads and muttering to one another. Rat

Face and Gold Chain followed after them as the four beat a path back to the mansion.

Mohawk stepped back inside the boathouse.

Porter looked over at Cooper. 'You speak Russian?'

'Some,' Cooper replied hesitantly.

'What's going on?'

'The cattle prod battery's dead. They need a charger. Plus something about supplies. Water, first aid kit, towels. Power tools. The guards are heading back to the house to fetch everything.'

'Why would they need four blokes for that?'

'It's a long list. And two of them are clocking off for the night. The new guys are having to go back and get everything themselves. They're pissed off that someone didn't call them over the net.'

Porter turned his attention to the four guards. They were already moving across the open ground towards the mansion. Gold Chain and Rat Face marching behind the surly twins.

A minute later they reached the patio doors and disappeared inside the mansion. Leaving only one guy on guard duty inside the boathouse.

Mohawk.

This is our chance to get Street, Porter thought. Before the guards come back. He turned to the others. 'This is it,' he whispered. 'Fucking move yourselves.'

He stood up. Stepped out from behind the shadow area of the trees.

So did Bald and Cooper.

Then they hurried towards the boathouse.

FORTY

They broke forward across the open ground.

Porter led the way. Bald to his right, Cooper at his six o'clock, the three of them moving at a brisk jog. There was no need for silence now. They had only a few minutes to act. As long as it would take for the HGH twins to retrieve the supplies from the mansion and return to the boathouse.

On a routine op, Porter and Bald would have stayed behind cover for at least a couple of hours before making their approach. They would have observed the immediate area and the guards' routine, establishing the weakest points and then launching their attack at first light. But there was no time for that now.

They had one chance to rescue Street from his captors.

If they failed, he would die.

Ten metres to the boathouse.

Ten metres to Street.

Bald and Porter scrabbled down the slope leading towards the lakefront, Cooper hurrying after them. Porter wasn't worried about being spotted by Mohawk, or anyone inside the mansion. Artificial light fucked with your natural night vision. Anyone looking outside at the garden, from a well-lit room, would see no further than a few feet away. The guards on the rampart weren't a problem either. Their attention would be focused solely on the ground outside the perimeter. They had orders to search for enemies attempting to enter the estate. Neither of them would be looking for a threat on the inside.

They hit the bottom of the slope, then slowed their stride as they approached the boathouse. The soft grass had masked their footsteps but they would have to exercise greater caution on the final approach. Porter hurried up the steps, keeping the noise of his boots on the treads to a minimum. There was no time to plan a sophisticated attack. It was all about speed now. Suppress Mohawk before he could raise the alarm.

Porter and Bald had their Yarygins stashed down the backs of their trousers. They couldn't risk using their guns to deal with the guard. A discharge would alert everyone else on the estate to their presence. They were going to have to use brute force to take him down instead.

Fifteen seconds had passed since the guards had returned to the mansion. There were plenty of people who would think long and hard before crashing through that door, but Porter wasn't one of them. Neither was Bald.

That's what makes us Blades.

He hit the top of the steps half a metre ahead of Bald. Cooper was lagging further behind, snatching at his breath, struggling to keep up with the others.

The door in front of Porter was wood-panelled, with a brace across the middle and a tiled canopy above. No window or spyhole. No lock either. Just a cast-iron bolt fixed at waist height. Zhirkov had apparently decided there was no need for a heavy-duty lock on his boathouse. Which made sense, from a security perspective. He had a bunch of armed toughs to patrol the grounds of his estate. They were all the deterrent he needed.

Porter yanked the bolt free of the receiver. It made a grating noise as it wrenched free. In the next instant he flung open the door and charged inside the boathouse.

He was light-blinded as he swept into the main room. A rank smell hit him, the putrid stench of shit, blood and piss. Porter squinted, his eyes adjusting to the fluorescent light as Bald rushed in at his six. He found himself in a brightly lit space with a low ceiling supported by timber cross-beams. Lengths of spare cordage and lifejackets hung from iron hooks fixed to the walls. To the left was a table with several knives laid out next to a set of pliers and a soiled rag. Next to the bloodstained tools Porter glimpsed a Motorola walkie talkie and a Makarov pistol.

Tied to a metal-framed chair in the middle of the room was Charles Street.

In the split-second that Porter focused on the ex-spy he saw the guy had been stripped down to his underwear. His hands were bound behind his back. Lengths of rope were tied around his ankles, lashing them to the rusting chair legs. A dark, sticky pool had collected between his bare feet.

Mohawk stood to the right of Street, gripping an iron hook in his right hand. He'd already half-turned towards the door, the sound of it door crashing open drawing his attention away from Street. A look of dumb surprise flashed across Mohawk's face as he saw Porter and Bald bulling towards him from three metres away.

Then he didn't wear any look on his face at all.

Porter lunged at the Russian, closing the distance between them to less than a metre. In the same motion he dropped his right shoulder and body-slammed into Mohawk like a rugby player tackling his opponent. Mohawk let out a gasp of pain as Porter smashed shoulder-first into the guy's solar plexus, driving the air from his lungs. The Russian stumbled backwards, crashing against the table before he fell away.

He grunted as he landed on his back, his spine crunching against the hardwood floor, the hook tumbling out of his stunned grip. Porter landed on top of Mohawk, clamping a hand over the guy's mouth before he could scream for help. Mohawk struggled manically under his opponent's mass, kicking out, rocking from side to side as he tried to throw Porter off. He fumbled for the iron hook but Porter knocked it out of reach before Mohawk could grab it.

'Fucking do him!' he shouted at Bald.

Bald surged forward in a blur and dropped down beside his mucker. Mohawk continued screaming and flailing as Bald grabbed the guy's right collar with his right hand, so that his knuckles were pressing against the side of Mohawk's neck. He reached for the left collar with his left arm, forming an X with his wrists.

Mohawk read his intentions. Realised what Bald was about to do. He let out a full-throated scream.

Then Bald yanked on his collar.

He pulled hard, bringing the guy's left collar across with his left hand, pressing his right knuckles against the right side of Mohawk's neck, compressing the carotid artery. Like a tourniquet being applied to a bullet wound.

A blood choke was quicker to execute than an air choke. Loss of consciousness took seconds, rather than minutes. Porter kept Mohawk pinned down beneath his knees, the Russian's eyes bulged as Bald pulled the sides of his collar tighter, cutting off the blood supply to his brain.

The guy screamed into the fingers Porter still had clasped over his mouth. He kept up the fight for a couple more seconds, until his oxygen-starved brain couldn't function any more. Then the colour drained from his face. His eyes veiled. He went limp.

Bald held the collar tourniquet in place for another few seconds, making sure the guy was out for the count. It took seconds for a blood choke to render a victim unconscious, but it would take minutes to kill him. Time that Bald and Porter simply didn't have. They needed to be in and out of the boathouse as quickly as possible.

'Let's get this fucker secure,' Porter said as he rolled off the Russian.

They worked fast. Bald dug out the set of plastic restraints from his back pocket and clinched them tight around Mohawk's wrists, binding his arms behind his back. At the same time Porter snatched up the filthy rag from the table to the left and stuffed it in the Russian's slack mouth. The guy would be out for at least four or five minutes. More than enough time for them to free Street and bolt out of the mobster's estate.

Bald and Porter turned their attention to Street. Under the harsh overhead lights Porter saw the full extent of his injuries. His chest and face were covered in painful-looking bruises and welts. His arms were blistered where Mohawk had given him a few bumps with the cattle prod. Street's left ear had been hacked off, leaving a knotted gout of cartilage.

'Bastards have done a real number on him,' said Bald.

Porter nodded. But he knew enough about the human body to know Street would survive his injuries. 'Quick. Give us a hand, Jock.'

Both operators set to work. Porter began loosening the rope binding one of Street's ankles to the chair leg. Bald dropped down beside his mucker and tackled the rope tied around his other ankle. Street made a weak groaning sound in his throat. His whole body shuddered with pain. Porter moved on to the rope binding Street's wrists, his hands working fast.

Almost there now.

His mind was turning to their escape plan. Once they had freed Street they'd have to leg it out of the boathouse, then back across the estate. Over the mound, through the pine forest and back to the G-wagon. If they made good time, they could be racing away from the mansion before the guards came back to find Mohawk bound and gagged on the boathouse floor.

Porter was still tackling the rope when he heard a familiar metallic click at his back.

He stopped what he was doing and lifted his gaze from Street. He saw Cooper standing just inside the boathouse doorway, gripping a Makarov semi-automatic pistol.

Aimed directly at Porter.

FORTY-ONE

Porter didn't move.

Bald had turned towards Cooper as well, frozen in mid-turn as he caught sight of the Makarov in his right hand. In his left hand, Cooper held the Motorola walkie talkie Porter had glimpsed earlier on the table, among the torture instruments. A sidelong glance at the table told Porter that both the walkie talkie and the pistol were missing.

Cooper must have grabbed them while we were busy choking the shit out of Mohawk, he realised.

Bald's pistol was still tucked away in the waistband of his jeans. So was Porter's. Out of reach.

'Make a move,' Cooper said, 'either of you, and I'll shoot.'

Bald's jaw muscles tensed. 'The fuck are you doing?'

'Taking you both prisoner.' Porter looked on, anger clawing at the insides of his guts as Cooper depressed the push-to-talk button on the walkie talkie. He jabbered a few words of fluent Russian into the unit. There was a burst of static, before a flurry of barked responses came back over the same channel.

'What the fuck's going on?' Bald demanded angrily.

Cooper smirked. 'Come on. Even someone as thick as you should be able to work that one out.'

'You led us into a fucking trap,' Porter said between gritted teeth. 'You were planning to turn us over to the Russians all along.'

'That wasn't my initial plan. After Charles was taken, I intended to cover up my tracks. The Russians were supposed to help in that regard. They had orders to kill you both. But then you survived and figured out my involvement. That's when I knew I had to leave the country.'

'Why Russia?'

'Why d'you think? I've got contacts here. I speak the language. And the Russians would never agree to extradite me to the West. Not after everything I've done for them over the years.'

'That's why you agreed to take us here,' Porter said, suddenly understanding. 'Why you went along with the plan. You had to get out of the US.'

'You were threatening to kill me. It's not like I had any choice. But once I agreed, I realised I had a golden opportunity to turn you two over. I just had to lure you here without suspecting anything. It's all worked out rather well.'

'We had a fucking deal,' Bald said.

'I'll get a better one here, I expect. Better than anything Vauxhall was offering me. After all, I've not only sabotaged an MI6 operation to rescue Charles, but I've captured two ex-SAS legends into the bargain.'

'You're a dead man.'

Cooper laughed. 'I don't think so. I'm about to become the hero of the hour. You two, on the other hand, are going to be in a world of pain. What they've done to Charles is nothing compared to what they'll do to you.'

Porter stared coldly at Cooper. Outside the boathouse, he could hear several approaching voices, coming from the direction of Zhirkov's mansion, shouting at one another in their native Russian tongue.

The guards.

Porter remembered his gun. He could feel the grip nudging against the base of his spine. He thought about reaching for it. Cooper read the look on his face and said, 'I wouldn't. We both know I'd kill you before you could reach for your weapon.'

'You can't nail us both. One of us would get the drop on you first.'

'Possibly. But the guards will be here any second. I've already alerted them. Even if one of you managed to take me down, you'd never make it out of here alive.'

Cooper's right, Porter admitted bitterly. He felt the anger swelling up inside him, boiling the blood in his veins.

'You won't get away with this,'

'Oh, but I already am.'

The pounding of boots announced the guards' arrival as they bounded up the steps. The HGH twins crashed through the door, brandishing Makarov handguns. Government-issue pistols. The two of them were pumped up with adrenaline and wounded pride, waving around their weapons and shouting at the three Brits.

Rat Face was next inside, shoulders squared to combat. Then Gold Chain. The man-mountain had to crowbar his enormous frame through the door. Further away, Porter could hear more voices carrying across the night as the remaining guards raced around the estate. There were a lot of raised voices, a lot of full-throated responses. Zhirkov's heavies were well drilled. That much was clear.

The twins said something to Cooper. He slowly bent down and placed the Makarov on the floor beside him. Then he stretched upright, raising his hands above his head. Bald and Porter mimicked him.

While the twins kept their weapons pointed at Bald and Porter, Rat Face patted them down. He snatched up their Yarygin pistols, their passports and wallets, plus the two burners. Handed everything except the guns over to Gold Chain. Porter figured he was the senior figure in the room. A lieutenant, maybe. The king of the heavies. Gold Chain casually flicked through their documents while he barked questions at Cooper. The two of them exchanged a few words. Cooper gestured in turn at Mohawk, Porter and Bald. Then he pointed to the Makarov and the walkie talkie. Painting a scene for Gold Chain. Filling in the blanks.

Once Cooper had finished explaining, Gold Chain got back on his walkie talkie. Relaying the agent's version of events to someone based at the house, presumably. The boss, or someone higher up in the organisation, at least. Giving them a blow-by-blow account of what had happened. There was a long back-and-forth that went on for a minute or so. The conversation finished.

Then Gold Chain shouted an order at the other guards.

Whoever was in charge at the house carried some serious authority, Porter decided. Because the Russians sprang into action with the urgency of men who lived in fear of their boss.

Rat Face ushered Cooper towards the door. Cooper strolled confidently outside ahead of the Russian, the walk of a man who was winning at life and knew it. Gold Chain turned to Porter and Bald, still holding their passports. The documents were the size of postage stamps in the Russian's fat hands. He had a dull, bovine face. The muscles on the left side of his face drooped downwards, like a punch-drunk boxer. His forehead was glossy with perspiration. From shifting around all that bulk, probably.

'You bitches are lucky,' he said in thickly accented English. He spoke like he moved, slow and heavy and full of menace.

'Yeah,' Bald said. 'We're fucking blessed.'

Gold Chain didn't seem to get the joke. 'You break in here, you two are usually dead men. We rip off your balls, wrap you in chicken wire, feed you to the fishes. Big laugh.'

He said this matter-of-factly, as if killing was no big deal to him. Like taking out the rubbish, or brushing his teeth. Porter stood rigid, the smell of blood and shit and urine thick in the air, coating his lungs.

'But not today,' Gold Chain went on. 'Today, your lucky day.'

'Why? What's going on?' Porter asked.

'Boss man wants to meet you.'

'Zhirkov?' Porter asked.

Gold Chain's lips parted into a sadistic grin, revealing a set of gold-capped front teeth to go with the chain around his neck. 'You see, bitch. Soon. Now move.'

One of the HGH twins shoved Bald in the back, underscoring the order. Porter and Bald didn't need any more encouragement. The pistols in the twins' bloated grips did all the talking. Either we do as these bastards say, Porter thought, or we're dead.

We might be dead anyway, the other voice in his head said.

Bald and Porter followed the rest of the party out of the boathouse. They trudged down the steps ahead of the twins, following Gold Chain, Rat Face and Cooper as they made their way up the slope leading up to the mansion.

The two guards Porter had seen at the front of the house were racing over to the boathouse. Gold Chain barked at them in Russian. They nodded and ran on, vaulting up the steps before darting inside the boathouse to check on Mohawk and Street.

293

Across the garden, more guards were rushing about in pairs, armed with pistols and torches, searching the shrubbery and outlying buildings. Porter counted half a dozen of them. Plus the four guards at the boathouse.

Ten guys.

He turned to Bald, recalling what Cooper had told them earlier. 'I thought Cooper said the mobster only had four guards on his detail.'

'Aye,' said Bald.

'So where did all these other blokes come from?'

'Fuck knows. But we've got bigger things on our plate right now.'

Porter nodded. *Zhirkov*.

'What do you think he'll do with us?'

'Take a fucking guess.'

'That bad?'

'Worse. The guy's a bloody nutjob. All the other mafia bosses are shit-scared of him.' Bald shook his head. 'He's not gonna be giving either of us a soldier's death, mate.'

Porter felt an icy tingle of dread on his neck as they reached the patio. We're about to meet the most ruthless mobster in Russia, he thought. Right after breaking into his estate and dropping one of his guards.

Jock's right.

This isn't gonna end well.

Two powerfully built guys stood guard in front of the patio doors. They were dressed differently from the mobster's other henchmen. Dark blue suits, crisp white shirts. Corporate grey ties. Earpieces. Zhirkov's inner circle, maybe. His most loyal heavies.

Porter thought again about the big security presence at the mansion. He wondered if someone else had made a threat against the mobster. Either that, or he was really paranoid. Gold Chain said something to the blue-suited heavies. One of them relayed the communication into his mike and stepped aside, making way for Rat Face, Gold Chain and Cooper as they stepped inside the mansion. Bald and Porter followed a few paces behind, with the twins breathing down their necks.

'Keep moving, bitches,' Gold Chain said.

They swept through a wide chandeliered living room. There

was a Steinway grand piano in one corner, images of religious iconography lining the walls. Porter absently noted a coffee table in the middle of the room with a Fabergé egg on display.

Gold Chain led them over to a room off to the right. He stopped in front of the door. Wrenched it open. Turned to the three Brits.

'Inside, assholes.'

Cooper and Rat Face went first. Then Porter and Bald, shoved into the room by the two hormone-enhanced heavies.

They entered a games room with a massive pool table off to one side. Vintage Turkish rug in the middle of the parquet wooden floor. A private bar in one corner, fridge stocked with bottles of Veuve Clicquot. Glass cabinets lined up along one wall of the room, displaying various Soviet-era weapons and bullets.

Porter glanced around. 'Where's Zhirkov?'

'Boss Man on his way,' Gold Chain said, flashing his gold-toothed grin. 'He'll be here soon. You wait.'

He stepped closer to Porter, his vast frame blocking out the light. 'No more questions now. You speak again, I break every bone in your hands.'

The dull look in his knife-slash eyes told Porter he wasn't fucking about. They went quiet as Gold Chain and Rat Face spread out across the games room, while the two walking adverts for steroid abuse stepped back outside, blocking the doorway, cracking their knuckles, posturing like tough guys in an eighties action film.

Several minutes passed. Porter's anger turned to ice in his bowels, his frustration giving way to a cold sense of despair. We're going to die out here, he realised grimly.

After everything we've survived. The battles we've fought together. All of it had been for nothing.

Now the best we can hope for is a bullet to the head.

Footsteps echoed in the hallway. The steroid twins straightened up, as if standing to attention in the presence of royalty. One of them said something to Gold Chain before moving away from the door.

'Boss man is here,' Gold Chain barked. 'Straighten your back. Show some fucking respect.'

A moment later, three figures filed into the room.

The first two guys were guards. Lantern-jawed and stern-faced and decked out in the same suits as the two guys who had been guarding the patio. They had the same earpieces, the same bovine expressions. The same weapon-bulges in their jackets. They took up their stations either side of the door.

Behind them, a third guy strode into the room. He was pale-faced and tall, dressed in a fine dark suit.

Not the mafia boss, thought Porter.

But a face he recognised instantly.

The Russian president.

FORTY-TWO

Viktor Gabulov, the president of Russia, stepped forward from his heavies and glanced briefly around the faces in the room. Porter stood rooted to the spot, fear and shock percolating down into the pit of his stomach as he stared at the president in disbelief.

Gabulov was taller than he had imagined from the news. Six-five, or possibly six-six. He was thin-lipped, with a high forehead and sucked-in cheeks. His skin was stretched so tight across his face you could almost see the veins and tendons beneath. The watch on his left wrist was a Blancpain Villeret. Fifty thousand pounds of Swiss watchmaking expertise, right there. More than Porter had ever earned in a calendar year.

This isn't happening, he thought.

Gabulov looked the two ex-SAS men up and down before he turned to Cooper. Something like recognition flashed in his eyes.

'Terence, my friend,' he said. He spoke English with an American accent, as if he was auditioning for a role as a mafia wise-guy 'This is a surprise, I must admit. I didn't expect to see you returning to your homeland so soon.'

Porter glanced over at Cooper. The guy looked lost for words, his mouth opening and closing in surprise.

'Mr president,' Cooper began, rediscovering the ability to talk. 'It's ... it's an honour ... I wasn't expecting ...'

Gabulov waved him off. 'It's okay, Terence. Tarasov has briefed me.'

He pointed out the lieutenant, Gold Chain.

'But Zhirkov ... I thought he was handling the operation.'

The question seemed to amuse Gabulov. 'Do you really think I'd leave something as important as this, to that fat sack of shit?

Zhirkov's job was to return the prisoner to me. Nothing more. He takes his orders from me. As do these men. As do you.'

'Yes, Mr President.'

Gabulov narrowed his eyes at Cooper. 'But you had no orders to return to Mother Russia yet?'

'I didn't have a choice, Mr President.' Cooper waved a hand at Bald and Porter. 'As I explained to your lieutenant, these men are ex-Special Forces, sent by MI6 to rescue Charles. They forced me to lead them here. They were going to kill me unless I cooperated.'

Gabulov slid his gaze over to Bald and Porter. His eyes were like marks somebody had engraved in a block of wood. 'These are the same pieces of shit who were helping you to find our friend?'

Cooper nodded eagerly. 'They hatched a plan to rescue Charles, after your men took him away. I played along and turned the tables on them as soon as I had the chance. If it hadn't been for me, they would have escaped with Charles.'

'Why didn't you warn us?'

'I tried. But they were keeping a close eye on me all the time, Mr President.'

'You shouldn't have brought them here. You should have stayed in America, Terence. That would have been much better.'

'But I couldn't. Not once these men figured out who I was working for. I had to leave. I thought it best to lead them here and hand them over.'

The president stared at Porter and Bald for a long moment, as if he was calculating something. Then he jerked his chin at Cooper.

'Who else knows these men are here?'

'Just their handlers.'

'No one else? No backup?'

Cooper shook his head. 'MI6 couldn't risk any official involvement. That's why they sent these two to do the job. They're deniable assets. No ties to anyone at Six.'

'I see.'

A faint smile spider-crawled up the side of Gabulov's face. His features relaxed. As if he'd reached a decision. A weight taken off his shoulders.

'You've done well, Terence,' he added. 'Under the circumstances. These two are a welcome gift.'

Cooper bowed slightly. 'Thank you, Mr President.'

'But it's unfortunate that you've decided to end our arrangement. We had big plans for you.'

'End the arrangement?' Cooper repeated.

'You just admitted to me that your cover has been blown. There's no way you can return to your position in America.'

'I can still be of service. I've spent my whole career at Vauxhall. I know all their dirty secrets.'

'Your friend has told us plenty of them already. He's proving very cooperative, as a matter of fact.'

'But I told you about the dossier,' Cooper said. Panic started to creep into his voice. 'Without me, you would never have found out about that stolen nuke.'

The last words ran through Porter like a knife. He glanced at Bald. The same question bit away at both of them.

'What the fuck are you talking about?' Bald snarled, looking from Cooper to Gabulov.

Cooper pressed his lips shut. Gabulov saw the confused looks on the operators' faces and smiled.

'Didn't Terence tell you about the dossier?'

'The sex tape?' Porter said. 'Terry Cooper told us you were gonna use it . . . to blackmail the US president.'

Gabulov chuckled heartily. 'Do you really think I'd go to all this trouble over some footage of that old fool screwing a whore? We're not even sure such a tape exists. My people tell me it's just rumours.'

Porter and Bald looked towards Cooper, both of them wearing the same angry expression. Cooper's face had turned pale, his feet shifting with anxiety. He had the look of a man who'd gambled heavily on black and had lost everything. 'If it's not a tape,' said Porter, 'what's this all about?'

'A mention of a portable nuclear bomb,' Gabulov replied. 'Stolen by one of my sworn enemies.'

The words hit Porter in the stomach like a one-two punch. A sick feeling coiled up inside him and spread through his guts. This whole time we had it wrong, he realised. Porter understood something else now too. Why so many Russians had been involved in the attack on the safe house.

They weren't after a sex tape.

They were after something much bigger than that.

'That's what you've been after all this time?' Bald said. 'Some report of a missing nuke?'

Gabulov's expression darkened. 'Not missing. Taken from me, by those in my country who wish to undermine my authority.'

Porter said, 'But if this stuff about a nuke was in the dossier, why didn't Street say anything about it?'

'Tell them, Terence.'

Cooper swallowed nervously. 'My old friend didn't know what he'd stumbled upon. When he came to see me, Charles was all over the stuff about a sex tape. I would have sent him on his way, but then I spotted the claim about the nuke.'

'What did it say?'

Cooper spoke as if reading from an autocue. 'A Russian criminal had acquired a portable nuke and hidden it at his dacha in the countryside.'

'That's it?' Bald asked. 'That's the whole story?'

'More or less. There were some other claims in there, but Charles said I should dismiss them. Including the report about the bomb.'

'But why would he leave that stuff in the report, if he didn't think it was true?'

'To pad it out, I suspect. Charles is notoriously lazy. Always has been, going back to our days in the service. He didn't take the claim seriously, that's for sure.'

'But you did,' said Porter.

Cooper gave a slight nod. 'Yes.'

'My people have been looking for that nuke for months,' Gabulov cut in. 'Ever since the traitorous fucks in my country stole the weapon from one of our storage facilities. Terence was our British contact. He had orders to keep his ear close to the ground, see if his colleagues at MI6 knew anything about it. We didn't want our enemies finding out that one of our nuclear packages had gone missing. For obvious reasons.'

Bald made a face at Cooper, like someone had pissed in his

300

soup. 'That's why you told Six a pack of lies about a sex tape. To stop them finding out what you were really after.'

'That was part of it, yes.' Cooper's voice was husky with fear. 'But I needed help to find Charles. I had to give Dom a reason to send someone over. So I told them the stuff about a sex tape.'

Porter shook his head. 'But why bother kidnapping Street? He didn't even know about the nuke claim, according to what you just said. He couldn't tell you a fucking thing.'

Gabulov smiled. 'Wrong, my friend. Street knew something very important. Something we had to have. The identities behind everyone he included in the report. Including the criminal with the stolen bomb.'

A memory flashed back at Porter. Something Tannon had told them in London. About Street masking the identities of the people named in the dossier. To protect his sources.

Charles was reluctant to give them up, Tannon had said. *Extremely*.

'That's why you took him here?' he said. 'To find out a name?'

'Not just that. The prisoner has many other secrets we wish to learn. Some of which he has already told us.'

Cooper spread his hands at Gabulov. 'That's why you need me, Mr President. 'Because of my contacts. Without my help, you wouldn't know where to find that bomb.'

'I'm grateful for your help. But that's in the past now.'

The president tipped his head at Gold Chain, aka Tarasov. The mob lieutenant stepped towards Cooper and slid a hand down to his belt holster, reaching for his Makarov.

Cooper's mouth gaped. 'What . . . what are you doing?'

'Terminating our agreement.'

'Christ, no.'

'Mother Russia is grateful for your service, Terence.'

'You can't kill me.'

'I'm the president. I can do whatever the fuck I want.'

Cooper backed away a step from Tarasov as the Russian drew up his gun arm. He looked pleadingly towards Gabulov. Desperation gleamed on the agent's face.

'Don't. Jesus, don't do this. I'm begging—'

Tarasov grinned as he pressed the muzzle against Cooper's

temple and pulled the trigger. A gunshot thunderclapped inside the room.

The side of the agent's head exploded as the 5.45x18mm round ripped through his cranium before punching out the other end. Blood sprayed out of the exit wound in a furious bright-red gush, like popping the cork after shaking a bottle of champagne. Porter felt warm droplets of Cooper's blood splashing against the side of his face. Cooper fell away like someone had just cut his strings. The president smiled in amusement, as if someone had told him an old joke that he still found funny. Tarasov stood over Cooper, grinning at the lifeless heap on the floor.

Then Gabulov snapped an order at the HGH twins in Russian. They barrelled inside the room and padded over to Cooper. Stooped down beside him, took an arm each and dragged him out of the room, leaving a glistening trail of blood on the vintage Turkish rug. The president waited for the twins to leave, then said something to Tarasov. The lieutenant holstered his Makarov, fished out the fake passports from his back pocket and handed them over. Gabulov flipped casually through the pages then passed them to one of his heavies. He looked back at Porter and Bald, his black, pitiless eyes searching their faces.

We're next, thought Porter. They did Cooper. Now they're gonna finish the job. *We're about to get slotted, and there's fuck-all we can do about it.*

'Terence said you're former Special Forces,' Gabulov said. 'Is that true?'

The question threw Porter. It took him a moment to compose himself. 'We used to be in the Regiment, yeah.'

'Regiment?'

'SAS.'

'Now you work for those pieces of shit at MI6?'

'On and off. Here and there.'

'You were stupid to come here alone, with no one else to help you.'

'We didn't have a fucking choice.'

Gabulov nodded at Tarasov. 'My lieutenant tells me you came close to stealing our prisoner. Made a mockery of our defences.'

Porter shrugged. He thought, I'm done talking to this madman.

302

Nothing they could say would make Gabulov change his mind. There was nothing else to do except brace themselves for the pain they were about to suffer.

'If you're gonna kill us, just get it fucking over with.'

A smile formed on the president's thin lips.

'I'm not going to kill you. I'm going to make you both an offer,' he said, his American accent intensifying. Porter had a passing suspicion that he was doing an impression of Marlon Brando in *The Godfather*. 'One you can't refuse.'

'We're not cutting a deal with you.'

'You will . . . if you want to save your friend.'

Porter felt a prick of curiosity. 'What offer?'

'We've been questioning the prisoner for many hours. He's already given up what we needed to know. I know the name of the traitor who stole the package from me. Now I want you to get it back.'

Bald did a double-take. 'The nuke?'

Gabulov nodded. 'You're going to go to that dacha, find that bomb and return it to me. Then I'm going to make my enemies pay.'

FORTY-THREE

The room went dead silent.

Out in the hallway, Porter heard low voices, the slither of Cooper's dead mass being dragged across the polished floor as the twins hauled him outside. Rat Face had left the room to help them. Gold Chain lingered by the door, arms folded across his front, like a bouncer prowling the entrance to an exclusive club. Gabulov stood between Heavy One and Two, watching the two former SAS men.

Waiting for their response.

Bald spoke up at last. 'Why would we help you?'

'Simple. If you refuse, I'll hand you over to Tarasov.' The president nodded at Gold Chain. 'No one is as skilled at torturing people as him. Or as loyal to me. Tarasov once ripped off a man's testicles with his bare hands. He's killed women, children. Hundreds. A few hours in his company, you'll be begging him to put you out of your misery.'

'How do we know you won't just slot us anyway?'

'You can trust me. I always keep my word.'

Porter shot a thirsty glance in the direction of the private bar. Above the fridge with the bottles of Veuve Clicquot his drinker's eye spied a rack of luxury spirits. Remy Martin cognac, Grey Goose vodka. Laphroaig thirty-year-old single malt.

The voice returned.

You need a drink right now, it whispered. *A fucking big one.*

'Why us?' Bald asked.

'Tarasov tells me you two were at the safe house. In America.'

'Aye. That was us.'

'You put up a hard fight back there. Took down some of my best foot soldiers. Then you came here and almost succeeded in stealing the prisoner. That took balls.'

'You're the president. You've got a whole fucking army on speed dial. You don't need us to get the nuke back for you.'

'I don't want to go to my own men,' Gabulov said. 'Not for this mission.'

'Why not?'

'Because the traitor is my brother. Alexei.'

Something like a knife twisted through Porter's guts. He remembered reading somewhere that the president had a younger brother. A mobster who had risen up through the ranks in the Russian prison system, while the president had been doing the same in the KGB. Nobody knew much about him.

'Why would your brother steal a stolen nuke?' he asked.

'Alexei is part of a group of hardliners. Fanatics who see themselves as the last defenders of the Christian world. They're determined to fight a new crusade. A global war to wipe out Islam completely. No survivors.'

'Ambitious,' Bald said. 'But fucking mad.'

Gabulov nodded. 'I tolerated the hardliners at first. It was safer to have them inside the tent pissing out. But lately they've been getting out of control. Working against me, funding my enemies. Spreading lies.'

'What do the hardliners want with a nuke?'

'Revenge,' said the president.

'Against who?'

'The Chechens. The hardliners want to make them suffer. Payback for the recent bombings. They want all-out war.'

A chill slithered snakelike down Porter's back as he recalled the footage he'd seen on the news back home. The suicide bombing at St Petersburg. Thirty-nine dead. The latest in a spate of terrorist attacks, the newsreader had said.

He remembered something else too. The hardliners on the streets of Moscow. Swastika tattoos and shaven heads.

Protesting against the Chechens.

He said, 'That's their plan? They're gonna drop a nuclear bomb on Chechnya?'

'Not there,' Gabulov replied. 'We think they're targeting Moscow.'

'Why would they detonate a nuke in their own back yard?'

'There's a slum to the north of Moscow, on the outskirts of the city. A shanty town. We think that's the target. Thousands of migrant workers live there. Chechens, Tajiks, Uzbeks.'

Bald frowned. 'That's madness. They'll turn every Muslim from here to Baghdad against Russia, if they get away with that.'

'Exactly. We'd all have targets on our backs.'

Porter shook his head. 'If you knew what these nutjobs were planning, why didn't you stop them?'

'It's not that easy. The hardliners have a lot of support in the army. Some of the generals, they're unhappy with my response to the bombings. They don't understand why we're not carpet-bombing the shit out of Grozny. Going against them is risky. Besides, we thought it was just a lot of talk. A general aim. Nothing specific.'

'Until Cooper told you about the document mentioning the Russian criminal with the nuke.'

'I knew he was up to something,' the president admitted. 'But Alexei has overstepped the mark this time. That fucking dog is going to suffer for his treachery.'

His eyes glowed, his hands trembling with rage as he spoke. Porter was left in no doubt as to the hatred that Gabulov felt towards his own brother.

'So put a bullet in his head and take the nuke back,' Bald said. 'Problem solved. What's the big deal?'

'I can't stop Alexei. Not officially. If the hardliners found out I'd ordered the death of my own flesh and blood, it would trigger an all-out war among the rival factions.'

'That's why you need us to grab the nuke?'

'Yes. Whoever stops Alexei has to come from outside my ranks. Completely deniable. It's the only way to prevent a civil war.'

Porter said, 'How did your brother get his hands on the nuke in the first place? It's not as if he could just order the fucker off Amazon.'

'He had help. A co-conspirator. Someone high up in the army. One of the generals, possibly. Someone who was in a position to steal the bomb without drawing attention.'

'They just smuggled it off the base?'

Gabulov said, 'The package was designed to be transported on foot. It could have been concealed in a truck, or in the back of a car.'

'How small are we talking?"

'Small enough to be carried in a backpack. Only one man needed to operate. We built them in the sixties. For use by Spetsnaz soldiers, behind enemy lines. We were going to use them to blow up strategic installations, in the event of a war with the Americans.'

The knife deepened in Porter's guts as he listened. He'd heard of similar weapons during his time in the Regiment. The Americans had rolled out backpack nukes at the height of the Cold War. Mk-54s, stashed inside H-912 military rucksacks. Special Atomic Demolition Munitions, otherwise known as SADMs. The closest thing the Allied governments could get to a suitcase bomb. Mechanical timer, one-kiloton yield. A two-man team would parachute in over enemy territory with the weapon, stash it at a dam or a bridge, arm the timer and then leg it out of the blast radius before it detonated.

Madness.

'Don't you need the codes to work them things?' asked Bald.

'They're stored in the same crates as the devices,' Gabulov explained. 'Whoever smuggled out the bomb also managed to get their hands on the codes. My brother has the complete package.'

Porter said, 'Those backpack nukes are like the world's biggest demolition charges. If that fucker goes off, it'll kill thousands.'

'Our best estimate is five thousand dead in the shanty town. Another fifteen thousand injured in the surrounding neighbourhoods. Most of the city would have to be evacuated.'

'Your brother's out of his fucking mind.'

'Maybe. But he has the tools and the will to succeed. Now you're going to stop him for me, or you're going to suffer a slow and painful death. Both of you.'

Porter glanced down at the bloodstains on the vintage rug and set his teeth on edge. This guy is capable of anything, he thought. Either we do as he says, or we're gonna end up like Cooper.

Or worse.

'If we do this,' he said, 'we want something in return.'

That prompted a mean chuckle from the president. 'You're in no position to negotiate with me.'

'Yeah, we fucking are. You need us. We're the only ones who can stop your brother without it coming back to haunt you. Either you give us something, or you can find some other cunt to do your dirty work.'

Gabulov's eyes narrowed. 'What do you want?'

'The prisoner. We get you the package, you give us Street.'

'That old spy? That's your demand?'

'Have we got a deal or not?'

The president pressed his fingers to his lips as he paused to consider.

'Deal,' he said at last.

'We want him alive,' Porter added.

'Don't worry. We'll return the prisoner without harming another hair on his head, as you English say.'

'Where's the nuke now?'

'Hidden at Alexei's dacha. In a village called Zukotka, to the south of Moscow.'

'What's the deal with security?'

'Minimal. Two or three guards. Token resistance.'

Bald made a face. 'I thought all those mobsters have big fuck-off BG teams.'

'Not Alexei. That piece of shit thinks he's untouchable,' Gabulov replied with a sneer. 'He knows no one would dare make an attempt on the life of the president's brother.'

'How long have we got?' asked Porter. 'Until the attack?'

'Not long,' Gabulov replied. 'We think the attack is going to happen soon. Before daybreak.'

'Based on what?'

'My people have been watching Alexei since we found out he was the traitor. He left for the dacha a short while ago. We think he's gone there to make his final preparations before the attack.'

'You're sure?'

'Alexei doesn't use that house in the summer. He spends his weekdays in his penthouse in the city, with his mistress. Some dancer at the Bolshoi Ballet. Suddenly leaving for the dacha late at night, alone, is strange behaviour.'

'If your brother is already at his country pad, he might launch the attack at any moment,' Bald pointed out.

'It won't happen. Not just yet.'

'How'd you know?'

'Alexei is sending his family and friends away. Out of the country, to Colombia. To protect them. They're booked in on flights to Bogotá. He won't launch the attack until they're airborne.'

'What time's their flight?'

'Five o'clock, tomorrow morning. We think Alexei will launch the attack any time after that. That's why you've got to leave immediately. This is the only chance we have to stop him.'

Porter said, 'How is he going to deliver the bomb?'

'We don't know. We're still trying to figure that out. Our best guess is a truck or van, parked in the basement.'

Bald shook his head. 'Those type of nukes are on a short timer. Whoever activates that package will never make it a mile out of the blast radius before it goes off. It's a suicide mission.'

'Alexei wouldn't kill himself. He's a schemer, not a martyr.'

'He must have some other way of delivering the bomb,' Porter said. 'There's no way you could set that timer and leg it out of the city in time to escape the blast, that's for sure.'

Gabulov said, 'Whatever his plan is, you've got to stop him. If you fail, five thousand deaths would be just the start. Every Chechen would rise up against us. I'd be forced to react. My brother and the hardliners would get their wish. They'd drag us into a long and costly war on our border. Many thousands more would perish.'

'What happens once we get the nuke?'

'You'll return it to my men. Once we have the bomb, I'll give the word for the prisoner to be released. He'll be dropped outside the British embassy twenty-four hours from now.'

'If the job isn't done?'

'Then, your friend will be killed.'

There was a glow in the president's eyes that suggested a limitless capacity for inflicting pain. Porter had seen that look only once before, seventeen years ago, on the face of a child soldier in the remote jungle of Sierra Leone. There were some people you just never wanted to cross. Viktor Gabulov was clearly one of them.

The president straightened up. 'You'll leave at once. Tarasov will brief you on the rest of the details.'

'What about your brother?' Porter asked. 'What do you want us to do with him?'

'We might have to rough him up,' Bald suggested. 'Find out where he's hiding that nuke on his dacha.'

'Torture him if you have to,' Gabulov replied coldly. 'But bring him back to me alive. I want to look that treacherous fuck in the eye. Then he's going to find out the meaning of pain.'

FORTY-FOUR

The president handed the floor to Tarasov. The three-hundred-and-fifty-pound man-mountain with the drooping facial muscles and the gold-capped dentures. He took over the meeting while Gabulov and his heavies filed out of the room, disappearing back down the hallway. Rat Face ducked out of the games room as well, returning several moments later clutching a rolled-up map which he unfurled on top of the pool table. Bald and Porter found themselves looking at a detailed layout of Alexei Gabulov's dacha.

Tarasov struggled to mask his disappointment as he pointed out security features, points of entry, cameras. Maybe the lieutenant is pissed off that he's not going with us on the op, Porter considered. Or maybe he'd just prefer to be torturing the shit out of us. On reflection, he decided the latter was the more likely explanation.

Bald frowned at the map and said, 'What kind of guns are his guards packing?'

'AK-47s,' Tarasov replied in his thick Russian accent. 'All three of them. Nothing else. They aren't expecting trouble.'

Porter said, 'If we're gonna do this, we'll need some weapons of our own. We can't go in there empty-handed.'

'No problem. We give you back your guns when you leave. The Yarygins. Okay?'

Bald pulled a face. Tarasov noticed it too and slanted his tiny black eyes towards him. 'Is there a problem?'

'Aye,' Bald said, 'there is. We're going up against heavies kitted out with assault rifles. We're gonna need more firepower than a couple of fucking pistols.'

'Is not possible. Boss Man says you only use guns you brought with you. Same deal with car. You are two Englishmen on your own, we don't know you.'

'Scottish,' Bald growled. 'I'm Scottish.'

Tarasov shrugged.

Porter thought, No Russian fingerprints. Nothing that could be traced back to President Gabulov or his men. *The only way to prevent a civil war. Completely deniable.* Like the countless ops they'd done for Six over the years.

Except this time, we're working for the enemy.

'This is bollocks,' Bald went on. 'We didn't sign up for this.'

'You have problem, take it up with Boss Man,' Tarasov replied, sounding like the world's most threatening customer service representative. 'He won't change his mind. This is how it's going down. You accept, or you can go feed the fishes.'

Porter took one look at the stone-cold look on the lieutenant's face and knew there was no point arguing their case. 'What's the area around the place like?' he asked.

'Zukotka is rich village. All big businessmen have country dacha there. Lots of private security. You make big noise, someone will call police. Make this job quick. Get in, then get out again. No fucking about.'

Porter said, 'What about the nuke? Where do we take it?'

Tarasov reached down to his jeans pocket, dug out a burner and handed it over. A flip-phone handset, manufactured by a Chinese company Porter had never heard of, pre-dating the burners they'd been given in London by maybe a decade. The kind of handset only ever used by taxi drivers on the subcontinent.

'You find the nuke, you call the number on this phone. We give you address. You take the bomb, bring to the location. Hand over to us. Then you go home, to your shit country.'

Bald said, 'What about Street?'

'Your friend will wait here. We'll keep him company.'

'Not gonna work. You bring him to the RV. We'll make the swap.'

Tarasov shook his head. 'Boss Man gave us instructions. We don't let him go until we have the bomb and the brother. Then we make the call and release him.'

'Fine. But you'd better not lay another fucking finger on him until he's free.'

The Russian smiled pleasantly.

'How long will it take us to get there?' Porter asked.

Tarasov rubbed his jaw with one of his huge hands. His fingers were gnarled and laced with scars. 'Three hours. Maybe less, if you drive like madman.'

Porter checked the time on his G-Shock. 0114 hours. If they left straightaway, they would hit the village at around four-thirty in the morning. According to what the president had told them, Alexei Gabulov was already en route to the dacha, but he wouldn't set off with the nuke until his loved ones were safely in the air and on their way to Colombia. Their flight departed at five o'clock in the morning.

That doesn't leave us a lot of time.

Tarasov reached into his jacket and pulled out a photograph from his breast pocket. 'You'll need this,' he said as he handed the snap to Porter.

Porter studied the picture. It had been taken some years ago, judging by the dated clothes and the bleached colours. The photo showed Gabulov and his brother on a hunting trip. They were kneeling beside a slain bear, smiling for the cameras as they celebrated their kill. Three other figures posed behind them, but their faces had been pixelated beyond recognition. Viktor Gabulov was kneeling to the left of the bear. Alexei was on the right, his face circled with marker pen. He looked shorter and fatter than the future president, with a bushy beard, bright blue eyes and thin, arched eyebrows. In the snap he wore a woodsman's cap and a camo-pattern hunting jacket.

Porter tucked the photo into his jeans pocket.

'One more thing,' Tarasov said.

'What's that?'

'Message from the Boss Man. You try to warn your friends at the embassy, we kill the prisoner. You try to escape, he dies. We find you too. Cut you up real bad. Cut off your noses. Then your ears, toes, fingers. Dicks. We send you to your families, bit by bit.'

The threat hung heavy in the games room, like hanging fruit. Tarasov still wore the same dull, flat expression on his face. A guy like that, thought Porter, he would do anything his boss told him too, no questions asked.

313

'Yeah,' he said. 'We got it.'

They wrapped up the briefing. Then Rat Face was called back into the games room. He swept in carrying the two MP-443 Yarygin pistols he'd taken from them at the boathouse, one in each hand. Tarasov handed over the fake documents belonging to Bald and Porter. Passports, wallets, cards. Porter felt like a convict being released from prison, collecting his valuables from the duty guard.

The wad of roubles had mysteriously disappeared. Which wasn't wholly surprising. The employee benefits of the average Russian henchman weren't great, Porter suspected. The pension plan was probably whatever you could get hold of and stash under your bed.

The two operators tucked away their documents and grabbed their pistols. Porter tucked the flip-phone in his trouser pocket and folded up the map. He cast a final longing look at the spirits behind the bar. More than twenty-four hours had passed since he'd slipped up at the safe house. Now he was in grave danger of getting the shakes – and causing the mission to fail.

He shut out the voice. Followed Tarasov and Bald out of the games room.

They left the mansion through the front door this time. Which looked a lot like the rooms at the back of the house, only with more gold leafing and bigger chandeliers. The G-wagon was waiting for them in the front drive. One of the twins had taken their keys and brought the vehicle round. Like a valet service, minus the friendly smile and the tip. The twin tossed Bald the keys and gave him a fuck-you smile. Porter swung round to the boot, flipped it open and took out the handheld GPS from the gym bag. Then he jumped into the front passenger seat.

At 0121 hours, they drove out through the front gate.

'This is a bad fucking move,' Bald muttered as he steered the G-wagon back down the approach road. 'Working for that mob.'

'We don't have any choice, Jock. You heard what Gabulov said. They would have killed us unless we agreed to the job.'

'They might do anyway.'

'They can't. Gabulov needs us.'

'Right now he does. But once we've delivered him that bomb, it's a different story.'

314

'You don't think the Russians will hold up their end of the deal?'

Bald pursed his lips. 'You don't know them, mate. I do. I've worked with the Russians before. They're slippery bastards. I don't trust any of them further than I can piss.'

'Me neither,' Porter replied, clenching his jaws. 'But our hands are tied. This is the only chance we've got of getting Street back.'

'Let's hope they stick to their word, then. Because when Vauxhall finds out we're doing the president's dirty work, they're gonna hit the roof.'

'We're trying to stop a nuke. They can't have a problem with that.'

'That's not how Six'll see it. They'll say we helped the enemy. Got involved with the Russian mafia. They'll have our heads for this.'

'Not if we give them Street, they won't.'

'Maybe,' Bald conceded. 'But they'll still be mad at us for going against orders. Either way, they won't be giving us a hero's welcome when we get back.'

Porter sighed. 'We can't worry about that now. All we can do is focus on getting hold of that package. If we fail, Six will definitely have our balls for breakfast.'

'If we fuck this one up,' Bald replied, 'Six will be the least of our worries.'

Zukotka was forty miles due south of Moscow, a short hop from the other major airport at Domodedovo. Which meant having to double back on themselves, making the long journey south again, on the same potholed stretch of road that had led them to the mansion, minus the Russian drivers. At one-thirty in the morning, the roads were empty apart from a few long-haul trucks. Bald and Porter had a clear run all the way to Moscow. The first bit of good luck they'd had on the op.

They drove on in absolute darkness past beaten-down fields, black under the huge grey dome of star-pricked sky above. Moon gleaming faintly behind ribbons of steel grey cloud. All around them was the brooding, hollowed-out emptiness of the Russian countryside. Bald pushed the G-wagon as fast as he dared, which was roughly twenty miles an hour faster than they had averaged on the drive up.

After an hour they stopped to refuel at an all-night petrol station, somewhere south of Sergiev Posad. Bald filled up the tank, giving them enough gas to make it to the dacha, plus whatever they would need for the onward journey to the RV with Tarasov. Then they raced on.

Bald kept the G-wagon needle hovering on the eighty per mark. Forty miles later they reached the Moscow ring road. They took the road south, motoring past Elk Island.

Fifty miles from their destination.

0319 hours.

Seventy minutes to the dacha.

This is gonna be fucking close.

Bald said, 'What's the plan once we reach the brother's place?'

Porter said, 'There won't be time to do a proper recce. We'll do a drive-by of the place before it gets light. Size up the defences.'

'It'll have to be a smash-and-grab job. Charge in, grab the package and get the fuck out of there.'

'Unless those Russians bug out before we rock up.'

'They won't, mate.'

'Let's hope you're right. Otherwise, we're in deep shit.'

'Like usual, then,' Bald snorted. 'One thing's for sure, I'm gonna need a drink when this is over.'

You and me both, thought Porter. His left hand was beginning to tremble. Drops of cold sweat formed on his brow. Withdrawal symptoms.

Another couple of hours, and he'd be feeling the shakes big-time. Once the shakes took hold, Porter knew, he'd be useless in a firefight. All he could do was pray that they retrieved the nuke before that happened.

'If we make it out of here alive, I'll be sticking to the orange juice,' he said. 'But I'll get the first round in. Least I can do, after you saved my bacon at the safe house.'

Bald stared at him. 'One pint, for saving your arse? Fuck me. And there I was thinking us Scots are tight-fisted.'

They shared a grim smile. Porter looked at his mucker, at the mate he'd known for longer than anyone, apart from his daughter. They'd survived some crazy shit together. Drug-fuelled rebel ambushes in Sierra Leone. Serbian hit squads. But none of it compared to facing down a Russian mobster armed with a back-pack nuke.

We might be going into the unknown, Porter thought, but I've got a mate by my side. Someone I can trust with my life. Jock's the best bloody soldier I've ever known.

The night sky was already beginning to lighten as they took the next exit off the Moscow ring road. Four o'clock in the morning, at the height of the Russian summer. An hour until dawn. Porter was sweating freely now. Nausea clogged his throat. The wound on his left forearm throbbed. He was exhausted and stressed and he needed a drink.

Just hold on for a little longer. Not long to go now.

They arrowed south to Zukotka, on a downward trajectory through mile upon mile of deserted motorway, flanked by corri-dors of steep pine forest. After twenty-two miles Porter directed Bald to make a right off the main road. They rolled west for three miles, then took the next left.

Twelve minutes later they reached Zukotka.

0417 hours.

The village was basically a road, with about twenty Soviet-era homesteads scattered either side of it. Timber-framed houses built shoulder-to-shoulder on tiny plots of land, the paint on the boards peeled, the sash windows broken or boarded up, the footpaths knotted with overgrown shrubs and weeds. Something that people had aspired to own forty years ago, now reduced to a derelict shack.

'This is where the brother's country home is?' Bald queried as he glanced out of his side window. 'It's not exactly the Four Seasons round here, is it?'

'Keep going,' Porter said.

They carried on for half a mile, until they reached the new part of the village. The old Soviet shacks were replaced by huge new developments set behind granite walls dotted with security cameras at regular intervals. Even the road was better, smooth and recently relaid. A demand by the new residents, perhaps. The new rich had certain expectations. They couldn't be expected to drive their shiny cars down rickety old tracks. So the blacktop had been relaid, probably at significant local expense, to stop the elite from upping sticks.

Money and power, thought Porter.

Same the world over.

Bald followed Porter's directions, making a quick left, then a right. Keeping to an even forty as they continued deeper into the village. Two minutes later, at 0426 hours, Alexei Gabulov's dacha slid into view.

The place was set thirty metres back from the main road, on a parcel of land the size of two football pitches, surrounded by a seven-foot-tall wire mesh fence topped with coils of razor wire. A narrow, rutted track led off the main road to the gated entrance at the front of the property.

'Slow us down,' Porter said.

Bald downshifted, dropping the wagon to ten miles per as they passed the dacha on a drive-by recce. As they crept along Porter buzzed down his side window and strained his eyes in the grainy half-light, scanning the entrance at the far end of the track, fifty metres away.

An iron gate guarded the front of the dacha. Two metres tall, painted black and decorated with ornate symbols, fitted to a pair of metal hanging posts. The style was English country estate. Grand and solid-looking, but not impenetrable. To the left was a wooden gatehouse. A hefty guard prowled the area in front of the gates. He was decked out in a tight-fitting black suit, his chubby hands clasped around an AK-47 assault rifle. The guard lifted his eyes to the wagon as it rolled past, his head cocked.

Fifty metres further back, on a slight incline, Porter glimpsed the dacha itself.

It was humbler than he had expected. A one-storey dwelling, situated north of the main gate, at the far end of a straight drive. The building itself was like something out of a Scandinavian furniture catalogue. Timber-framed and wide, with floor-to-ceiling windows and a roof shaped like a skateboarding halfpipe, flat in the middle, curved upwards at the corners. Security lights covered the open ground to the front and sides of the dacha, making a stealthy approach impossible.

A hundred metres beyond the dwelling, the muddied ground slanted down towards a lake, grey as lead in the pallid light before daybreak. Picturesque on a warm summer's evening, probably. But at four-thirty in the morning it looked cold, bleak and hostile.

There was an outlying shed forty metres behind the dacha, next to an ornate gazebo, white as icing sugar. Both were linked by a footpath to the rear of the main dwelling. Porter knew from the description Tarasov had given them that there was a helipad situated directly to the rear of the dacha, on the shores of the lake.

A Dartz Kombat T-98 sat idle in the carport to the left of the front door. Armoured SUV of choice for the Russian elite. Through the tall windows Porter could see several lights glowing brightly inside the dacha. He thought, There's still time.

We're not too late.

'Someone's home. We're in business.'

Bald said, 'How many guards are we looking at?'

'One on the gate.'

'Carrying?'

'AK-47.'

'Any sign of the others?'

'No.'

Bald chewed on that int for a second. 'Must be inside the gaff. Helping to load the nuke.'

'That's what I'm thinking.'

'Looks like Tarasov was right They're not expecting trouble.'

Porter turned to his mucker. 'What do you reckon?'

'The gate's the weak point. No way we can climb over that fence. We can't sneak inside either. Not with all them security lights. We'd be spotted before we could get near to the building. But if we crash through that gate, we can hit the fuckers hard. Deal with them before they can get their shit together.'

'What about the guard?'

'Run him over. Easy.'

'But the other guards in the dacha will hear us. Soon as we breach the gate. They'll come running out.'

'We could ram the dacha.' Bald grinned. 'Use the wagon as a

battering ram, like. Put a hole in the front of it. Drop the guards, grab the brother and the nuke.'

Porter glanced at the digital clock on the dash as they rolled on past the entrance. 0428 hours. Thirty minutes until Alexei Gabulov's friends and family boarded their flight to Columbia. Porter could feel his heart beating steadily faster now.

Bald said, 'There's no time to OP the shack. We've got to go in now, mate. No fucking choice.'

Jock's right, Porter told himself.

We'll have to go in hard and fast.

The way we were trained in the Regiment.

'Let's do it,' he said.

Bald rolled on past the house for fifty metres. Then he yanked the steering wheel hard to the right and K-turned in the road, so the nose of the G-wagon was pointing east again, facing the dacha entrance.

As they moved slowly forward, Porter reached into the glove box and took out the two MP-443 Yarygins he'd stored there. He tugged back the sliders on both pistols, checking that both weapons had a round of 9x19mm 7NS brass nestled in the chamber.

Eighteen rounds in each clip. A total of thirty-six bullets. To deal with three guards on the BG team, plus whatever firepower the president's younger brother might be packing. It wasn't much. But it would have to be enough.

'Ready?' Bald asked.

Porter nodded at his old friend. 'Let's go,' he said.

Bald steered the Mercedes G-Class east. Back down the main road.

Towards Alexei Gabulov's dacha.

FORTY-FIVE

The first pale glimmer of dawn glowed on the horizon as they approached the dacha. Porter could see the track leading to the front gate, forty metres ahead of the G-Class, to the left of the road. There was a barren field to their right, littered with mounds of rubble and worn car tyres. In the distance, more new-build compounds crowded the horizon. A lot of people were moving to the area, evidently. Muscovites fleeing the city in search of cleaner air and cheaper prices.

As they hit the turn in the road, Porter ran through the plan in his mind. Their attack depended on speed. They would smash through the gate in the wagon, running over the guard. Bullet up the driveway towards the dacha and breach it using the G-Class. Overrun the other guards inside, then seize Alexei Gabulov. Bald and Porter had been given no indication about where he might be hiding the nuke at his dacha, so they'd have to torture that information out of him. Once they had the package, they would bug out, race to the RV. Make the handover, get Street released. Then return to the British embassy on the banks of the Moscow River for the debrief.

If it all went to plan.

Bald steered down the track at a steady clip. Metal signs were staked into the ground either side of the track, carrying stark warnings. White Cyrillic text against bright-red backgrounds. Some of the signs had crosses through them. Porter couldn't speak Russian but the implication was obvious.

Keep out.

They drove on.

Twenty-five metres away, the guard saw the approaching wagon and lumbered forward from the gatehouse. He moved like he was

321

wading through a foot of snow. Every stride was slow and heavy and exaggerated. The guy took up his position a metre in front of the gate, his legs planted wide apart, his right arm thrust out with the palm facing Bald and Porter. Left arm by his side, gripping the AK-47.

An aggressive stance. The guard was putting on a show for the driver of the G-Class rumbling towards him. Staking out his territory. Sending Bald a message.

Stop.

A predictable move. But also a mistake. Because that stance also made him an easy target to hit.

Fifteen metres to the gate now.

Bald slowed down until he was edging along in first gear. A deliberate tactic. He didn't want to alarm the guard. A sudden burst of speed would persuade the guy to jump out of the way, or hoist up his weapon and discharge a burst at the windscreen. But at five miles per hour, Bald wasn't presenting any kind of threat.

Not yet.

The guard in the tight-fitting suit still had his right arm extended. Totally unaware of the pain that was about to come his way. At ten metres, he shouted something at Bald in Russian. A throated, guttural command. A verbal extension of the thing he was doing with his hand. Some sort of threat.

Bald kept going.

The guard in the undersized suit still stood his ground. Presenting himself as a target, dumbly assuming that the wagon would stop.

At seven metres, he realised his mistake.

He brought up his AK-47, training the barrel on the windscreen.

'Floor it!' Porter shouted.

The rifle muzzle sparked as Bald hit the gas. Porter and Bald ducked low in their seats as a four-round burst of hot lead starred the windscreen. Porter didn't see where the shots landed but he heard the cracked-ice shattering of glass, the muffled feathery thump of rounds tearing through the head rests a few inches above them.

Three more rounds punched through the glass, one glancing

off the bonnet. Bald kept the pedal to the floor, the engine roaring as the wagon catapulted forward.

Two metres to the gate now. Through the fractured windscreen Porter glimpsed the guard lowering his rifle before he dived out of the way of the onrushing motor. A last-gasp calculation. He was fast, but not fast enough. The front corner of the G-Class clipped the guard as it bulleted past, sending him into a tailspin and knocking the rifle out of his grip. He landed on his back next to the gate house. In the next instant the front bumper collided with the gate, crashing through it with a furious clanging of broken chains and flying sparks, tearing it free from its hinges. As soon as they were through Bald hit the brakes, the G-wagon lurching as it skidded to a halt a couple of metres beyond the shattered gate. In his side mirror Porter could see the guard writhing on the ground, the AK-47 just out of his reach.

'Fucking do him, mate!' yelled Bald.

Porter sprang the door handle and slid out from his seat, thumbing the safety on his Yarygin down to the Fire position. He jumped down and whipped round to his right. The guard was three metres back from the wagon, next to the busted gates. He looked up, caught sight of Porter charging towards him and thrust an arm out, reaching for the assault rifle he'd dropped.

Porter was on the guy in a flash, sidefooting the weapon away before he could snatch it up. Then he dropped low and gave the guard the double-tap special to the back of the head. His body made a death-spasm before he stilled. Then Porter grabbed the AK-47 and pounded back across the ground to the G-Class. Bald was already gunning the engine as Porter hurled himself into the front seat.

'GO! FUCKING GO!'

The wagon roared as they tore down the front drive. Fifty metres of brightly lit blacktop stretched out ahead of them. At the end of the drive stood the dacha, the entrance lit up by a bank of security lights. Carport to the immediate left of the dwelling. Shed and gazebo forty metres further back from the carport, ninety metres from Bald and Porter. No signs of activity at either structure.

Eighty metres beyond the main building stood the leaden grey lake, flat and wide. Dense forests of pine and other conifers extended along both sides of the shore, like black arms hugging the water. The lights were still glowing inside the dacha, Porter saw Which meant the Russians were somewhere inside.

That's where Alexei and his heavies must be, he told himself. That's where we're going to make our attack.

The G-Class picked up speed as Bald accelerated towards the dacha. The enemy would have heard the gunshots at the front gate by now, Porter reasoned. They were probably grabbing their weapons at that very moment, rushing to the front door to deal with the intruders.

We've got only a few seconds left to breach the dacha, he thought. Stun the Russians and brass them up before they can put the drop on us.

Thirty metres to the dacha.

Twenty metres.

Ten.

This is it now.

No going back. We're committed.

Porter braced himself as the wagon smashed into the front of the dacha like a motorised battering ram. The G-Class must have weighed over two thousand kilograms and it bulldozed into the front of the wooden dwelling with a tremendous crashing noise, tearing the door off its hinges. Porter heard the timber cladding splitting, the shatter of the headlamps as the wagon ploughed into the main room. Debris rained down on the bonnet from the roof, a pitter-patter of loose tiles and torn metal and broken glass. Bald shifted into Reverse, dragging the wagon back from the damaged wall. In the same movement Porter burst out of the vehicle, raising his AK-47 as he bulled through the hole into the smoke-filled space inside, sweeping the rifle's s iron sights from left to right in a broad arc as he scanned for his first target.

Porter found himself in a living room eight metres wide by six deep, with wood-panelled walls and a beige corner sofa next to a couple of bucket chairs. Flat-screen TV the size of a cinema screen fixed to the wall. Wide corridor at the far end leading past several rooms towards the kitchen at the rear of the dwelling, fifteen metres away.

No sign of the guards.

Or the brother.

Bald was hurrying forward from the wagon, armed with the other Yarygin. He stormed through the gap between the G-Class and the hole in the front of the dacha, scanning the area to the left of the breach.

Nothing.

'Room clear,' Bald said.

'Shit,' Porter said.

Where's the nuke?

And the brother? They tore across the living room and moved quickly down the corridor, clearing the rooms either side. Like they'd done countless times before in the Regiment, in training exercises at the Killing House down in Pontrilas. Bald going first, sweeping to the left. Porter hard on his heels, clearing the right-hand side of the entry point, shouting when the room had been cleared. Working as a team. They tackled the bathroom first, then the two smaller guest bedrooms. Moved further down the corridor and checked the master bedroom too. All the rooms were decorated with the same modernist furniture and colourful fabrics. Like sweeping through an IKEA showroom.

The rooms were empty. But also chaotic. Chests of drawers in the guest bedrooms had been pulled open. Bundles of clothes taken from the master bedroom closet and dumped on the bed. The bathroom cabinets had been cleaned out. As if someone had left in a hurry.

The last room on the left was the study.

Bald went first. Then Porter.

He took a step inside and twisted to the right. Saw something in the corner of the room, beside the floor-length curtains. A large safe, built into the floor. The patterned rug covering it had been rolled back and the safe door was open. The contents had been removed, Porter noticed. Another safe fitted to the wall above the study desk had also been cleared out.

Bald glanced briefly at the emptied safes, then spun towards Porter. 'Where the fuck is everyone?'

Porter didn't answer. He swung back out of the study and carried on towards the kitchen at the rear of the dacha, dread tightening in his stomach.

Maybe we're too late, he thought.

Maybe Gabulov and his heavies have already got away.

Then he caught sight of the back door.

The door was on the left side of the kitchen, next to the old gas stove. It was hanging open. Through the gap, Porter glimpsed the grounds at the rear of the dacha.

As he drew near a distant whining noise reached his ears. It was swiftly followed by a dull, incessant thrumming. A sound Porter recognised at once.

The relentless *whump-whump* of helicopter blades turning.

FORTY-SIX

Porter ran over to the kitchen door, his heart hammering madly inside his chest. Bald sprinted after him as Porter charged through the open doorway, looking out across the open stretch of ground between the dacha and the wide grey lake a hundred metres to the north. Security lights dotted around the estate illuminated the land. Like floodlights on a football pitch.

Then Porter saw it.

An Ansat light helicopter, black with white stripes down the side of the fuselage, parked on a helipad, eighty metres beyond the kitchen door. The four blades on the main rotor were spinning as the engine droned. The heli was turning and burning, preparing for take-off.

A figure was running towards the chopper from the direction of the dacha, seventy metres ahead of Bald and Porter, decked out in the same type of dark, ill-fitting suit as the guard on the front gate. He had a black duffel bag slung over his shoulder, weighing him down as he sprinted the last few paces to the heli.

Two more figures had almost reached the Ansat, Porter saw. They were bolting over from the garden shed fifteen metres due west of the helipad. The pair of them were two metres from the heli now. Another guard in a black suit, shaven-headed. And a third guy, short and squat, with a thick beard, wearing a hunting jacket and a woodsman's cap. At a distance, he looked like a smaller, fatter version of the Russian president.

Alexei Gabulov.

The guard racing alongside Gabulov was also carrying something on his back, Porter noticed. A military-green rucksack, with some sort of bulky cylindrical object stuffed inside it.

The nuke.

So that's where he's been hiding the bomb.

In his garden shed.

There was no time to put the drop on them. Gabulov and the guard at his side reached the Ansat before Porter could line up a shot with the AK-47. A moment later the guard with the duffel bag joined them. He dumped the bag on the floor between their legs and climbed into the main compartment alongside the other two.

Is there another nuke in that thing? Porter asked himself.

Has the president's brother got two bombs, instead of one?

The cabin door on the side of the Ansat slid shut. The main rotor blades began turning faster and faster.

'Shit,' Bald said. 'Fuckers are getting away.'

Several thoughts flashed through Porter's head at once. His professional eye told him there was no way they could stop the Ansat from lifting off from where they were positioned. Not with the weapons they had to hand. Several well-aimed bursts into the engine block from a heavy machine gun might do the trick. But a nine-milli pistol and an AK-47 weren't going to do any serious damage to the machinery. Not at this distance.

There was only one way they could stop the heli.

One chance to stop the enemy from escaping.

Porter spun away from the Ansat.

'Get to the wagon!' he shouted. 'On me.'

'Why?' Bald said. 'What's the plan?'

'There's no time. Move!'

Porter spun around and darted back through the kitchen door, scrambling back down the corridor. He was thinking clearly now. The booze shakes had gone. So had the voice in his head, replaced by a cool, focused determination to stop Alexei Gabulov from succeeding in his plan.

The stopwatch in Porter's head ticked away as he raced towards the front of the dacha. A light chopper, cocked and ready to fly, would take about sixty seconds from firing up the engine to skids in the air. Which didn't give them much time to implement his plan.

We've got to stop them, Porter told himself.

It ends here.

I'm not gonna let these bastards win.

He bolted through the breach hole a metre ahead of Bald. The front end of the G-Class had suffered some heavy damage from the impact. The bonnet was buckled and bent out of shape and smoke was gushing out of the grille. Cracks starred the windshield, like bullet holes. But the vehicle would be looking a hell of a lot worse shortly, if his plan worked.

Porter leapt behind the steering wheel and dumped the AK-47 on the dash. He turned the ignition key as Bald dived into the front passenger seat alongside him.

'The fuck are you doing?' he said, catching his breath. 'They're getting away!'

'Hold on, mate,' Porter replied. 'It's gonna get bumpy.'

He shifted the gear lever into Reverse and hit the gas. Debris skidded off the bonnet as the wagon dragged itself clear of the wreckage at the front of the dacha. When they were four metres clear of the breach point Porter threw the wheel hard to the right then hit the brakes, bringing the vehicle to a halt at an angle, with the front end pointing towards the carport. Then he upshifted and accelerated, crunching through the gears as he sped towards the rough ground to the west of the dacha.

Forty seconds since the pilot had fired up the Ansat.

Twenty seconds before lift-off.

The wagon rocked and lurched as Porter steered off the smooth blacktop of the drive, onto the bumpy ground beyond. As soon as they'd sped past the western edge of the carport Porter threw another hard right, making a wide turn around the side of the dacha. The wagon shuddered as it slewed round the corner. Porter wrestled with the wheel, won a hard-fought victory, then straightened out so that they were bulleting past the western side of the dacha, heading north. Towards the grounds at the rear of the country house, the garden shed and the brilliant white gazebo.

Towards the helipad.

Fifteen seconds to go.

The chopper was sixty metres ahead of them, rotor blades whirlwinding. The engine thrum was deafening.

Realisation flickered across Bald's face as he grasped the plan. He glanced at Porter. 'Jesus. You're fucking mad.'

Maybe I am, thought Porter. *But sometimes, the maddest bastard wins.*

'Grab the AK,' he said. 'When I give the signal, you jump out and get ready to brass them guards up.'

'You're gonna get yourself killed.'

'Just do as I say.'

Bald shut his mouth. Porter gripped the wheel tightly as they hurtled towards their target. He thought about the backpack nuke. About a bomb with a one-kiloton yield being detonated over a densely populated city. *Tens of thousands of casualties*. Not enough to destroy Moscow. But sufficiently powerful to reduce an entire neighbourhood to rubble and ash.

There would be enforced evacuations, to mitigate against radioactive fallout. Widespread terror. One of the biggest cities in the world, turned into a ghost town.

If this works, we're heroes.

If we fail, it's a fucking global disaster.

They were twenty metres from the Ansat now. The heli engine reached a high-pitched crescendo. Another ten seconds until it took off. The skids were already beginning to leave the ground. Porter fought to keep the wagon on target as he bore down on the heli at a frightening speed. Through the main compartment window he glimpsed Alexei Gabulov, screaming at the pilot in the cockpit.

'NOW!' Porter bellowed.

Bald tugged open the side door and scooped up the rifle resting on the dash. Then he threw himself out of the vehicle, rolling on to the ground twelve metres from the heli. Porter jerked the wheel, the open wagon door swinging back and forth like a pinball flipper as he adjusted course, aiming straight for the tail rotor fixed next to the fin. The most vulnerable part of any bird.

Porter braced his legs in the footwell as the G-wagon rammed into the back of the chopper. The rear rotor blades exploded as they struck the bonnet. They made a real mess of the front end of the wagon, grinding up the crumpled metal, striking against the radiator. Porter heard the hiss of steam inside the engine, the clang of the front wings as they struck against a section of the heli tail boom. Torn metal shrieked. The windscreen, already starred with bullet holes, fractured in a million places. Porter crouched low, keeping his head below the dash as the tail blades ground down the front end of the vehicle.

The Ansat engine groaned under the strain. Like a wounded beast. The fuselage shook violently. Without the counterbalancing torque of the tail rotor, the heli became an unstable platform, pitching and rolling as the pilot struggled to maintain control. Then he lost, and the chopper canted sharply to the left. The four main rotor blades pivoted down at an angle, slicing through the roof of the G-wagon, shredding it, peeling it back like a lid on a can of peaches. The front and rear windscreens exploded. Porter ducked lower as he felt the powerful downward pressure from the blades cutting through the air above.

There was a jarring shudder as the rotor mast came loose. The airfoils struck against the hard ground and sheared off, throwing up clumps of dirt and fragments of rotor blade. Then the Ansat pitched, rocking from side to side. A terrible screaming noise pierced the air as the main engine shaft shattered. The heli bounced up and down once, breaking apart the landing skids located beneath the fuselage. The chopper briefly threatened to topple before it came to a rest on its side, with the broken stumps of the four blades propping it up.

Porter looked back and spied Bald twelve metres behind the heli, just beyond the semi-circle of blade-churned turf. With the blades slowing to a rest Bald was moving forwards, gripping the AK-47 as he approached the stricken heli.

The thud of a door reached Porter's ears, snapping his attention back to the Ansat. On the opposite side of the heli from the G-wagon he spied the pilot jettisoning out of the cockpit. The guy sprinted away from the chopper, making a run for the forest at the edge of the dacha.

A second later the door on the main compartment sucked open.

The engine crank continued to scream as one of the bodyguards staggered out of the cabin, blood streaming from a wound to his scalp. The guy with the shaven head. He was following the basic human instinct for anyone sitting in a wrecked piece of machinery, surrounded by highly flammable fuel. *Get the fuck out of there.*

Bald was ten metres away from the Ansat now. Weapon raised.

Shaven Head didn't appear to spot him. Not at first. The guy's

331

senses were overloaded with fear, Porter guessed. His eardrums would be splitting from the terrifying shriek of the engine, he would be disorientated after being thrown about inside the heli. He wasn't thinking about anything beyond the next three seconds. The bodyguard didn't know or care about what might be waiting for him on the other side of the cabin door. He just wanted to get the hell away from the heli.

He stepped outside, looked up. Saw Bald nine metres away, his index finger clinching the AK-47 trigger. The bodyguard reached down for his holstered pistol. Never got there.

Bald fired a three-round burst. The muzzle flash lit up the churned-up soil and shattered rotor blades. The rounds struck the shaven-headed bodyguard in the chest region in a close grouping, giving him a trio of bullet holes to go with the head injury. Open-heart surgery, Regiment-style. He gargled a death note as he fell away.

Through the window, Porter glimpsed the remaining body-guard wrenching open the main cabin door on the other side of the heli. Alexei Gabulov was in his seat, grappling with his safety belt.

They're not getting away. Not this time.

Porter sprang open his driver's side door and jumped down to the ground, gripping his MP-443 Yarygin. The engine shriek died down to a rattling whine as he circled around the tail of the Ansat, racing towards the cabin door on the side of the chopper facing away from the G-wagon. Porter glanced across to his left and saw Bald six metres further back, hurrying after him.

Porter faced forward and increased his stride. He knew what the Russians were thinking. They would have seen the other bodyguard getting dropped and instinctively decided to try their luck by escaping through the other exit. But it wasn't going to save them.

Not today. As Porter swung around the rear of the chopper he glimpsed the pilot at his three o'clock, thirty metres into the distance and counting. Running towards the forest. Not a tactical withdrawal. A desperate retreat. He wasn't any kind of threat. Porter ignored him and trained the Yarygin's rear sights on the cabin door.

The door had been wrenched open. The remaining bodyguard had emerged from the heli. The guy who had been lugging the backpack nuke. He had his back to Porter as he reached into the cabin, helping Alexei Gabulov out of his seat.

The guy must have glimpsed Porter's movement at his nine o'clock. Because he instantly dropped his hands and turned away from the cabin door, whipping round to face the operator standing next to the knackered tail, six metres away.

Just in time to see his killer's face.

Porter fired twice. The first round smashed into the bodyguard's leg just above the shin, shattering his kneecap. The second landed about two feet higher, clipping him in the midriff and doing all kinds of damage to his internal organs. He gasped and melted to the ground. Porter raced over and gave him a tap to the head, just to make sure.

Bald swung into view round the back of the heli a beat later. Shouting at Porter at the top of his voice as he ran over.

'The brother! Get the bastard! Get him out of there!'

Porter rushed forwards, sprinting over to the cabin door ahead of his mucker. The door was tilted slightly from where the chopper had come to a rest. He clambered up, scanning the interior.

Alexei Gabulov was slumped in one of the rear-facing seats in the main compartment, struggling with his seat buckle. The military rucksack and the black duffel bag squatted by his feet, along with a smaller grey backpack. Some sort of emergency go-bag, Porter guessed.

Gabulov looked up. He saw the gun in Porter's hand. Saw the two dead BGs on the ground either side of the wrecked helicopter, and quickly formed a decision.

The president's brother threw up his hands.

'Don't shoot!' he cried.

FORTY-SEVEN

Porter stared at Alexei Gabulov for a long beat. Up close, the guy in the grounded heli looked different from the picture Tarasov had shown them. His face had filled out and was pitted around the cheeks. From too much drinking or too little exercise, or some combination of both. His arched eyebrows were bushy and wild. His beard was now tinged with grey hairs. About the only thing the Gabulov brothers had in common was their taste in luxury watches. Alexei wore a gold-cased Richard Mille watch, visible on his left wrist.

'Please,' he said, keeping his hands raised. 'I surrender.'

Bald had caught up with his mucker and peered into the cabin. 'How the fuck does he know we're English?'

'I heard you,' Alexei Gabulov replied in a wobbly voice. 'Just now. Talking outside.'

The Ansat engine stopped whining and finally gave up. Porter lowered his pistol, stuffed it down the back of his trousers and grabbed hold of the younger Gabulov by his hunter's jacket. The mobster grunted in pain as Porter hauled him out of the helicopter cabin and turfed him onto the ground next to the slotted BGs. Alexei Gabulov fell forward, landed on his hands and knees, then scrabbled away from the corpses of the bodyguards. Like getting shot in the head was infectious. Something he could catch.

'Watch this prick,' Porter said, cocking his head at Bald. 'I'll fetch the package.'

'Better hurry it up, mate. The neighbours will have woken up by now. We'll have company soon enough.'

Porter hurried back over to the heli cabin, leaving Bald to keep watch over Alexei Gabulov, his gun trained at a spot between the guy's small, black eyes.

He went for the military rucksack first. The backpack nuke. It was nestled between the black duffel bag and the go-bag. At first sight, it looked almost identical to the Mk-54 SADMs the Yanks had developed. A metal housing container shaped like a forty-gallon drum, encased inside a rugged green canvas, secured with various ropes and padding, with a battery pack strapped to the side of the canvas, connected to the main unit by a series of wires. Porter grabbed the nuke by the straps, hefting it up. Carefully. He was sure the containers had been designed to absorb the occasional bang, but he didn't want to accidentally set the bastard off.

The bomb was heavy. Thirty kilograms or so. Ten kilos more than the Bergen that SAS candidates were required to carry during Selection. Portable, but only just. Anyone less than supremely fit would struggle under the weight of it. Not the sort of thing you wanted to lug around a battlefield for any length of time.

Porter set the rucksack down next to the chopper.

Which is when he heard the ticking noise.

He glanced down at the nuke. There were several switches and knobs on the lid of the metal casing, connecting it to a firing unit. Some sort of code-decode lock, requiring a complicated sequence to initiate. The kind of thing you needed a manual for. A very old setup, from another era. From a time when Amstrad computers were state-of-the-art, and everybody expected the world to end in a nuclear apocalypse.

Next to the switches was a mechanical timer. A cream-coloured dial, notched with a black marker and encircled by a series of points numbered from zero to sixty. Like minutes on a clock face. The dial had been twisted clockwise, Porter noticed. To the thirty-minute mark. There was a red light next to the dial, flashing repeatedly. Below the light was a single word in Russian, but Porter didn't need Google Translate to tell him what the word meant.

Armed.

Bald looked over at his mucker. 'What is it?'

Porter didn't respond at first. He stared down at the timer as it continued to make its soft rhythmic tick. A sick feeling brewed inside his chest.

'This fucking thing is on a timer,' he said after a beat.

Bald frowned but stayed next to Alexei Gabulov, keeping his weapon pointed at the Russian. 'Why the fuck would he activate the nuke before taking off?'

Porter glanced at the chopper. Then back at the nuke. Several dots connected inside his head.

'The heli was the delivery system,' he said. 'He was gonna set the timer, get vertical, then drop the nuke somewhere over the city. Then clear off before it detonated.'

Which made several kinds of sense. Kicking out the bomb over a built-up neighbourhood was a more effective delivery system than a truck or a panel van. The guys in the heli could drop the package on the rooftop of a house or tower block, hit the throttle and get away. If they timed it right, they stood a reasonable chance of clearing the blast radius. Better than by delivering the package on foot, at least, with the added potential risk of being slowed down by traffic and crowds. Any witnesses on the ground would be incinerated in the land burst.

Five thousand dead.

Revenge.

'What's the timer on that thing say?' asked Bald.

'Twenty-nine minutes.'

'Shit.'

The timer continued ticking.

'Check the other bag,' Bald added. 'We need to know how many of these things we're dealing with.'

Porter ducked back inside the cabin and retrieved the duffel bag. The one they'd seen the bodyguard carrying across from the dacha. It felt even heavier than the backpack nuke. He struggled to lug it out of the chopper.

The bag jangled as Porter set it down next to the military rucksack. He pulled back the zipper, moving fast, fighting to ignore the anxious thumping inside his chest. Every second they wasted at the dacha meant less time to get away from the resulting blast.

Something gleamed dully inside the duffel bag.

Not another nuke. But something else entirely.

Gold bullion bars.

Each one was the size of a brick, stamped with the logo of the Swiss Bank Corporation, with a serial number at the top and the metal purity percentage at the bottom. Each brick weighed one kilo. A market value of thirty-five thousand pounds per bar. Porter figured there had to be at least thirty bars stuffed inside the bag. Maybe more.

'Gabulov's getaway funds,' he said.

'Jesus. That's what he must have had stashed in them safes.'

Porter spun away from the bag of bullion. They had more important things to be dealing with. Namely, the one-kiloton nuke on a timer delay, two feet away from them. He marched over to Alexei Gabulov, hauled the Russian to his feet and shoved the pistol muzzle against his cheek.

'How do we stop that thing from going off?' he demanded. 'Tell us, or I'll put a fucking hole in your head.'

Alexei Gabulov sneered. 'You think that's the first time someone's put a gun in my face? You don't know shit.'

'We know more than you think. We know you were gonna drop that nuke over a slum. Kill thousands of Chechens.'

Gabulov's expression tightened. His eyes shrank to pin-pricks.

'Viktor sent you? I should have known. That little bitch was never loyal to his motherland. He doesn't know the meaning of the word. The only loyalty he ever had was to his wallet.'

'You've lost,' Porter said. 'It's over.'

'I don't think so. Zukotka is home to a lot of oligarchs. Friends of my brother. They die, Viktor will take the blame. My people will put out a story that the Chechens planted a bomb at my house. Viktor will be forced to act. Take action against the Muslim filth polluting our great country. Bomb Chechnya to shit. We'll still win.'

A surge of hot rage swept up inside Porter just then. Alexei Gabulov was right. If the bomb detonated anywhere close to a civilian population, it would cause mass casualties.

We'd lose. Street would die.

'I don't know who you are,' Gabulov went on in heavily-accented English. 'But I can make you an offer. A more generous one than my brother has made to you both.'

'The fuck are you talking about?'

The Russian tipped his head at the bullion bag. 'There's a million in gold bars in that bag. Half of it is yours. Two hundred and fifty thousand each, if you take me across the border, to my friends in Minsk.'

'I've got a better idea. I'll make *you* an offer. Tell us how to deactivate this fucker, or we'll beat the shit out of you.'

'No fucking way.'

'Tell us!' Porter thundered.

That merely drew a demented laugh from Alexei Gabulov. 'You think you can scare me, with your pathetic threats? I'm not afraid of you, or my brother. Those Chechen pigs are going to suffer for what they've done. I'd rather die than give up that code.'

He stared evenly at Porter. The president's brother had the cold, calm look of a madman. There was no inner torment going on there. No hint of self-doubt or questioning of actions. Just complete conviction in the righteousness of his own twisted beliefs.

'We don't have time for this, mate,' Bald muttered.

Porter held the MP-443 Yarygin against the Russian's cheek for a beat. Then he lowered his gun.

'What are we gonna do?' he said, turning to Bald.

'We can't leave the nuke here. This nutter's right. It'll level the area. We'd be looking at hundreds of dead. Thousands, maybe.'

'We could load it up in the wagon. Drive it somewhere.'

'But where? There's towns and villages in every direction.'

Bald had a point, Porter acknowledged bitterly. The heli was fucked. Without the rear rotor blades there was no way that thing could take off. Which meant they would have to transport the bomb by car. They were in the Moscow suburbs. A twenty-minute drive to the west or south would only take them as far as the next major towns. East of the village was the international airport at Domodedovo. North was the city centre.

'Even if we did find somewhere out in the sticks,' Bald went on, 'we wouldn't have enough time to dump the package and bug out. We'd get caught in the blast.'

Porter looked around the dacha in frustration. 'There must be something we can do. There has to be.'

338

Bald didn't reply. He wasn't looking at Porter. He was gazing out across the lake, twenty metres to the north of the helipad. It looked huge. As big as the North Sea. Down by the lakefront, a wooden jetty extended out a short distance across the lake. At the far end of the jetty a sleek wooden motor boat was tethered by a line to a stout mooring post.

'One of us is gonna have to drop the nuke in there,' Bald said, pointing to the motor boat. 'Take it out in that craft and dump it in the middle of the lake.'

'Would that work?'

'If it's deep enough, aye.'

Porter stared out across the water. A lake that big could be deep enough. At its deepest point, it might contain the explosion. Or at least enough of it to reduce the bomb's impact. The lake itself would become a radioactive soup, and the immediate surrounding area might sustain some heavy damage from the initial blast. Some of the houses nearby would get soaked in radiated water, inevitably. But significant loss of life would be avoided. It was the least-worst option.

A handful of deaths, instead of five thousand.

Porter said, 'Whoever goes out on that boat won't have much time to get themselves clear, once they've tossed the nuke overboard.'

Silence fell between the two operators. Like snow.

In the corner of his eye, Porter noticed Bald glancing down at the duffel bag beside the backpack bomb.

The timer continued to tick.

'I'll go,' said Bald.

Porter stared at him in disbelief. 'You can't.'

'Somebody has to.'

'It's a bloody suicide mission.'

'It's the only way of isolating the blast,' Bald countered. 'Either one of us dumps that bomb in the lake, or this area's going up in smoke. It'll make Chernobyl look like a fairy tale.'

'I'm not leaving you here with a fucking nuke, Jock.'

'There's no choice, mate. You need to take this wanker to the RV.' He gestured at Alexei Gabulov. 'Hand him over before the Russians execute Street.'

Porter couldn't believe what he was hearing. He looked from the rucksack to the lake, then back again, frantically racking his brains. 'There has to be some other way.'

'There isn't.'

'At least let us give you a hand loading that thing. It'll be quicker if there's two of us.'

'There's no time, mate. You've got to get out of here now. Put some serious distance between yourself and the blast site. If this thing goes wrong, you want to be well clear of this place.'

Porter tried to think of something to say. Some argument or plan that would dissuade his mucker from what he was about to do. But he couldn't think of anything. Bald was right. They had to dispose of the nuke. The lake was their best and only bet.

Twenty-five minutes.

At the back of his mind he thought, Bald's the last person I'd expect to sacrifice himself for others. It's just not his fucking style.

'You sure about this?' he asked quietly.

'We don't have a choice,' Bald replied. 'It's the only way of stopping this thing. Now get moving.'

There were no handshakes or big speeches. Nothing that needed to be said between them. Just a brief nod of respect from one old Regiment man to another.

Then Porter turned away from his mucker. Bald kept an eye on Alexei Gabulov while Porter patted him down. He found what he was looking for in the side pocket of the Russian's combats. The keys to the Kombat T-98 parked in the front drive. The SUV would be their best bet as a getaway vehicle. Marginally less conspicuous than the trashed wagon they'd just ploughed into the chopper.

Porter dug out the spare pair of plasticuffs he'd been carrying. The second of the two sets they'd been given, when they collected the G–Class from their contact at the airport. Less than nine hours ago, but it felt more like a month.

He bound Alexei Gabulov's wrists together behind his back, making sure the plasticuffs were pulled tight. Then he grabbed the guy by the arm and set off at a brisk pace, heading for the carport at the front of the dacha. Away from the dead BGs and the wrecked Ansat heli, and the nuclear bomb stuffed inside the rucksack.

'You're making a fucking big mistake,' Alexei Gabulov rasped. 'You do this, you're only going to help those Chechen dogs. Take my offer. Put yourself on the right side of history.'

Porter said nothing.

'I have friends in Minsk. Patriots. They can get you whatever you want. Money. Women. Boys. You name it, it's yours. Just get me across that border. You'll be rewarded.'

Porter still said nothing.

He blanked out Gabulov as he glanced over his shoulder. He saw Bald sixty metres back, hefting up the backpack nuke. The guy had slipped his arms through the straps, shouldering it like an army Bergen. Bald stood on the spot for a moment, adjusting the clips and straps, checking to make sure it was securely fastened to his back.

Then he set off towards the jetty.

Porter watched him for a moment. Then he turned and carried on towards the dacha. Alexei Gabulov was still protesting, issuing threats. Making offers. Trying to cut a deal.

As they reached the Kombat parked up in front of the carport Porter tapped the unlock button on the key fob and popped the rear door open. Then he shoved the president's brother towards the back seat. The guy resisted.

'In the car,' Porter growled.

'Wait. Where are you taking me?'

'Your brother. He wants a family reunion.'

A look of terror briefly registered on the captive's face. Then his expression hardened, like cement. 'You're a fucking dead man. When my friends hear what happened to me, they'll hunt you down. Your and your family. You're all going to pay for this.'

'We'll see. Now get in and shut up.'

Porter bundled the Russian inside the back of the Kombat and slammed the door shut before the guy could reply. He paced around to the front of the SUV, stopped by the driver's side door and cast one final look towards the back of the dacha. At Jock Bald, his old mate and the least likely martyr in Regiment history, carrying a nuclear bomb over to the jetty.

Porter slid behind the wheel.

341

Twisted the keys in the ignition.

Then he hit the gas.

Twenty-three minutes until the nuke detonated.

Ninety metres to the south, Bald scrambled towards the jetty.

He moved as fast as he could with thirty kilos of nuke strapped to his back. Which wasn't that fast. His body had slowed down in the years since he'd left the Regiment. A combination of exhaustion, age and general wear and tear. Bald could feel his leg muscles burning under the strain of the nuke-filled backpack.

He hit the jetty in two more strides and hurried along the worn timber planking. The jetty extended for eight metres from the edge of the land across the gunmetal lake. At the far end, the wooden motor boat was sitting in the water alongside the mooring post. It was a fine old vessel, constructed from mahogany and leather. Eight metres long and two-and-a-half metres across the beam, with an outboard motor and a storage locker aft of the cockpit. A Russian flag dangled from a metal pole forward of the windscreen.

Bald reached the motor boat with twenty-two minutes on the clock.

He slid his arms out of the shoulder straps, set the rucksack down on the jetty and clambered into the cockpit. With his feet firmly planted on the decking, Bald reached back over to the jetty, grabbed the nuke by the straps and lowered it carefully into the boat, setting it down next to the storage locker. He unhooked the length of rope tied to the forward cleat, chucked the rope aside and turned his attention to the outboard motor.

The mechanical timer ticked away as Bald operated the shift lever, moving it to the neutral position. He pumped the bulb on the fuel primer line several times, clearing the air out of the length of black tubing. Advanced the hand grip on the throttle lever to the start position and pulled out the choke. He pulled on the starter handle, until he felt the rope give a little tug. Then he yanked hard on the rope. Like starting an old diesel lawnmower.

It took three attempts to get the motor running. Bald pushed in the choke and unhooked the rope from the aft cleat. The craft began to drift away from the jetty as Bald twisted the throttle and shifted it to the forward mark, pulling away bows-first. He stuck to a low speed until he was well clear of the jetty, getting a feel for the old motor boat.

As soon as he reached the open water, Bald pushed the tiller away from him, swinging the stern of the boat towards the port side, so that the bow was pointing out towards the middle of the lake. Then he accelerated, twisting the grip like a motorbike throttle. The boat picked up speed, her bow riding high, humping over the lake's surface and leaving a foamy trail in its wake. Bald pushed the throttle harder. A few seconds later the vessel planed out, skimming along the surface as he accelerated towards the open water. Engine chainsawing, the bomb ticking.

Twenty minutes.

If Bald succeeded, thousands of people would wake up tomorrow, without ever realising how close they had come to death. He would be a hero, and no one would even know his name. He didn't complain. This was the life he'd known in the Regiment. What he'd signed up for, all those years back. You don't push yourself just to win a fucking medal. You don't do it for the individual glory.

You do it to win.

Bald closed out all thoughts of death from his mind. He simply told himself, *I didn't come this far to lose. Not to Gabulov and his extremist mates.*

It took him seven minutes to reach the middle of the lake, guiding himself by his night vision and the black mass of the surrounding land, and the faint illumination from the pre-dawn sky.

Thirteen minutes to go.

Bald shifted down to neutral as he approached the mid-point of the lake. He twisted the grip away from him, turning it to the stop position. Hit the kill switch. The engine sputtered out as the boat slowed to a halt on the still water. Once he was in position, Bald manoeuvred around to the aft storage compartment. The boat rocked from side to side as he dropped to his haunches, gripped the rucksack by the straps and carried it over to the gunwale on the port side. Then he shoved it overboard. The backpack hit the water with a loud splash. It bobbed for a moment on the surface, before the weight dragged it down towards the bottom of the lake.

The dark slimy water closed up around the top of the bomb, like a mouth. Then it was lost to sight.

There was no chance of the water damaging the firing unit, Bald knew. Those nukes were designed to be dropped with paratroopers out of the back of a cargo plane. They were waterproof and shockproof. Nothing would stop that bomb going off.

Bald swung back round to the outboard motor. Twelve minutes to go. He thought: Seven minutes back to the jetty. Five minutes to leg it out of the blast radius. *No time. No fucking time at all.* The odds against him surviving were a million to one.

Worse, even.

He had to try anyway.

Bald gripped the starter rope. Fired up the motor boat's engine. Then he got moving.

Porter was six miles away when he heard the blast.

He saw it unfold out of his side window as he drove north. A giant column of water surging high into the air, close to the horizon. The column expanded outwards, like a bubble about to burst. There was a low, deep rumble as a mushroom cloud bloomed upwards from the crown of the bubble, into the lightening sky. The rumble boomed across the land, quaking the road, triggering nearby car and building alarms. Then the water bubble burst, collapsing into a radioactive mist that drenched the surrounding landscape for miles in every direction.

Even as he looked, Porter knew there was simply no way Bald would have survived that explosion.

Jock's dead, he thought. The realisation hit him like a punch to the throat. As he looked on at the dissipating bubble, he knew he'd underestimated Bald.

All these years, I thought the guy only ever gave a shit about himself. But I had him wrong.

Porter drove on with a hollow feeling in his stomach. He pulled over at a rest stop and called the number he'd been given on the burner. A voice he didn't recognise told him to head to a place he didn't know, seventy-one miles away from his location according to the Kombat's built-in GPS. As he pulled out onto the motorway, dozens of police cars and ambulances and army trucks tore past in the other direction. Racing south towards the explosion. Their sirens wailing in the distance, like electric screams.

He reached the RV two hours later. Another dacha, to the west of Moscow. Porter was beginning to wonder how many places the Russian president owned. Hundreds, probably. He probably had more cash sitting in the bank than Apple.

Viktor Gabulov wasn't there. Tarasov showed up in his place, along with several heavies and a convoy of Land Rovers with tinted mirrors. The president was back in the Kremlin, the Russian man-mountain explained. He had to be seen to be handling the nuke crisis personally. An important part of his strongman image. Hands-on leadership. His lackeys were busy figuring out how to spin the explosion to the world's media. There was talk of blaming it on an earthquake. Or a comet. A crashed UFO. Conspiracy theorists were already hard at work on behalf of the government, peddling theories on Twitter and Facebook. The Russians weren't about to admit to a stolen nuke going off in the vicinity of Moscow.

Porter didn't care. He was done.

I just want to get the fuck out of here, and never come back.

The heavies dragged Alexei Gabulov kicking and screaming out the back of the Kombat. The hardliner turned out to be just as shit-scared as everyone else, when he was faced with the prospect of a slow, agonising death. The heavies gagged him, gave him a few sharp digs to the ribs, then shoved him into the back of one of the Land Rovers. Tarasov made a call. To someone back at Zhirkov's mansion, Porter figured. Telling them to drop Street off at the British embassy.

Porter half-expected Tarasov to slot him. But the bullet never came. The guy just signalled to his heavies, and they climbed into the Land Rovers and pulled away.

There was no debrief at the British embassy. No slaps on the back or congratulations. Six wanted Porter out of the country immediately. There was talk of a big inquest when he got back. The rescue of Charles Street was something of a coup, but questions were being asked back in Whitehall about how much int Cooper had shared with his Russian counterparts. Intelligence officers were going through past ops with a fine-tooth comb, searching for potential leaks. Vauxhall was in damage-limitation mode. Nobody was punching the air in celebration.

They gave Porter painkillers and a new dressing for his wound. A new passport, and a ticket back to London. The airspace around Moscow was closed off, so they put him on a train from Leningradsky station to St Petersburg. From there he caught a BA flight back to London.

He slept through most of the flight. For the first time since he could remember, Porter didn't crave a drink.

Eighteen hours after the bomb went off, Porter found himself sitting on the Tube at Heathrow airport.

Somebody had left a copy of the *Evening Standard* on the seat next to him. The first four pages were filled with news about the mysterious blast in a village outside Moscow. The first English-language report Porter had read since it had happened. The lake had absorbed most of the initial explosion, leaving a massive crater at the bottom. Much of the immediate area had been soaked in the radioactive mist created by the bomb. Clean-up crews were sent in. Zukotka and the surrounding villages were evacuated. The death toll stood at sixteen, but a government spokesperson said it could have been far higher.

There was a long list of theories about the cause of the blast. So-called experts weighed in. The comet theory was high on the list. So was the UFO conspiracy. One or two voices had suggested it could be a backpack nuke, but a spokesman for the Kremlin denied such weapons existed. If they did, he added, they would have been decommissioned a long time ago.

There was nothing in the news about Bald. Which was no surprise. But at the bottom of the page, a single line caught Porter's eye. One of the clean-up crews had made a curious discovery in the woods near the scene.

A single gold bar.